First published 2020

First printed edition published 2023 by Drollery Ltd.

Copyright © Alice Coldbreath, 2020

ISBN 978-1-916736-04-7

More books available by Alice Coldbreath:

The Vawdrey Brothers Series:

Book 1: Her Baseborn Bridegroom

Book 2: His Forsaken Bride

Book 3: An Ill-Made Match

The Brides of Karadok Series:

Book 1: Wed By Proxy

Book 2: The Unlovely Bride

Book 3: The Consolation Prize

Book 4: Her Bridegroom, Bought and Paid For

Book 5: An Inconvenient Vow

Book 6: The Favourite

The Victorian Prizefighter Series:

Book 1: A Bride for the Prizefighter

Book 2: A Substitute Wife for the Prizefighter

Book 3: A Contracted Spouse for the Prizefighter

Sitwell Place, Pimlico, London

"A toast," said Uncle Josiah jovially. "To the prospective bride and groom!"

Everyone scrambled to pick up their tumblers of water. Lizzie Anderson raised hers aloft like the rest of the company, though she thought there was precious little to celebrate. Cousin Betsy had lost her mind. Why else would she go and throw herself away on a reprobate like Benedict Toomes? There could be no other explanation for it, Lizzie thought as her gaze traveled from her pretty, dimpling cousin to the dark male specimen lolling in his seat next to her.

Benedict Toomes's shoulders were twice as broad as any other man sat there, and maybe that was supposed to excuse the fact he had seen fit to remove his jacket in polite company and unbuttoned the top of his shirt. To Lizzie, it just looked slovenly. Uncle Josiah would never sit to supper in his shirtsleeves. Then, too, he had barely spoken a word throughout dinner, though his every pore radiated an ill-bred arrogance that set Lizzie's jangling nerves on edge. Instead of trying to ingratiate himself to the company at large, like a decent man would, he looked, if anything, rather bored.

How did he dare to sit there so silent and scornful, she fumed, when he was surrounded on all sides by good Christian folk? Lizzie's bosom swelled with indignation as she unfolded her napkin. She knew full well he had been released from prison only two months ago for common affray, yet instead of looking even remotely abashed, he sat there bold as brass with those cool hazel eyes of his and a faint curl to his sensual full mouth that spoke of pride and disdain.

What did he have to be arrogant about, that's what she'd like to know! From what Betsy had told her, he was nothing more than a common prizefighter, and though her cousin had airily talked of his having money to invest and enough put by for a house of his own, Lizzie would believe it when she saw it! Men like that were soon parted from their money by fast living. She only hoped that Betsy would not rue the day she had decided to let flashy good looks overrule good sense.

Lizzie could not for the life of her understand why Uncle Josiah had permitted the man a seat at his table, let alone to become engaged to his only daughter. Of course, she knew a repentant sinner must be welcomed back into the fold, but Benedict Toomes did not look remotely repentant, and besides, he had never *been* part of their fold! Sometimes she even wondered if he was a regular churchgoer at all!

Her gaze sought out the reassuring presence of Reverend Milson, who sat at the opposite end of the table in his somber black robes. From her seat, she could just about make out his melodious voice informing his neighbor of the charity fundraiser he was currently devoting his energies to. Lizzie hoped the rich Mrs. Lessing would prove receptive to his cause. Although a wealthy widow, she could be extremely mean with her largesse and liked to keep her prospective beneficiaries dancing constant attendance on her.

How shocked dear Reverend Milson must have been to find himself having to share a meal with the likes of Benedict Toomes, Lizzie thought, yet you could not tell from his wonderfully serene expression. Everyone knew the good reverend had regretfully declined to read the banns in his own church after Benedict had refused to formally pledge himself a member of their congregation. Lizzie had never been so shocked as when she had learned that poor Betsy was having to be married out of a neighboring parish. Lizzie did not know

2

how Betsy could bear the indignity after being raised in the same church all her life. It must have been a cruel blow, yet her cousin seemed determined to forge ahead on this dubious path in life.

The only consolation was the proof that their pastor was indeed a man of principle, she thought, looking at how Reverend Milson's pale hair swept back from his noble brow. He knew a sinner when he saw one, and he did not flinch from his duty. Fortified by this thought, Lizzie reached for her water glass and took another refreshing sip. It was overcrowded tonight in the Andersons' dining room, and she was starting to feel a little hot in the face.

"Lizzie, my dear," Mrs. Hedgcomb addressed her with a kindly smile. "I wanted to thank you for that pretty shawl pattern you dropped by yesterday. Why, it's just the thing for my niece Hilda's new baby."

Lizzie leaned forward. "I'm so glad, Mrs. Hedgcomb," she replied. "I've made it several times, and it always turns out very nicely indeed."

She turned and apologized to old Mr. Scott, who she had inadvertently jostled. There were so many extra seats crowded around the dining room table tonight, it made it hard to avoid scraping elbows.

"Not at all, my dear," he assured her, patting her arm. "Don't give it another thought." Lizzie smiled back at him and steeled herself to ask after his elderly father, who suffered from the gout.

She was not sure at which point her attention started to wander. Mr. Scott always went into so much detail about his father's maladies, and the buzz of conversation around the table somehow made it easier to disassociate from the gently

3

plaintive voice as it unhurriedly ran through the elder Scott's various ailments.

Lizzie nodded absently, her thoughts miles away as her eyes wandered over the flowers and the dishes of wax fruit stacked down the center of the table. She had just noticed that someone had spilled gravy on Aunt Hester's pristine table linen when her eyes were dazzled by a flash of light. Glancing up, she saw the candlelight had caught Mrs. Lessing's diamond brooch as sly fingers plucked it from her black lace shawl and dropped it into a discreet breast pocket.

Lizzie blinked, her disbelieving eyes traveling up from the breast pocket to the serene features of Reverend Milson as he smoothly continued his conversation with Mrs. Lessing without even pausing to draw breath. She gasped. *What just happened?* Her eyes traveled back disbelievingly to Mrs. Lessing's plump bosom. The shawl was bare of adornment, for the brooch was gone.

"Lizzie, my dear?" She turned back blankly to Mr. Scott. "You must not take on so, my child," he said with an indulgent chuckle. "He is a very old man, and it's only natural that he feels his years at ninety-one."

She nodded dumbly. "It s-seems hard the old gentleman should have to suffer so," she managed to stammer from lips that felt strangely numb. Her mind was reeling. What had she just seen? Could Mrs. Lessing have asked Reverend Milson to take her brooch for safekeeping? she wondered. Could the brooch pin have become loose? Or a stone have fallen out? Madly, she scrabbled for a reasonable excuse for the vicar to have legitimately removed the brooch, but all the while, in the back of her mind, she kept remembering how his lips had flowed with speech while his fingers surreptitiously removed and pocketed the brooch.

4

Lizzie's spirits plummeted. A horrible, cold voice told her it was undoubtedly theft. But it could not be! She argued with herself all through the next course as her hands turned clammy and she felt herself starting to perspire. She pushed the food around her plate, unable to put a single forkful into her mouth. What was she going to do? She had no choice. She would have to ask Reverend Milson to explain himself, she thought desperately. She would draw him quietly to one side and ask him what his purpose had been. There must be some reason she was not aware of, some motivating factor that would become clear to her with time.

It was as the last course of marbled jelly and cheese straws was being tidied away that Lizzie heard Reverend Milson clear his throat. "But my dear Mrs. Lessing," he said in an upraised voice. "Where is your brooch? I could have sworn you had it on before supper." Lizzie caught her breath in her throat as all eyes turned toward Mrs. Lessing.

"My brooch! My diamond brooch! It's gone!" the shaken widow shrieked. There was the sound of chairs being hurriedly dragged back as people inspected the floor and immediate area for the missing jewel.

Aunt Hester stood up and, in an awful voice, called Annie back into the room. The unfortunate maid had only reached the hallway and was still holding an empty tray of crumbs. She hurried back and was soon reduced to incoherent tears.

"Every time I turned around you were hovering at my shoulder, girl!" Mrs. Lessing squawked.

"That was just to serve you vegetables, madam!" Annie wailed.

"Turn out her pockets!" Uncle Josiah ordered direly. Aunt Hester had soon whisked around the table and divested the

5

servant of her starched white apron and turned out the pockets of her black cotton gown.

Lizzie sat in stupefied silence, her heart pounding, her pleading gaze barely leaving Reverend Milson's composed face. She kept expecting him to reveal the location of the pilfered brooch, like a conjuring trick. Was there some kind of moral they would be expected to draw from the way they were conducting themselves? she wondered dumbly. Was this a lesson in false accusation? Was Reverend Milson, even now, composing next Sunday's sermon?

Poor Annie had collapsed into a heap and was sobbing into her apron. It struck Lizzie suddenly, that as the unfortunate maid had briefly left the room, her name was not really cleared by her pockets being found empty. Suspicion would remain hovering over her, and glancing around, she could see their guests were starting to whisper behind their hands at each other.

"Annie has been with us for over ten years," she heard herself say weakly to Mr. Scott, but it was at this point she saw it was not Annie he was eyeing askance but Benedict Toomes, and he was not the only one. As though in a nightmare, Lizzie saw the hardening gazes of the company directed as of one accord toward the outsider sat among them. Of course, she thought dully. He was the only relative stranger in their midst. Everyone else present was friends of long standing and belonged to St. Joseph's church. As though on cue, Uncle Josiah stood up, tugging on his waistcoat, his expression very grave.

As he cleared his throat to speak, old Mr. March jumped up from his seat. "I won't sit idly by while we all eye our neighbors with suspicion. We have only one stranger in our midst this night, and I beg pardon, Josiah, but we all know he's a relative heathen!"

Lizzie froze as murmurs of agreement filled the room. She would have to act now, or things would be said that could never be undone. She surged to her feet. "I saw who took the brooch!" she announced croakily. "I saw the whole thing." She felt her color rise as all eyes now swiveled to look at her.

Both Mr. March and her uncle dropped back into their seats, leaving her with the floor.

"That's it, girl, speak the truth and shame the devil!" Mr. March uttered.

Feeling her mouth suddenly dry, Lizzie turned in mute appeal to Reverend Milson, willing him to take over now with some explanation for his seemingly inexplicable actions.

For the first time, Lizzie saw a crack in his tranquility. A little color crept into his cheeks and his eyes darted left to right. *Oh no*, she thought incredulously as her heart sank. There *was* no reasonable explanation, and he wasn't going to confess. The realization was like a cold bucket of water being poured over her head. She felt as though she were in the midst of some awful dream.

"Speak out, Lizzie!" her uncle ordered strictly. "As the good book says, 'Speak up for those who cannot speak for themselves; ensure justice for those being crushed.'"

Lizzie raised a trembling hand, before dropping it again. "It was Reverend Milson," she said hopelessly.

Those who did not gasp drew in sharp breaths of disapproval. Mr. March uttered a faint cry.

"Lizzie!" her aunt burst forth in shocked censure.

"It's in his breast pocket," Lizzie added, briefly closing her eyes against the angry, hard stares of her family and friends. "I saw him put it in there. I believe it is there still."

"I believe I speak for all present," her uncle said shakily after a moment's stunned silence, "when I say that nothing could induce me to ask the good reverend to turn out his pockets!"

"Not quite," cut in a cool, hard voice. It was Betsy's fiancé, Benedict Toomes. Lizzie felt his sardonic gaze dwell on her for a moment before he turned it on the vicar. "If no one else will, I believe I'll have to insist upon it." The room was instantly silent as the grave.

"Oh no, Benedict!" Betsy protested, turning toward her fiancé and plucking at his sleeve with agitated fingers. He neither acknowledged her words or actions with so much as a glance.

"Empty it," he said in a voice that could cut ice. "Now."

Reverend Milson turned an unflattering shade of puce. "I really must object…" he bleated, even as his fingers obeyed the demand, fluttering to his breast pocket. He licked his lips and pulled out the corner of a large white handkerchief and in the process dislodged the brooch, which fell with a heavy thud onto the tablecloth where it glittered up at him accusingly.

Shocked silence reigned for one awful moment, and all that could be heard was the steady tick of the grandfather clock. Then Mrs. Lessing pounced on her brooch with a suppressed squawk and lifted it to press it to her lips. "Thanks be!" she breathed reverently.

Reverend Milson drew himself up. "How did that get there?" he blustered, raising his eyes heavenward. "Good gentlemen, I assure you I have no earthly notion."

He was lying. As her faith in her idol withered away, Lizzie dropped like a stone into her seat and sat winded as the babble of excited conversation rose in a deafening swell. She felt like a puppet whose strings had been severed. Her limbs felt weak and strangely heavy.

"Someone must have placed it there!" said Mrs. Hedgcomb shrilly. "It's an outrage to try to discredit a man of the cloth and besmirch his blameless character. Hester Anderson, I'll not set one foot in this godless house again, and I'll warrant I am not the only one!" Her words were greeted with a chorus of indignant agreement from the company at large.

Aunt Hester's mouth fell open, and she looked about in dismay at the angry faces of her guests. "B-but, Ada!" she stammered, wringing her hands. "No one could think that dear Reverend Milson could ever do such a wicked thing!"

"You seem to forget," Benedict Toomes's voice cut across them all like the crack of a whip, "that there is a witness here present who saw Reverend Milson steal the brooch."

Lizzie drew a pained breath as, once again, she felt the burning gazes of reproach of everyone present fall upon her. She raised her eyes from contemplation of her hands in her lap to meet them.

"Lizzie," intoned her uncle sternly. "Do you mean to say you stand by this outrageous assertion of yours?" He was coldly furious, Lizzie realized. Furious with her.

Lizzie stiffened her spine. "I do," she said simply. "I must. I saw Reverend Milson take the brooch and slip it into his own pocket." She met first her uncle's eyes, then slowly went around the table meeting everyone else's. All fell away from hers, save for Benedict Toomes. His bored into her so searingly that she felt almost scorched.

"May the good Lord forgive you," said Reverend Milson piously, though he gazed at some point over her left shoulder, steadfastly refusing to meet her eye.

"And you," Lizzie responded automatically, as though in church.

"Lizzie!" her aunt choked out, deeply shocked.

Benedict Toomes gave a nasty laugh, and the whole table erupted into chaos.

He must have been mad to think he could marry into this lot, Benedict reflected, watching the polite folk filing their way out of the Andersons' hallway, from his seat just inside in the drawing room. A bunch of meek-faced hypocrites, the lot of them. Not one of them had the guts to look the devil in the eye. No, that wasn't quite true, he thought musingly, one of them did. That sanctimonious bitch, Betsy's cousin, had courage enough, though precious little else to recommend her to a man.

He had felt Lizzie Anderson's disapproving gaze on him all through supper, when she wasn't gazing starry-eyed at that thief of a preacher, that was. There was a rich irony to the fact her fervent admiration had led to the man's unmasking. Ben savored the fact for a moment. That stricken look on her face as she had denounced her idol would have been enough to wring sympathy from the flintiest heart, but all it afforded him was a dark sort of amusement. He knew damned well she had counseled Betsy against marrying him.

His fiancée came hurrying back into the room, the color high in her cheeks. "I'm so vexed I could scream," she said, crossing to stand by the window. She hitched a lace curtain and watched their guests pouring out into the street. "If Mama does not handle this, we will be given the cut direct by all our friends and neighbors!"

"And just how do you suggest she 'handles' it?" Benedict drawled.

Betsy turned to look at him in astonishment. "Why, Lizzie must be forced to retract her ridiculous claims, of course!"

Benedict reached into his jacket pocket and extracted his silver cigarillo case. "Your cousin saw him take it, Bets. It was in his pocket."

Betsy shook her head so vehemently her blond ringlets bounced. "It's all a plot against Reverend Milson. A conspiracy! Papa agrees with me."

When Benedict raised his eyes to hers, she flushed and turned away. "Why would there be a conspiracy against Reverend Milson?" he asked coolly. "You know your cousin was keener on him then anyone. Didn't you tell me she spends her spare time embroidering him slippers and handkerchiefs?"

"Exactly!" Betsy said, eagerly seizing on the fact. "He must have spurned her affections, so she turned against him. Old maids can be bitter, you know."

For a moment, Benedict was so taken aback he could not speak. The idea of Lizzie Anderson flinging herself at a man was so ridiculous he almost laughed. She'd been mad for the reverend alright, but Lizzie Anderson was an old maid of the mitten-knitting variety, not the man-hungry type. He would swear an oath on it.

He remembered the conflicted look on her face as she confronted the reverend. She'd been almost begging him with her eyes to give her a reason why he'd taken it. Any reason would have sufficed. She would gladly have swallowed any ridiculous lie he might have uttered, but the reverend had faltered when confronted with so many onlookers and turned craven. The shattered look on her face was still fresh in his mind's eye. She'd had a hell of an awakening. "I thought you and she were much of the same age," he said at last.

Betsy pouted. "I'm an engaged woman," she pointed out. "Lizzie's never had so much as a gentleman caller in her life."

"You won't be engaged much longer if you keep this up, my girl," he said softly.

Betsy gasped. "Benedict!"

He narrowed his eyes. "You saw how those jackals turned on me. They were a hair's breadth away from denouncing me at the table."

"No!"

"If there was a conspiracy, very likely it would have been against me, not your precious reverend."

"How can you say so?" Betsy flung at him, her bosom heaving. She looked at her best animated, but at this very moment, he could not remember admiring her less. "After my parents received you into their home, despite your—" She broke off with a dismayed gasp.

"Record?" he suggested, striking a match and lighting his cigarillo before draping an arm over the back of the sofa. "Or do you mean my prizefighting?"

Her chin rose. "Yes, despite *both* of those things."

He breathed out a curl of smoke from his lips. "Very magnanimous of them," he agreed. "If I was honest and penniless, I doubt they would have felt the same way."

Her eyes filled with sudden tears. "You have no cause to say such a thing!"

"Haven't I?"

"Oh, Benedict darling," she cried and crossed the room to sink onto the sofa beside him. "Please don't let this horrid evening come between us. We are to be married in four days' time." She placed a soft white hand on his sleeve, and he had to suppress the impulse to shrug it off. "This has been the worst evening of my life. Please don't add to it now by forcing a quarrel between us."

Before he could reply, a footfall in the doorway announced his prospective father-in-law's arrival on the scene.

"I trust I'm not interrupting," Josiah Anderson said, clearing his throat. "But you must allow me to apologize for this dreadful evening's entertainment, Mr. Toomes."

"Oh, dearest Papa," Betsy said, rising and moving to his side. "It's not your fault. No one could think so." She slipped an arm through his and looked at Benedict meaningfully. "No apologies are needed between family."

Benedict contemplated the end of his cigarillo before rising to his feet. "I believe I'll take my leave of you now," he announced, to his betrothed's consternation. He remained distant during their goodbyes. Mrs. Anderson did not appear; apparently, she was too busy taking her recalcitrant niece in hand. On the twenty-minute walk back to Winchester Street, Benedict wondered if she would succeed in browbeating Lizzie into taking back her damning words. Thinking of that stubborn and principled damsel, he was surprised to find he had some doubt.

He threw a penny to a beggar sat huddled on the corner and discarded the butt of his smoked cigar. On the surface, Lizzie Anderson would have little choice but to accede to her uncle and aunt's wishes. From the confidences Betsy had poured in his ears, he knew Lizzie had been taken in by them at age four as an orphan. She was wholly dependent on her uncle's goodwill and her aunt's charity. They had always been loud in their assertions that she was a second daughter to them. He wondered how true this statement would prove, now the chips were down.

14

On reaching the quiet, affluent street on which the tidy red-bricked villa he had purchased little more than a month ago stood, he paused. Betsy still believed him to reside in lodgings, but he had bought the house as a surprise, in anticipation of their impending marriage. He contemplated now the double-fronted exterior and decorated gables. Buying it had been quite an achievement, a farewell to his former life. Contemplating its solid respectability now, he felt rather flat.

Was this what he wanted? To live surrounded on all sides by doctors, dentists, and solicitors? Perhaps there was a good reason he had not told his prospective bride of its purchase. Was it possible he was holding back, reluctant to commit to this new life? When, after walking out for only a month, she had vowed to stick by him during his incarceration, he had been filled with the conviction that pretty Betsy was the one for him. Since his release, however, it had been brought home to him on several occasions that he had been locked away for the majority of their courtship. There was little true sympathy of mind between them. Did that matter? He had not thought so, but now he was starting to wonder.

Letting himself into the house, he struck a match and lit the lamp on the hall table. It illuminated the checkered floor tiling, and he turned and secured the front door with its stained-glass panels. Still the little voice whispered in his head, refusing to be quieted. Perhaps the price of respectability *was* too high if it meant being saddled with the likes of the Andersons. Had he shrugged off one troublesome family only to pick up another? Lifting up the lamp, Benedict walked through to the parlor and poured himself a liberal dose of whisky. Of course Betsy's people would be teetotalers, he thought with a twist of his lips. He knocked back his whisky and grimaced.

Quitting boxing before he reached thirty had always been his goal, and he was now twenty-nine. Going respectable though?

15

He wasn't sure when that notion had taken root. Maybe it had been those two long years he had spent in the workhouse as a child. His expression tightened, as did his hand on the whisky glass. His brothers would never understand that part of his life, as they had never been subjected to the humiliation and privation of those years. As always, he slammed the door on recollection of those times before they could overwhelm him with a tide of bitterness.

It had been almost eleven months since he had seen Frank and Jack, but he knew full well where he could find them should the need arise. It would be Easter this weekend, which meant the annual fairs would be starting up again and they would be traveling with the family boxing booth from April till November. He felt a strange pang in the vicinity of his chest when he thought of the red-striped tent and the peeling sign proclaiming The Toomes Brothers Boxing Saloon.

Easter meant they would be pitched at Greenwich Fair for three days, just as August meant Bartholomew Fair, October was Hull Fair, and November the Goose Fair in Nottingham. In between were a whole seven months of touring the smaller fairs throughout England. Of course, he had vowed he had served his last season taking on all comers and brawling between posts hammered into a field. His brothers had not believed him at the time. A third of the stall was still his, as neither one of them had jumped to buy him out. As for his youngest brother, Jack still hadn't paid him back for lending him the brass to buy his own stake five years previously.

He just hoped to God their father hadn't rolled up and persuaded Frank to let him back into the family business. Ben's lip curled. Frank was soft when it came to the old man. Pa would have another "wife" in tow, no doubt, and likely a few more grubby, miserable-looking kids. It was always the same old story. Nothing ever changed where their old man was concerned, just the faces of those he dragged in his wake.

Shedding his jacket, Benedict threw it over the newel post and made his way upstairs. As he unbuttoned his cuffs, he wondered wryly what his welcome would be if he *were* to pitch up at Greenwich without so much as a by your leave. He'd avoided the usual haunts since his release from jail, and none of the Toomeses were letter-writers, even those of them who could write. Then, too, was the fact not one of them had a fixed abode. They tended to winter in lodging houses of varying degrees, depending on the plumpness of their pockets after touring the fairs.

He could have found them, of course. If he'd wanted to, that is, but the fact was he didn't. He'd burned his bridges with the boxing world after his arrest. He'd wanted distance and to go it alone, so he'd resolutely turned his back. He'd spent half his savings on this house and gotten engaged. Then he had started looking about him in earnest for some concern to invest the rest of his money in. But nothing had taken his fancy, from stocks and shares to shipping, diamond mines to ranches in South America, nothing really appealed.

Clem Dabney, a fellow prizefighter he still spoke with, had tried to interest him in some "supper and song" establishment with showgirls and liquor. Clem also thought they needed to invest their money now, before it ran through their fingers. They had seen too many examples of broken-down fighters who ended on the scrap heap, penniless, after squandering the money they'd made at the height of their fame. Benedict had been sorely tempted to throw his lot in with Clem, who had a good business head on his shoulders, but he was glad now he hadn't committed himself to some mad scheme on impulse. The last he'd heard, Clem had been looking at theaters, and God knows those places gobbled up money and could go bust in the wink of an eye.

He'd been ripe for mischief, he realized now, on release from prison, or he never would have set his foot halfway into the parson's trap. Betsy Anderson was pretty enough with her heart-shaped face and dimples, but if those same charms were already starting to pall on him, then what chance did a lifetime of marriage have of holding his attention? He looked about at the tasteful decor, the expensive wallpapers, and carpeting as he made his way to the master bedroom. He felt almost as if he were seeing the place for the first time, like he'd been sleepwalking the past two months. What the hell had he been thinking?

Setting the lamp down on his bedside table, Ben started undressing as he considered his options. He could sell this place easily enough. Property was never a bad investment, they said, so he would not allow himself to feel too much regret about purchasing it. He could speak to Edwards, his legal man, about putting the place back on the market. Or he could rent it out, or even do nothing at all and let the dust settle before making up his mind.

By the time he climbed into bed and stretched out with his hands behind his head, he felt calmer. He'd find a way to extricate himself out of this mess, preferably without getting sued for breach of contract. He wouldn't put it past Betsy's grasping family to try to screw him out of every penny they could lay their hands on.

Before the betrothal had been approved, he'd been obliged to meet with her father and his legal man to give assurances about his financial standing and fitness to take a wife. They had agreed on a sum Benedict should settle on her once they were married in the event of his death. He would need to put a stop to such proceedings on the morrow, he thought grimly. He would rise early and drop around to his man of business's office on Chancery Lane first thing in the morning. Whatever happened, he now had no intention of marrying Betsy Anderson in four days' time.

3

Lizzie stood on the doorstep, stunned, as the door was slammed in her face. Her last glimpse was of Aunt Hester's thin lips tightly pressed together as she slung the carpet bag containing all of Lizzie's worldly possessions out onto the path beside her. Lizzie wasn't sure how long she stood there, staring at the smart green paint of the door, the gleaming brass door knocker, and the etched numbers showing the numbers thirty-two, which had been her address and safe haven in the world for over twenty years.

She wasn't roused from her stupor until she heard the crunch of gravel on the path behind her. Turning blindly, she saw that it was Mr. Benedict Toomes and fell back a step. No doubt her aunt and uncle would allow Betsy's fiancé admittance, even though they had turned out their niece. She bent down to retrieve her bag and hurried past him down the path, her cheeks flaming, refusing to meet those hateful, mocking eyes of his. She had her dignity left if nothing else.

It wasn't until she'd reached the end of the road and turned left that she realized she had absolutely no notion of where to go. The only friends she could call her own were also friends of her family and were moreover also members of Reverend Milson's congregation. Her footsteps faltered as she realized the true horror of her situation. She had no one to turn to. Not even the mercy of the church. She had very little money and even fewer items of value that she could sell. She had nothing.

Her fingers gripped the handles of her bag tighter with every step, and almost without conscious thought, she found herself turning away from the shabby gentility of Pimlico and toward the slums of the East End, where she carried out her charitable work every Wednesday without fail.

It was funny, but walking these streets alongside her aunt and cousin, carrying their covered work baskets, she had always felt secure in both her station and respectability. As if she were protected in some kind of bubble from the ragged inhabitants of the slums. Today it was quite a different matter. She clutched her bag and pulled her cloak tight about her as though trying to conceal herself from the stares of passersby.

As the streets grew narrower and dirtier, she fancied the glances turned her way grew more curious and speculative. She was a lone female, quite unaccompanied and out of place. Except, she thought dully, her own circumstances were now just as straitened as their own, if only they knew it. The meanest beggar could scarcely be worse off, she thought, blinking back tears.

"'Old up, darlin'," a hoarse voice said nearby, almost making her scream. Before she could react, a meaty hand had taken firm hold of her forearm. "You must be lost, I reckon, sweet little dove like yourself."

Lizzie looked up from the hairy hand to find a rough-hewn man with a purple complexion leering down at her. "Release me at once!" she demanded, her outrage filling her with courage.

"Now don't you take on so, I only wants to be friends, see," he responded with horrid familiarity, and Lizzie got a blast of alcohol fumes as he lowered his face to peer inside her bonnet.

"Get off me!" she yelled shrilly, attempting to wrench her arm back. When this did not work, she swung her carpet bag in the direction of his head and landed a heavy whack to the side of his face. Evidently, Aunt Hester had not confiscated the large leather-bound bible they had given her for her last birthday. If she was not mistaken, that was what caused the loud thump when it connected with his temple.

Her assailant bellowed with rage and swung his other fist in her direction. Even as she flinched back and attempted to put her carpet bag between herself and the blow, someone else entered the fray. There was a blur of black, Lizzie's arm was released, and she staggered back with a cry. Setting out a flailing hand, she steadied herself against the railing as she heard a procession of muffled blows and pained grunts. Pausing only to straighten her bonnet, she turned back to find her assailant rolling on the cobbles, groaning.

Lizzie gasped and whipped around to behold the man stood behind her. Her heart pounded loudly as he lowered his fists. "Mr. Toomes!" she uttered in blank astonishment. "What on earth are you doing here?"

"I followed you, Miss Anderson," he replied coolly. "All the way from Sitwell Place. Not that you noticed," he added witheringly. "It's a dangerous place to be oblivious to your surroundings. This bastard has been tailing you for the last two street lengths." He illustrated his point by setting a booted foot on the wretched man's shoulder and shoving at him. The fellow rolled into a defensive huddle.

Lizzie was far too flustered to object to his coarse language; however, she could not allow the insult to her self-awareness to stand. "Evidently, he did not notice you following me either," she pointed out tartly. "And *these surroundings* must be his natural habitat," she concluded with a faint note of triumph.

He narrowed his eyes at her retort. "What the hell are you doing here, Lizzie? This is not the sort of neighborhood a gently reared woman should be traipsing about unaccompanied."

Lizzie! She was so shocked by his calling her by her Christian name that she regarded him open-mouthed for a moment before flushing with chagrin. Was she no longer to be afforded any respect now her circumstances had changed? She swallowed, then lifted her chin. "I—that is, I have an acquaintance that lives nearby," she admitted.

He snorted and lifted a skeptical eyebrow. "What acquaintance?" he asked as if it was his perfect right to interrogate her.

Lizzie drew an indignant breath to let him have a piece of her mind before remembering that he had just saved her from a common street attacker. Swallowing her sharp retort, she answered "Mrs. Louisa Napp" instead. "She lives just around that corner in lodgings on the second floor."

He followed the direction she pointed with his eyes, though he looked frankly suspicious. "And just how is it that you have an acquaintance in the East End?"

"I visit her every Wednesday," Lizzie flung at him in some defiance.

His frown cleared. "Oh," he said dryly. "Good works." She bristled at his tone but made no reply. "You're hardly in a position now to give her charity," he pointed out, rather cruelly to Lizzie's mind.

"I was hoping she might be able to point me in the direction of employment," Lizzie admitted with as much dignity as she could muster. "Mrs. Napp sews shirts to be sold on commercially. I have a neat hand at the needle myself and—"

"You mean she sells to a slophouse?" Benedict cut in dryly. "It's backbreaking labor and they barely make ends meet. Why else do you think she needs the aid of your church?"

Lizzie was uncomfortably aware he spoke nothing but the truth, but what other option did she have? "Mrs. Napp accepts apprentices and trains them up in her trade," she said, thinking of the young girls who were sat around pale and pinched as they stitched up the garment pieces in Mrs. Napp's chambers.

"For a price, I'll wager," he answered, stooping down to pick up her bag. When she held her hand out for it, he ignored it. "I'll accompany you," he said shortly.

"That's really not necessary," Lizzie replied without conviction. In truth, she would like nothing less than to be left alone at present. She fell in step beside him and steadfastly ignored the knowing look he cast her. They stepped around the fallen man and made their way toward the corner.

"Mrs. Napp is a widow and has to support five children," Lizzie told him, rallying her spirits. "At least I do not have any dependents and must only feed and clothe myself."

He inclined his head slightly as though conceding the truth of this before asking silkily, "What makes you think Mrs. Napp will stick her neck out to help you when doing so will only provoke her church benefactors?"

Lizzie hesitated, wondering how to admit that Mrs. Napp was not exactly a fan of her aunt Hester. "Mrs. Napp and my aunt are not always in perfect accord with one another," she admitted delicately.

Benedict smirked at her choice of words. "You mean she would not object to spitting in your aunt's eye, if the opportunity arose."

Lizzie winced. "Most likely not," she confided. "Aunt Hester says Mrs. Napp is a low, vulgar creature and would be struck off the charity register if she had her way. She suspects Mrs.

Napp takes a drop of gin when the opportunity arises and that—" Lizzie broke off, aghast at what she had been about to repeat.

"And that, what?"

"I—er, oh, I forget now," Lizzie lied, casting about in confusion for something, anything else other than the awful thing she had been about to repeat. That her children did not all share the same father. She was talking too much. Why was she doing that? Likely her nerves were quite overset.

Benedict gave a short laugh. "There's nothing so nasty as that which a narrow mind can conjure up," he said softly.

Lizzie darted a surprised look at him. Did he think Aunt Hester was narrow-minded, then? Her heart was beating fast by the time they entered the narrow passageway and started the climb up the rickety staircase. What would she do if Mrs. Napp turned her away from the door? Even worse, what if she answered the door and someone else had been there before her to poison Mrs. Napp's mind against her?

They reached the scratched, scruffy door, and Lizzie rapped upon it. "It's Monday," she said nervously. "So she won't be expecting my visit."

They heard voices from within. "Susan, answer that door!" Mrs. Napp's strident tones rang out. "Do stop your dallying!"

The door stepped open and six-year-old Susan stood bare-footed in the doorway. "Mam, it's that Miss Anderson!" she bawled back over her shoulder.

"On a Monday?" replied Mrs. Napp. "Well, let her in! Don't keep her stood out there in the draught."

"Thank you," Lizzie murmured as she stepped over the threshold. "Good morning, good morning," she greeted the

25

assembled company of young women who were sat around on the bare floorboards industriously sewing. There were only three chairs in the room. Mrs. Napp sat in one and her eldest daughter, Lucinda, on another. Seeing Lizzie had brought a guest with her, Lucinda rose from her seat and sank down between two of her younger sisters on the bare floorboards.

"Sit and welcome," Mrs. Napp said, eyeing Benedict with interest. "I didn't expect to see you till Wednesday. You've not got your cousin with you today, I see, nor that aunt of yours," she added, pursing her lips.

"This is Mr. Toomes," Lizzie said with an awkward gesture toward him as she removed her bonnet and cloak. "He is betrothed to my cousin." She sat in a chair, which immediately pitched her forward. Looking down, she saw one leg was clearly shorter than the other. By the time she had righted herself, she found Benedict Toomes lolling back in his own chair with an easy athletic grace she could only envy. He looked entirely unruffled by the fact he had thrust himself into a roomful of strangers.

Lizzie smoothed her hair and took a deep breath. "I was hoping to ask your advice this morning and enquire about your terms for taking on apprentices," she started rather breathlessly. "You see, my circumstances have changed, and I must now fend for myself and earn a living."

Mrs. Napp drew in a sharp breath. "They've never tossed you out on your ear!" she exclaimed. "And them purporting to be fine Christian folk!"

Lizzie sent her a pained look. "I'm afraid there's been a difference of opinion between myself and my family," she said lamely.

The other woman looked at her hard a minute before sucking in her cheeks. "I don't doubt you've got a neat hand with a needle, Miss Anderson," she said, shaking her head. "But if you'll take my advice, you'll seek employment elsewhere. We're at it from eight in the morning till ten at night here, and it's as much as I can do to keep body and soul together. A nicely spoken girl like you could get shop work if you put your mind to it. You got to have better prospects open to you than this life, I'm sure."

Lizzie fidgeted in her seat. It seemed only the brutal truth would work in this instance. "I have no money and lack even a roof over my head at this minute," she admitted hoarsely. "Moreover, I have no one that would recommend me or stand witness to my good character. That bag there contains all I own in the world."

Mrs. Napp narrowed her eyes as though assessing her words. After a moment, she sighed. "You got anything in there you can pawn?" she asked, nodding at the carpet bag.

It was five minutes later that they had separated her meagre possessions into two piles. The first had a change of clothes, her nightgown, bible, and woolen shawl. The second comprised of her best dress of green taffeta, her decorated wooden hairbrush, a tortoiseshell hair comb, and a small enamel brooch.

"I don't say as you'll get much for 'em," Mrs. Napp said doubtfully, pushing the second pile toward Benedict Toomes. Lizzie flushed as he rolled the items inside her dress. She had been wearing that dress at supper last night. It seemed very wrong watching him put his hands all over it now.

"I won't be long," he said, bundling it under his arm, for he had been nominated to take the items to the pawn shop. Lizzie wondered how he'd find his way, for he asked no directions of Mrs. Napp. Was he familiar with the East End, then? If he had been raised here, she could detect no accent.

He shut the door behind him, and Mrs. Napp turned immediately to her middle daughter. "Liza, go and fetch what's left of that jug of beer," she instructed. "And two mugs. You'll take a drop with me now, Miss Anderson." When Lizzie went to object, for she never accepted refreshment from any of her charity cases, she was summarily overruled. "Nonsense," the older woman said briskly. "I'd offer you water, but it's not safe to drink round these parts."

Lizzie took the mug Eliza solemnly handed her and watched as it was half filled with flat-looking beer.

"Your health," Mrs. Napp said and drained her own cup.

Lizzie took a cautious sip. "And yours," she replied feebly. Strange to say, she did feel fortified after she drank a little more. "I must warn you, Mrs. Napp," she said forthrightly. "If you do offer me shelter, you would not be advised to admit as much to any of my former acquaintances."

"Cast you off and all, have they?" Mrs. Napp snorted. "Well," she said comfortably. "If we gets a knock on the door, you'll have to slip into the back room and make yourself scarce. And mind," she said, raising her voice and looking about at her children and apprentices, "you're not to breathe a word about Miss Anderson when we gets any callers from St. Joseph's."

Before anyone could make a reply, she turned back to Lizzie. "Now quick, come and tell me before 'e returns," she said. "What you been up to, blackening your name so deep?"

Lizzie flushed and darted her eyes at the younger occupants of the room. "I'd rather not say in front of current company," she said primly. The thought of even repeating her tale made her heart quail. Mrs. Napp looked more intrigued than ever.

28

Luckily, it was not long before they heard a sharp rap on the door. Lizzie was half out of her chair to fly into the other room, but it was Benedict Toomes returned already. He held his hand out to her and dropped a bunch of coins into her hand.

"Thank you." She turned immediately to Mrs. Napp with them. "Is this enough?" she said, showing her the money.

Mrs. Napp's eyes widened, and she shot a speculative glance at Benedict. "Just give me this for now for your food and lodging for a week, and we'll see how we go on from there," she said, taking a silver sixpence. "Tuck the rest of it away," she recommended, and Lizzie made haste to do so, buttoning it into an inner pocket in her carpet bag.

"I'll be getting along now," Benedict Toomes said. "I've got to see a man across town at eleven, then I thought I'd call in at Sitwell Place."

Lizzie flushed at the mention of her late home. "Of course," she said, holding out her hand to him. "Thank you for your aid this morning. It was very good of you," she said, wishing she sounded less stiff and awkward.

He glanced at her hand but made no move to take it. "I'll be back later," he said, astounding her.

"Oh." It trembled on her tongue to demand why, but she didn't quite have the nerve to ask. Did he mean to act as intermediary then between herself and her family? She regarded him doubtfully a moment. Quite frankly, she could not imagine a less likely peacemaker.

He nodded at Mrs. Napp and made his way out of the door, his progress closely followed by the eyes of all ten occupants of the room.

"Quite the gent, ain't he?" Mrs. Napp commented, sticking her tongue in her cheek. "Wouldn't kick him out in the cold, would you?" One of her daughters giggled and was nudged by another. Lizzie, who had never considered him a gentleman in even the loosest sense, folded her lips. "Said he was engaged to that pretty little cousin of yours, didn't you?"

"Yes, he and Betsy are to be married in three days' time," Lizzie answered repressively. She did not want to encourage this topic of conversation if she could help it.

"What's his trade, if I might make so bold as to ask?" Mrs. Napp continued, drawing a pile of shirts toward them. Lizzie noticed the way all the apprentices' gazes swiveled curiously to her. Why were they so intrigued about Mr. Toomes? she wondered in bewilderment.

Lizzie cleared her throat. "He is a prizefighter," she admitted. "Or rather, I should say he *was*. I believe he is currently looking about for a more settled living, in anticipation of his marriage."

"Prizefighter?" Mrs. Napp looked impressed. "Never say so! And him so handsome! I always thought they had cauliflower ears and broken noses."

"Like that Mr. Chapman, Mam," chimed in Susan. "What lives above the grocers."

"Yes, him, luv," agreed Mrs. Napp absently. "They say he made a powerful amount of money back when he was in his prime. Lost it all, of course," she sniffed. "And none of those pretty gals what flocked around him when he was plump in the pocket stuck around once it was spent."

Lizzie drew her chair closer as Mrs. Napp passed her a needle and thread. She was glad to see the subject of prizefighters seemed closed for now.

"Now, the girls here has cut out the shirt pieces," Mrs. Napp explained, gesturing. "Aggie is sewing the cuffs and Jessie is on the yokes. I'll put you to setting the sleeves into the shoulders. It's fiddly work, and you can't be taking an age over it," she cautioned. "Not if we're to make our daily quota." Lizzie nodded and watched painstakingly as Mrs. Napp demonstrated the technique she must employ.

4

Benedict felt restless. It had been two whole days since the disastrous meal at Sitwell Place, and it had not been as straightforward to wind up affairs as he had initially imagined. He had been with his legal man for a full morning giving his new instructions. The house on Winchester Street was now viewable by appointment to prospective tenants. Edwards already had someone lined up who might be interested in taking it for a twelvemonth.

Then, and only then, had he devoted his energies to breaking off his betrothal. He had called at Sitwell Place directly after lunch the next day and then spent all afternoon needling its inhabitants into a state of self-righteous ire. The inevitable explosion did not take place until almost suppertime.

In truth, he had enjoyed prodding their sore spot and had informed them with malicious amusement that he knew the whereabouts of their cast-off niece. The rigid displeasure they displayed at this information alone would have informed him they thought the subject off-limits, but ignoring all social cues, he forged ahead regardless, disparaging Reverend Milson's character at every opportunity.

Finally, old Josiah had not been able to stand it any longer and had informed him stiffly that unless he could guarantee such sensitive topics would remain off his lips, then he would not be welcome to join them. Benedict had paused at this. "Not welcome at your supper table or as a member of your family, Mr. Anderson?" he had asked deliberately.

Josiah had bristled up at this lack of tact. "Why, as to that, sir, I must answer to either or both as you may choose to take it!" he had responded wrathfully.

Benedict had glanced then at Betsy, who had raised her chin in defiance. "And you, Betsy?" he asked thoughtfully. "Do you agree with your father's sentiments?"

"You have been most offensive all afternoon, Benedict," she had answered crossly, and he wasn't sure she didn't stamp her foot. Her ringlets jiggled with agitation. "How dare you lecture my parents on their duty! I declare the words you have spoken about Reverend Milson this day have wounded me quite beyond repair!"

Her mother had patted her hand indulgently. "There now, daughter. I am sure Mr. Toomes needs only a little nudge in the right direction to modify his behavior to that which would please you. He surely did not mean to cause us all such grievous offence."

"Beyond repair?" Benedict repeated loudly as though Hester Anderson had not spoken. "I am inclined to believe you are right about that. Indeed, I am starting to think things are beyond repair myself."

Betsy stared at him, open-mouthed. "You mean—" The dawning comprehension in her eyes as he levelly met hers caused a spark of anger to ignite in their blue depths. Wrenching her hand from her mother's, she groped at her finger for the engagement sapphire cluster ring he had given her. "Then, sir, I must return this to you forthwith!" she cried in a high dudgeon.

Calmly, Benedict had held out his hand, and she dropped it into his palm. He had closed his fingers around the ring and dropped it into his inner breast pocket before she could change her mind. Then with a brisk bow, he had turned on his heel and headed for the door.

Behind him, all had dissolved into chaos as Mrs. Anderson announced in a shrill voice that quivered, "Josiah, the invitations have all gone out! The disgrace!" There was the sound of a wail and a crash as the small occasional table was overturned. Josiah bellowed, but whether it was his wife or his daughter that had gone off in a swoon, Benedict found he neither knew nor cared.

He had wrenched the door open and found the maid crouched down listening at the keyhole. She straightened up and took a hasty step back to make way for him. Benedict grabbed his hat and coat and got outside of the house as fast as his legs could carry him. When he got to the top of the road, he thought he heard running footsteps, and someone call out "Wait." He did not even hesitate but had sharply turned right and not looked back.

Benedict slept soundly that night for the first time in a long while. The next morning, strangely enough, his thoughts had turned to Lizzie Anderson, wondering how she was faring under Mrs. Napp's roof. He smiled grimly, doubting a shared room and likely a bedroll on the floor would be suiting her somehow. How the mighty had fallen!

After breakfast, he headed on impulse to an auctioneer house and spent the rest of the day viewing horses and wagons. He felt restless. The idea of upping sticks appealed to him. More and more his thoughts turned to Greenwich Fair and the red and white boxing booth that would stand proudly among the fluttering tents. Why should he not join his brothers there? What was to stop him?

One last season under the canvas would give him time enough to ponder his next move *and* find a buyer for his third of the business. He could hardly consider himself out until he had sold his share. As he walked around the wagons and carts, with a keen eye for a bargain, he found himself making his mind up. He would go to Greenwich. He would settle things with his brothers, and he would complete one last season on the fairs.

His shoulders felt all the lighter now he had made his decision, shed his fine house, and cut loose his fiancée. He was footloose and fancy-free. He was his own man again. He had sold the engagement ring that morning and wound up purchasing a sturdy Irish cob and a wagon with the proceeds. It had been lived in by farm laborers while traveling for work and was a bit beat up and tatty looking, but Benedict didn't want anything showy or new for his last season. What was the point? He had no one to impress, and besides, it did not do to encourage folk to think you might have something valuable inside when you were leaving it unattended all day to work the booth. The previous owners even threw in some cast-iron cooking utensils and pots, and he was satisfied he'd got himself a good buy.

The wagon had two large fixed wooden trunks to store everything away inside and a wooden bed frame of decent size. That afternoon, he bought a sprung mattress, new bedding, a basin and jug, a hurricane lamp, and a box of candles and thought himself well equipped. Why then, did something niggle away in his mind telling him he had forgotten something?

It wasn't until he lay abed that evening that he realized what nature the unfinished business was that tugged at his memory. Tomorrow was to be his wedding day. He doubted very much that anyone at Sitwell Place had thought to let the parson at St. Mary's know the ceremony was no longer required. The Andersons had very much looked down on that humble church of red brick, so different to the austere gray stone of their beloved St. Joseph's. At eleven o'clock, it was likely the vicar would don his cassock and look in vain for the bride and groom.

Once again, his thoughts turned to Lizzie Anderson. He would go and see her on the morrow and see how she was bearing up, he thought with cruel amusement. He smiled to himself, and it was not a particularly nice smile. She would likely be fit to drop by now, as the true hopelessness of her situation dawned on her. Or maybe not, he thought with a twinge of interest. She was no coward, to give her her due. She would fight, alright, and go down fighting to the death sooner than admitting defeat.

She was a scrawny, sanctimonious, holier-than-thou know-it-all, but craven was one thing Lizzie Anderson was not. He recalled how gamely she'd swung that tatty carpet bag of hers at her attacker's head. She had not shrunk from confrontation as so many with her upbringing would. If he hadn't been there, she would have suffered a nasty blow for her pains, but he doubted even that would have daunted her for long. No, she was not faint-hearted, he thought with a flicker of something he could not quite identify as the clock struck midnight in the quiet house.

In fact, if she'd only agreed to take back her testimony against Reverend Milson, she could have remained in the familiar comfort of Sitwell Place. She must know that as well as anyone, but Lizzie Anderson would never retract a statement she knew to be true. Even on their slight acquaintance and despite the fact he did not like her, he knew this for a fact. She had faced down that table full of detractors and hypocrites with a stout heart, even though her face had been red and her expression dismayed.

Even under duress, she would not alter her story. Though it cost her her home and her family and every friend she'd ever possessed, Lizzie Anderson would not tell a convenient lie. Unlike Betsy, who must know deep down that the precious reverend was guilty as sin and her flesh and blood quite blameless. Placing his hands behind his head, he pondered that two first cousins could be so unalike. One so full of grace and charm, the other full of piss and vinegar. They could not be more dissimilar.

Betsy and Lizzie. Lizzie and Betsy. Despite the obvious differences, their names were, in fact, the same—Elizabeth Anderson. He remembered once that Bets had told him both were named in memory of their shared paternal grandmother. A cog somewhere turned slowly in his brain. *Elizabeth Anderson.* The banns that had been read at St. Mary's the last three weeks had been for Benedict Toomes and Elizabeth Anderson.

He sat up in bed, frowning into the dark. Why did that thought now strike him as significant? He was breathing hard, his brain racing as he let his mind run amok over the crazy scenario that now occurred to him. After all, why should he not substitute one bride for another? The vicar would likely not notice, especially if Lizzie wore a veil. She was a little taller than Bets, two years older, and her figure decidedly sparer, but again, in a dimly lit church, would the vicar make that distinction? Neither one of them were members of his regular congregation.

Benedict ran over the details they had given the clergyman at the time of their registering. Elizabeth Anderson, spinster of Sitwell Place, Pimlico, to marry one Benedict Toomes, bachelor of Winchester Street, Clapham. That much would still be entirely factual, and none could say different. He doubted very much that any of the Andersons' friends and acquaintances would turn up now. In fact, he was damn sure that among their circles precious little else would have been discussed for the past three days.

The church would likely be empty, and it would not be until signing the register that things such as their date of birth and parents' names would be recorded. Ben fell back on his pillows. Had he gone stark raving mad? Or was he seriously considering suggesting Lizzie Anderson take her cousin's place by his side at the altar?

His heart thudded in his chest at the prospect, though why that should be, he had not the faintest notion. He frowned. Having a wife in tow *would* fend off unwelcome questions from his brothers about what he had been doing with himself since he had been out of jail. He could use a new wife as a welcome deflection. Given what a thorn in his side Lizzie Anderson had been for the past couple of months, it would serve her right if he used her now for his own ends.

Didn't she deserve some retribution for the many freezing looks and cold blasts of disapproval she had directed his way? An unholy gleam entered his eye. He wouldn't be bored while he extracted his pound of flesh from her, that was for certain. If he meant to get her up the aisle, he would not have to mention how he intended to spend the next nine months. She would not like the wagon nor the noisy fairs, he reflected. Nor being the wife of a common fairground bruiser. He contemplated the prospect of her humiliation with some relish. But after all, what choice did she have left? Her own stiff-necked principles had left her wholly without future or prospects.

He stared up at the shadowy ceiling anticipating her reaction to his proposal and how he would counter every argument she might make. Because for some reason, it now seemed he was set on taking Lizzie Anderson to wife.

When he finally dropped off to sleep, he did so with a smile playing about his lips.

The next morning, he rose early, dressed in his black suit, and set off for Mrs. Napp's rooms. To his surprise, his knock on the door was answered by a harassed-looking Lizzie. She was pale and drawn, and her hair was not yet neatly pinned in a coil at the nape of her neck. Instead, it hung loose about her shoulders, thick and waving like pale gold.

Seeing the direction of his gaze, Lizzie colored and stepped back to allow him to enter. "I'm afraid you find me at sixes and sevens this morning, Mr. Toomes. I've been up all night finishing my share of the dress shirts," she said wearily. "They had to be finished for this morning."

Benedict entered the room, glancing about. "Where is everyone?" he asked.

"Mrs. Napp has taken the shirts to her supplier, and the other girls are still sleeping," she told him, glancing at the door to the next room. "I was going to try and join them and get my head down for an hour or so, but I suspect they'll be rising soon."

"I doubt you'd sleep now the sun's up in any case."

Lizzie gave an unladylike snort. "I could sleep on a window ledge right now!" she retorted. "If I ever see another shirt, I swear I'll scream."

A smile tugged at his lips. "You're not finding it to your tastes, then? The slopwork?"

Lizzie's face went blank. "I daresay I shall get to grips with it eventually," she told him bravely, but he could see at least a dozen tells that she was scared out of her wits at the prospect. From the nervous way her fingers curled into her palms to her red-rimmed eyes, she was a mass of nervous agitation.

"How's your money lasting?" he asked with a faintly malicious edge as he walked over to the window and gazed out onto the street below. People were just starting to appear on the cobbles, scurrying off to their places of work.

Lizzie swallowed. "Not terribly well," she admitted. "I had to buy my share of the candles to work by and coal for the fire. Then there's jugs of beer for everyone to drink and my share of the food… It all adds up…" Her words trailed off despairingly. "I was wondering," she began awkwardly. "If you would be willing to take my spare dress along to the pawn shop for me. Just to tide me over."

"You'll end up with just the clothes on your back at this rate," he said coolly, glancing her over.

Lizzie bridled a moment before her shoulders slumped. "After all, what does it signify?" she said hopelessly. "I have more pressing needs right now than a change of clothes." He shrugged as though acknowledging the truth of this statement. "How—how do you find everyone at Sitwell Place?" she asked with a slight tremor in her voice.

"As firm in their belief of Reverend Milson's innocence as ever," he replied dryly. "They are immovable on that subject."

Lizzie nodded, but her gaze skittered away. "I see," she whispered, her eyes gazing blindly over his shoulder.

"Betsy and I have broken our engagement off," he said without expression.

Lizzie started at his words and stared at him. Her lips moved for a second before she found her voice. "Over Reverend Milson?" she asked faintly.

He shrugged. "I refuse to join my lot in life with someone whose mind is so closed; they cannot accept plain truth when they hear it."

Lizzie gaped. "But—but—"

"Which brings me to my next point," he said ignoring her interruption. "You're someone who doesn't flinch from hard facts." For once, Miss Anderson seemed lost for words. When his interrogative stare told her he wanted a response, she nodded dumbly. "How do you fancy the job, then?" he asked softly. "Think yourself equal to it?"

"Job?" She looked bewildered at the turn the conversation had taken.

As well she might, he acknowledged to himself wryly. "In short, I have need of a wife," he said briskly. "You have shown yourself to have a backbone, and believe me, any wife of mine will need one."

She blinked. "Am I to understand—" She raised a hand waveringly to her forehead and pressed it there. "I think I must be sleeping right now," she muttered.

"Is it such a dream of yours to receive an offer of marriage from me?" he asked.

That was a step too far, even for Lizzie Anderson, who was quite crushed in spirit. She dropped her hand smartly. "Hardly!"

He smirked. "You're in a fix and so am I," he responded. "Why not help one another out, to our mutual benefit?"

"Just what kind of a fix are you in, Mr. Toomes?" she asked with a flash of her old suspicion.

Benedict shrugged. "My family expect me to show up with a new bride in tow. I've avoided them since my release. A fresh marriage will ward off unwanted questions and spare me any embarrassment over wasting two months in fruitless courtship."

"So, you have need of a wife?" she repeated slowly and gave her head a quick shake as if trying to dispel a fog.

41

"I do," he agreed smoothly. "And you have dire need of a paying occupation and a roof over your head. I think you're honest enough to admit this situation isn't really working out for you." He glanced around the shabby, overcrowded room.

Lizzie looked down at her hands. "I—yes," she agreed with that innate honesty he was starting to admire. "I'm not even sure how long Mrs. Napp can afford to keep me on."

"The church is already booked for eleven o'clock," he pointed out. "I don't think we should let it go to waste, do you?"

5

Lizzie tugged at the skirt of her green taffeta dress, so recently reclaimed from the pawn shop, and wished there had been time to properly get the creases out. A strange odor clung to it, a sort of vague mustiness which filled her with distaste. She did not like to think where it must have lain these past three days and in what company. Suddenly, she remembered the silly rhyme Betsy had pored over for days before picking out her own wedding gown: *Married in green, ashamed to be seen.* Lizzie bit her lip. Of course, Betsy had chosen a very pretty ice blue for her own dress. *Married in blue, he'll always be true,* her cousin had recited smugly as she had primped herself in the looking glass.

Not that Lizzie believed in such nonsensical superstitions, she reminded herself. And just as well, for the past week had been filled with nothing but ill omens. When he had returned her best dress to her, Benedict Toomes had also handed her a heavy veil of ivory lace. She had not liked to ask him where he had got it, though she suspected it was probably from the same pawn shop.

It could have belonged to some jilted bride for all she knew. It was nothing like Betsy's pretty mantilla veil; she knew that much. Then again, she had none of her cousin's accessories, the wrist-length white kid gloves, the silk stockings, or the necklace with a drop pearl. In truth, she was surprised that Benedict Toomes had thought to get her a veil. Their marriage was a business transaction, nothing more. He had described it to her in terms of a way to pay her way in life. In truth, many marriages operated along similar lines, so she had little to feel uneasy about on that score.

It just felt so unreal, she thought distractedly as Mrs. Napp's apprentices helped her drape and pin the veil in place over her bonnet. They did so with many exclamations and nudges to one another. They had all been agog at the news that she was to be married that day. Mrs. Napp had called her a "sly puss," pinched her chin, and declared it was little wonder that the Andersons had thrown her out of their home if she had stolen their daughter's bridegroom!

When Lizzie had tried to protest, Mrs. Napp had laughed heartily. "Don't waste your breath, my girl," she'd recommended. "I don't blame you. If I was a few years younger, I'd have a go at stealing him meself!" This had been greeted with giggles and whispers, and Lizzie glanced uneasily at Benedict. Mercifully, he did not appear to be paying attention. "Me and Lucinda will come with you to the church and act as your witnesses, and I can't say handsomer than that," Mrs. Napp had continued with satisfaction.

When Lizzie had tried to say that this was not necessary, Mrs. Napp had turned insistent. "Isn't the bride being married out of me own home?" she had asked belligerently. Benedict Toomes's eyebrows had risen, but it seemed he had taken the hint and duly sent for some celebratory refreshments which had greatly impressed the girls. They fluttered around in excitement at the sight of the jellied eels, fried pigs' trotters, and pickled whelks from the street vendors. Lizzie's stomach had turned, though she had tried a cup of "rice milk" which seemed to be extremely thin rice pudding with sugar and spices added to it.

Eliza had run down to buy more beer and returned with a very large pink rose which had become detached from its stalk. "Let me 'ave it for a ha'penny, the flower seller did," Eliza announced proudly as she presented it to Lizzie. "On account of it's snapped clean off, but it was still the biggest flower she 'ad." Lucinda snatched the bloom from her sister and pinned it to Lizzie's bonnet. "I wanted her to have it for a bouquet!" Eliza objected with spirit.

"She can't carry a single rose head down the aisle," her older sister told her witheringly. "Have some sense, do!"

"Now, girls," Mrs. Napp said from where she was mixing a rum punch with fruit peelings, treacle, and nutmeg. "You stop that squabbling. Today is Miss Lizzie's wedding day, and we'll not have any quarreling. Susan, you fetch that poker from the fire and mind you don't burn yourself."

Susan wrapped her petticoat around the handle gingerly and withdrew the poker before carrying it to her mother. No sooner had Mrs. Napp taken it than she plunged it determinedly into the jug of rum punch. The beverage bubbled and hissed, and all the girls clapped with delight.

"Now fetch the cups. Some of you younger 'uns will have to wait your turn, but we must all toast the health of the bride and groom," Mrs. Napp announced.

Lizzie glanced at Benedict, but his face gave nothing away. He accepted the cup proffered to him and paused for the toast. Lizzie found herself doing likewise, as though there was nothing irregular about it. She knew for a fact the bridegroom was not usually permitted so much as a glimpse of a bride before the wedding, let alone to sit in the same room and watch her as she prepared for church. As for the toast, Lizzie was sure that was supposed to happen *after* the wedding, not before.

Still, they would have no wedding breakfast celebration like the one so carefully planned at Sitwell Place, with an iced plum cake, cold pheasant, and oysters. She really ought to make the most of her current fare, she thought, remembering belatedly that she had not eaten since lunchtime the previous day when she had partaken of stale bread and a rather hard cheese. She had felt too sick with worry to join the others in a bowl of stew at suppertime.

"Long life and happiness," Mrs. Napp said solemnly once the amber-colored contents of the jug had been sloshed into every cup.

"The bride and groom," Lucinda said loudly, and everyone took a swig. The smaller children were then given the dregs, which they enthusiastically downed. Lizzie wet her lips and then handed hers surreptitiously to Eliza, who was quick to swallow it before anyone else could lay a claim to it.

Benedict reached into his waistcoat pocket and withdrew his watch. "We'd better be setting off," he commented. He turned to Lizzie. "You ready?"

Lizzie nodded and looked about her. There was no spray of lilies for her to hold. It seemed strange to have no reticule to carry, but he was returning her here straight afterward to finish off her week with Mrs. Napp while he wound up his business affairs, whatever they were.

He was far too handsome for her, she thought distractedly as she eyed his upright figure, which looked so well in his understated dark suit. She was surprised Betsy had not insisted he wore a dress coat and top hat for the ceremony, but then again, he had never seemed the sort that could be bossed around.

Married 'neath April's changeful skies,
A checkered path before you lies.

She felt a shiver run down her spine. She'd never longed for orange blossoms or a bridegroom, yet here she was stepping into her cousin's place as a last-minute substitute. For a moment, her head seemed to reel at the sheer improbability of it. Then Benedict Toomes offered her his arm. She hesitated an instant, then took it. After all, it wasn't like she had a whole array of options open to her.

Scarcely an hour later, they were married in an empty church. Lizzie had been profoundly grateful that none of the St. Joseph's congregation had turned up, either through ignorance or to denounce her for a husband stealer. Benedict Toomes slipped a brass ring on her finger and promptly returned her to Mrs. Napp's lodgings with an assurance he would be back to fetch her early on Easter Sunday.

"Seems a funny sort of way to spend your wedding night," Mrs. Napp sniffed after Lizzie changed out of her green taffeta and back into her navy blue cotton dress.

"We thought it would be best if I finished out my week with you," Lizzie murmured, taking the seat next to her hostess and resuming her sewing. She could hear the apprentices whispering to each other as she threaded her needle. "He has some business to sort out, and besides, nothing can really be done over the Easter weekend."

"When I was a girl, it was frowned on to marry at all during Lent," Mrs. Napp commented. "Still, times is changing and not for the better," she sighed. She had made another jug of rum punch from the feast Benedict had provided and signaled now for Suzy to refill the cups. "We'll toast your health again, Miss Lizzie."

"She ain't Miss Lizzie now, Mam!" Lucinda reproached her. "She's Mrs. Benedict Toomes! You saw her wedded yourself not two hours ago!"

"Well, so I did," Mrs. Napp agreed. "But she don't seem a married woman to me yet, and that's the truth!"

Lizzie gave a strained smile as the cups were held up solemnly toward her. One was pressed into her own hand. She took a cautious sip. This concoction tasted more of gin than rum.

"And where's this 'usband of yours taking you on Sunday, if I might be so bold?" the older woman asked. Lizzie felt all eyes present swivel to her. She opened and closed her mouth. Well, really, she thought with surprise, she had no idea! "Hopefully to church," Lizzie said smartly. When they all continued to gaze at her expectantly, she added slowly, "I believe Mr. Toomes is currently in lodgings. So, he will likely take me along there."

Mrs. Napp shrugged. "Churching's all very well," she said dismissively. "But you'll want to get established in your new home with your things set up around you."

What things? thought Lizzie. As of now, she owned a bible and precious little else. She nodded as though she knew what the other woman was talking about.

"That's a fine punch," Mrs. Napp said, smacking her lips. "Suzy, add a little more nutmeg to the mixture. We'll eke out another jug before it's done." The girls murmured with approval at this idea, and Suzy ran to throw the last of the ingredients into the jug. "I think you said Mr. Toomes was undecided about his current line of business?" Mrs. Napp pried. "'E'll need to make his mind up sharpish, now he's got a wife to support. I'm not so sure I'd let my Cindy marry a fellow what hasn't got an established trade."

Lucinda preened while Lizzie struggled to quell the wave of uneasiness breaking over her. Really, she knew next to nothing about the man. Recalling he was now her wedded spouse gave her a nasty jar. She glanced down at the brass ring and found her finger was turning green underneath it. Had he been intending to give a brass ring to Betsy? She did not think her cousin would have been pleased with anything but gold. Vaguely, she remembered the flashy engagement ring which had been her cousin's pride and joy. Maybe it had been a fake? It had been rather large.

Lizzie bit her lip as the thought occurred to her that Benedict Toomes could well be one of those confidence tricksters that you read about in the newspapers. He was good-looking enough, and Lizzie did not think highly of her cousin's mental faculties. Betsy was a fool for a pretty face and a glib tongue, though she did not think Mr. Toomes was glib exactly. He had no patter of cozening talk to take a body in. Just those disquieting eyes of his that rested on you and made you feel all of a quiver. What if he had up and left her just as he had Betsy?

"'E's got a trade, Ma," Eliza piped up from where she sat between two of her sisters. "'E's a fighter. Miss Lizzie said so. Like wot Mr. Chapman was."

"So she did," Mrs. Napp agreed amiably. "'Spose there's nuffink to stop him falling back on that by way of making a living. Needs must when the devil drives."

"'Sides," Suzy added. "Cindy would take him alright, trade or no! I seen the way she looks at 'im through 'er lashes!" The apprentices greeted this with smothered laughs, but when Lucinda swiveled on her seat and pinned a fierce gaze on them, they cleared their throats and bent back over their sewing.

Mrs. Napp coughed. "Well now, there's no 'arm in looking. I daresay Miss Lizzie will agree." She stuck her tongue in her cheek. "There must ha' been plenty of looking and more besides to make 'im up and switch brides at the last minute!"

Lizzie blushed up to the roots of her hair. It was no good pointing out she never hankered after Benedict Toomes. After all, who would believe her?

"Now don't you take on, girl!" Mrs. Napp begged her. "There's no account for you to take on die away airs. All's fair in love and war, ain't that what they say? If you managed to lure him away from that pretty cousin of yours, then more power to your

49

elbow!" Lizzie didn't know where to look. "I daresay you'll make him a sight more capable wife in the long run," Mrs. Napp concluded comfortably. "A man like that needs more than a pretty face to keep him on the straight and narrow." Lizzie looked up sharply. Now just what did Mrs. Napp mean by that? The other woman chuckled. "Oh-ho, I don't doubt but you'll have to keep a lively eye on that man of yours."

Lizzie's stomach dipped. "Why do you say that?" she croaked.

"Just a certain something about him," Mrs. Napp said airily. "Wot's 'ard to pin down."

Lizzie had a terrible feeling Mrs. Napp spoke nothing but the truth. She went to bed long before the others, for she had not slept a wink the previous night. Thankfully, from the moment she lay down on the borrowed quilt in the back room, Lizzie slept. She did not wake when the others crept in by two and threes to join her. She did not stir when the lowliest of the apprentices rose to lay the fire. When she did finally wake, she did so suddenly and with a lurch of stark terror. She lay a moment, her heart racing, her eyes staring up at the ceiling as she listened to Mrs. Napp's gentle snores. What had she done?

Had she really walked up that aisle with Benedict Toomes the previous day? She raised a shaking hand and gazed in horror at the brass ring on her finger. Even in the gray morning light of the bedroom, she could see it. She must have been mad! She had been worn so ragged she had scarcely been able to string her thoughts together or known what she was doing! *Married…* She gulped. *Oh Lizzie, how could you have done anything so imprudent?* The sheer weight of her anxiety felt like it was crushing the very air from her lungs.

Bleakly she contemplated the drudgery of the day that lay ahead of her, struggling to set the sleeves into two dozen dress shirts, and shuddered. By the time she lay down on the hard floorboards at night, her eyes were tired with strain and her fingers stiff and cold. Whichever way she looked at it, her life had transformed into a living nightmare. Who could say if she had chosen a better or a worse fate by marrying Benedict Toomes? She shut her eyes with a faint groan. It was Good Friday. She had only two more days before he would return for her. And then what? Hopefully, he would prove a disinterested sort of husband who would set her in his house and then forget all about her!

Her eyes popped open. Had he told her his plans and she forgotten? She could remember nothing, try as she might to recall his words. All she could bring to mind right now was his claiming to be in a tight corner and needing a wife. She frowned. He had said something about fending off his family's curiosity, but that didn't seem to make a whole lot of sense in the cold morning light. Was he expecting an imminent visit from them, then? She felt quite at sea about the whole thing.

She must have been operating under some sort of brain fog the day before, which had blunted her thinking faculties. As soon as he had mentioned marriage, she ought to have run in the opposite direction and fast! *Too late for that now, my girl,* Lizzie told herself bracingly. *You've made your bed and now you have to lie in it.* The thought gave her an unwelcome shiver. A married woman did not generally sleep in her bed alone, she thought with some trepidation.

Lizzie's fingers tightened on the edge of her blanket. It was unlikely he wanted her for *that,* she told herself firmly. If so, he would have picked another pretty bride, like Betsy, not the likes of her. Lizzie knew herself to be plain and thin as a rake. She always had been. Men's gazes did not warm for her, as they did for desirable women. Benedict Toomes's gaze had never dwelt on her with admiration or pleasure and nor did she want it to!

He was the most alarming man she had ever met, more so even than that brutish specimen who had accosted her mere days ago in the street. After all, Mr. Toomes had sent him sprawling in the dirt with very little effort. So, what did that say about him, then? She knew him to be a convicted criminal for he had served nine months at Her Majesty's pleasure in Exeter jail.

In vain, she tried now to remember what reason Betsy had given for his deplorable behavior of brawling in a public place. Her cousin had maintained the incident had been some kind of misunderstanding. How scornfully she had listened to Betsy's excuses for her intended, she recalled now with uncomfortable clarity. She had thought her words a lot of humbug for an ungovernable nature, and yet here she was, now his legally married wife!

Lizzie took a deep breath. This was no good; all she was doing was scaring herself silly. If Mr. Toomes had viewed her with any sort of illicit desire, he would hardly have left her here to sleep on the floor since their marriage! Certainly, she rallied, he had shown himself to have no interest in consummating their hasty union.

She could see no reason why that should change any time soon. He had married her for convenience. Likely he meant to set her in charge of running his house and keeping it comfortably, she told herself firmly. She could certainly do that, she reflected, so all this panicked conjecture was fruitless and likely pointless. She would be a glorified housekeeper, nothing more.

Feeling a little comforted by such thoughts, she rose, dressed, and took a hasty wash with her sponge which had been soaked in vinegar and water. Lucinda had shown her the trick of it for washing when there was no regular supply of fresh water. She had twenty-four shirts to work on before her new husband fetched her on Sunday. If she intended to meet her obligations she had better set to work at once.

6

By the time Easter Sunday arrived, Lizzie was exhausted and practically dead on her feet. She had barely managed to fulfill her needlework obligations, and her eyes felt gritty and tired. When Lucinda shook her awake, she had scarcely managed to snatch three hours' sleep.

"You'd best be getting up now, Lizzie," Lucinda whispered urgently. "He'll be coming to fetch you shortly. I left you as long as I could."

Lizzie thanked her and dressed hurriedly in her navy gown. By the time she emerged into the front room, Lucinda had buttered her a piece of bread and made her a cup of black tea. Lizzie accepted both gratefully and took them over to the window.

"Eh, you do look a wan, pale thing," Lucinda told her critically, looking her up and down. "Mr. Toomes will think you go in mortal terror of him."

A mouthful of bread went down the wrong way and Lizzie went off in a coughing fit. When she could speak once more, she apologized and swiped at her watering eyes with her handkerchief.

"Now you look like you've been crying your heart out half the night too," Lucinda added, clicking her tongue.

"I'm just tired," Lizzie answered quickly. "I'm unaccustomed to large quantities of sewing under such time constraints."

Lucinda nodded, accepting this. "You would have made a go of it, given time, I daresay."

"Do you really think so?" Lizzie was doubtful. "I always thought myself a decent seamstress, but this experience has rather humbled me in my opinion of my abilities."

Lucinda smiled wryly. "I'll let you in on a secret—Mother threw you in the deep end. You should never have started on setting sleeves. You're supposed to work up to it."

"Oh!" Lizzie lowered the teacup in surprise.

"Me or Mother does it usually, so you've spared us a job." Lucinda shrugged.

Lizzie felt a flash of indignation, but it quickly dispersed. After all, the Napps had taken her in when no one else would. "Well, you don't have an easy time of it, earning a living through this means."

"I won't disagree with you," Lucinda said easily enough. "But at least you're out of it now."

Lizzie shifted uncomfortably. "Yes," she murmured, wondering if she was jumping out of the frying pan and into the fire.

A knock on the door startled them both. Lucinda started wordlessly to answer it, and Lizzie hurried to fetch her cloak, bonnet, and bag.

Five minutes later, she was following Benedict Toomes out into the street. He had hold of her bag, and it was as much as she could do to keep up with his long strides.

"A post boy is holding my horse," he said, looking at her over his shoulder. "And I don't mean to keep him waiting long."

"Your horse?" Lizzie echoed blankly. He made no reply. "Are we traveling far?" she persisted.

"No," he said briskly. "Only to Greenwich."

"Greenwich?"

"Do you mean to repeat everything I say to you?" he asked, glancing back at her. He narrowed his eyes. "What ails you?"

"I'm just tired!" Lizzie said defensively. "I did not know you lived in Greenwich."

"We will both live there for the next week," he answered, and she thought he looked grimly amused by his own words. She was just opening her mouth to question him further when they rounded a corner and he hailed a muscular young man who was stood murmuring to a sturdy-looking horse.

It was not the horse that captured Lizzie's eye, but rather the strange contraption that it was hitched up to. At first glance she had taken it for a large delivery wagon, but now she noticed that in place of a scrolling advertisement of wares on the side, there was instead a small shuttered window. Lizzie blinked. In shape it resembled a regular tin loaf and was painted a dull bottle green. Lizzie stared at it until it sunk in that it was a tiny home on wheels.

"*This* is your house?" she gasped incredulously before she could stop herself.

Luckily, her husband was addressing the youth and passing over a coin. "Lizzie, come!" he said, turning impatiently and addressing her rather in the manner of one summoning a terrier dog. He held out a hand to her irritably. "I'm keen to be off."

This snapped her out of her stupor. Hurrying forward, she accepted his hand and was helped up a step onto a footboard before a curious little door. Were they to go inside? she wondered. She tried to peer in through a little window at the top of the door, but it had sacking hung over it instead of curtains, obscuring her view.

"You need to sit on this," Benedict said, patting the footboard and settling down on it to demonstrate. He had the reins in his hands and eyed her impatiently as Lizzie lowered herself with exaggerated care.

"Is this safe?" she blurted. "To sit perched here while we are in motion? There is no guard rail."

"It is perfectly safe," he answered coolly. "Brace your feet as I do, against the struts."

Following his example, Lizzie placed her booted feet against the wooden contrivance by which the horses were attached to the wagon. This did help her feel more secure, she had to admit. "Yes, that is better," she agreed cautiously.

"You had better put your arm through mine," he said, casting a disparaging look at her, "if you're scared of tumbling off."

Lizzie opened her mouth to refute this offensive claim when he tugged the cap he wore on more firmly and shook the reins. "Let her have her head," he called to the youth.

The lad sprang back, and then with a lurch, they were away. Lizzie gave a small screech and scrabbled to grab at Benedict's arm. With her other hand, she reached for her bonnet, despite the fact she knew the ribbons to be firmly tied. Once she had a tight grip of both husband and bonnet, she felt a little better. His arm was so solid with muscle that she could not fail to feel securely tethered.

It was not until they reached the end of the street and swung out to turn into the next that Lizzie managed to relax her clutching fingers. She was surprised he had voiced no objection to her death grip, she reflected in embarrassment, though she could not bring herself to thank him for his forbearance.

Soon, Lizzie's eyelids were drooping, despite her precarious perch. The clip-clop of the horse's hooves was strangely soothing, and they were moving at such a sedate pace that the jolting of the wagon hardly jarred her at all. The cumbersome size and shape of the little house on wheels no doubt accounted for this, but even so, she was profoundly grateful for the fact Benedict Toomes was not reckless at the reins.

"Lizzie!"

Hearing her name so sharply spoken, Lizzie straightened up with a gasp. "What is it?" she mumbled.

"How much sleep did you get last night?"

Lizzie reddened. "Not more than three hours," she admitted. "I had too much sewing to do for sleep."

"Well you can't sleep here," he admonished. "Get along into the back."

"What do you mean?" She glanced over her shoulder at the door.

"There's a bed in there," he said. "Go and get your head down for a couple of hours."

"A bed?" she blurted in surprise, before realizing she was repeating his words again.

"Aye, go and get in it." She stared at him stupidly for a moment before she managed to collect herself. "Reach up and open the door," he instructed, "and then crawl in on your hands and knees."

Lizzie gave herself a little shake and then reached up to open the little green door. It swung inward and she turned about, placing her palms inside the door and then inching forward until she could swing her legs up onto the footboard. It felt vastly

58

undignified, and she did not dare glance at Benedict Toomes. More than likely he got an eyeful of her petticoats in the scramble.

She had barely managed to maneuver herself inside when he yelled at her to close the door. Lizzie scrambled to her knees and did so maintaining a dignified silence. Once inside, she gazed about her with bemusement. As both windows were covered, the interior was dimly lit, and it took a moment for her eyes to adjust to the gloom. She could make out a bed and what looked like two large trunks.

Staying on her knees, for she did not trust the motion of the wagon would make a reliable floor, she made for the bed. To her surprise, she could feel fresh, clean sheets already made it up. Climbing onto it, she removed her cloak, bonnet, and shoes, set them on the top of one of the large trunks, and then rolled onto her side, letting her weary eyes drift shut.

When next she woke, she realized immediately that they had come to a halt. She blinked a moment, rolled onto her back, and gazed up at the wooden roof above her. They must have arrived at whatever destination Benedict Toomes had intended. But why had he not roused her from her sleep?

She sat up and peered around her at the strange surroundings. She could hardly believe this wooden box with windows was his house. Betsy would have been appalled to find this as her new home, she reflected. As for herself, living in two shabby rooms with the six Napps and their four apprentices had taught her to be grateful for any roof over her head, however strange.

Tentatively, she set her foot over the edge of the mattress onto the floor and took a step. In her stockinged feet she tiptoed over to the covered window and, lifting one edge of the sacking, peered out.

To her astonishment, the sight that met her eyes was a great open field full of wagons and tethered horses and campfires. The field beyond in the distance seemed to be full of what she thought at first were canvas sails flapping in the wind, like little boats bobbing in the sea.

Had he brought her to the coast? she wondered with a lurch of excitement. Her aunt had once been persuaded to take a rest cure at Brighton after a bout of influenza, but Lizzie had not been permitted to accompany her. Then she frowned. Surely, they were not boats, but rather *tents*.

Then she remembered he had said they were going to Greenwich, not the seaside. *Greenwich at Easter*, she thought, piecing the puzzle together distractedly, when suddenly she let out a gasp. Surely, he could not have meant the infamous Greenwich Fair?

Her heart thudded as her spirits plummeted to her stockinged feet. Oftentimes, she had heard her uncle holding forth on the immorality and excesses of those springtime revels. No woman of respectability, he had always intoned gravely, would permit herself to be escorted to such a bacchanalia of wickedness. Of course, at the time, Lizzie had never thought there would be the slightest chance of her ever attending.

A sudden knock on the side of the wagon almost made her cry out with alarm.

"Lizzie, come out, my family's here to meet with you," called out her new husband's voice.

Lizzie froze. *His family?* She did not recall Betsy ever mentioning that he even had one. Pausing only to shove her feet back into her ankle boots, she crossed to the door, squared her shoulders, and swung it open.

"Here she is, my four-day bride," Benedict said in an expressionless voice, and Lizzie felt her color rise. Stood on either side of him were two men between whom she could see bore a very strong family resemblance to Benedict. They stood looking her over critically, Lizzie thought. Rather as if she were a mare one of them had bought at a horse fair.

When she stood hovering on the footboard, one of them was moved to speech. "Nay, lass, don't be shy," said the one stood to Benedict's right who sported a fine pair of sideburns. "We're your new brothers-in-law. I'm Frank and this here is Jack," he said, motioning to the third brother, who had a moustache. Other than the facial hair, their coloring was like her husband's, with their tanned skin and curling brown hair. Like him, they were tall and wore dark breeches and waistcoats, their shirt collars open at the neck.

"Cat got her tongue?" Jack asked rudely, sticking his hands in his pockets and looking at Benedict rather than to her.

Benedict smirked. "She's usually got plenty to say for herself," he said, coming forward, seizing her about the waist, and swinging her down onto the ground.

Lizzie bit back her exclamation of annoyance at this treatment and instead straightened herself, for she had realized her dress was disheveled from sleep. Even worse, she had forgotten her bonnet and her hair was straggling about her having come out of its neat bun.

Seizing her courage, she turned resolutely to Frank, who seemed the more civil of the two. "How do you do," she said with polite formality.

He grinned at her and offered his hand which she shook. "It's nice to meet you, Lizzie," he said cheerfully. "Welcome to the family."

"Thank you."

She turned to Jack, who pulled his hand out of his pocket. "Likewise," he drawled.

"Charmed, I'm sure," said Lizzie dryly as she shook his hand. Frank threw back his head and laughed heartily, though she thought Jack looked a little taken aback.

"You'll have to bring her over to the campfire tonight to meet Ma," Frank said. "And take your supper with us."

Benedict shrugged. "We'll have to see how we go."

"You coming with us now to help us set up the booth?" Jack asked. "If you want back in the business, you'll have to do your fair share." Lizzie saw Jack quail at the look Benedict turned on him.

"Ready to pay me now for your third of the business, are you?" Benedict asked in freezing tones. "The way I look at it, I legally own the lion's share."

"None of that now," Frank said heartily. "None of that! We all know Ben's always pulled his weight and none could say any different. As for what Jack owes, he's good for it. Not going anywhere now, is he?"

Jack flushed and looked away and Benedict relaxed. Lizzie quickly deduced Frank must be the peacemaker, and she wondered what their birth order was. If she had to make a guess, it would be that Jack was the youngest.

"We're heading over to the booth now," Frank added affably. "It's as good an opportunity to show it to Lizzie before it's full of—" He bit back the words he'd intended. "Punters," he finished after a moment's hesitation.

Benedict cast her a speculative look which immediately put Lizzie on her guard. "Aye, that's true enough," he conceded. "Fetch your cloak." He turned away and started a low-toned conversation with Frank before she could raise any objection to this plan. *And what, pray, did they mean by "the booth"?*

The manner he had of barking out orders was certainly not likely to endear him to her any time soon, she thought grimly as she jammed her bonnet on her head and threw her cloak about her shoulders. As soon as she rejoined them outside, the four of them set off across the field toward the flapping white tents she had initially mistaken for sails.

As they grew closer, she saw the size and shape of the tents varied. Some were as big as a marquee and their signs gave wild boasts that they contained a whole theater troupe or even a ballroom. Others were so small, they were little more than a sheltering tarpaulin pulled over a table piled high with oranges or gingerbread.

Lizzie gaped with rounded eyes at the painted banners which made their grand boasts. "Returning from a triumphant tour of the Americas" claimed The Philmore Players. She turned to Benedict, wanting to ask him if the tent really held a portable stage, but he was deep in conversation with his brothers, so she held her tongue.

"That's our pitch over there," Jack said suddenly, pointing to where a loaded cart sat squarely in the middle of an area marked out by wooden stakes hammered into the ground.

Benedict narrowed his eyes. "It's a fair spot," he said grudgingly. "Though we're next to the clowns."

Lizzie followed the direction of their gaze and saw a strange assortment of people arguing over a pile of poles and strings.

Frank shrugged. "They draw a crowd; you can't deny that, Ben."

"I can't stand clowns." Benedict scowled.

Lizzie, who had never been to see such an act, stared hard. She found it hard to believe that so quarrelsome and tense a bunch could be capering clowns. Not one of them looked remotely merry. Suddenly one of them threw down his armful of sticks and began jumping up and down on them in an explosion of wrath. His fellows quickly fell silent and avoided each other's eyes as they went about their tasks in perfect silence.

Benedict and Jack walked past them without acknowledgment, though Frank raised a friendly hand which was ignored. When the Toomeses reached their wagon, they immediately began unpacking the contents.

Lizzie stood to one side. "Is there anything I can do?" she asked, clearing her throat. She was still wondering exactly what the Toomes brothers were purveyors of.

"Just stand there and look pretty," Frank quipped with a wink.

Not bothering to make a reply to so foolish a comment, Lizzie turned instead and looked with interest at the industrious activity all around her. As far as the eye could see there were stalls and tents being erected. She was flabbergasted that Greenwich Fair could be such a huge event. She'd had no notion that it could be so vast.

Opposite her, a man was hammering a post into the ground with a sign bearing a naked depiction of Adam and Eve, made decent only by the judicious placement of fig leaves. She was just wondering what their business could possibly be when another started unloading crates of bottled beers and liquors and carrying them inside. It was a public house, she realized with

64

disbelief, her mouth falling open. Her bosom swelled with indignation at their daring to take a biblical name for their den of iniquity!

"Told you we had a prime spot," Jack said, nodding toward the beer tent.

Behind her, the Toomes brothers were moving purposefully and briskly as their own booth started to take shape. It was a large square tent of off-colored white, and to Lizzie's eye, it looked rather devoid of interest. All around her she saw colored flags and bunting, but there seemed precious little to entice a passerby into the Toomeses' enclave.

"Here," said Benedict, thrusting a rolled-up pile of fabric into her arms. "Unfold this."

He picked up another and started to unfurl it as Lizzie shook out the large banner he had given her. The Toomes Brothers Boxing Saloon was spelt out on it in large red and black letters. Well, at least she knew what their act was, she thought with a sinking heart. After all, she had known he was a prizefighter.

From each corner of the sign was a length of string, presumably for attaching it to the tent. Lizzie had just sat herself down onto the grass and started unknotting the strings when Benedict turned with a snarl toward his brothers.

"What the fuck is this?" he demanded, holding his own banner aloft.

Frank and Jack looked at each other furtively before they turned back to their brother. Lizzie looked at the long sign painted in red and yellow with the interest. The Battling Burnett Sisters, it proclaimed jauntily.

Frank scratched the back of his neck. "We had to take on another turn, Ben. While you were serving your stretch. Me and Jack weren't enough to carry the show. Not on our own."

"We're the Fighting Toomeses," Benedict pointed out coldly. "Not a freak show."

"Now don't be like that," Frank sighed.

"We knew you wouldn't want us letting Pa back in the act," Jack piped up. "He came sniffing round as soon as he knew you weren't on the scene."

Benedict immediately went rigid. "You'd better not have," he growled.

"Of course we didn't!" Frank scoffed, but Lizzie could see he looked uneasy.

"Did you give him any money?" Benedict persisted.

"Course he did!" Jack burst out contemptuously. "You know what he's like where the old man's concerned."

"He is our father," Frank said wretchedly. "And he—"

"Save it!" Benedict growled. "I don't want to hear it! If I see him anywhere about, I'll ram his teeth down his throat with my fist."

Lizzie gasped at the visceral image this conjured. She had never dreamed such filial impiety was even possible.

Benedict threw her a warning glance before he continued. "And this?" he hissed, holding up the yellow banner.

Frank gazed back at him appealingly. "They were a real draw, Ben. We made more at Hull last year than we have in a long time—"

"They're still a fixture, then?" Benedict ground out furiously.

"Sadly not," Jack replied. "Would you believe someone only went and reported us the next month at the Goose Fair?" He sounded aggrieved. "The law showed up, slapped a heavy fine on us, and forbade them to box."

"It's prohibited for women to box publicly," Frank added. "It's alright so long as no one sells you down the river, but we got stung good and proper."

"Apparently," said Jack contemptuously. "There's those that think it's an affront to public decency. As though Ma didn't tell us she watched Elizabeth Wilkinson back in the day fight both men and women and gouge and kick as good as any man."

Benedict glanced briefly at Lizzie. "Those were different times," he muttered, throwing the banner down onto the ground contemptuously, flinging off across the field without so much as a glance in her direction.

Lizzie sat a moment, wondering if she should scramble to her feet and follow him. Then with a shrug, she decided to finish untangling the knotted strings instead.

"Jesus, I'd forgotten what a moody bastard he could be," Jack said, wiping his brow. "I hope you know what you've let yourself in for."

Lizzie ignored him. Whoever had torn the banner down at their last show the previous year had done so with a shocking lack of care. For some reason, she suspected Jack was the culprit.

"He was bound to take it hard," Frank said fairly. "We didn't consult him after all."

"What happened to them?" asked Lizzie curiously. "The Battling Miss Burnetts, I mean."

"We had to let them go," Frank replied absently, stroking his full sideburns. "It was a damn shame, but that fine really cut into the profits and we do the bigger fairs, so it's not like we could get away with going unregulated."

"They'll be touring the smaller fairs now," Jack explained. "Maybe have gone abroad. Prime pair of girls they were, too, and decent boxers, whatever Ben thinks of it."

Lizzie nodded and carried on tugging away at the knotted string until she had eased all the snarls out.

7

Benedict only made it to the end of the field before he stopped with a muffled oath and swung back around again. After all, what's done was done. He hadn't been around last season, and things had moved on without him. What was the point in cutting up rough? Especially when he was planning on abandoning the family business for good at the end of the season.

It was good, he told himself, frowning ferociously, that Frank had some new ideas. He'd need them in the future when Benedict wasn't there to carry them anymore. Jack was a feckless idiot, and Frank was too busy trying to juggle his roles as husband, older brother, and dutiful son to really be successful in any of his endeavors.

By the time Benedict had made his way back to the booth, the main red and black sign had been affixed to the tent and the yellow one had disappeared. Jack had sprung onto the pony's back, and Frank was offering to hand Lizzie up into the cart.

"She'll walk back with me," Benedict said dismissively.

"We'll see you this evening, then," Frank persisted. "At supper."

He shrugged a noncommittal reply as Lizzie stepped back and the horse and cart trundled away. Jack gave him an ironic salute which he ignored, turning instead to Lizzie.

"We'll walk back the roundabout way," he said. "You can get your bearings that way."

She looked surprised, but quickly fell in step alongside him. "I don't understand. How does boxing for your living work?" she asked after a few moments' silence. "Does the general public pay an admission fee to watch you fight?"

"Yes." Feeling her eyes on him, he turned to look at her. "It's a ha'penny entrance."

"I see," she said with a frown. "How many people do you suppose you could fit in your tent?"

"Forty," he hazarded. "Maybe fifty."

"And you and your brothers box each other for the entertainment of the crowd?" She frowned. "Do they not grow bored of watching the same matches? Do you have no other boxers on the roster for variety's sake?"

He cast a glance at her. "We sometimes spar each other, but in general it's volunteers from the crowd."

"I don't understand."

"Usually someone in the audience fancies their chances."

She gave an exclamation. "You mean, you box with visitors to the fair?" She sounded shocked.

"The fair moves around. We box with all comers—miners, colliers, navvies. We don't discriminate."

"It hardly seems sportsmanlike," she pointed out primly. "If they have not had formal training in the art."

A reluctant smile tugged at his lips. "The science," he corrected her.

"I beg your pardon?"

"Some would say boxing's a science rather than an art."

70

"Oh?" She sounded dubious but did not argue. Instead, she gazed at him frankly. "I cannot fathom why anyone should challenge you so foolishly."

This time he could not prevent his smile. "You have to put yourself in their shoes," he said after a moment's pause. "They're on a half day holiday and likely liquored up. Or maybe they're a big fish in a small pond."

"You mean," she said slowly, "that they might believe themselves proficient in fisticuffs?"

"A man usually knows if he can hold his own in a fight."

She shuddered. "It all sounds positively barbaric!"

"There's a money prize to be taken into account too," he pointed out. "If they can go three rounds with one of us, they win a pound."

"A pound?" Lizzie echoed in shock. He said nothing. "That is a great deal of money. But what is a round?"

"You'll see tomorrow when the gates are opened," he said dismissively, catching her arm and drawing her toward a nearby stall. "What will you have?" He nodded toward the array of pies and buns on display. She opened her mouth as though to decline.

"You've not eaten since this morning. I'll take two," he said, nodding toward the pies.

"Mutton or beef?" asked the vendor.

"I would like a currant bun, please," Lizzie interrupted him.

He amended his order and passed her the glazed bun. They walked the rest of the length of the field as they ate in companionable silence. Then he bought a bottle of beer for himself, though Lizzie insisted she would rather have orange juice. He looked skeptical and she pointed out the many orange stalls littered about the field.

"You'd get precious little juice out of most of them. They boil them to make them look fresh."

"Boil them?"

"Just one of the tricks to spruce them up. How about a lemonade?" She looked relieved and accepted this offer gratefully. He bought her a cup of the cloudy stuff and they carried on their way. "You know where we are yet?"

She glanced about and shook her head. "No," she admitted regretfully. "It just looks like a sea of tents in all directions to me."

"It'll be ten times worse tomorrow. All you'll see then will be people as far as the eye can see." Her eyes widened and he pointed into the distance. "The camp field is that way."

"I'll have to take your word for that," she said, and at this point, he was hailed by an old acquaintance.

"Ben! That you, love?" The woman who had been sauntering past them halted so abruptly that the large decorated hat perched atop her burnished curls quivered violently.

"Connie, aye, it's me."

She clasped his arm and beamed up at him, touching his cheek with a lilac glove. "Frank said he hoped you'd be joining them this season. How are you, love?"

"Good, yourself?"

"Oh, I'm grand," she said heartily. "I wintered at Brighton. Took the air like a proper lady and now I'm back better than ever."

"Frank tell you I'm married?" he asked casually, knowing full well he wouldn't have had the chance.

Connie's painted mouth fell open. "I was just wondering who this must be!" she exclaimed archly, turning to survey Lizzie appraisingly.

"Connie, this is Lizzie, my wife. Lizzie, this is Connie, an old family friend."

"How do you do?" Lizzie asked with scrupulous politeness.

"Pleased to meet the woman who got him up the aisle," Connie said humorously. "So, you stood by your man in his time of need, did you?" the older woman carried on, casting Lizzie a puzzled look. She might as well have said *You don't look the type*.

Benedict watched Lizzie's face redden. "We've only been wed four days," he said to cover her confusion.

"Why, you're still a bride," Connie said with a laugh. "Small wonder you're so covered in blushes!" She prodded her parasol into Lizzie's side and laughed uproariously at her obvious discomfort. "Wish I could still blush like that," she said with a twist of her lips. "Mine comes out of a rouge pot these days. You'll have to stop by our tent. I've got a couple of new girls, but Niamh's still with me and I've got a new girl for Salome. I'm expecting her to really draw the crowds." She lowered her voice. "Her last *keeper* was a lord of the realm, no less."

Benedict cast a quick look at Lizzie. "How about Alfred?" he said, steering conversation into safer waters by asking after Connie's hired muscle.

73

"Oh, Alfred," she answered with a spasm of irritation. "That great lummox ran off with my Amazonian she-warrior at the end of last season. I've not seen hide nor hair of either of them since."

Ben grinned. "Well, he deserved some luck. Always unlucky with the ladies was Alfred," he reminisced.

"I hope she robs him blind!" Connie snapped, forgetting her benevolence a moment. "Properly left me in the suds he has! Anyway," she said, "I can't stand here gossiping all day. Got to get back to my girls. Without me there to keep an eye on them, they'll be sitting around on their arses, the lazy mares!"

"See you, Connie."

"Cheerio!" She waved an airy farewell and moved away in a cloud of perfume.

Lizzie stared after Connie, and he wondered idly what she'd made of her. He could almost see the words trembling on her lips.

"Wondrous Females of the World," he said in answer to her unspoken question.

Her head swung around. "I beg your pardon?"

"You were wondering what her attraction was."

Lizzie frowned. "And just what are Wondrous Females?" she asked after a moment.

"Last time I looked, a snake charmer, a spotted woman, and a giantess."

Lizzie was struck speechless for a full moment. "And people pay to see those things?" she asked in a faint voice.

They were approaching a gate at the end of a field, and Benedict held it open for her. "They do," he said briskly as she passed through. He followed and they proceeded along the track until they reached a hedge leading to the camping field. He held out his hand, and Lizzie took it before clambering over the stile. She delicately averted her eyes when she had to lift her navy cotton skirts, revealing her petticoats.

As those garments looked to be more practical than decorous, he lifted an eyebrow at her excessive modesty. Still, he had to admit, she was taking things in her stride. Not many women of her station would still be standing after the week she'd had. She'd seen so many changes, it was a wonder she didn't have whiplash.

He knew damned well she had not known of his fairground connections, for he had never told Betsy of them even. His previous fiancée had claimed she wasn't interested in his past, but only his future, and in light of his recent custodial sentence, he had been glad of the fact.

He knew Betsy had tried to draw a discreet veil over his background wherever possible. She'd once described him as a "man of business" in his hearing, and he'd had to pull her up sharply about it. If prizefighting was a social embarrassment, then he suspected fairgrounds would mean utter disgrace.

On the whole, he reflected, he thought it for the best that he had taken Lizzie to wife instead. He watched her marching her way through the next field resolutely. Her social ruin had been complete the moment she had been thrown out by the Andersons. Left to fend for herself, she would have been in dire straits, so she could hardly complain at the situation she now found herself in. In fairness to her, she hadn't even tried.

By the time they had reached the camp field she was looking about with interest. "Is it this way?" she asked, pointing in one direction. He nodded and she looked pleased. "Yes, I thought I recognized it," she said with satisfaction.

"You think you could find your way back to the main arena?" he asked.

"Certainly," she answered with assurance.

"Good." She cast him a quick glance, though she said nothing. "Likely you won't want to hang about the boxing tent all day," he added. Her lips formed a wordless *oh*. Sure enough, she seemed to be struggling how to put something into words.

"What will I be doing?" she asked as they made their way past a cluster of gaily painted caravans such as circus performers used. "While you're pummeling day-trippers?"

He shrugged. "I'm sure we'll think of something." She fell silent at that, but he had the feeling she was biding her time.

"Frank is the oldest of you three brothers, I think," she ventured.

He shot her a look. "That's right," he said shortly.

"And Jack the youngest?"

"Also correct."

She hesitated. "I don't recall my cousin mentioning that you had brothers." He said nothing and she tried again. "Did—"

"The subject never came up," he interrupted her.

She pursed her lips. "I see," she murmured. "And if we go to supper with your family tonight, they mentioned I would meet your mother, I think?"

"My grandmother," he corrected her. "Ma Toomes."

"And she lives with your brothers?"

"I don't know the current arrangement," he said dismissively. "This is our wagon." He pointed, and she gave up whatever question had been hovering on her lips.

After that, he made himself busy gleaning flat stones and branches and building a small campfire nearby while Lizzie went inside to "tidy herself." Then he went and fetched water both for washing and for boiling and set the pans down next to the fire. He was in two minds about that evening, but it might be best to get it over and done with, he thought grimly, though God only knew what Lizzie would make of Ma!

If they stayed here, Lizzie wasn't the type to sit meekly by, he thought. She'd start poking and prying and want his whole damn life story. He glanced up, seeing her emerging from the wagon, her hair now neatly braided and looped under her ears and twisted up into that neat arrangement at the back. She looked so bloody respectable he almost winced.

Still, at least she didn't look fit to drop anymore. The sleep she'd caught up on had taken that unnatural pallor away, and her eyes weren't red-rimmed or dull like they'd been when he'd married her in that empty church.

He'd caught the puzzled glances his brothers had sent her way. They didn't understand how he'd ended up leg-shackled to a prim miss like Lizzie Anderson, but that didn't bother him overmuch. He'd never worried about the opinion of others, and he wasn't about to start now. He adjusted the chain suspending the water over the flames.

"The water will be hot enough for you to wash in a bit," he said as she jumped down from the footboard. He should probably get some steps, he reflected as she righted herself self-consciously.

"Thank you," she murmured.

"You'll need to share my blanket," he said. "The ground's damp."

"Oh." She advanced toward him and gingerly lowered herself onto the blanket. "This looks a very neat setup," she commented, looking curiously at the fire and assorted pots and pans. He made no comment. "I noticed some of those other wagons had chimneys. Would they be for fireplaces?"

"Stoves," he answered briefly.

"They have stoves inside?"

He turned to look over his shoulder at her. "Yes," he said heavily.

She seemed to pick up on this cue and fell into silence. Strangely enough, he did not find it a companionable one. After a moment, he cleared his throat. "We'll go to supper with my family tonight," he said grudgingly.

"Very well."

"I'm not—" He wasn't sure how to continue. "Close with my family," he finished. Then again, he wouldn't say he was exactly close to anyone.

"I see." She paused. "I thought I was," she said, surprising him. "But I was wrong."

What reply could he make to that? He glanced back at her again. She was leaning forward toward the fire, her arms wrapped around her knees. "Are you cold?" he asked.

She shook her head. "Not on the outside," she said quietly, making him frown.

"What does that mean?" As soon as he uttered the words, he realized his mistake. The last thing he wanted was for her to tell him. She shook her head again and lowered her chin to her knees. Feeling sorry for herself, he supposed. For just a moment, he considered telling her he could always take her back to Mrs. Napp, but something stopped him. He wasn't sure what.

"What will we tell them?" she asked in a low voice, turning her face toward him. "About how we met, I mean." At his blank look, she added, "They're sure to ask."

"The easiest thing is to tell the truth and just omit the tricky parts. Try it," he said when he saw her frown. "How did we meet, Lizzie?"

She hesitated. "A—a mutual acquaintance introduced us?" she asked in a strangled voice.

He nodded. "Good. Now you ask me a question."

She lifted her head, coloring faintly. "How did you know I was the woman you wanted to marry?" she asked with more than a hint of challenge in her voice.

He considered this a moment. "You had certain qualities I admire."

"Really?" She sounded skeptical.

He nodded. "Now I'll ask you. How did you know?"

She swallowed. "How did I know I should marry you?" she asked, looking nervous. "I—well, you seemed to me the best prospect under the circumstances," she said scrupulously.

Against all odds, a smile twitched on his lips. "They'll likely guess your back was to a wall," he commented, and Lizzie's face flamed bright red. "Don't worry, they won't ask you that."

He reached over and dipped a fingertip into the pan of water. "It's warm enough. You wash first."

Not long after, they made their way into the next field where his brothers had two covered wagons parked next to each other and a pair of large piebald cart horses tethered. Frank hailed them both heartily and led them to the campfire which already had a large pot of stew bubbling away for supper.

Some packing cases had been set around the fire, and Frank even dusted off a cushion for Lizzie. She thanked him and arranged her skirts about her demurely. One of the tarpaulins was jerked back, and his grandmother clambered down, eyeing Benedict sardonically.

"So, you're back, are you?" she commented, squatting her straggly figure down next to the fire and stirring the pot with a large ladle.

"As you see," Benedict answered coolly. "This is Lizzie. Lizzie, this is my grandmother, Ma Toomes."

"Pleased to meet you," Lizzie said promptly, though God alone knew what she made of the old woman, he thought, watching Ma pull a pipe out of her pocket and demand a light. Jack obliged, rolling his eyes as he struck a match and leaned forward.

Ma puffed furiously on the clay pipe and gave a sharp nod of satisfaction when smoke began to rise from the bowl. "What?" she demanded when she noticed all eyes on her. "She'll have to get used to our ways if she plans on sticking around." She eyed Lizzie malevolently and looked disappointed to evoke no answer.

"Her bark's worse than her bite," Frank said with an awkward laugh. He started pouring a concoction which looked like a gin

80

punch into cups and passing them round. Lizzie took hers with a polite thanks.

"Here's to cheating the devil," Jack proposed with a grin, holding his cup aloft. "May we never arrive, but always be on our way."

Benedict's gaze flickered to Lizzie, who blinked at the toast but took a cautious sip of the brew all the same.

"You'll arrive alright!" their grandmother cackled as she tossed back her drink in three gulps. "Never doubt it, you young imp." She started ladling out the thick stew into bowls, and Benedict wondered idly where Frank's wife, Maggie, was. She had done all the cooking in recent years, and Ma happily retired from such duties to swig her gin and smoke her pipe.

He cast a sidelong look at the wagon, but it seemed they were all assembled already.

"Daphne made the stew," Jack said as though in answer to his unspoken question.

"Daphne?" Benedict repeated blankly.

"Aye, Daphne."

"And who the hell is Daphne?"

Frank coughed. "Her mother's the one Pa's taken up with at the moment. He left Daphne behind when they cleared out last summer."

Benedict narrowed his eyes. "Why should he leave her behind with you?" he asked sharply.

"You know what he's like, Ben," Frank said wearily. "He didn't ask permission."

81

"And where is Daphne this evening?" asked Lizzie suddenly.

"Oh, Daphne's taking her supper with a couple of those actresses from The Philmore Players tonight. They're old acquaintances of hers by all account."

"Actresses!" spat Ma with disgust. "That's a different name for it!"

"Ma," Frank cautioned.

"One of those actresses is uncommon pretty," Jack said thoughtfully as he took his bowl of stew. "Lips like a cupid's bow and hair that gleams as gold as a guinea."

Frank gave a short laugh. "Careful, Jack, you'll be following Ben here into the parson's trap."

Benedict took a mouthful of stew, refusing to rise to the bait. When he'd swallowed it and still no one spoke a word, he asked, "Where's Maggie anyway?"

If anything, the silence grew more pronounced. Ben had never been much affected by mood, so he listened to the crackle of the logs unconcerned as Frank replied in a low voice.

"She up and left me."

"When?"

"Must be some eight months ago now," Frank said gruffly.

Benedict's eyebrows rose. "You make any effort to retrieve her?" he asked.

"Where's the sense in that?" Ma interrupted sharply as Frank ducked his head.

"She's his wife," Benedict answered. He gave his brother a hard stare. Frank's face was averted and mostly in shadow. "You

82

seemed happy enough last time I saw you. What happened?" His brother stiffened, but still did not speak.

"Drop it, Ben," Jack urged.

"She made her choice." Ma scowled. "She couldn't hack the life; there's not many that can. Your own mother turned tail and Maggie was the same. Quitters with soft hands and heads full of dreams," she jeered. "This one of yours is no different, I'll warrant," she said, nodding toward Lizzie with a scornful twist of her lips. "I could tell as soon as I clapped eyes on her! You Toomes men are all the same. Too fond of a pretty face to pick wisely."

Benedict glanced at Lizzie, who was tucking into her stew. "I'm not much of a one for dreams," she said mildly. "As for my hands, they're toughening up by the day."

He laughed. He had to give it to her, she had plenty of self-possession. Betsy would have fallen apart at the seams confronted by a malevolent old hag like Ma. Realizing his brothers were looking at him curiously, he cleared his throat and held out his bowl for a refill. "How about another drink," he suggested.

Maggie's disappearance was glossed over, and the rest of the meal passed without too much friction. When they finally took their leave, Lizzie rose with a murmured thanks and good night and they started toward their own wagon.

"Well?" he asked, breaking the silence when they were out of earshot of his family.

"I'm not sure they knew what to make of me," she admitted, pulling her shawl tight about her shoulders.

Her reply surprised him. "And what about you? What did you make of them?" he asked, realizing he actually wanted to know.

She was quiet. "I'm not sure," she prevaricated. "It's difficult to get a full picture from just one meal," she said hesitantly. "It feels incomplete." At his mocking look, she grew defensive. "After all, you could scarcely have formed much of an opinion on me after dining at Sitwell Place a mere handful of times."

"Oh, couldn't I?" he replied dryly and saw her bristle. They walked in silence a moment.

"I collect," she said, "by your tone, that you did *not* form a good impression of me, Mr. Toomes."

He shrugged. "You made your own feelings about my presence at your table plain by your every disapproving feature, Mrs. Toomes."

He heard her breathe noisily in and out. "I wonder, then, that you even—" Whatever she had been about to say, she bit off, clearly thinking the better of voicing it. "That is to say, your grandmother may have had a very salient point," she said instead bitterly.

It was his turn now to catch his breath. He came to an abrupt halt, seizing her arm and swinging her about to face him. "What did you say?"

Lizzie glared up at him. "Betsy has a vastly pretty face," she panted. "But if you had set her down on a packing case to eat her supper in the middle of a field, she would have burst into tears and we both know it!"

He stared down at her, her flashing eyes, pink cheeks, and the heaving bosom that even her drab dress could not conceal. "Well then, it's a damned good job I didn't marry Betsy, isn't it?" he pointed out crisply.

"Some might think so!" she flung at him, and he marveled that she could have so little notion of self-preservation.

Maybe it was high time that someone taught Miss Lizzie Anderson—nay, his wife, he amended silently—a cautionary lesson. It seemed one was long overdue. He released her arm only to seize her roughly about the waist and drag her up bodily against him. She huffed and exclaimed but was too stiff with shock to put up much of a struggle.

"What are you—" His mouth put an abrupt stop to her words. Her indignant squawk was muffled as he explored the shape and taste of those pert lips, which ought to taste tart, but were instead cool and sweet, drawing a low rumble of pleasure from him.

As his one hand tightened at her trim waist, the other slid into the silky pale hair at the nape of her neck, urging her closer still as his tongue slid into her gasping mouth. The blood pounded in his ears when Lizzie grew pliant in his arms, and he forgot that he was supposed to be teaching her anything other than how to kiss so you forgot where you were.

A cough behind them in the darkness brought him back to earth with a bump. Lizzie gave such a violent start, it was as well he had a firm hold of her. "Who's there?" he asked gruffly, peering into the shadows.

"It's me," his brother Jack held up a lantern. "I came after you—thought you might need a light to see your way."

Benedict cleared his throat, though he did not let go of Lizzie, who was attempting to set herself to rights. With reluctance, he gave her the space, but seized hold of her hand instead, anchoring her to his side. "Good of you," he growled, anything but thankful.

Jack nodded and came alongside them, though he did not meet Ben's accusing gaze. "I—er—thought I'd better tell you about Maggie leaving," he said. "Frank doesn't like to talk of it."

Ben was silent a moment. "What happened?" he asked.

Jack shrugged. "Just one of those things. She got quiet and discontented and withdrew more and more each day. Bartholomew Fair it happened, last August." Jack hesitated. "Pa joined us for a few days with his new doxy and Daphne." Ben stiffened and Jack plunged on. "A loud-mouthed piece she was, and none of us liked her. Maggie was barely talking to any of us by that point. The third and final day, she just slipped away and disappeared into the night."

Ben grunted. "She leave any word where she was going?"

"Nope," Jack said, scratching the back of his neck. "I tell you, you could scarce get a word out of her. Even me. Frank was devastated, Ben; it really rocked him. He wasn't expecting her to walk out on him, however bad things had got between them. Pa tried to tell him to snap out of it and he'd find another woman in the next town, and Frank sent him sprawling, told him to get out of his sight and that he never wanted to see him again. Ma had to get between them, and Pa took off with his tail betwixt his legs after that."

Slightly mollified by the idea of Frank knocking down their father, Benedict unbent and the three of them started walking again in the direction of their wagon. "She ever get in touch after that?" Benedict prompted.

"She wrote to him two months after that at Weyhill. Said she wasn't coming back, and he wasn't to try and find her." Jack pulled a face. "Poor old Frank hasn't really bounced back from it all." Ben said nothing. "It wasn't Frank's fault, Ben," Jack insisted. "It wasn't like it was with Pa and our own mother."

"Oh, wasn't it?" he asked dryly. "So, Maggie wasn't expected to cook and clean for all her husband's family, as well as him? She didn't have to put up with Ma day in, day out, scolding her and telling her she wasn't good enough for a Toomes and never would be?"

Jack looked away. "You know that's just the old girl's way," he muttered.

"Tell me, has Frank taken up with this Daphne girl?" Benedict pursued coldly.

"Lord no! Nothing of that sort, I'd swear an oath on it."

Benedict snorted. "Frank's a fool if he didn't try to get Maggie out of it years ago. She deserved better than the life he gave her."

Jack stopped abruptly in his tracks. "Aye, well," he said sharply. "There's not everyone can turn their backs on their family as readily as you, Benedict," he said harshly. He held the lamp high. "This is you here, isn't it?"

Benedict didn't answer, just towed Lizzie in the direction of the wagon, bundled her up the step, and slammed the door shut behind them.

8

Lizzie woke gradually the next morning to the awful realization that she was pressed against a man's warm back. Staring with horror at Benedict Toomes's broad, tanned shoulder blades, she hastily snatched back her arm that had been firmly wrapped about his waist. What was she doing? She shuffled back from him as surreptitiously as possible. Luckily, the sheets were not the crisp linen she was used to but were instead a soft flannel which did not rustle.

She hoped devoutly Benedict was still fast asleep and unaware of her sleepy embrace. It must have been due to the cold in the night, she told herself firmly. It had certainly had nothing to do with the kissing. *That kiss*. Her fingers touched her mouth distractedly. If it could be thought of as a kiss. Before last night, Lizzie had thought of kisses as a chaste salute bestowed upon a relative's cheek. She'd had no notion that men could twist something so simple and wholesome into something…altogether different.

Her cheeks burned when she remembered how she had allowed him to take such wanton liberties with his tongue. She had not protested or even tried to stop him, she thought guiltily. She had simply held still and let him have his wicked way. She pressed her hands to her face. Oh, why had she not pushed him away?

Thank heavens he had not sought to further his *acquaintance* with her by such methods once they had returned to the wagon. It seemed his brother's news had dampened his ardor, for he had turned his back while they had mutually undressed and they had climbed into the bed alongside each other in perfect silence.

Rolling on her back, Lizzie reached down to untangle the cotton nightgown which had wrapped itself about her legs.

"Keep still, can't you," rumbled a low voice, startling her considerably. Lizzie froze, catching her breath. He was awake? When she made no response, he turned to look over his shoulder at her. "What are you doing?" he complained. "Get back here."

Lizzie stared at him. "What do you mean?" she faltered.

He shot her an exasperated look. "I've another half hour before I need to get up. Come back and keep my back warm."

Lizzie was aghast. When he turned his back to her again in wordless expectation, she gazed at him a moment before reflecting it could be a good deal worse. Inching closer, she checked the ribbon ties at her throat were still secure and then stopped before they actually made physical contact.

"And the rest," he prompted irritably.

Lizzie leaned the rest of the way forward with a protesting murmur, acutely aware of the fact she was naked beneath her long nightgown. The thin, well-worn cotton was the only barrier between them, for though he had kept his long underwear on last night, his upper body was entirely bare.

"You should wear a long-sleeved vest to bed," she told him, wishing she did not sound so breathless. "Then your back will not be cold."

He grunted. "This is better."

Lizzie blinked, but there was really no response she could make to that. At least he wasn't demanding that she hug him around his middle. Had he drifted back off to sleep? The steady rise and fall of his breath seemed to indicate as much.

Lizzie marveled that he could be so comfortable with a strange bedfellow when she felt most peculiar all over. She was not sure she would ever grow used to sharing a bed with a man, though common sense told her this was now her reality as a married woman. She lay still as possible, barely breathing in the hope Benedict Toomes would forget what was plastered to his back, namely her.

She was just starting to breathe a little easier when he gave a sigh and sat up in the bed. Lizzie rolled back in alarm, blinking up at him. The morning light was barely showing through the covered window, but she guessed it was early. He rubbed his eyes and yawned, then swung his legs over the side of the bed. "You may as well stay abed awhile," he said, standing up and scratching his muscular belly.

Lizzie hurriedly averted her eyes. "Are you going into the fair already?"

He murmured some agreement as he washed in the cold water leftover from the previous evening and dragged on his clothes. "I'll be back in an hour or so and bring you some breakfast," he said, glancing at her. "Get some more sleep, but first come and bolt the door after me."

Lizzie nodded, though she doubted she would sleep so much as a wink. He opened the door and ducked out, slamming it shut after him. Lizzie lay in the still-dark interior and breathed out a sigh of relief. She had shared a room with her cousin, but never a bed. The intimacy would take some getting used to. She crawled out of bed and bolted the door before returning to the mattress where she flung out her arms and legs in a full stretch. She had only a single cot in Sitwell Place, not a wide one like this one. She would close her eyes awhile and then ponder what to do.

When next she woke, it was to a banging on the door of the wagon. She gasped and cast about her in confusion a moment before remembering where she was. Sitting up, she threw back the covers and stumbled toward the door, pausing only to throw her shawl about her shoulders and conceal the nightgown.

Peering out cautiously, she saw it was old Ma Toomes scowling up at her ferociously. She wore a large coal shovel bonnet this morning to match her shabby black dress. Lizzie could have sworn she had been wearing a man's cap the previous night, but it had been dark next to the campfire so she could not be sure.

"What?" she squawked, catching sight of Lizzie. "Still abed, my fine lady?"

"Benedict told me to sleep in," Lizzie replied with as much dignity as she could muster.

"Huh!" the old woman snorted. "Well get up, then; you can't loll there all day. We've things to do."

Lizzie paused a moment before shutting the door again and hurrying to dress. She washed her face in the bowl of cold water, hurriedly donned her navy dress, and brushed her mussed-up hair which she had not even braided before bed the previous evening, instead shoving it under her lacy nightcap. As such, it had a few tangles. She had only just managed to roll and pin it to her nape when a scraggy arm banged on the door again.

"Come on, girl! We ain't got all day!"

Lizzie swung the door open and noticed it struck against a small package left on the step. Stooping down, she found it was a flaky pastry in a twist of paper and a bottle of lemonade. Had her husband returned with something for her to eat and found her still sleeping? The thought warmed her, and she had to give herself a stern talking to as she replied to his grandmother. "I just need to don my bonnet and cloak and I'll be ready."

91

"Don't bother," Ma told her curtly. "I've got one for you. 'Ere," she said. "Put this on." She passed Lizzie a hugely enveloping black cloak with a large pointed hood lined in red silk.

"What is it?"

"It's a cloak, what's it look like?" was the retort.

Lizzie climbed down from the step and took it from her. "And what am I to do with it, pray?"

"Put it on, didn't I say so?" asked the older woman sharply.

"Why?" Lizzie asked. "It's not raining, and I have my own cloak."

"You needs a costume, if you're to tell fortunes."

Lizzie's eyes widened. "I have never told a fortune in my life. I wouldn't know where to start," she spluttered in horror.

"Listen," Ma snarled, thrusting her withered face close to Lizzie's. "If yer a part o' this family you'd best be prepared to earn yer way or you'll be out on yer ear faster'n you can wink an eye!"

Lizzie stared back at her. She had been overgenerous in her appraisals of Benedict's grandmother's character the night before, partly, she knew, because the old woman had lumped her in with Benedict's mother and sister-in-law as being useless but pretty.

No one had ever said so much about Lizzie's rather plain face before. She knew the old woman had meant it as a scathing indictment, but she could not help but be perversely flattered. She knew she was not pretty, but perhaps not being constantly contrasted to her cousin would mean she would no longer suffer from such comparisons.

"I shall certainly speak to my husband about this!" Lizzie said aloud as the old woman continued to glare at her ferociously.

"You do that!" Ma cackled. "But I think you'll find this preferable to prancin' around in yer knickers advertising the booth."

Lizzie stared at her. Prancing about in her knickers? "I don't know anything about that!" she gasped. "Benedict certainly never asked me to do any such thing!"

"Not yet, he hasn't," Ma muttered direly. "But you just wait. If you've got any sense, you'll find another way to earn a penny and sharpish."

Lizzie swallowed. Was the old woman telling her that her husband would eventually prostitute her out? She stood speechless a moment before swinging the old cloak about her shoulders. Ma Toomes nodded her head in satisfaction.

"There's buttons on the inside; fasten it tight so it covers you neck to toe," she instructed. Lizzie hastily complied. "Now put these gloves on and this headscarf, see?"

Ma Toomes passed her a red silk headscarf edged in small gold discs like coins. When Lizzie fumbled with it inexpertly, it was whipped out of her hands with a muffled curse. "Not like that, you little fool!" the terrible old woman scolded. She wound it about Lizzie's head like a turban so it covered her pale hair completely and left only her face uncovered. "Yer face looks too young," she grumbled. "But it will have to do for now."

Lizzie dragged the fingerless mittens on over her hands. They looked a bit grubby to her and like they could do with a wash. Glancing at Ma's black fingernails, she shuddered. "Well?" she asked with a slight edge to her voice. "Anything else I can do for you?"

Ma Toomes surveyed her. "It's a good thing yer not easily cowed," she said mildly. "But we'll see if yer still as feisty in six months' time, my fine young lady." She gave an evil cackle. "Now you follow me and do everything I tells you, got it?"

Lizzie gave a reluctant nod before remembering her breakfast. "One moment," she said, hopping back up onto the step and retrieving the pastry and bottle. She offered half to the old woman, who pulled a disgusted face and turned abruptly on her in a sprightly march toward the main field. Lizzie trailed along behind her with severe misgivings.

The pastry at least was buttery and delicious and filled with flaked almonds. If she hadn't been wearing the horrible mittens, she would have licked her fingers. Another coating of grease would hardly affect them, she told herself, uncorking the lemonade and drinking it thirstily. The camping field was now a hive of activity with people bustling about and children running hither and thither.

After they climbed over the stile, Lizzie saw a procession of folk trickling in from the opposite direction. These people weren't dressed in working clothes but in their Sunday best. She saw frills and flounces and hats covered in flowers as well as pinstripe suits and watch chains and polished leather boots. When the groups of two and three started coming thicker and faster, the trickle of arrivals becoming more of a deluge, Ma seized her arm.

"We stay on the edges for our turn," she said, hanging back. "Ain't no point us going into the throng. There's precious little takings there unless yer a pickpocket. Not when you needs to use yer tongue to make yer money." Instead of proceeding into the field of stalls and booths, Ma drew her to one side. "Over there, see, where they're taking a breather."

Lizzie glanced across to see some day-trippers were congregating around a picturesque knot of trees. Ma nodded at two couples who were lingering at the edge of an ornamental pond. Lizzie pursed her lips, for she didn't like the look of them.

Both girls were giggling, and one was tugging the handkerchief out of her beau's top pocket, while he tried to catch her about the waist. The young men had too much pomade in their hair. They looked rather like shopkeepers' assistants on their day off.

Ma was already headed resolutely toward them, so Lizzie pocketed her empty bottle and hurried after her. "Care to have your fortune told, my dearies?" Ma wheedled in a sickly sweet voice.

One of the young men's face hardened. "Be off with you!" he said sternly. "We want no beggars here, old woman."

"Beggars?" screeched Ma. "You'll be feeling my curse on you for your impertinence, young man!" Lizzie blanched, hardly knowing where to put herself.

"Oh, Bert!" one of the young girls cried in lively distress. "You mustn't, oh indeed, you must not! I read a story in a magazine where this happened, and oh, it was awful what befell them!"

Ma wheeled about on her at once. "Aha!" she cried out. "You're a clever one, my pretty. You needn't despair." She stretched out her fingers. "A bright star shines at your brow and fortune smiles down upon your path in life."

The young woman's mouth fell open. "Oh," she breathed. "Does it really?"

Lizzie rolled her eyes.

Ma Toomes nodded gravely. "If you care to hear more from Granny, dearie, you'll need to cross my palm with silver."

"Oh." Her face fell. "But I spent my last sixpence, Clarence," she said, turning crestfallen to her companion.

He grimaced but reached into his pocket all the same. "Here," he said shortly and flipped a coin. Quick as a flash, Ma snatched it out of the air. She turned an ingratiating smile upon the young woman.

"Sweets to the sweet," she crooned. "Let me see that pretty palm." With only the slightest of hesitations, the girl held out one rosy upturned hand. Ma Toomes seized it and frowned over it over a moment. "Ah yes," she muttered, one finger hovering in the air and twitching as she seemed to trace some map only she could see there. "I see a Valentine," she said, squinting closer.

"Oh yes," the girl breathed. "I received one this year." She blushed and glanced at Clarence, who turned a fiery red.

Ma nodded. "From your true love and fated one."

The girl gasped. "Is it really?"

Lizzie saw the other young man, Bert, give a start. A look of annoyance crossed over his face, and she realized both young men must be keen on the same girl.

"I see the letter *C* written in the stars," Granny said in a faraway voice.

"Oh, that's me," the young woman squeaked excitedly. "My name is Clara, you see."

"No, it's not for Clara, though it's close," Ma continued, sounding puzzled. "The fates are drawing back a curtain now for me to see…" She squinted. "The name is…"

"Clarence!" the girl squeaked.

Granny nodded and smiled. "Clarence," she repeated. "I see I'm telling you nothing you do not already know deep down in your heart."

Bert was practically gnashing his teeth by now, though Clarence looked foolishly gratified.

"Oh, but I didn't!" the girl marveled. "I was ever so unsure, but now I know," she said, casting a glowing look at Clarence. "Oh, thank you, thank you, you wonderful old lady!" she gushed. "Oh, Clarence!"

Clarence whipped out his handkerchief and handed it to Clara, who dabbed daintily at her eyes.

"Oh, I'm so glad we came," Clara gushed. "This is a hundred times better than those old swing boats!"

Clarence laughed heartily as Clara slipped her arm through his and they moved away, leaving Bert to stare after them sourly.

"Well, you've properly queered my pitch!" he grumbled.

Ma rocked back on her heels. "Your fortune don't hold love," she told him comfortably. "Only that what glitters."

"Let's get after them, Bert," the other girl said, coming forward and grabbing his arm. "We'll get left behind."

He shook her off. "Get off, Trudie. What do you mean, that what glitters?" he demanded, turning back to Ma Toomes. She held out her palm, and grudgingly he dug into his pocket. "Here," he said and dropped a coin into her outstretched hand.

Ma Toomes sniffed, glanced at the coin, and then seized his palm. "Yer not built for love," she said, flashing him a cunning look. "But I do see riches and a ship docked at a port."

"A ship?" He looked annoyed. "What's that to me?"

"But, Bert," said Trudie. "Don't you see? That must be the ship that Mr. Pratt has docking at Liverpool next month." Bert inhaled sharply. "He offered you passage on it as a clerk, didn't he?"

"I turned him down flat," Bert said slowly. "I thought—" He flushed, and Lizzie guessed he had thought to pursue the fair Clara instead.

"That's the path laid out before you by the fates," Ma Toomes intoned solemnly. "If you deviate from it…disaster." She spoke the last word with hollow emphasis.

Trudie gave an alarmed gasp, but Bert still looked unconvinced. "I'm not sure," he prevaricated. "The only time I ever took a sea voyage I was sick as a dog."

"Got to find yer sea legs, haven't you," Ma said with a callous shrug. "That don't take long."

"And if I do take this course? You can guarantee I will meet with success?"

Ma peered once more at his outstretched hand. "Yer fortune will be made," she wheezed. "Sure as eggs is eggs."

Bert drew his hand back, looking half-dazed.

"Come along," Trudie urged him, casting a fearful glance at Ma Toomes. "Or we'll never catch them up." He allowed himself to be led away, and Lizzie watched after them in some bewilderment.

"See how it's done, girl?" Ma Toomes asked sharply.

"But how can you guarantee he should take that position?" Lizzie asked. "Or the identity of that young woman's true love, if it comes down to it?"

Ma Toomes snorted. "Either love or money. You has to predict one or t'other."

Lizzie eyed her narrowly. "You mean, in fact, that you saw neither?"

Ma Toomes shrugged. "I just says what pops into me 'ead, girl," she answered prosaically. "Who's to say that's not a gift?"

Lizzie regarded her speechlessly. "I'm not going to be able to do this," she said stiffly. "I don't have a ready tongue; I can't read palms and I am not good with strangers."

"You'll learn, if you has to," Ma Toomes predicted. "And you do have to."

"It's not just that, but also approaching people," Lizzie objected in an urgent undertone. "I simply could not bring myself to do such a thing. I can hardly threaten them with curses as you do! It would never work for me!"

"Threaten 'em?" squawked Ma Toomes. "How dare you? A poor soul like me what never threatened a body in her life?"

Lizzie regarded her half indignant, half despairing. "You're an old woman and seem to pose no real threat to anyone," she pointed out tautly. "I can hardly go sidling up to people, cajoling and cackling at them as you do. I'd soon be clapped in irons and thrown into bedlam!"

Ma Toomes threw up her hands angrily. "And that's the thanks I get for trying to help you find your way, is it?" she demanded angrily. "Ingratitude! You'd best get practicing kicking them legs of yours up in the air if you think yourself too good for the likes of this."

Lizzie flushed. "So those are my choices in life, are they? Either tricking people out of their pennies or displaying myself to all and sundry? Well, you needn't think I'll take *your* word for it, you horrible old woman!"

Ma Toomes's eyes bugged out and her mouth worked indignantly for a moment, but she could not seem to find the right words. "You little ingrate," she spat, looking Lizzie up and down with disgust. "You won't last two minutes here! Ben must have rocks in his head to have taken up with the likes of you!"

Lizzie stared back at her through a miserable haze. She had a feeling that for once Ma Toomes was speaking nothing but the truth. She wasn't cut out for this sort of life. How on earth was she going to survive? She pressed a finger and thumb to her brow a moment, warding off a headache, as Ma Toomes yelled "Pah!" clawed furiously at the air with her bony fingers, and spun in a furious whirl of rags, flinging herself across the field and promptly abandoning her.

Lizzie watched her sail away in some dismay. Likely she should have chosen her words more carefully, but she had been in such a wretched panic at the idea of telling fake fortunes that she had spoken too frankly and offended the old woman.

What would she do now if old Ma went running to her husband and told him Lizzie had called her a "horrible old woman"? She blushed; after all, she could hardly deny it. There was no getting away from the fact her besetting sin was a too-ready tongue.

She had learned over the years to choke her hot words back before they sprang forth, even though she felt like it half choked her some days to do so. The shocked virtue of her aunt and uncle had eventually schooled her against impetuous speech. Why then now had the floodgates opened with a vengeance? It must have just been panic that had induced her to act so badly, Lizzie reflected guiltily. She had better get a handle on it, or she would be lost to all shame.

She had started walking aimlessly along with the direction of the crowd. She was in no hurry to return to the dingy little wagon. In truth, she wished she could just keep walking and never go back, she thought, tears starting to her eyes. There was a sort of anonymity in the faceless crowd that appealed to her right now.

"Excuse me, miss," a timid voice quavered nearby. Feeling a touch on her shoulder, Lizzie wheeled about in surprise. A middle-aged woman hastily withdrew her hand. "So sorry," she squeaked. "My employer, Miss Halperton, bade me approach you," she said, wringing her gloved hands together. "I meant no offence."

Belatedly, Lizzie remembered the red headscarf with the gold coins she was wearing on her head. *Oh.* So much for the anonymity of the crowd! "That is quite alright," she said, drawing herself up and sticking her chin in the air. Clearly her haughty manner and excessive politeness had not been what the other woman was expecting at all. She blinked at Lizzie in confusion.

"Oh dear," she faltered. "Miss Halperton quite thought—that is, she imagined you might be *one of the entertainers*," she twittered delicately. "Do forgive me if we are laboring under a misapprehension."

Lizzie looked the woman over cautiously from her sensible tan gloves to her mousy hair. "Where is your employer?" she said after a moment's pause.

The companion pointed to a proud-looking woman with a prominent nose, wearing an elaborate outfit of purple silk trimmed with black. Miss Halperton was long past the first flush of youth and looked to be in her midforties with a commanding presence. "You are her companion?" Lizzie asked.

The woman gave a small gasp. "Yes," she answered in a frightened voice, and Lizzie realized she thought Lizzie was using supernatural powers of deduction, rather than simple logic.

"She has quite a retinue," Lizzie remarked dryly, noting the two people hovering solicitously at Miss Halperton's side. One was a rather florid-looking younger man in a loud check suit. The other was a meek-faced woman dressed very severely, as though to detract from her looks rather than enhance them.

"Yes, Miss Smith is her nurse," answered the woman with a muffled constraint that made Lizzie's ears prick up. Clearly there was tension between the companion and her nurse. "And Mr. Abney is, well, a trusted *friend* of Miss Halperton's," the companion fluttered in embarrassed accents. "Would you—that is, my employer was wondering if you would be so kind as to give her a consultation," she finished in a breathless rush.

Well, thought Lizzie. This could be her own test. Sink or swim, she could see if she was up to the challenge. Inclining her head, she indicated her willingness and followed the twittering companion to where the woman stood a good way back from the crowd.

"Good day," Lizzie wished her coolly, not particularly caring for the slightly contemptuous smile playing about Miss Halperton's mouth. "You wish to consult me, I understand?"

The mustachioed young man chortled. "That's one way of putting it, eh, Becky?" he said with a familiarity that made

Lizzie's eyebrows rise. He must be a good twenty years younger than Miss Halperton, and if he was merely a friend, then there was no familial bond to account for his manner.

Noticing Lizzie's raised brow, Miss Halperton flushed faintly. "Draw aside, Harry," she commanded. "I do not require you at present."

Harry Abney's color rose with chagrin, and Lizzie saw him flash a warning glance at the nurse. *Interesting*, she thought as a little color entered Miss Smith's cheeks, making her look a good deal prettier. "Of course," he answered, and caught Miss Halperton's gloved hand, raising it fawningly to his lips. "Fair Clorinda, you will not keep me waiting overlong," he said throatily. "You are too kind for such tricks."

What a dreadful mountebank, Lizzie thought contemptuously. If Miss Halperton were half as proper as she clearly thought herself, she would not allow him to act thus in public. Miss Halperton tossed her hair. "I will keep you waiting as long as it takes," she answered coolly. "You too, Smith, away with you."

Miss Smith bridled, but instead of following Mr. Abney to a nearby copse of trees, she walked in the opposite direction to stand staring at the view. *Methinks the lady doth protest too much*, sprang into Lizzie's mind suddenly. Something was clearly going on between the nurse and the gentleman caller for all the pretended indifference between them.

"You can stay, Timms," Miss Halperton said sharply when her companion started to shuffle off. "Your presence will hardly signify."

Miss Timms looked gratified, and Lizzie could only suppose she took it as a compliment, though in truth, her employer spoke of her rather as though she were an old spaniel than a trusted companion.

103

"So," Miss Halperton said boldly, eyeing Lizzie up and down. "How does this work? I must say, you do not look Romany."

"I am not," Lizzie agreed. "I never said I was."

Miss Halperton frowned. "I quite understood they usually were," she said airily. "At fairgrounds."

Lizzie gazed back. "If you would take off your left glove," she said at last. For it seemed to her that it was the left hand that Ma Toomes had favored. The other woman held out her arm toward Miss Timms, who made haste to unfasten the row of jet-black buttons and remove the expensive-looking glove.

"You shall not pay me now," Lizzie said slowly as the thought occurred to her. "But only at the conclusion. And then you will simply render what you think my services are worth, nothing more, nothing less." That way, she thought, she need not feel bad about her subpar fortune-telling.

"I see," responded Miss Halperton blankly. "How very droll."

She had rather large hands, Lizzie thought, staring down at the square palm and strong-looking fingers. "You are a capable woman, Miss Halperton," Lizzie said musingly. "But you have grown complacent about your abilities and need to show more care who you permit into your inner circle." Lizzie saw the woman stiffen and realized she needed to throw in a bit more mysticism to soften her words. "Danger lurks," she added vaguely. After all, she told herself, there was always danger when a woman was rich. Sharks circled close under such circumstances. "It grows ever closer by the day."

"Danger?" Miss Halperton echoed shrilly. "From whom?"

Lizzie thought again of the look that had flashed between the bluff suitor and the colorless nurse. "From those who would deceive you. Two are very close to you," she said in a low voice. "Deceivers both."

Miss Timms gave a small cry of alarm but was ignored by her employer, who was gazing at Lizzie intently now. "You see who they are?"

Lizzie shook her head. "All I see are two masks dangling from their strings," she said, feeling inspired. "One is that of modesty and the other…"

"Yes?" Miss Halperton demanded.

"The lover. Both are false."

Miss Halperton gasped. "I don't know who you can mean!" she lied, hot color rushing to her cheeks. "There is no one like that in my acquaintance! No one at all!"

"You must protect yourself," Lizzie told her levelly. "This is a warning only." She shrugged. "You are under no obligation to heed it."

Miss Halperton glared at her angrily, snatching back her hand and rubbing at her palm as though to wipe away something written there. "This is all nonsense!" she scoffed. "I won't pay you a penny!"

Lizzie shrugged. "I told you I would accept only what you saw fit to give. If that is the case, then farewell." She nodded and started to turn away.

"No, wait!" Miss Halperton blurted, her bosom heaving. "Papa always said payment must be made for services rendered." She turned imperiously to her companion. "Timms, take out my purse." She thrust her reticule at her companion, who hastily began untying the strings. "You say you will accept however much I think your consultation is worth, is that not so?"

Lizzie nodded, drawing her hood up and over her head. She was starting to feel a little conspicuous in the red headscarf. She certainly did not wish to tell any more fortunes, she thought fervently, heartily sick of the whole charade.

"So, that means you will not complain if I pay you a simple ha'penny?" Miss Halperton persisted triumphantly as she pulled on her black glove.

"That is so," Lizzie agreed. Suddenly, all she wanted to do was disappear into the crowd and find her way back to the wagon. She'd had enough of this disagreeable woman and the situation she had embroiled herself in. She glanced over her shoulder. Was it her imagination or had the noisy crowd grown closer since she had been stood here?

"I don't believe you!" Miss Halperton replied with a curl of her lip.

"Well, there is one way to prove it," Lizzie said irritably. "Pay me a ha'penny now. I assure you I will accept it with thanks."

Miss Halperton gazed at her keenly. "I believe you *are* in earnest," she blurted after a moment.

"I can't wait around here all day," Lizzie said, gathering her cloak about her. She had some dignity left to her and would wait no longer on this woman. "I'll bid you good day, ma'am."

"Wait!"

Ignoring Miss Halperton's cry, Lizzie started to hurry away. She felt suddenly overwhelmed with embarrassment over the role she had just played. When had she ever been so fanciful? What had she been thinking letting her imagination run riot like that, and even worse, giving voice to her suspicions which may well have been unfounded? She pressed her hands to her hot face and wondered if she was starting to lose her mind!

106

She almost screamed when a hand seized her elbow. Wheeling around, she found it was Miss Timms again. The poor woman was panting like she had run the entire length of a field.

"Please—" she puffed. "Don't run away—Miss Halperton— sends this—with her regards." She held out a glove of sensible tan leather, and Lizzie met it reluctantly with her own mittened hand. After all, a ha'penny might come in useful at some point. The coin pressed into her palm felt a good deal more substantial than a ha'penny, however. Lizzie glimpsed it briefly before closing her fingers around it tightly. It was a golden sovereign!

Miss Timms was regarding her almost fearfully. "How did you *know*?" she whispered. "I never dared to speak of what I saw in the orangery."

Lizzie stared back at her. "What did you see?" she could not prevent herself from asking.

"Mr. Abney and Miss Smith *in an embrace*," Miss Timms confessed shakily. "But I knew that Miss Halperton would never believe me, and indeed I would never have had the nerve to tell her of it. She would have dismissed me in a towering rage at the very suggestion, but now…" She shook her head. "Do you know, I believe she will actually throw him over." Miss Timms's voice shook with suppressed emotion, and she dabbed at her eyes with her handkerchief. "I am so relieved, you cannot imagine! A gazetted fortune hunter, that's what he is! And that cunning, sly wretch of a girl, dripping her poison into Miss Halperton's ear. You cannot imagine the weight that has lifted from my shoulders at the prospect of their dismissal. Thank you, thank you a thousand times, thank you!" the poor woman twittered. "Your great gift is truly a blessing!"

Lizzie swallowed and wondered what Miss Timms would say if she knew it was only a reckless mixture of guesswork and instinct that had led her to the truth. Deciding such an admission would be ill advised, she nodded at Miss Timms, and the other woman clasped her hands to her bosom and stood watching her with stars in her eyes as Lizzie made haste to disappear once more into the crowd. She would walk once around this busy arena and then make for the entertainers' field.

That way she should shake off any other pursuers, she thought, thinking for instance of a freshly spurned fortune hunter who might bear a grudge against her. She had entered the first of the fields now and gasped aloud to see how much busier it was today from the previous. Now there were people everywhere, as far as the eye could see; a teeming crowd of day-trippers on pleasure bent.

Lizzie felt her anxiety mounting as she picked up her pace and gazed about for a landmark she recognized. It did not matter how much she told herself she was being fanciful; she felt a sort of lurking dread sneaking up on her as she hurried around the field full of strange and bizarre attractions. Finally, she spied the Adam and Eve sign and realized where she was. Spinning around, she saw it, the Toomeses' boxing tent. This Easter Monday it looked full to capacity. In front of the booth, a tall, strapping brunette, her hair piled high on her head, stalked up and down, her voice upraised.

"Come and see the Harbinger of Doom!" she boomed. "'E takes on all comers, 'e's not fussy! Fancy your chances, lads? Go three rounds with the Harbinger and win a pound for your trouble! Be a local hero! A legend in your own time, gents! Sir, you look a likely young bruiser, ever boxed?"

Lizzie watched her importune a passing young man who seemed more interested in looking her up and down than trying out bare-knuckle fighting. And small wonder, for she was a handsome woman, Lizzie thought, though her dress was cut rather low and showed a good deal of frilly chemise along with her ample charms.

Whatever the young man said, she laughed and tossed her head. "Maybe if you stop by later, my fine gent." She winked and turned to hail another gaggle of young men. "You look the very thing, my lads, I'll bet there's a sports fancier or two between you. Surely you'll be keen to see the triumphant return of Benedict Toomes himself to the ring?"

"Toomes?" repeated one of them, lowering his bottle of beer. "Thought he was in Newgate, last time I heard?" Lizzie could not help but wince at this as she slipped past them, making for the tent.

"Bless you, luv, it weren't Newgate," the brunette started to explain, before noticing Lizzie. "Oi!" she yelled after her. "Where do you think you're—"

But Lizzie did not stop to listen. Instead, she hurried forward and ducked inside the opening. A heavy sense of impropriety descended on her as soon as she stepped inside the tent. For one thing, she was the only woman present that she could see. For another, the milling crowd was a rough company of men in flat caps, jostling and jeering without any discernible sense of propriety. Cigar and pipe smoke and curse words peppered the air, and she scarcely knew where to put herself as she looked about in vain for a face she knew, be it either her husband or new brothers-in-law.

Guessing that any entertainment must be at the front of the tent, she pushed forward, gathering the heavy folds of the black cloak about her and pulling the hood down low over her face. She did not make much headway, however, and it wasn't long before she realized that the crowd was thickest in the middle of the tent.

She was a good five or six rows back from the front when she realized she could proceed no further forward and came to a halt. Going up on her tiptoes and peering over the shoulder in front of her, she made out an area in the center which was roped off. It was square in shape, and standing at one end was a figure she knew only too well. It was that of her husband, Benedict Toomes.

He stood bared to the waist with his arms folded across his chest as his brother Frank whipped up the crowd. Lizzie could barely make out his words the crowd was so noisy, but after a moment or two she managed to drown out the catcalls and laughter and to focus on Frank's words.

"Here he is, gentlemen," Frank announced. "Take your fill. The Harbinger of Doom himself! Benedict Toomes, fresh from his sojourn at Her Majesty's pleasure!" A smattering of laughter greeted this witticism, and Lizzie was shocked to her core to hear such a thing joked about so shamelessly. His recent incarceration seemed to be a selling point rather than anything else. "Has prison softened him, gentlemen?" Frank pondered aloud. "Let's find out. Surely there's one among this fine company who will go toe-to-toe with this reformed convict who stands before us a new and better man?"

Another ripple of mirth went through the crowd at these words. Benedict stood, coolly impassive. His cold eyes, though, passed over the crowd with a sort of calculated consideration that reminded her of a coiled snake which had stared at her once through the glass with a venomous intent that had filled her with frozen horror.

Was he sizing up possible opponents? she wondered and gazed about her uneasily. What kind of fool would take one look at this man and think they wanted to tangle with him? If they had any sense of self-preservation, they would not set one foot over that rope.

To Lizzie's astonishment, however, she noticed several flurries of activities in the crowd as men started stripping off their jackets and rolling up their sleeves, making for the roped-off area. Her jaw dropped in surprise to see at least three burly types approaching Frank, who was clapping them on the shoulder, congratulating them on their courage and determining their experience.

When she glanced back toward Benedict, she suffered another shock, for instead of watching his competition, his hazel eyes were fixed now on her. Lizzie gasped and ducked her head. He surely could not have noticed her, she thought, clutching her hands into fists and wondering why her heart was beating so fast.

And why had she come over so bashful all of a sudden? He had told her that she would see how the boxing operated on the morrow, so it wasn't like she was doing anything she ought not by coming here. When she had steeled herself to raise her eyes again, Frank was conferring with him, and he was nodding in agreement over whatever was being said.

She breathed a sigh of relief and was then jolted again when the crowd started up as the first of the contenders stepped forward. "Give him a hiding, Dan!" yelled out a booming voice, and several others joined it, raised in encouragement for the blond-haired chap who nodded and raised a large hand in acknowledgment of the crowd's support.

Benedict still had his arms folded as Frank led the newcomer into the center and pointed to something on the floor which Lizzie could not see. He seemingly positioned himself against it with his fists upraised, and Frank turned beaming to the audience.

"Gentlemen, if you will please show your appreciation for Mr. Daniel Smith of the parish of Spitalfields in this here great city of London."

A cheer went up, Lizzie supposed from those fellow inhabitants of that borough, or perhaps anyone who associated themselves with either the East End or London itself. To her surprise, Benedict did not immediately join his opponent in the center of the ring, and a good deal of the spectators seemed to surge toward another corner of the tent where she now noticed Jack Toomes was set up on the top of a packing case. It was on the tip of her tongue to ask the man next to her what was occurring when the fog lifted. They were gambling on the outcome, she realized, watching Jack draw a notebook out from his waistcoat and start making notes as he took bets from the men milling around him, holding their money aloft as they called their wagers.

Hearing Frank's voice raised above the babble, she realized he was extolling Mr. Daniel Smith's various qualifications as a fighter. Apparently, he was the owner of a meat cart and used to hefting about great carcasses over his shoulders as part of his daily toil. That accounted for the strength of his build, Lizzie supposed.

Frank drew the audience's attention to Smith's great fists and the musculature about his neck, which was, Lizzie noticed, rather overdeveloped. It made him look like he did not have much of a neck, in her opinion. A babble of heated discussion rose up to the roof of the tent as the crowd debated his points.

"I like the look of the fellow!" a man on the other side of her yelled in his companion's ear. "Looks a steady chap. Great, mighty thews on him. Don't like to tell you your own business, Nat, but maybe he'll give Toomes a run for his money. What do you say?"

Glancing over, Lizzie saw his friend was wearing an improbably colored yellow tailcoat teamed with a waistcoat of blue and silver decorated all over in the pattern of seashells. He looked amused by his friend's opinion. "Care to make a wager on the outcome, old boy?" he suggested.

The first man turned cagey at this, fingering his chin. "Dash it, Nat, I promised Maud I wouldn't speculate," he grumbled. "But I suppose, if it's just between the two of us…"

Bit by bit, the buzz died down, and the press of the crowd returned as all bets were laid. Lizzie noticed Jack's broad grin as he nodded in reply to Frank's look of enquiry.

Finally, Benedict lowered his crossed arms and deigned to join his opponent in the center of the tent. He, too, seemed to line himself up with what Lizzie could only guess was some mark she could not make out from her vantage point.

To her mind, his body was a good deal better proportioned than the other man's and put her rather forcibly in mind of some ancient Greek statues she had once viewed in a museum before her aunt's muffled shriek had alerted her to the fact that particular exhibition was not intended for a lady's eyes. She had been hastily redirected to a textile display upstairs instead.

Still, she had filed it away in her memory and called it forth now to compare the body of Benedict Toomes to those highly idealized depictions of masculinity carved in white marble. She did not think he suffered by the comparison in any way, she reflected as her eyes traveled over his broad shoulders and well-muscled arms.

Unbidden, she remembered just how it had felt to be pressed up against that warm, tanned flesh when she awoke that morning and felt her face grow hot. Oh dear, she thought, when had she started noticing such things? Before the shocking event at

Sitwell Place that fateful night, she had thought the Reverend Milson was the height of manly perfection and that had been based purely on his moral superiority and supposed piety.

If anyone had told her she would be ogling Benedict Toomes's bare chest a mere week later, she would have laughed such an idea to scorn.

When he assumed the stance, hunching over and raising his fists, it seemed to Lizzie he held them a good deal closer to his head than his opponent. To Lizzie's surprise, it was Mr. Smith who threw the first punch, wielding his meaty fist like a sledgehammer.

"That's it, man!" her neighbor bellowed, making Lizzie jump and turn her head. "Let him have it!"

Benedict neatly ducked, avoiding the blow, his left fist snaking out with a counterpunch to the other's ribs that Smith absorbed with a grunt.

Lizzie watched as Benedict sidestepped and bobbed, avoiding his opponent's heavy roundhouse swings as he moved around him, jabbing him far neater blows to the jaw that made Smith's head snap back but did not seem to inflict any great damage to the other man's great slab-like face.

"Damned fellow's as slippery as an eel!" her neighbor objected bitterly as his friend in the pretty waistcoat chuckled, striking a match to light his cigar.

"I believe Toomes is an exponent of Mendoza's scientific method," he said, puffing elegantly on a slim cheroot.

"Aye, but if Smith were only to land one good solid haymaker, that's the thing," the first one said plaintively.

Lizzie could not help but agree. Every punch the meat-carter threw looked to be enough to knock a man clean off his feet, whereas Benedict's looked more like to sting than render a man wholly insensible.

"Just you wait," the second man predicted, blowing out a plume of smoke, and indeed after several minutes of this, it seemed even to Lizzie's untutored eye that Benedict's actions were becoming quicker and more decisive as his opponent's efforts grew clumsier and started to lack conviction as he ran out of steam. The crowd grew louder in its shouts of both encouragement and derision.

"Damn me, but that brute's as slow as a carthorse!" complained Lizzie's neighbor. "I was sadly misled by his bulk and sinew!"

"Don't mistake the fact, Toomes has a commanding left," his companion corrected him. "And is defensively very sound. In a regular mill, your carter would be lethal. Against a professional, however..." He shook his head. "He's entirely out of his depth."

Lizzie could only be grateful that she had happened to stand next to someone who knew what he was talking about. Otherwise, she surely would have been as ill-informed as the first gentleman and thought the eventual outcome determined by a lucky punch.

Though she found it hard to follow the blur that was Benedict's left fist, she could see, with the help of these pointers, that the combination of his defensive right and the way he moved his body about ensured that he received minimal punishment while inflicting maximum damage.

Another minute of this had Lizzie wincing in sympathy for the carter, who slipped down onto one knee, not once, but twice under the steady onslaught. Each time this happened, Benedict

115

stepped back, and Frank stepped forward. Lizzie guessed the older Toomes brother was talking to Smith, who furiously shook his head and clambered to his feet to the approving cheers of the crowd.

Each time, the burly carter positioned himself in the center of the square again, although by the third time, he seemed to have some difficulty in finding the right place, and a trickle of blood ran down the side of his face, making him squint his eye.

"Poor chap's done for," the fancy waistcoated man sighed. "Just won't accept the fact."

"Damn and blast it," the first man objected. "Great, hearty fellow like that should have a jaw of granite!"

"He does, Barney, you fool," his companion said affably. "If he did not, he would have been down in the first minute."

Lizzie cast a curious glance their way and caught the eye of the natty dresser. He winked at her and tipped his hat. Had he realized she was listening to every word he spoke? Lizzie flushed and faced resolutely forward. *How embarrassing.* Though, she comforted herself, it was practically impossible to follow social conventions in such an environment.

It was just as well she turned back when she did, for the carter was attempting to struggle back to his feet again. When it became apparent that he could not manage it, Frank Toomes came forward and, crossing his forearms together, pulled both hands in a downward motion. A groan went up from the spectators.

"It's over," said her neighbor sourly. "Deuce take it, I should have listened to Maud!"

Lizzie ignored him, watching Frank hook his arms under the fallen man and drag him to the side where his friends crouched

116

over him, splashing water in his face, and arguing hotly among themselves.

"A most valiant effort, I'm sure you'll all agree!" Frank cried, returning to the center. "Mr. Daniel Smith, gentlemen! One of Spitalfields' finest! And only the first of our three volunteers!"

"Oh?" murmured Lizzie's neighbor. "Maybe I'll recoup my losses, Nat, what say you to that?"

His friend merely laughed. "By all means, Barney, though I should probably warn you that the next two will suffer the self-same fate."

"Nonsense!" Barney cried. "Why, you haven't even clapped eyes on them yet!"

"Doesn't matter, Barney, my boy. The next one could have arms like tree trunks and I still say Toomes will dispatch him in just the same fashion."

"I tell you, Toomes is not fresh like he was!" Barney cried. "He goes into this next bout at a distinct disadvantage!"

"Does he look tired to you?" his friend asked laughingly, and glancing up, Lizzie had to admit that Benedict looked just as cool and unruffled as he had at the outset. He tipped back his head to take a drink of beer from a glass bottle, and she watched his Adam's apple bob as he drained it. When he lowered the bottle, she could have sworn his gaze met hers again before she looked hurriedly away.

Frank was now parading another contender for the crowd. Lizzie barely listened this time, for she found she believed the gentleman with the decorated waistcoat. This must indeed be how these things worked, she thought dazedly. But how many times a day did they repeat this process of filling the tent with both audience and prospective volunteers?

Again, there was the rush toward Jack Toomes and his betting book. Lizzie wondered if they only allowed bets against the house, or else surely Jack would still be trying to sort out who he owed money to from the first fight? She looked about distractedly. More spectators seemed to be drifting in by the minute, and the air, which had been thick enough to slice from the start, was now taking on a distinct odor of beer which she could only suppose was courtesy of the Adam and Eve.

Oh, for a cup of tea, Lizzie thought wistfully and wondered if any of the tents sold the superior beverage. If they did, she had not seen any sign of it so far. She was just pondering this when she felt someone tapping her shoulder.

"Excuse me, madam!" It was the handsome brunette from outside. The rush to place bets meant there was now room enough for her to make her way through the tent. "You owe me a ha'penny!"

Lizzie turned to face her. "That's my husband in the ring," she explained.

"I don't care if he's King Solomon himself," the brunette answered in strident tones. "You still got to pay your ha'penny or I'll sling you out on your ear." Lizzie found she believed the belligerent young woman and had just opened her mouth to clarify who she was when an arm was slung around her waist, and she was dragged back against a half-naked body.

"Who the hell are you to threaten my wife?" snarled Benedict, and the woman recoiled in alarm.

Lizzie gasped. He must have leaped over the ropes quick as a flash. "It was just a misunderstanding, I'm sure," she blurted.

"It had bloody better be."

118

Frank hurried over, an alarmed expression on his face. "Daphne, I don't think I've had the chance yet to introduce you properly to my brother Ben and his wife, Lizzie."

Daphne looked stunned by this, but she rallied fast. "Pleased to meet you, I'm sure," she said promptly. "And I apologize for not realizing who you was."

"Not at all," Lizzie responded.

"Daphne is a sort of stepdaughter of Pa's, Ben," Frank explained, not quite meeting his brother's eye.

Benedict's lip curled. "I don't give a damn who she is," he said in a hard voice. A crowd had started to form around them now, so transferring his grasp from Lizzie's waist to her wrist, he tugged her behind him down to the front.

"I was perfectly well where I was," Lizzie attempted to protest. Looking around, she saw Daphne looking after her with an aggrieved look on her face. Frank appeared to be placating her. Lizzie would miss the commentary of the gentleman in the waistcoat, she thought, looking about in vain to spot him.

"You were about to be slung out," Benedict growled at her. "Stand here," he said, depositing her in the front row between two men who looked her up and down in surprise. "If anyone says anything, tell them you're with me," he said with a menacing look which had both men quickly facing front again. He stepped back over the rope before she could think of a reply to this.

Lizzie stood glassy-eyed through the next two fights, neither of which lasted as long as the first. The crowd seemed even noisier as the morning wore on, and the man stood to her right was smoking a particularly noxious cigar which caused her eyes to water and the back of her throat to tickle.

When the third man proved unable to get back to his feet, Lizzie went off in a coughing paroxysm and missed Frank's closing speech altogether as she groped for her handkerchief and wiped her streaming eyes. By the time she had recovered herself, Benedict was stood before her. He thrust his shirt and vest into her arms and started wiping a wet cloth over his face and shoulders.

"Have you no towel?" Lizzie asked, raising her voice above the babble of the dispersing crowd. As though in answer to her words, Frank Toomes appeared beside them with one and a heavy frown. He handed the towel wordlessly to Lizzie, and unsure what else to do, she started dabbing at Benedict's neck with it.

"Finished him off a bit fast, didn't you?" Frank asked, resting his hands on his hips. "What was the rush?"

Feeling his eyes on her, Lizzie looked up. Frank looked away.

Benedict shrugged. "You put them in the wrong order."

"No, I didn't," Frank disagreed. "You just didn't want to oblige for some reason."

Benedict lowered his cloth and eyed his brother sardonically. "I was the one trading punches, not you. I say the third was weakest."

Frank snorted. "You could have drawn it out, Ben. You *should* have. You know well enough how the game's played."

Benedict ignored him, angling his head so Lizzie could reach his wet hair. She rubbed his hair vigorously with the towel, and Frank clicked his tongue but otherwise grew quiet.

Jack came hurrying over, brandishing his book. "Not bad takings," he said cheerfully and slapped his brother on the back.

"That was a strong finish, Ben. I reckon you've improved, if anything."

Frank snorted but was otherwise ignored as Benedict shrugged into his long-sleeved vest and then his shirt.

"I'll see you at two," Frank called after them as Lizzie found herself towed in the direction of the exit.

"What time is it now?" Lizzie asked as they emerged from the tent into a patch of bright sunlight despite the chill in the air.

"About half past twelve. What's that cloak you've got on?" Benedict asked critically.

Lizzie flushed. "It's your grandmother's," she explained.

He stopped in his tracks and reached over to tug back the hood, revealing the red and gold scarf. "Take it off."

"It's too cold to go without a cloak," Lizzie objected.

"I'm not talking about the cloak."

Catching his meaning, she reached up for the headscarf, but he was already before her, unknotting it and tugging it free from her hair. "That's better," he pronounced.

"Give it to me." Lizzie held out her hand. "I'll tuck it in my pocket so I don't lose it."

He handed the headscarf over but narrowed his eyes. "Do I want to know what you've been up to this morning?" he asked.

Lizzie considered this. "Attempting to find my place?" she ventured.

This seemed to give him pause. After a moment, he reached for her hand again. "Well, it's not in the boxing tent," he said roughly, pulling her alongside him. "I know that much."

121

She could not help but be grateful at this pronouncement. "Where are we heading now?"

"For some refreshment," he answered shortly, but she saw they had eschewed the rowdy Adam and Eve altogether.

Instead, they made for a tea and bun tent called Mother Grimley's. Lizzie sank into her seat with a sigh of relief. "I would love a cup of tea," she admitted as a girl came bounding over in an apron.

"Two teas and two buns."

"What kind?" the girl responded chirpily. "We got currant, saffron, ginger, or lemon or we does a nice Banbury cake or there's our specialty two-penny bun."

Benedict shot a look of enquiry her way. "A lemon bun, please," she requested, wondering what could distinguish the two-penny bun so much as to cost twice as much as its fellows.

"Two lemon buns," he rumbled, sitting back in his seat. As he did so, he rolled his right shoulder as though he might be experiencing some discomfort in it.

"Does it pain you?" she asked, noticing the neat little maid had looked back over her shoulder at him as she retreated to fetch their order. He shook his head. "I could pay for these," she offered, reaching into her pocket and showing him her gold sovereign.

His eyebrows rose. "Dare I ask?" he drawled.

"Your grandmother took me with her to learn how to tell fortunes."

He rolled his eyes. "I can't imagine you'd be well suited for such a thing."

Lizzie stared down at the faded tablecloth, tracing a tea stain with her finger. "I agree," she said in a strangled voice. "And yet…" She trailed off miserably. "Why do you say I would not be suited to it?" she asked instead.

"You're too truthful," he replied at once, and Lizzie felt the words on her tongue shrivel and her cheeks grow hot.

"Lizzie?" he asked.

"I haven't anything else to add," she said in a small voice.

He snorted. "The old lady scolded you, I suppose, but you needn't attend her."

"Well, but how am I supposed to keep myself busy all day?" she asked reasonably. "I have to pull my weight somehow. Everyone else seems to have their own role."

"Don't lump us together with them," he said sharply. "We're separate. Our own entity."

Lizzie was startled by his vehemence. "So then—"

"You answer to me and no one else," he retorted.

She considered this. "I wasn't *bad* at the fortune-telling, precisely," she admitted. "It was just that I rather alarmed myself by getting carried away."

He narrowed his eyes at this. "How do you mean?"

"Well." Lizzie took a deep breath. "Once I started, I couldn't seem to stop." He seemed at a loss how to respond to this confession, and finding the silence difficult to bear, Lizzie plunged on. "I—I told some woman that her suitor was a fortune hunter and her nurse not to be trusted."

"Why?" Benedict asked as she squirmed with embarrassment.

"Because that was how they struck me," she said wretchedly. "It was like—" She broke off. "Oh, I don't know how to describe it!"

"Are you saying you were divinely inspired?" Benedict asked with heavy sarcasm.

"Of course not!" Lizzie was profoundly shocked by the idea of such blasphemy. "It was more like someone giving me free rein to say exactly what was on my mind. For one as opinionated as I am," she admitted frankly, "I think that might be rather dangerous."

Benedict laughed suddenly, startling her a good deal. "You may be right," he conceded. "So then leave off the fortune-telling in future."

"Really? Your grandmother may not be pleased after she took the time to tutor me in the art."

He shrugged. "It doesn't sound like you minded her much."

"How can you tell?"

"You're supposed to tell them what they want to hear," Benedict pointed out dryly. "It sounds like you did the opposite."

Lizzie brooded on this a moment.

"Well, then what else can I do?" she asked slowly, remembering how Daphne had paraded up and down the front of the boxing tent, accosting passersby. She shuddered. "I—I do not think I am cut out to approach people. I do not have a particularly engaging manner."

A smile tugged at his lips. "No, you don't, do you?" he admitted softly, and for some reason, that, too, discomforted her. Luckily, the girl returned at this point with a tea tray and set down their pot of tea, two cups and saucers, and a plate of buns. Benedict paid her but otherwise ignored the admiring looks she was casting at him through her lashes. Finally, the girl retreated with a last wistful glance.

Lizzie found she did not truly wonder at it as she once did. She had judged Betsy harshly, she thought, for being taken in by Benedict Toomes's flashy good looks. Now she had seen him stripped to the waist, she had to admit he was an admirable male specimen.

Benedict had to be the poorest dressed man in the tent in his black waistcoat and faded shirt. He did not even wear a collar at his neck, let alone a cravat or tie. Instead, he had a loosely tied kerchief completing his workaday outfit. But still, she thought, letting her eyes wander around the tent, he was commanding plenty of attention from the female quarters.

"Lizzie," he said suddenly, and she returned her gaze to his face. "Your tea's growing cold while you gape at all and sundry."

"I wasn't gaping," she protested as she lifted her cup to her lips.

"What was it?" he said, half turning to look over his shoulder. "A hat you admire? A gown?"

"Certainly not! I hope I am not so caught up in worldly things that I sit gawping at another lady's finery."

"It better not be a man," he uttered direly.

Lizzie spluttered on her mouthful of tea. *A man!* "It is not my habit to sit and s-stare at gentlemen!" she assured him freezingly, but a slight stammer revealed her discomfort.

"You were staring at me earlier. I could feel your eyes burning into me," he said, looking at her over the rim of his teacup.

125

Lizzie felt her face grow scarlet. "Well, you were on display!" she pointed out hotly. "Everyone was looking at you, not just me!"

"I did not care about anyone else," he answered smoothly.

"Well, then perhaps you will be so good as to inform me where I *should* have directed my gaze?" she said smartly, setting her teacup back in its saucer with a rattle.

"Oh, you were looking exactly where you were supposed to," he assured her. "What did you think?"

Lizzie was momentarily thrown. Surely, he was not expecting her to comment on his physique? She reached for a teaspoon and distractedly added a lump of sugar to her tea. She did not even take sugar usually, just lemon, however they had only been supplied with a small jug of milk. She cleared her throat. "I—er—do not have extensive experience about such matters," she prevaricated, feeling a complete fool. "I once attended a viewing of antiquities that it put me in mind of," she admitted, desperately groping for some experience to draw on.

"Antiquities?" Now it was Benedict's turn to look blank. "I don't think I follow."

"N-naked statues," Lizzie blurted. "Classical ones." Benedict stared at her in seeming bemusement, and she grew even more flustered. "I don't mean a Greek god or anything of that nature," she assured him hurriedly. "But they had—er—games and such pursuits even in those ancient times."

"They had boxing?" he asked lightly, his eyes gleaming in a manner she found deeply disconcerting.

Lizzie took a deep breath. "I'm not sure," she admitted. "They certainly had wrestling and—um, gladiatorial entertainments in arenas and things," she finished off lamely.

A smile curved his lips, and she found herself remembering, rather inconveniently, his kiss from the previous evening. "Is that so?"

Lizzie forced herself to take a bite of her bun. At least chewing on that gave her an excuse not to enmesh herself even deeper. He must think she had been shamelessly ogling him, she thought, feeling mortified. Swallowing, she asked him quickly, "What did your brother Frank mean by his comments at the close of the match?"

He shrugged. "You don't need to pay that any heed." She looked at him curiously. "What?" he asked.

"It's nothing."

"Tell me," he insisted.

"It's just, I thought you would want me to pander to your family more," she admitted. "I called your grandmother a horrible old woman earlier."

He gave a choked laugh at that. "I daresay she asked for it."

"I'm not so sure; I think I was just in a flat panic." Lizzie sighed, peering into the teapot. "There's enough for another cup," she informed him.

"You have it." Lizzie poured the last of it into her cup through the strainer. "The boxing tent's too rough for the likes of you," he said abruptly. "We'll find you something else to do."

"What?" asked Lizzie, gratefully gulping her tea.

"Something," Benedict answered with the faintest glimmer of a smile playing around his lips. "Where you don't have to make yourself too agreeable to others. I'll put my thinking cap on."

"And what will I do this afternoon?" she asked, lowering her cup.

"You can sit inside the entrance and take the ha'penny fee."

9

In truth, Benedict knew he had given Frank cause for complaint that morning. The first fight had gone to plan, but he *had* rushed the second and the third. His mind had been on other things. Namely, his new wife. For some reason, he had imagined he would feel quite indifferent to Lizzie's struggles to find her place in his life. But that had been before…

Now he was faced with the reality of Lizzie Anderson as his wife, he felt quite differently about the matter. Frank had clearly recognized as much, for when Benedict had said Lizzie would require a chair, his brother had made no complaint, but merely fetched her one and handed her a jar for the ha'pennies. "Daphne will drum up custom," Frank announced. "And Lizzie can take the entrance fees. Jack, you keep an eye on her."

Their younger brother had nodded in agreement, and Daphne had made her way back outside the tent to start hollering. Benedict had found himself hovering a moment until he had seen that Lizzie was settled and then returned to the ring.

Even now, as Frank touted the next prospect, Benedict was fighting the impulse to turn and crane for a glimpse of her sat in the doorway. God alone knew why. He knew what he would find. Her neat figure sat ramrod straight. The demure braided head of hair. The lips pressed primly together. He wanted another taste of those lips. Damn Jack for interrupting them last night when he had finally got her where he wanted her. Namely, in his arms.

Just when had he started hankering after Betsy's correct cousin? he wondered with a quick shake of his head. Desire had crept up on him and taken him unawares. She had spent the night in his bed since then and, what's more, had left it as innocent as she had entered it, more's the pity.

It had been a pleasant awakening that morning though. She wasn't so starched up when she was sleeping. Lizzie Anderson had been sweet and clinging in the early hours when her arm had stolen around his waist and her breath had tickled the back of his neck. Her trim figure had felt womanly enough, though in truth, he had always thought her on the skinny side at Sitwell Place, stood next to her comely cousin.

Frank sauntered Benedict's way and, still beaming at the audience, clasped his shoulder in a tight grip. Had he noticed Benedict's abstraction? "Our first volunteer has boxed a bit before, so watch your step," he murmured, before turning back to the crowd. "Gentlemen, we have a treat for you! A veritable treat! Can we get another volunteer or two before we start this afternoon? Come! There must be some hot-blooded bruisers among you, keen to prove your mettle to your fellows!"

Benedict let the patter wash over him. He had heard it all so many times after all. He'd never heard anyone compare him to a Greek statue before though. That had been a new one. He found he liked to think of Lizzie's stunned gaze running over him, comparing him to the only example of masculinity she had heretofore been exposed to. A statue. A smile tugged at his lips as he rolled his shoulders.

He wanted her eyes on him now, he realized, though in truth, it was probably just as well they weren't. Otherwise he might feel inclined to impress her by dispatching his challengers as speedily as possible. Again. And he had a livelihood to earn, he reminded himself, especially with a wife to support.

Irresistibly, his gaze returned to the entrance. Was someone arguing the fee with her? he wondered, straightening up. Two men hovered there, talking with boisterous loudness. Nay, they

130

were coming into the tent now, all smiles and jocularity. What the fuck were they smiling about? He scowled. He'd like to see one of them climb in the ring with him, and he'd wipe that smile off their face.

Benedict decided he would take particular satisfaction in pummeling the bastard in the stovepipe hat. He turned a hard stare on his brother Jack. What the fuck was his brother going to do about it? If he wanted to make himself useful, he could try turning his eye on his new sister-in-law and making sure she wasn't being harangued by all-comers. He watched his brother cast a bewildered look about him. Bloody young idiot was less than useless.

The afternoon crawled along. It didn't matter how many times he glanced at the doorway, Lizzie's attention was either trained outside the tent, or on the person handing her their fee. Only once did he catch her looking his way, and on that occasion, she looked away so fast he barely had time to register the fact. It vastly improved his mood though.

There was a break between the early and late afternoon show, but Benedict dared not distract himself by going to her. If he had, he would not want to return to the ring at all. Instead, he stayed where he was and accepted the bottle of beer Jack fetched him. Out of the corner of his eye he could see Lizzie sat alone with her lemonade. That Daphne had not approached her once, and after fetching her drink, Jack gave her a wide berth.

In truth, they did not need two women working the outside of the tent. It probably deterred as many customers as it attracted. He would need to find some other occupation for Lizzie. But what? What was she fit for in this world so outside of the one she knew? He ran through the list of prospects, but nothing seemed a likely fit. The theater tent, such as it was, was full of hecklers and revelers that would no doubt shock the living hell out of her.

The acrobats would have no use for her, and even the food stalls would expect her to share a laugh and joke with their customers. Something he just could not imagine Lizzie doing. If anyone told her a bawdy jest, he had no doubt it would likely be met with disapproval and outrage. Though why that should make him smile, he had no notion.

It was between the eighth and ninth crowd volunteer that inspiration struck. Connie and her Wondrous Females of the World. Had Connie not told him herself that Alfred, her muscle, had run off and left her in the lurch this season?

Though Connie's booth relied on titillation, she fostered a strictly "hands off" policy and cultivated at least a surface appearance of heavy respectability. Partly, this was to circumvent decency laws, and partly, because outright touch would expose the fact that most of her "wonders" were out and out frauds.

In the past, Alfred's hulking presence with his cauliflower ears and broken nose had been intended as a deterrent to those who would seek to either importune Connie's girls or expose them outright. What if Lizzie were to patrol the tent instead? She could freeze a man at twenty paces with one of her looks, and it wasn't as though she would shrink from ticking anyone off who crossed a line.

Alfred, for all his bulk, had been awkward and bashful when it came to telling young ladies to stand back or to prevent them from peering behind the curtains. Benedict could not imagine Lizzie showing a similar reluctance. She would wade right in given half the chance.

Again, he found himself inclined to smile at the thought, greatly startling Frank, who he realized had just given the chilling "he'll seal your doom" speech of introduction for him. Hastily, he rearranged his features into a fearsome scowl. It only occurred to him as they were clearing away that he had spent most of the afternoon thinking about Lizzie.

She appeared silently by his side as he fastened the last of his shirt buttons. "Do we tidy away the roped-off area too or leave that up for tomorrow?"

"Leave it up," he answered. "No one will disturb it."

She held up her jar of ha'pennies. "What shall I do with this?"

"Frank will sort the takings for the day," he said, looking around for his older brother, who was already looking through Jack's betting book with a frown of concentration on his face. Lizzie carried it over to him. Benedict watched his brother take it with a nod, and Lizzie returned to his side.

"I don't think Daphne really needed me on the door with her, you know," she commented without rancor.

He grunted, knotting his kerchief about his throat. "I've thought of something else for you to do on the morrow."

"Oh?" She sounded wary.

"I need to speak to someone first tomorrow morning, but I think it will suit."

"Not now?" she asked.

He shook his head. "Not now." He let his eyes wander over her as Lizzie frowned distractedly.

"It doesn't have anything to do with my legs, does it?"

"Your legs?" He frowned. "I don't think I—"

"It doesn't matter," she said hurriedly. "Forget I said it. So what happens now?" she asked. "Does the fair shut down for the night?"

He gave a short laugh. "Far from it. Come on. Let's go find something to eat." He offered her his arm and Lizzie took it. He was pleased to see she took less time to pause each time. Heading for the exit, he called a brief goodbye to his brothers.

"You coming back later?" Jack called after them. "You can watch me in the ring, see how I've improved."

"We've got better things to do," Benedict replied as they passed outside into the milling crowd. They had walked to the end of the row and turned into the next before either one of them spoke.

Lizzie cleared her throat. "You don't need to return to the tent this evening, then?" she asked.

"No, I've taken my turn in the ring for the day."

"How will they manage without you? Who will take over the betting book if Jack is boxing?"

He shrugged. "Frank probably."

"Does Frank never box himself?"

Benedict felt a twinge of irritation. "Do you want to talk about my brothers all night?" he asked and even he heard the edge to his voice. *Damn it.*

She was quiet a moment, then asked, "Well, what *do* you want to talk about?"

"Us," he answered gruffly and heard her indrawn breath. Perhaps that had been a bit too direct. "What do you fancy for supper?" he asked, nodding in the direction of the stalls they were passing.

Lizzie glanced that way, looking grateful for the change of subject. At that moment they were passing a coffee stall that also sold hot eels and pea soup as a sideline. "The Napps were very fond of pea soup," she commented. "It was a good deal cheaper in the East End," she added critically, noticing the scrawled sign. "And those cups look rather small. Mrs. Napp used to buy a whole pint for a ha'penny and thought it very nutritious."

"They hike the prices up at the fairs," he answered. "But I refuse to buy you pea soup for supper when there's fried fish to be had."

"Fried fish? Is that your favorite, then?" she asked, looking at the bewildering array of stalls on offer.

"It is," he replied promptly. "They fry it in a batter made with beer."

"It sounds…interesting," Lizzie conceded.

They ate their fried fish out of newspaper sat on wooden crates. It was served with a buttery baked potato on the side and sprinkled with salt.

"Good?" he asked curiously, watching her lean back with a sigh.

"Very good," she conceded. "I haven't had fish cooked this way before." Having finished her food, she gazed around in bemusement at the teeming crowds. "Is it always this busy?" she asked after a moment.

He withdrew a handkerchief from his pocket and passed it to her. "Always. Greenwich is one of the biggest fairs in the country."

Lizzie dabbed the corners of her mouth delicately before handing it back. "I collect that you and your family tour the fairs all year long."

He nodded. "Though in truth it's nine months in all, not twelve."

"Have you always lived like this?" she asked curiously.

"Since I was a lad. My grandfather started the act, but me and Frank took over as soon as Frank turned eighteen." He could see her suppress further questions only with an effort. "I don't get along with my father," he said shortly.

She drummed her heels against the crate softly. "I'm an orphan," she volunteered.

He already knew this but made no comment. "I went to prison for public affray. Did you know that already?"

His words seemed to take her aback. "Betsy did say something of that nature," she admitted. "What happened?"

He shrugged. "Someone insulted me; it was just my bad luck the peelers happened to be around at the time."

"Peelers?"

"Police," he explained. Her lips formed a soundless *oh*. "It won't happen again," he found himself adding, though he was blessed if he could say why.

After a moment, she asked, "So, we will be touring now until November?"

He gave her a keen look, but her expression was guarded, giving nothing away. "How does that prospect strike you?" he asked, keeping his own tone impassive.

"A little daunting," she admitted. "But I am sure I will find my way." To his surprise he found he believed her. "With time," she added conscientiously.

He grunted, taking the newspaper from her and scrunching it up with his own and throwing it into a crate nearby that was being used to collect rubbish. "Come on," he said. "Let's go get something to drink."

Naturally, Lizzie chose ginger beer.

"What do you want to do now?" he asked casually. "Walk around the fair some more or go back to the wagon?"

Lizzie lowered her drink. "Go back to the wagon," she admitted thankfully. "It feels like it's been a long day."

Benedict frowned. "You're tired, then?" he asked.

She must have caught something in his tone, for she glanced at him in surprise. "Well, I would have thought that you must be exhausted after all those fights."

"Not especially. I'm used to it."

"Then, you wish to view more of the attractions?" she ventured hesitantly. He shook his head. "So, you also want to return to the wagon, then?"

He nodded his head. "Aye, but not to sleep," he said gruffly. "I think it's about time we got to know each other a little better, don't you?"

Lizzie's frown deepened. "I thought that was what we had been doing."

He pulled a face. "Well, there's getting acquainted and there's getting acquainted."

She exhaled noisily, coming to a complete halt where she stood. "You mean—" She broke off to suck in a deep breath, glancing around her furtively before she spoke. "Do I take it you mean in the biblical sense, Mr. Toomes?"

"Call me Benedict," he said, catching hold of her arm and tugging her alongside him. There wasn't enough room to spare for her to come to a complete stop. Not without causing a traffic jam.

"*Is* that what you mean?" She sounded so uncertain it was almost laughable.

"Of course that's what I mean." He glanced her way and saw the stunned look on her face. "This surprises you?" he asked carefully.

"Well, yes, quite frankly!" she answered roundly. "I had no notion—that is, you have given no indication that you found the prospect even a remotely attractive one!"

"The prospect of bedding you?" he asked with raised brows. "I don't know where you got that idea."

"Well," she spluttered. "I spent our wedding night on Mrs. Napp's floor!"

He tipped his head to one side to regard her frankly. "That was a result of circumstances, nothing more."

"But you—you always made your dislike of me quite plain when you called at Sitwell Place!" she rallied hotly.

"As did you of me," he pointed out, narrowing his eyes.

"Precisely!"

"Things change," he said, his gaze wandering over what he could see of her beneath that enveloping black cloak.

"Not that quickly!"

"Oh yes they do, Lizzie Toomes," he said, lowering his voice. "I'm attracted to you, alright. You need have no doubts on that score."

"Since when?" she flung at him. "I don't believe you!"

"I've wanted you since you faced down that parson at your uncle's table," he retorted, surprising himself as much as her.

Lizzie stared at him. "Since—" she repeated blankly before swallowing her words. "But…" Again her words led nowhere. He waited impatiently. "But that's preposterous! I mean, it makes no earthly sense!" she persevered, clearly struggling for words at this point.

"I can make you want me too, given the chance," he said in a low voice. Lizzie gasped and turned to stare straight ahead. He felt her arm tremble where he touched her, and it encouraged him, for he did not think it was with fear precisely. At least he hoped it was not.

"Well, it is your right, of course," she admitted jerkily. "I just never imagined you would claim it."

Now it was his turn to be surprised. "You never imagined I would want to bed my own wife?" he asked skeptically.

"Not when I was simply a last-minute substitute you felt forced to take."

"Forced?" he repeated, blinking. "And just who do you imagine forced me?"

139

"Your own sense of chivalry, I suppose," a clearly flustered Lizzie responded.

"My sense of what?" He was so startled by this he actually laughed out loud. Lizzie clenched her fists, a spark entering her eyes, but just then a rowdy bunch of young men came barging past them, waving paper flags and singing loudly.

The song was a bawdy one, and their voices raucously upraised. Benedict reached out and drew Lizzie close against him until they had surged past. She did not struggle to break free, and he kept his arms about her as the song faded into the jostling crowd.

"The way you put it, as I recall," she said against his top shirt button, "was that we were both backed into a tight corner and could use each other to our mutual advantage."

He frowned. "Was that how I put it?" He could scarcely remember now as he felt her breath tickling his throat. He just knew he had been determined to pursue her. His vehemence had struck him, even at the time, as a little odd. When the crowd had dispersed, he released her, retaining a firm hold of her arm.

"You recall yesterday when you said I possessed certain qualities you admired?" Lizzie asked in a stifled voice.

"Yes."

"Did you speak the truth?"

He stole a sideways glance at her, but her gaze was trained straight ahead. "I did."

"What were they?"

"You don't back down from a fight," he answered promptly.

140

She looked at him then but almost immediately turned away again. "I see," she said, though he had to concentrate to hear her voice against all the shouted laughter and background noise. Suddenly, she came to an abrupt stop. "Very well, then," she said. "Let's return to the wagon."

She didn't need to tell him twice. Immediately on their return he set about building a small fire to heat the water for washing. Wordlessly, Lizzie joined him in collecting nearby branches and twigs. Once it was lit and he'd encouraged the flames to take, he collected the pail from the wagon to fetch more water.

"Don't stray far," he warned, and she nodded. Perhaps, he pondered as he walked the five minutes to the well, he should have put their wagon closer to those of his family. There was safety in numbers, and he did not like to think of Lizzie left alone and unprotected at the wagon. Then again, proximity to his family had its own drawbacks.

This business of campfires seemed, for the first time in his life, an onerous task when he had better things to do. Perhaps a small stove, such as the ones circus performers used, would serve better. He had never considered purchasing one before, and a chimney would have to be installed, he thought with disfavor. Still, it was an option.

When he returned, Lizzie was patting their horse which was tethered near the wagon. Seeing him, she approached and threw the last of her branches into the fire. "Shall I fetch more?" she asked.

He considered the fire. "No, this should last long enough for our needs."

"In that case, I just need to slip into the field opposite." She did not meet his eye, and he guessed her meaning.

141

Damn it, maybe he should have bought a chamber pot too. He'd never had to contend with maidenly modesty before. "Don't go far." When she returned, he had a pot of water hung over the fire and was spreading a piece of sacking over the damp ground. "Come and sit here with me while we wait for this to boil," he said. "I've something here for you."

Lizzie joined him, sinking down beside him. "What is it?" He retrieved the packet of tea from his pocket and tossed it into her lap. "Tea leaves?" She sounded pleased.

"There's no milk, but I got the other things you'll need," he gestured toward the blue enamel tea set he had bought that morning while she still slept.

"And cups!" Lizzie picked up the pieces, turning them over. "They're made of metal," she exclaimed with surprise.

"Not what you're used to," he said wryly. "But bone china doesn't fare well in a moving wagon."

"I'm sure this is much more functional," she agreed, inspecting the tea strainer and spoons with interest. "Thank you." She looked up. "And I always prefer lemon to milk, in any case."

"I haven't got lemon either."

"Well no," she conceded. "But what I meant was that I'm used to drinking it black."

Once the first lot of water was boiled, she set about brewing the tea, and Benedict refilled the pot. By the time their beverage was ready, they drank it with their shoulders touching to guard against the decided nip in the air.

"What is the horse's name?" she asked. "You never told me."

"Florence."

"She's very large. What kind of horse is she?"

"An Irish cob. You should turn in after this. It's getting cold."

She gave a murmur of agreement. "Do you have such a thing as a hot water bottle?" she asked. "My aunt kept stoneware ones for the winter months. There were most effective, I always found."

"No," he answered after a moment, giving her a meaningful look. "You won't need one now, Lizzie. You've got me instead."

She cleared her throat. "Well, yes, there is that, I suppose," she agreed in a stifled voice.

"Get along inside," he recommended. "I'll bring in the water for your wash once it's hot enough. Take these matches," he said, passing her a box. "To light the lamp so you can see what you're doing in there."

She took the matches from him and clambered to her feet, hurrying over to the wagon and shutting the door behind her. Sitting alone, he found himself running over her words from earlier. What was that comment she had made about her legs? he wondered, mystified. It did not do to let your mind wander when it came to conversing with Lizzie, as she tended to go haring off in another direction.

With a shrug, Benedict added another branch to the fire and rested his forearms against his knees. It was good he had a few moments now to collect himself, for in truth he felt over-keen to join her and needed some breathing space to pull himself together.

His heart had nearly leaped out of his chest when Lizzie had said they should come back early tonight. It was her boldness he liked, he told himself, that was all, and he'd always enjoyed a challenge. That had to account for it. He shifted uneasily and peered beneath the lid of the pot. It needed another five minutes at least.

Breathing out slowly, he went over all the reasons why tonight's consummation was bound to be a disappointment. She was a straitlaced virgin, and she had about twenty years of a puritan upbringing to shrug off before she'd make him a halfway decent bedpartner.

When that did not dampen his enthusiasm as it ought, Benedict had a strange realization. A good deal of his excitement was simply the prospect of getting his hands on her. Added to that was the heady prospect of *her* hands on him. God, he actually wanted that, he realized, feeling dumbfounded.

All those weeks of seeing Lizzie's sour face during his tiresome courtship should not have wrought this effect on him. Back then he had imagined her disapproving eye had all the warmth of a fish on the slab. He had found Betsy's spinster cousin about as appealing as a dunk in a cold trough of water. Yet here he was slavering after her.

Betsy, he thought with a start. He had not even thought of her once in the last day or so. And yet he had been so close to marrying her. It wasn't until that godawful dinner at Sitwell Place that he had realized he absolutely, beyond a shadow of a doubt, could not go through with it. Perhaps he should thank providence or that light-fingered vicar for showing him a way out. No, he amended with a faint smile, it was Lizzie's gimlet eye which had spared him an awful fate.

The lid of the pot rattled, letting him know it was boiling. He poured the water into the large wash jug and knocked on the door of the wagon. Lizzie opened it, swathed in her white cotton nightgown and shawl, and took it from him with thanks.

144

Benedict kicked earth over the remains of the campfire and went to relieve himself in the wooded area behind them. Then he smoked a cigarillo, giving her time to ready herself before his return. When he knocked on the door again, she yanked it open at once.

"Where have you been? I thought you'd changed your mind or got lost."

"Changed my mind?" he echoed as he climbed in and pulled the door shut behind him. "I was being considerate and giving you time to wash and undress."

"Undress?" Lizzie echoed, blinking. She looked down at the nightgown buttoned up to her neck.

"Get in the bed," he recommended. "There isn't room to swing a cat in here, and it's my turn." He poured the remaining water into the bowl and started unbuttoning his waistcoat. Behind him he heard her move over to the bed and climb in.

"I wonder where that saying comes from," her muffled voice remarked from the bed. "Why would anyone swing a cat about in any event? It makes no sense as well as being inordinately cruel."

"I believe," Benedict remarked as he flung his waistcoat on top of one of the wooden boxes and started unfastening his shirt, "it refers to a cat o' nine tails."

"Oh." Lizzie sounded impressed. "So, it refers then to flogging?"

"Apparently."

"Room to wield the whip," she pondered. "Yes, I suppose that does make sense. Though, of course, it is still a very cruel metaphor."

145

He added his shirt to the pile, plunged his hands into the basin of water, and started to vigorously wash his face and neck. By the time he was shaking the water out of his ears, she had thought of some other line of enquiry.

"I wonder how your family contrive to sleep in just two wagons," she remarked. "I suppose your brothers must share."

Benedict set the bar of soap aside and unbuttoned his trousers, stripping down to his long underwear. "They manage," he said shortly. Then he remembered she was likely nervous and forced himself to elaborate. "In the summer they build a tent with branches and a leather cover, and Jack sleeps in that."

"How curious."

He stripped and washed the rest of himself in record time and even considered for a moment climbing *back* into his underwear. Glancing over his shoulder, he found her staring up at the ceiling in any case. There seemed little point in putting them on only to take them off again. Instead, he made for the bed and climbed in. When his naked body came into contact with hers, he let out a sigh of relief between his teeth, despite the enveloping nightgown.

Lizzie lay stiff as a board as he shifted against her side. Small wonder, for she must feel what was poking into her hip. He wound an arm about her, drawing her closer as he breathed out, striving to calm himself. His excitement was disproportionate. He needed to calm down. "I suppose I'm the first naked man you've seen," he commented. "Except for those Greek statues of yours." Lizzie gave a nod. "Were they wearing fig leaves?" he asked huskily.

Lizzie cleared her throat. "The exhibition wasn't intended for a female audience," she replied in a slightly strangled voice.

146

"Which means?" he prompted.

"They weren't wearing fig leaves."

There it was again. He liked how she didn't lie however tempted she might be. "So, mine isn't the first cock you've seen, then?"

She gave a horrified gasp. "I didn't look! At yours, I mean," she added conscientiously.

"So, you did look at the museum?" he laughed softly.

Lizzie plucked at the coverlet. "Well—yes," she admitted in a rush.

"And what did you think?"

Her color deepened. "I didn't really know *what* to think." She ventured a glance at him. "Would you say art faithfully represents the appendage?"

Benedict felt inclined to laugh again. Not a pastime he indulged much in. "I don't know about that," he said unevenly. "I'm not much of an art connoisseur." He rolled onto his back. "Why don't you tell me?"

She gave him a scandalized look as he drew down the sheets, baring himself to her shocked gaze. He didn't feel cold at all right now. He felt blazing hot as he displayed himself for her pleasure, or rather, he should say, for her edification. For all her embarrassment, he noticed her gaze was riveted to what curved away from his thighs, standing for her attention. Her eyes widened, then flew to meet his, then returned once again to contemplate his erection.

"How do I compare?" he asked curiously as the moment stretched out. She must be impressed, he reflected. He couldn't remember a time he'd been more aroused.

147

Lizzie sucked in a breath. "They did not have hair there as you do," she observed quietly. "Or if they did, not much of it. And they weren't—um—" She faltered, her eyes averting delicately. "That is, they did not—"

"They weren't hard as I am," he supplied when words apparently failed her.

She frowned at that. "I believe they were made of marble. You are made of flesh."

"They weren't hard for a woman, I should say," he corrected himself. "In everyday life, mine is not stiff like this, or it would never fit it in my breeches."

She looked much struck by this. "Well, no, I suppose it would not."

"Anything else?" he asked. When she hesitated, he asked curiously, "What?"

"They were altogether neater in proportion," she blurted. "I can't see how that could possibly"—she floundered a moment before concluding in failing accents—"fit."

Benedict struggled, but this time could not entirely contain his laughter. "It will though," he assured her. "We just have to make sure you're ready to receive me."

She mulled this over a while before asking "How?" rather pointedly.

"We have to—" He paused. "Kiss and touch a bit."

She blew out a breath. "I don't see how that would help."

"You haven't asked *where* I need to touch you yet."

Lizzie regarded him, the misgiving plain to see on her face. "Where?" she asked.

He grinned at her. "It's your turn to show me yours now, Lizzie."

"What?" Her voice was little more than a squeak at this point.

"You heard me. Draw down the covers and show me what you've got."

Her expression was aghast. "You're not serious."

"Oh, but I am," he assured her, reaching for the pillows and piling them up behind her. "Lean back. You can keep your nightgown on if you want."

Her expression told him that she had no intention of losing her robe. Casting him a quelling look, she pushed the blankets down, exposing her white-clad body. Then she reached down and started to draw the demure nightdress up over her shins.

Benedict caught his breath. What was it she had said earlier about her legs? Had he ever figured that out? She had nice legs, slender, but well formed. Without even thinking about it, he reached out to wrap his fingers around her ankle and slide them up her shapely calf. Lizzie gave an exclamation and started violently.

It occurred to him that he was likely the only man who'd ever touched her. For some reason, that thought had him breathing even harder. "Higher," he said hoarsely when the hemline paused at her pretty knees. The thought gave him a momentary pause. When had he ever thought to appreciate a woman's knees?

Lizzie gave an almost audible gulp. Then she closed her eyes, fell back against the pillows, and yanked her nightgown up to her waist.

Benedict kept his eyes on her averted face. "Look at me, Lizzie." She shook her head. "I'm not going to do anything until you do."

One eye flickered open at that. "What do you mean?" she croaked.

"I won't look or touch until you're fully with me in this." She opened both her eyes at that. "How about a fair exchange?" he offered. "And we each get to touch the other." He waited for her to tell him she didn't want to touch him, so he could convince her otherwise. But to his surprise, the words never came.

"That...sounds fair," she conceded. He kept his eyes on her face. "You can look at me now," she prompted him. "I looked at you, so it's only fair."

He allowed his gaze to dip down to where her pale thighs were pressed together below a triangle of light brown hair. His eyes dwelt there a moment appreciatively. "Nice," he said on an outward breath. She gave a choked sound. "What?" He tore his eyes away to meet hers.

"It seems an odd thing to say, that's all. There's not really much for you to—well—*see*. Not like yours, I mean." She must have seen the change in his expression for she asked at once, "What is it? Why do you look like that?"

He hesitated. "That's because I go inside you." Clearly, she knew that already from her earlier concerns about his size, but he wasn't sure how far her knowledge extended of such things. When she said nothing, he lifted his hand from where it rested,

150

lightly tracing the soft skin of her calf. "Can I touch you now?" he asked hoarsely.

She nodded, and he reached across to carefully cup the mound between her legs. Lizzie gave the same startled sound she had made when he touched her leg.

"Are my hands cold?"

She shook her head. "Female statues don't have hair either," she commented breathlessly after a moment. "I always wondered about it."

"Maybe it's hard to sculpt," he answered absently as his thumb sifted through her curls.

Her breathing hitched. "N-no, that doesn't make sense. They show hair on their head, just not…"

"Between their legs?" he supplied. Hearing the pillow rustle, he guessed she was nodding. "This hair is much more delicate though," he pointed out. "Maybe the models didn't let the artists get close enough to make it out."

"Benedict!" she squeaked as his hand slipped between her legs, gently tracing her there.

He lifted his head and shifted over her. "Yes, my Lizzie?" he murmured, lowering his mouth to hers in a kiss that coaxed and teased. For the first time he let his tongue trace lightly over her lips even as his fingers did the same below.

When Lizzie gasped, he slid his tongue into her astonished mouth, even as he carefully explored her hidden folds and felt her quivering response until his fingers were coated in a warm, wet welcome that had him groaning aloud.

"Wait," she gasped. "Wait." He stilled his fingers at once, tilting back his head to look at her.

151

"Too fast?" he asked raggedly. *Jesus*. He didn't know if he could go any slower.

The look in her eyes was conflicted. "I don't know what I'm doing!" she said shakily, her cheeks poppy red, her blond locks escaping from her braid.

"You're doing just fine."

Her chest heaved beneath the cotton nightgown. "I am?" Her eyes sought assurance from him. Whatever she saw in the depths of his own seemed to work, for she relaxed.

"Just kissing and touching, remember?" he assured her, withdrawing his hand from between her legs. He wanted to taste his fingers, but he didn't want to shock the holy hell out of her, so instead, he stared at her lips which were reddened from his kisses.

He'd never really noticed her lips before. They weren't the cupid's bow that popular songs extolled, but they were delicate and surprisingly sweet. He wanted to crush them under his own instead of sipping from them like some lovesick swain. She nodded and started to say yes, when he hungrily took her mouth, bearing her back onto the pillows and covering her body with his own.

This time he did not hold back, but gave her the kiss he wanted, rough and tender at the same time with plenty of tongue. Lizzie squeaked and panted underneath him, and he was sure she was shocked as hell at the way he pressed his manhood into her hips and belly, rubbing and straining against her.

He told himself he was getting her acquainted with it, but in truth it was as much for his own relief as anything. The noises she made seemed to make him even wilder for her. He ran his hands down her slim back and over the swell of her bottom before tugging her body flush against his and grinding against the cradle of her hips. "Are you going to touch me now, Lizzie?" he whispered raggedly. "Don't make me wait any longer."

Her hands, which had been close to her sides, rose to loop around his neck. "Where?" she asked against his jaw. Even the touch of her featherlight breath made his dick jump.

"Everywhere." His voice was so gravelly he scarce recognized it. He shuddered when her palms skimmed down his spine and circled his shoulder blades before sliding around to his chest.

"You've hair here too," she murmured, scraping her fingers through his chest hair. "I saw it this afternoon when you boxed."

"I liked you looking at me," he admitted raspily. Where the hell had that come from? Her hands slid down his sides and stopped at his hips, lightly clasping him there and making him growl. He thought she would stop there or await further instruction, but instead, she shifted away from him, putting space between them.

He reached for her at once.

"I can't see what I'm doing," she murmured. "You're practically on top of me."

He frowned. "I know I am."

"Then how am I supposed to touch you everywhere?"

"You want to touch me there?" he rasped. *Christ,* he wasn't sure he would withstand much of that.

"I thought that was the idea."

He must have been mad. Blowing out a breath of air, Benedict lay back down on the mattress. He glanced down with a grimace at his engorged shaft. Lizzie shuffled closer until their sides were touching. Carefully, with exaggerated slowness, she reached across him and he felt her fingers brush lightly against him there. Steeling himself for more, he sucked in his breath. Again, she ran her fingers tentatively down his length, rather in the manner of one stroking a dog you were unsure of. He should find it amusing, but instead, he was stimulated almost beyond belief. Very, very lightly she cupped his balls, and Benedict nearly arched off the bed with a strangled oath.

"Did that hurt?" she asked, releasing him in alarm.

"No," he panted. "I just…you took me by surprise, that's all." She looked at him doubtfully. "Do it again," he ordered thickly.

Very gently she did so, and Benedict felt himself break out into a light sweat. *Damnation*. There was no way it should feel this good. "Take me firmer in hand." She did so, lightly squeezing. "Fuck," he groaned aloud. "It feels good," he added before she got the wrong impression and backed off again. He lifted a hand to show her. "I'm going to touch you now too, Lizzie. Alright?"

She nodded and he slid his palm over her flat stomach and down between her legs until he found the slickness there with his questing fingers. Lizzie let out a whimper as he stroked and sought out her hidden pearl. "You like it there?" he asked as she bit off a sob.

"Y-yes," she answered breathlessly. "Oh, I don't know. It feels strange."

Luckily, her own hand grew slack as his ministrations increased. He was way too stimulated now for her to be tickling his balls. Closing his eyes, he concentrated on finding out her likes as her cleft grew increasingly wet, enough for him to push a finger up inside her.

"Ohhhh!" she moaned, but it wasn't in protest. The blood pounded in Benedict's ears as he felt her convulse around his finger. She was coming. *Damn, that was fast.*

"Good girl," he praised her as her legs stiffened and shook. "Clever Lizzie. Let it happen, that's it." He stroked her sensitive little bud until she gave a choked sound and fell back, her face wet with tears and her expression dazed.

He was surprised. For such an uptight little prude, she had reached the peak with surprising swiftness. He'd have to be careful to build her up slower next time, he thought, taking advantage of her relaxed body to slip a second finger inside her.

He grunted. Jesus, she was wet. Gloriously wet and tight. Maybe he could even work himself inside her already, he thought, drawing in a shuddering breath. He pumped his fingers tentatively, and the sound of her slickness made his head reel. "Open your legs, Lizzie," he ground out. "I want to see what's mine."

She groaned, but her pale thighs fell open, taking his breath away. He shifted down, cursing the fact the lamp was turned down so low. Ah God, he could come just at the sight of her pretty cleft stretched out on his thick fingers. "Fuck," he breathed again and saw her shiver. Interesting. Was she cold…or? He brushed his thumb through her folds, seeking out her tender bud. Lizzie gave another suppressed whimper.

He looked up sharply and saw her quivering eyelashes and flushed cheeks. His heart began to beat twice as loud. "Ah, Lizzie," he said richly. "What a lucky man I am. Such hidden sweetness and it's all mine." He lowered his face, inhaling her musky scent. His mouth was watering. He'd never intended to

155

push her so far on her first foray, but Christ, he wasn't made of stone and his self-restraint was shot to hell. He lowered his mouth to her with a groan and started lapping and sipping at her wetness with indecent enthusiasm before sucking her bud between his lips and laving it with his tongue.

Lizzie gave a muffled shriek, and he felt his embedded fingers gripped so tight in her juicy cunt that he almost came on the bedsheets. Her whole body convulsed this time, and he had a hard time anchoring her with only one hand free.

"Ohhhhh!" she wailed, her legs thrashing. He gripped his fingers into her waist and pinned her as best he could while the storm had her in its grip. They were both breathing hard by the time she stilled, her chest rising and falling beneath the bunched-up nightgown.

"Do you think you could do that a third time?" he asked her hoarsely as he slid up her body. "With me inside you this time?" He yanked the nightgown up and over her head, tossing it to the floor as his eyes roamed over her small, high breasts.

She blinked at him as he ran the broad tip of his cock between her wet nether lips. "Fuck, Lizzie, but you're a firecracker between the sheets," he said, lodging himself inside her with a grunt. He wasn't sure if it was the words or the action that roused her, but her head lifted off the pillow.

"Benedict!" she muttered in faint reproach. He groaned as he pressed his hips forward and felt himself start to slide into her hot unused channel. Then he hit what remained of her maidenhead. "Ouch!"

"Shhh, it's done now," he consoled her gruffly. "We won't have to worry about it again. Still with me?" Thankfully, she gave a nod, as he wasn't sure he wouldn't cry if she demanded he pull

156

back now. The sweat was beading his forehead, and he was precious close to losing control.

Bracing his forearms against the mattress, he held his weight off her as he covered her body with his. "Wrap your legs around my back," he urged, shifting over her. He wanted deep inside her, but her shaky breath and clutching fingers at his waist made him mindful of her discomfort.

The sensation of her limbs wrapped around him made him feel surprisingly giddy. "Now your arms," he ordered gruffly. She slipped one around his waist, the other gripping his shoulder tight. "Yeah, like that," he grunted. Inexplicably, he found himself seeking her lips again. As he stroked his tongue against hers, he thrust inside her, once, twice, until he was gloriously seated to the hilt. Lizzie gave a muffled squawk into his mouth, but it was drowned in his own groan of overwhelming pleasure.

She surrounded him. All he could taste and touch and see was her. He drew back, wanting to see her expression, but her face was in shadow. Her glorious pale hair was spread out across his pillow though, and that sight caused his heart to squeeze. Without stirring another inch, he tipped over the edge and found he was coming so hard he could scarce catch his breath. *Fuck.*

Luckily, Lizzie held on tight, entirely unaware he was disgracing himself. He shook violently through his release, eyes shut fast and jaw clenched in a vain attempt to stem the flow, but it was pointless. He could no more stop his seed from bursting from him than he could turn back the clock and change the object of his wooing. As though he had been craving Lizzie all along, he came inside her in a heady rush, and it was as much as he could do to prevent himself from shouting in triumph as he emptied himself into her.

In short, he was lost to all shame, and all he could do now was ride it out. He allowed himself a few shallow dips of his hips as he bit his lip and gave the last of himself to her, swallowing back the filthy curse that sprang to his lips. She would not appreciate it, and really it was the least he could do.

Only by a supreme effort did he prevent himself from collapsing on top of her like a felled oak. Instead, he gathered her in his arms and rolled onto his back, taking her with him. Lizzie lay limply atop him, catching her breath. After a moment, he felt her turn her head so her cheek lay against his bare chest. He knew he should speak, but by this point he lacked the effort to muster his thoughts. Instead, he allowed his eyes to drift shut and gave up even the attempt.

10

Lizzie woke the next morning to someone shaking her shoulder. She gazed blearily up at Benedict, who was already clean-shaven and dressed.

"There's hot water here for you to wash," he said, setting a bowl down beside the bed.

Lizzie gazed about in bewilderment. "What time is it?" she croaked, sitting up. Feeling a draught at her back and a decided stickiness between her legs, she lay back down again with haste. Where was her nightgown?

"Not long after seven," he replied. "I've got the water back on the boil for tea." When she lay there like a stunned mullet with the blankets held up to her neck, he added wryly, "Maybe I should have made you the tea first."

She could barely meet his eyes this morning. "I'd love a cup," she mumbled. It was only recently she'd realized what a luxury it was having Annie bring her one every morning. His gaze seemed to dwell on her a moment and Lizzie colored. "But I can make it," she stammered. "I don't expect you to wait on me, and it won't take me long to wash and dress."

"Take all the time you need," he answered and let himself out of the cramped confines. Lizzie breathed a sigh of relief as the door closed behind him. She must have slept like the dead for him not to have woken her when he rose. And small wonder after the way he'd used her the previous night. Her face flamed as she felt herself sore and aching in unaccustomed body parts.

What had he been looking at? she wondered self-consciously. She had no mirror to check, but she fancied it might have been the tumbled mass that was her hair this morning. She cursed the impulse that had made her leave it loose about her shoulders the previous night. She never had this problem when it was braided neatly under her nightcap. What had she been thinking of leaving it loose?

She lingered over her wash, scrubbing herself from head to toe, and felt much refreshed after it. By the time she had climbed back into her petticoats and sensible navy blue gown, she was feeling more herself again. Her hair was extremely tangled, but she labored over it until she could smoothly arrange it into a roll at her nape and secure it with pins.

Her self-possession had returned, or something like it as she had clambered out of the wagon, and she felt able to face Benedict Toomes. He was crouched next to the fire, pouring hot water into the teapot.

"Just in time," he commented, gesturing to a small three-legged stool.

"I just need to…" Lizzie gestured vaguely toward the woods and his lips quirked.

"I'll set the tea to brew."

Lizzie headed off with her cheeks on fire. When she returned, he was setting out the teacups on an overturned crate. She took her seat gratefully and watched him pour.

"So, what was the plan for this morning?" Lizzie asked, looking anywhere rather than her husband. He slid her teacup toward her on the packing case, and in her haste to take it, she inadvertently brushed her fingers against his. "Oh, I'm so sorry!" she blurted, drawing back her hand as though stung.

"No need to apologize, Lizzie." A smile lurked in his eyes that she found most discomposing. "You can touch me all you like. It's your God-given right."

160

The oddest recollections from the previous night kept flashing into her mind's eye, badly rattling her. Raising her teacup to her lips with shaking fingers, Lizzie promptly burnt her mouth, choking on a mouthful of scalding-hot tea. She blanched and set the cup down so fast she nearly overset its contents. *Pull yourself together, Lizzie!* Giving her head a quick shake, she asked, "Y-you were saying?"

"I was?"

"About your plans for me today," she said awkwardly.

Benedict frowned. "Oh, that," he murmured. "I've half a mind to simply keep you with me now." His expression as it lingered on her made Lizzie's pulse race.

Oh God no, she thought with dread. She couldn't possibly stand around all day watching him half-clothed from close quarters. Not after what they'd done last night! She cleared her throat. "I did not care overmuch for the boxing tent," she said stiltedly. "The clientele is not the sort of company I am accustomed to."

"Neither am I what you're used to," he reminded her. "But you're doing a grand job of getting used to me." The warmth in his eyes astonished her. She took another distracted swig of hot tea and winced. "You're not too—uh…" He broke off and scratched his neck. "Sore this morning?"

Lizzie was so aghast at him referring to such things, her mouth dropped open. She gazed at him, speechless with horror. When Benedict's eyebrows rose, she realized he was waiting for an answer. "No, no indeed," she replied in stifled accents.

"Good," he responded, his eyes traveling over her face as though measuring the veracity of her words. Lizzie gulped the rest of her tea, feeling thoroughly unnerved. He pushed the teapot toward her. "There's enough for another cup." Lizzie

161

poured it gratefully. "I suppose I'll have to take you to Connie, then," he said without enthusiasm. "If that's what you really want."

"Connie?" She seized on the notion eagerly. "Is that not the lady you introduced me to yesterday? In the hat?"

"It is. I had some idea you might act as curator for her tent." He shrugged. "I'm not so sure it holds up in the cold light of day, mind you."

"I think it sounds a very good idea," she argued staunchly. "Her tent comprises of female acts I think you said. I'm sure their society will suit me much better than that of boxing enthusiasts."

"The acts may be female, but their paying guests are mixed," he pointed out dryly. "You'll be required to remind them of their manners."

"Oh, I'm sure I could do that!" Anything, she told herself, would be better than gazing on Benedict Toomes's half-naked body all day, a-prey to mortifying recollections. Maybe in a couple of years she would be able to think of what they had done without flinching, but right now…

Twenty minutes later they were stood outside a round tent whose banner proclaimed it housed The Wondrous Females of the World. A scrawled piece of paper was pinned to the tent flap, stating their doors were currently closed but they would return shortly. The acts were listed in a scrolling hand painted onto a brightly colored banner on the side of the tent.

Lizzie surveyed the list with sinking spirits. A tattooed lady, a "living goddess"—whatever that meant—and a snake charmer were advertised. Lizzie's eyebrows rose higher with each one. Top of the bill was Salome—"she wears nothing but a smile"—

162

who apparently owned "the finest head of human hair you've ever seen." Lizzie gasped at the lurid picture showing a naked woman strategically covered by great swathes of hair which hung down to her feet.

"The acts listed seem different to the ones you mentioned yesterday," she commented. "Didn't you say something about a giantess?"

Benedict finished the last bite of the pastry he had bought on the way. Lizzie had wrapped hers in the paper bag and slipped it into her cloak pocket uneaten. "She has to swap them out regularly to keep the public interested," he told her and pulled the tent flap aside, ignoring the sign.

Lizzie followed him inside, wide-eyed with curiosity in spite of herself. An inner voice warned her that Connie's clientele would be no more genteel than the ruffians in the boxing tent. The only difference would be that they were seeking salacious means of entertainment rather than violent ones. Still, she had wanted an occupation and breathing space, and that was what this tent would provide.

Inside, the tent was draped with many painted hangings with mystical depictions of stars and evil eyes and many of semi-clad women with lurid claims under them. One of them was for a live mermaid in a tank and another for a "living doll." Lizzie could only suppose that the banners of past acts were hung as decoration once they had left.

Various empty plinths stood about that had oval curtain rods rigged above them suspended from the ceiling of the tent. These were hung all about with draperies, some silky and filmy and others of heavy velvet. Curiously, to one side was a velvet fainting couch. Lizzie wondered if the spectators were offered a seat while they marveled over the Wondrous Females. One of the platforms had a pile of cushions on it and a woven basket.

163

Pointing to it, she asked in failing tones, "Please tell me that basket does not contain a snake."

Benedict barely spared it a glance. "The snake charmer would hardly leave behind something her livelihood depended on. Not when someone could easily nip in and pinch it."

"Unless they intended for it to act as a deterrent to thieves," Lizzie pointed out. "Who would be mad enough to steal a snake?"

Benedict lowered his mouth to her ear. "I'm telling you this in the strictest confidence," he murmured, and feeling his breath on her neck made her shiver right to her toes. "The snake's probably not real."

Lizzie blinked, wondering at the strangeness of the sensation. "Really?"

He shook his head. "Extremely doubtful."

"Oh."

The flap that served as a door to the tent swung open. "Who the bleedin' 'ell—" Connie started wrathfully. Then she recognized Benedict and fell back a step, suddenly wreathed in smiles. "My, my, I am honored! Mr. Benedict Toomes and if it isn't his little bride."

Something about the way she said "little bride" had Lizzie narrowing her eyes, but the other woman was all affability as she listened to Benedict's suggestion, if a little skeptical.

"Think you can keep my punters in line, do you, my dear?" she asked, cocking her head to one side as she considered Lizzie in her plain garb and bonnet. She must be wearing an awful lot of hat pins, Lizzie thought, watching the large arrangement of wax fruit balanced on her brassy head. It did not move an inch.

"If you ask me, I think you're in for a rude awakening," Connie continued gustily. "But you're free to try, by all means. Far be it from me to throw a damper on your scheme. And I never could refuse one of the Toomes boys, now, could I?" she said, brushing the front of Benedict's waistcoat and eyeing him with a good deal more warmth than she had Lizzie.

Lizzie's spine stiffened, but at that instant, Benedict stepped back.

"Pastry crumbs, my dear," Connie said. "Someone ate his breakfast on the move."

Benedict smiled perfunctorily and extended his hand to Lizzie. "Walk me out." She accompanied him outside the tent. "You're sure you want to try this?" he asked, turning to her as soon as they were out in the cold morning air. "You could just come with me. If you don't like taking the entrance fee, you could do something else," he said vaguely.

"Such as?" Lizzie asked, feeling strangely touched by his inclination to keep her with him.

He shrugged. "Hold my shirt while I box," he suggested with a glint in his eye.

"A chair could do that," Lizzie pointed out.

He glanced quickly round, then caught her about the waist. "Give me a kiss, then, to be going on with," he demanded gruffly.

Lizzie squeaked as his hand cupped the back of her neck, bringing her face close to his. She scarcely had time to utter his name before his lips were upon hers, hot and demanding. Lizzie's head reeled. This was not a goodbye kiss in her opinion. When he abruptly released her, she would have stumbled if the tent pole had not been conveniently close.

"I'll fetch you for lunch," he said. "About one."

Lizzie nodded, striving to catch her breath. She watched him stride away in the direction of the boxing tent, feeing all of a flutter.

"He's knocked your bonnet crooked," said Connie dryly. Lizzie whipped around and found the older woman watching her from just inside the tent. "You set yourself straight before anyone turns up. Run a respectable establishment, I do." She sniffed. "You needn't think you can stand around mooning after that fine husband of yours neither! If you're here, you're here to work. I got no time for idlers."

Lizzie reached up and adjusted her bonnet. "Of course, Mrs. Brown," she answered, wondering where Mr. Brown might be.

"You'd best call me Connie," the other replied without enthusiasm. "And I'll warn you now, little lady. If you don't work out, I shall tell your husband so, and you needn't think my fondness for a handsome face will prevent it."

Lizzie felt herself suddenly in the grip of the oddest sensation. For the veriest instant, she pictured herself snatching Connie's ridiculous hat off her head, flinging it on the floor, and jumping up and down on it until it was flat as a pancake. When she regained control of her riotous thoughts once more, she breathed in deeply. "I am sure we will both of us give the other a fair trial," she answered coolly.

Connie gave a mirthless laugh. "Look lively. Here's Niamh and the twins," she said briskly as a tall redhead ducked into the tent followed by two slender dark maidens of identical appearance.

"Good mornin' to you," the redhead started heartily. "But who's this?" she asked, looking Lizzie up and down in surprise.

166

"The new girl," Connie answered briskly. "She's Alfred's replacement."

"Alfred?" Niamh echoed and gave a deep laugh. "You're joking!"

"Not at all, she's going to keep our paying visitors in check, ain't that right, Lizzie my girl?"

"Certainly," Lizzie answered, inclining her head. "I am happy to make your acquaintance."

Niamh blinked. "Fairly got the grand manner, hasn't she?" she said, addressing Connie. "Looks like she could freeze a duke at ten paces."

Connie looked much struck by this observation. "She has," she said slowly. "Indeed, she has got something of the governess about her," she admitted, tapping a finger against her chin. "Perhaps we could use that to our advantage?"

The twins approached Lizzie, catching her hands and holding them extended out by her sides. "She needs props," one of them said eagerly.

The other nodded, turning to Connie. "Where is Zuleika's parasol?"

"That old thing?" Niamh cried. "She'd look a regular ratbag carrying that tatty thing about!"

One of the twins released Lizzie's hand to scurry over to a large trunk. Flinging open the lid, she delved inside until she retrieved a rather battered-looking parasol of black lace and silk with a fringe hanging down. "Here!" she said, brandishing it with a triumphant flourish before hurrying back to offer it to Lizzie.

Lizzie took it hesitantly, though to be honest she privately agreed with Niamh's scathing pronouncement. The parasol had indeed seen better days. Hefting it in her hand, she had to admit it was a good substantial weight.

"I 'spose if anyone was to get handsy she could whack 'em on the wrists wiv it," Niamh said doubtfully.

One of the twins shook her head so her glossy black braids flew. "Ankles," she corrected the redhead. "If she struck their hand, she would surely break their wrist!"

Connie snapped her fingers. "Agatha's bonnet!" she said. "Would be the very thing to complete the look!"

"What? That ugly old poke bonnet?" Niamh gasped. "Why, she'd look a fright in it!"

Lizzie stirred uneasily as the other twin flew to the trunk and drew out a misshapen black bonnet, trimmed fussily with velvet and tulle.

"It is *very* ugly, is it not?" the girl said as she turned it over in her hands and cast a sympathetic look at Lizzie.

Indeed, Lizzie thought, taking it from her hands, it must have been exceedingly ugly even when it was new, let alone now it was past its prime. She was used to plain things, but she hoped she'd never had such lamentable taste as to choose a hat such as this one.

"Just the thing," Connie pronounced with satisfaction. "Here, let me take yours, and you can wear this one. I'll put yours safely in the trunk."

Lizzie watched her own bonnet, sensibly trimmed with a navy ribbon, disappear into the box of junk. Suppressing a shudder of distaste, she drew the bonnet over her head.

"I dunno," said Niamh. "You can hardly see her face in that dark cave!"

"Gives her a slightly sinister air," Connie said approvingly. "Which will stand her in good stead when dealing with the cheeky blighters we get in here."

"You look much better than Agatha did in it though," one of the twins said, giving Lizzie's hand a consoling pat.

Niamh went off into choking laughter. At Lizzie's quizzical look, she pointed wordlessly to a nearby poster which boasted "The Living Skeleton. She has a skull for a head."

Lizzie's eyes widened, and she wrenched the bonnet off her head. "You mean this bonnet belonged—"

"She wasn't really a skeleton!" the other twin assured her hastily.

"Course she wasn't!" Connie burst in, sending Niamh an irritated look. "Just a little gaunt was Agatha, with hollowed cheeks and sunken eyes. We played it up with a bit of greasepaint, that's all."

"What happened to her?" Lizzie demanded.

"Her sister opened a boarding house," Niamh said with a shrug. "Aggie went to live with her there and help her run the place."

Assured that the bonnet's previous owner did not have some fatal wasting disease, Lizzie set the hat back on her head.

"Shame we ain't got a fancy black cloak for you," Connie lamented. "That navy one of yours doesn't match."

"Ma Toomes has a black cloak she lent me," Lizzie volunteered, thinking of the cloak she had not yet returned to Benedict's grandmother.

169

Connie brightened. "Maybe you could bring that one with you tomorrow," she said optimistically. "If you work out, that is," she added with a frown as though annoyed she had been swept away with the tide of enthusiasm the twins had brought with them. Connie clapped her hands. "Alright now, girls. Let's get this place set to rights."

Lizzie fell back as the twins and Niamh busied themselves drawing out screens and diving behind them to disrobe and don their costumes.

"Lizzie, you can help me ready Salome's grotto," Connie said, gesturing to a basket full of rolled-up canvases and artificial roses pinned to streamers. She led the way to the raised platform with the pink velvet fainting couch.

They spent the next five minutes pinning the streamers to the gauzy curtains and unfurling reproductions on canvas of fleshy Venuses surrounded by clouds and cupids and not wearing much by way of clothing.

Lizzie bit her lip. "Whose couch is this?" she asked. The twins had reappeared from behind their screen, their skin painted gold and wearing the most extraordinary garments of voluminous red which contrived to both expose and cover them at the same time. They wore rubies in their bared bellybuttons, beaded slippers with turned-up toes, and pointed headdresses which looked like exotic tiaras about which their braids were woven.

"It's Salome's, didn't I say so?" Connie responded briskly.

"And who, pray, is Salome?"

Connie pursed her lips. "She's our regular star turn this season, that's who," she said, standing back and setting her hands on her hips as she surveyed the effect they had achieved. "Good enough, though I declare a pair of plaster of paris cherubs would set it right off." She clicked her tongue and sighed. "Lizzie, drape that bit of curtain over the back of the couch. That'll do," she said with a quick nod.

Niamh emerged from behind her screen, and Lizzie was astonished to see she now wore only her chemise and stays and a pair of lace-trimmed bloomers which extended down no further than her knees. More astonishing than this was the fact that the skin of her exposed arms, décolletage, and legs was heavily decorated with intricate designs that looked at first to be black lace, but on closer inspection appeared to be ink drawings of butterflies and birds and flowers.

"They're tattoos," Niamh said by way of explanation.

Lizzie flushed. "I shouldn't stare," she stammered. "I apologize."

Niamh laughed. "Lord bless you. If I minded, I wouldn't be displaying them to all and sundry, now would I? I'm a contortionist too, as well as a tattooed lady."

At that moment, the entrance to the tent was swept open and a very dapper little man in a green tweed suit with a pointed beard appeared. "She comes!" he announced dramatically in heavily accented English. Lizzie thought he must be Swiss, like a visiting pastor she had once met, though she was not sure. "My sister, she arrives!"

Turning back, he held the entrance open as a tall, substantial figure came sailing into the tent in an extremely expensive outfit of yellow silk trimmed lavishly with swansdown. She had a simply breathtaking face, rather like a Botticelli painting.

"I am come!" the radiant vision announced, sweeping a white muff wide as she beamed at everyone present. "Indeed, have no fear for I am now come, dear Mrs. Brown!"

171

"About time too," Connie muttered under her breath. "How was your night at the inn, Salome?" she asked aloud, coming down the steps to exchange greetings. The little man frowned to hear his sister addressed thus, but the amiable smile on the newcomer's face did not waver. The two women kissed the air in the vicinity of each other's cheeks.

"Oh, such a quaint little inn!" Salome responded delightedly, clasping her hands to her bosom. "They could not do enough for me. The landlord, how he fussed to have a guest from the Continent! Is that not so, Jakob?"

Jakob grimaced. "The chimney smoked in our rooms," he said fretfully.

"Ah, nonsense!" his sister boomed. "Always you must make some complaint, Jakob!" She regarded him fondly. "It is a most charming inn. Most quaint and we will enjoy our stay there very much. The way they serve the roast mutton with the mustard and the roasted potatoes is most delicious and to be commended." She broke off her ruminations as she noticed Lizzie in her sober garb. "But who is this?" she asked, turning reproachfully to Connie. "You are allowing in my public already? I am not yet ready!"

"No, no," Connie assured her. "This is Mrs. Toomes, who is to be our new *chaperone*," she said with emphasis on the word. "I could not help but be aware the crowds were not respectful of the rope barrier yesterday and pressed rather close. I could not have my star attraction being *breathed* on by the common masses."

Salome's eyes grew wide as her brother interrupted. "This is good, very good. Yes, my dear Mrs. Brown, I am most glad to hear you take my dear Ada's safety to heart."

172

Salome, or should it be Ada, Lizzie wondered, gave a gusty laugh. "And how will this little female hold back my public?" she asked genially. "She looks as though a breath of wind would blow her away—*poof*!"

"I assure you, I am not so insubstantial," Lizzie piped up.

Salome's pale blue gaze passed over her, and she gave an expressive shrug, effectively dismissing the subject. "And now I must undress," she proclaimed. "Ah, you have anticipated me, I see, my good Mrs. Brown."

Lizzie turned and saw that Niamh and the twins—she really must learn their given names—had combined their screens to cordon off an area substantial enough for Salome's ample figure to undress.

"Jakob," she said, turning to him and passing him the large white muff and her delicate gloves. "Mrs. Brown, you will help me now to disrobe."

Connie's eyes rolled but she followed Salome's lead and disappeared behind the screens.

"It will be too draughty," Jakob fussed. "My poor sister will be taking the chill."

"Fat chance of that," Niamh said sotto voce. The twins giggled.

Jakob glared at them and turned to Lizzie. "You, woman," he said. "You will be most assiduous to your duties, I trust. My sister must be protected at all costs. She is not used to such"—he broke off, his lip curling—"surroundings."

Lizzie gazed back at him impassively. "My name is Mrs. Toomes," she replied coolly. "And you may rest assured that I *always* do my duty, Mister...?"

He drew himself up to his full height. "Wurtzel," he rapped out.

Lizzie nodded. "Mr. Wurtzel." She walked past him and stalked over to where Niamh and the twins stood. It seemed to her that there was an invisible line drawn between the inhabitants of the tent. Those that the Wurtzels knew the names of and those they did not.

"Good for you," Niamh whispered, nudging her in the waist.

11

Benedict felt unaccountably annoyed. He regarded Lizzie over the top of his teacup and decided he should have elected to go for a beer. God alone knew why he had felt the need to please her by returning to a bloody tea tent. His selfless action was wholly unappreciated, he thought, listening to her rattle on about her new blasted job.

"—and only fancy." She leaned forward confidingly. "Niamh said she does not believe that Mr. Wurtzel is Salome's brother at all!" She sat back in her seat, her face flushed. She really did look surprisingly pretty with a bit of color to her face. For the first time he noticed that the bonnet framing it was not her own. "In point of fact, her name is not really Salome either. That's just her stage name. Apparently, Connie has had three Salomes in the past twelve months, but none of them have drawn a crowd like Miss Wurtzel."

"What's that on your head?" he grunted, cutting through her excited chatter.

"Oh." She reached up and touched the faded trim. "I quite forgot to change it. It's awful, isn't it? But you see"—her eyes gleamed—"it's part of my costume. I have a parasol too, but I left that in the tent. No one would steal it for it's simply the ugliest old thing."

Benedict eyed her moodily. It seemed to him that she *ought* to have given her appearance a second thought, when she knew she was meeting up with him. Hadn't he fully buttoned his shirt and even combed his hair before leaving the ring?

Jack had seemed highly amused to see Benedict tidying himself for his own wife. *You're surely past the courtship stage*, he had joked. *You'll be taking her a bunch of flowers next.* Benedict had glowered at him, but in truth, Jack wasn't to know that Lizzie had never been wooed.

"I'm a sort of an old-fashioned *duenna*, you see," Lizzie explained, setting down her cheese sandwich. "My role is protectress of the girls, ensuring the spectators do not encroach on their private space."

I know, thought Benedict sourly as he clattered his cup back into his saucer and added a second sugar lump to his tea. *I was the one who thought of it. Bloody fool that I am.* Aloud he simply said, "So, you're thinking you'll stick with it for now?"

"Oh yes!" She regarded him with some surprise before giving him a reassuring smile. "I'm perfectly content with my lot."

Perfectly content. He should be reassured by that, but strangely, he was not. He didn't *want* her to be content. *He* wasn't content, he realized with a frown, watching her take a bite of scone. He felt edgy and restless, like he'd neglected some duty or overlooked some detail. What was it niggling away at the back of his mind?

Lizzie dabbed her mouth with a napkin and took a sip of tea, wholly oblivious to his inner turmoil. "How about you?" she asked politely. "You said your morning went well. How did you find your brothers?"

"They're fine," he said shortly, and seeing her frown, he forced himself to elaborate. "Though Frank looked a little rough first thing. Maybe he's missing Maggie setting his clothes out for him of a morning."

Lizzie fiddled with her napkin, clearly unsure of her footing when it came to commenting on his brother's broken marriage. "And your bouts this morning?" she ventured. "They went well?"

"Fine."

"You won them all?"

He felt a spasm of irritation. "Of course."

Lizzie shot him a look. "Only you seem a little…"

"What?"

She shook her head a little. "How was Daphne?" she asked instead brightly, and Benedict scowled.

She made polite conversation as he walked her back to Connie's tent, and it was as much as he could do to mutter ill-natured replies. It wasn't until he was headed back to the Toomes Brothers Boxing Saloon that he realized why he was in a sulk. He wanted her attention on him, not anyone else, unreasonable brute that he was. The problem was, Lizzie didn't get it. She'd never walked out with a man before, so she had no clue how to make up to one.

It wasn't enough, he realized dimly, to avoid Frank's mistakes with Maggie. He needed to actually make his interest known to Lizzie. Clearly, she viewed their marriage as some kind of agreement they had struck up between them to make the best of a bad bargain. And why wouldn't she? he reflected irritably. That *was* how he had presented it to her, but he felt somehow quite differently now.

Laughter and music spilled out of the large ballroom tent, the aptly named Fiddlers Green. Should he try to take her dancing of an evening? he wondered idly. At night it was a shilling entrance, but there was an orchestra of sorts, a cold supper to be had, and country dancing. In such a tight squeeze, he could slip his arm about her and no one would be any the wiser.

Did Lizzie dance? He had no notion. Betsy certainly had, but she had been happy enough to sit out when he had declared himself an unenthusiastic partner. He would grit his teeth and fling Lizzie about the floor if it was something she enjoyed though, he reflected. The next tent along was The Philmore Players. Ben eyed the banner boasting of its touring successes. Would she prefer a play? At that point, Jack came sauntering out of the theater tent and the two brothers eyed each other warily.

"What you doing here?" Jack asked, taken aback. "Not hanging out after an actress, are you?"

"Course not!" Benedict found himself snapping. "I was just looking to see what they're performing."

Jack regarded him with surprise. "What for?" Patronage of the arts was not precisely a Toomes trait.

"Just thinking of bringing Lizzie to see a show," Benedict admitted. Even to his own ear, he sounded a little sheepish.

Jack's eyebrows nearly shot off the top of his head. "I swear if I didn't know better, I'd think you hadn't yet tied the knot."

"I didn't get much chance to court her beforehand," Benedict answered grudgingly.

His brother scratched his ear. "So that's why you're doing it now, so late in the day?"

Benedict grunted. He didn't exactly want to encourage his brother's line of questioning.

"I've just been to see Cora," Jack said with a grin. "That actress I mentioned at supper the other night."

Benedict ignored this. Jack had always had an eye for the pretty girls. They all had, even Frank before he'd settled down. None of them were ever in the picture for long. "What play are they putting on presently?" he asked, glancing back at the tent. He hoped to God it wasn't Shakespeare.

"Damned if I know." Jack shrugged. "I've never actually sat through a show."

They started back toward the boxing tent together.

"You got any fights lined up?" Jack asked conversationally. "Real fights, I mean."

Benedict shot him a glance. "No."

"I guess you and Nat Jones didn't exactly part on speaking terms," Jack continued. "He contacted you at all since you got out?"

"No."

"Oh. Well." Jack finally seemed to pick up on his brother's pointed silence. He cleared his throat. "Me and Frank boxed a few times for him this past year," he said casually. "Early on in the evening, of course, not as headliners." Benedict grunted. "He always rated you highly though."

"Not enough to give me a shot at a title," Ben pointed out bitterly.

"Frank always figured he was working up to it."

"Frank was ever an optimist," Benedict said dryly.

179

"I ain't so sure he is anymore," Jack commented frankly. "He takes a drop too much of an evening now. Turns in early with a bottle most nights."

Benedict shot his brother an incredulous look. "Frank? He's no drinker."

"Maybe he wasn't," Jack corrected him. "But that was before. Before Maggie left him, I mean."

Benedict turned this over, remembering Frank's untidy appearance that morning. "He seems to be holding things together," he said with a frown.

Jack looked unconvinced. "I thought so, too, at first. He—er— went out a bit. Squired a few women about for a while, but I think it was just bravado."

Benedict's eyebrows snapped together. "He's still a married man," he heard himself point out like some kind of puritan.

Jack snorted. "So is Pa, but it's never stopped him picking up a new woman every year or so."

"Frank's not like Pa, and don't you ever think it."

"Damn it, I know that, Ben. None of us are!"

They continued in silence a moment before Jack broke it with a cheerful, "You'll never guess who *has* got leg-shackled this past year. Will Nye, to some schoolteacher, and properly gone over the edge about her, he has too. Froths at the mouth if anyone so much as looks at her too long. He nearly planted me a facer for passing the time of day with her last spring. It was touch and go for a minute, and you know what a nasty left hook he has."

"Nye, married?" Benedict asked with a flicker of interest. "I thought he'd buried himself in the wilds of Devon somewhere."

"Cornwall," Jack corrected him. "He took over his father's inn. They host an evening of bouts there once a month. Mayhap you'll get a spot at some point."

"Doubtful." He cast a look at Jack. "I've seen a bit of Clem since I got out," he admitted.

"Clem Dabney?"

"Aye."

"What's he up to?" Jack asked. "I've not seen him since last November."

"When last I saw him, he was on the brink of buying a theater. Tried to get me to go in with him as a matter of fact."

"Clem's bought a theater? What the devil for?" Jack asked, sounding astonished.

"He doesn't want to end up in the workhouse," Benedict answered dryly. "You know as well as I do, how most of our profession end up, Jack. You've got to play the long game."

His brother gave him a hard look. "You've not blown it all, then? Your winnings? Only Frank and Ma thought you must have, and that's why you're back here."

"With my tail between my legs?" Benedict interrupted him sarcastically. "Well, then they're dead wrong. That's not why I'm back."

Jack fell silent a moment. "You say Nat wouldn't give you a title shot, but he got you a lot of top-paying gigs, Ben. You must have been getting top dollar for some of those fights. That one against Meaks, and that Frenchie, Pfeifer."

"He did," Benedict agreed. "And yes, I got good money. Enough to retire on."

181

His brother gave him a quick look. "Nat never got those kinds of fights for Frank," Jack said, raising his chin pugnaciously. "He never got the chance to earn those kinds of purses. Yet you don't see him getting into brawls about it or burning his bridges with Nat."

Benedict came to a standstill. His brother halted a couple of steps away. "No, Frank didn't," Benedict agreed harshly. "And you know why, don't you, Jack?"

Jack flushed and looked away. "He ain't good enough," he admitted tightly. "Neither am I. Not for top of the roster."

"But *I* was good enough, Jack. I was damned good, and deep down, you and Frank know it and so does Nat. But I wasn't given my shot because my face doesn't fit."

His brother gazed at him. "Is that really what you think, Ben?" he asked, shaking his head.

"What else?" Benedict snarled.

"It's not your face, Ben, but your stinking attitude that's the problem. So, Nat expected you to show off for a few of his rich backers. Would it have killed you to show willing? To turn up at a few dinner parties and smile?" Benedict glared at his brother, but Jack didn't even pause to draw breath. "As for Frank, he may not be as talented with his fists as you, but by God! He has other strengths you'll never possess! Loyalty for one thing! Unwavering loyalty to his family!"

"Maybe," Benedict conceded through gritted teeth. "But it cost him his wife, Jack. Not a mistake I'll be making any time soon, I assure you!"

The two brothers stood facing each other with rigid expressions and clenched fists as the crowds drifted past them. Finally, Benedict relaxed his stance. After all, what was the point in falling out with Jack? "Come on," he said grimly. "Frank will be expecting us for the afternoon bouts."

Jack followed suit and they made their way wordlessly back to the booth.

12

The last of the stragglers left the tent, and Niamh let out a great sigh of relief, hopping down from her plinth. "Well, thank gawd for that, I'm stiff as a post."

"I'm famished," complained one of the twins from behind her sister. As "the living goddess" one of them had to stand obscured behind the other, only showing as an extra pair of slim brown arms adorned in golden bangles. Her sister turned around and started unfastening the obscuring black curtain to free her.

Ada Wurtzel's brother hurried across the tent to help her up from the couch she was draped across with only her long hair for a covering. At least, Lizzie had thought it was only her long light brown hair that preserved her modesty, but as she caught a glimpse of Ada straightening up, she did seem to be wearing some flesh-colored fabric over more crucial parts of her anatomy.

Lizzie hurriedly looked away from the abundance of naked pink skin as Jakob Wurtzel covered his sister in a frothy wrapper. Ada yawned. "I almost went off into a nap," she declared, sweeping her hair over her shoulder.

"You were not cold, my Ada?" Jakob asked anxiously.

"Ach no," she replied heartily, and Lizzie wondered at it. She could feel a definite nip in the air herself for it was early March and the weather frigid. As though guessing the reason for Lizzie's expression, Niamh nudged her.

"You haven't got Salome's padding," she said slyly with a wink. Lizzie cleared her throat and went to store her parasol and bonnet in the trunk, retrieving her own hat in exchange.

"Not a bad day's work," Connie said, looking her over critically. "You can come back tomorrow after all."

"Such grudging praise!" fired up Niamh. "Lizzie was wonderful! Didn't you see the way she challenged that fellow with the red nose who tried to pull Zaya off her stand? Escorted him right out the tent she did and gave him a fine scolding to boot!"

"Yes, that is so," the first twin said, clambering down from their display. She turned back to help her sister down before joining them. "Miss Lizzie was magnificent!"

"And I nearly burst out laughing," Niamh put in, "when you prodded that corpulent gent in the side and then said, 'Excuse me, sir, I thought you were a chesterfield. Could you please move along.'"

"Please, what is a chesterfield?" asked the second twin.

"It's a kind of sofa," Niamh told her. "Like Salome's couch over there." The twins went off into peals of mirth.

"He did look like a couch!" exclaimed one in delight.

"And his eyes were two deep-set buttons!" chimed in her sister.

Mr. Wurtzel turned from the screens he had folded around his sister for her to dress. "You are to be commended, Mrs. Toomes," he said curtly. "I will confess, I was much impressed with your manner and work ethic."

"Thank you, Mr. Wurtzel," she answered, feeling pleased in spite of herself to receive such universal praise. He gave a quaint little bow and returned to fussing over his sister's gloves and hat.

Setting her hat on her head, Lizzie bade them all farewell and made her way toward the boxing tent. Just for an instant, she

185

thought she caught sight of Ma Toomes on the edge of the crowd, but when she looked again, the wizened old woman was nowhere to be seen. She would have to go and see Ma soon, Lizzie thought uneasily. To return that headscarf for one thing, then, too, she needed to ask if she could keep a hold of the black cloak.

Lizzie noted the attractions as she walked past them. The next tent along from Wondrous Females was a tent which boasted the world's finest waxwork show, Bluebeard's Chamber. The painted advertisement hanging on the side of the tent looked so hideous with its array of grisly female bodies that Lizzie gave a violent start when she heard a blood-curdling scream from within. As she clasped a hand to her thudding breast, a gentleman came hurrying outside, carrying a swooning young woman in his arms.

"She needs air!" he cried, depositing his fair burden onto the grass. "Make way, make way! The horrors within are not fit for the eyes of any gently bred female!" As he assiduously fanned the stricken woman with his hat, more and more people came hurrying over with their pennies to queue for the attraction.

"Ohhhh," moaned the woman. "Do not leave me, Harold! I declare, I shall not sleep a wink tonight!"

"I 'ope it scares me to 'igh 'eaven!" one young woman said, turning excitedly to her companion, who stuck his thumbs into his braces.

"Never fear, Polly old girl. If you gets too afeard, you can cling on to me arm!" he offered obligingly.

"It's Pauline to you, Gerald 'Awkins, don't you get so familiar," she reproached him, though Lizzie noticed she seized hold of him and clung on for dear life as they approached the entrance.

Lizzie passed on by the Farini Family Acrobats. A mournful-looking clown in a multicolored suit stood next to the entrance holding a hat for the entrance fee. When he saw Lizzie, he gave her a terrifying grimace which she could only hope was his approximation of a smile.

Lizzie carried on her way, narrowly avoiding a barrow painted a bright yellow and piled high with little white saucers containing an array of pickled salmon, whelks, cockles, and mussels swimming in a greenish liquid. The smell quite turned her stomach, and Lizzie hastily swerved aside to escape the stench. How anyone could merrily tuck into such things she could not fathom.

The crowd seemed to be getting thicker here, so Lizzie put her head down and marched, not even noting the next few tents and whatever spectacles they might contain. Then suddenly, the crowd thinned again, leaving her ample room to maneuver between the strolling visitors.

Lizzie had just sighed with relief at this reprieve when she spied a tall bony man dart in front of her bellowing with rage and raising a whip high above his head to bring down on a dark gray shaggy creature he had cornered against a stand selling spiced nuts.

"Stop that at once!" Lizzie cried out in swift reaction, for she could never stand by and see one of God's creatures abused. The man didn't even glance at her as he brought his whip hand smartly down, but the animal was too fast for him. It wheeled about, snapping its huge jaws and catching the whip squarely between its sharp teeth. The rapid movement of its large body overset the cart, and the stallholder howled with rage as a pile of nuts went cascading over the side of his stand.

"Look out!" someone cried as the creature violently shook its head and flung the bony man from side to side like a rag doll.

187

"Let go of that whip!" Lizzie shouted. "He'll have you over in a minute!" She knew a moment's fear that if the animal got him on the floor, he might tear out the man's throat, so viciously did the creature regard its attacker.

With a yell of anger, the tall, thin man relinquished his grasp on the handle and backed away, cradling his wrist in his other hand, his features contorted with rage.

"Halt!" Lizzie cried imperiously at the animal; she hardly knew what it was, so outlandish was its appearance. It had crouched down as if to spring at its enemy, but by some miracle, her words seem to stay the beast. Its large ferocious head swung in Lizzie's direction, and its savage gaze fixed on her intently.

"Is this your dog, madam?" the stallholder huffed, clearly incensed. "I'll have an action against you for reckless endangerment! Look at me nuts!" he cried indignantly. "All over the floor in a heap! How am I 'sposed to sell 'em now?"

Lizzie opened her mouth to deny any claim of ownership, but at that instant the stallholder caught sight of some officials passing in a crowd. "Hie!" he called, summoning him. "Officers! Over 'ere, good sirs! Help!"

Lizzie kept her eyes trained on the unfortunate creature a moment before turning back to the tall, thin man. He was wearing a faded red coat and dirty buckskins, and she wondered now if he was one of the entertainers. Glancing over in the direction he had appeared from, she saw a small tent with a faded banner proclaiming Overton's Menagerie. "Have you taken hurt?" she asked, for though she did not like the look of him, it was no more than her Christian duty to enquire.

He scowled back at her. "Mind your own business, woman!" he seethed through a mouth of crooked and yellowing teeth. He glanced furtively first at the stallholder and then toward the

188

approaching officials. Lizzie saw his eyes dart from side to side and perceived he was looking to make good his escape.

"Is this your beast?" she asked him.

A look of fury sprung to face. "You—" he choked out, before seeming to get control of himself with some effort. "So that's your game, is it?" He spat and gestured about him. "These folk will testify the animal responds only to your command, and yet you try to hold me responsible for it!" he blustered. "You will not succeed!"

"Don't look like no dog what I ever saw," someone in the crowd murmured, and Lizzie was forced to agree. Turning back toward the animal, she saw to her surprise that it was now slinking toward her.

Lizzie stiffened, but no sooner had the beast reached her side than it dropped to its haunches, its tongue lolling out harmlessly to one side. She eyed it doubtfully. Was it really a dog? In truth, it looked more wolf than dog with its long muzzle and light eyes, but everyone knew there had not been wolves in England for hundreds of years.

"See!" the tall man howled triumphantly. "See how the vicious beast returns to its rightful owner?"

"What seems to be the trouble?" asked a black-suited man with large mutton-chop sideburns. He was flanked on both sides by other men dressed neatly in sensible tweeds. One held a large leather journal and was scribbling in it industriously with a pencil. "Write this up, Jones," the first said irritably, pulling out a gold pocket watch. "Well, be quick about it, man," he said with a contemptuous twist of his lips. "I haven't got all day to stand dallying with the likes of you. I've got miles to patrol, crammed full to the brim with incidents that need writing up! What's your name? And what seems to be the trouble?"

189

"It's Wilkins, sir, of Wilkins Finest Quality Nuts. And this lady's dog's been and upset me wares, that's what's up!" the stallholder protested hotly. "Just look at the mess it's made of me spiced nuts!"

The man turned censoriously toward Lizzie. He eyed her dubiously, and Lizzie felt her face flush at the picture she must present. She had jammed her bonnet over her head with scant thought of how tidy she looked after a day patrolling Connie Brown's tent. "Well, madam," he demanded. "What reparation do you mean to make for your animal's mishap?"

Lizzie gazed back at the official and then glanced toward the craven menagerie owner. His eyes flashed with malignant triumph, and Lizzie turned back to the official. "My name is Mrs. Elizabeth Toomes," she said concisely. "Enter that if you will to your record. And it was this man," she said coldly, "who is responsible for the entire misfortune. He approached the animal with his whip upraised and moved to attack him without provocation." She turned back to the crowd. "Will no one here bear me witness?"

"He did have a whip wiv 'im," someone piped up. "That's it on the ground, lying there."

The crowd turned as one to look at the discarded whip.

"Is this your whip, sir?" the official asked direly.

The man in the red-tailed coat let out a yell of fury. "That animal was clearly out of control!" he roared.

"He upset the cart only after *you* cornered him!" Lizzie countered sharply.

"That's true enough," the stallholder said grudgingly. "I saw 'im come chargin' across wiv his whip. Thought he was coming for me for a minute, I did." He tugged at his neckerchief and

190

eyed Mr. Overton reproachfully. "He looked like a ravin' loony!"

The man scribbling the details down in his book looked toward the irate gentleman. "What is your name?" he asked blandly. "I need it for the official record."

The man vibrated with anger, but when he spoke, he did so in a barely audible mumble. "It's Stanley Overton," he said grudgingly.

"Overton?" the official repeated distinctly. "Are you not the owner of that menagerie tent over yonder?"

Stanley Overton ground his teeth. "I am," he admitted. "But I have never seen that *dog* before, so don't you try and pin the blame on me!"

The first official stroked his sideburns thoughtfully before turning back to Lizzie. "No, we have established the animal belongs to this lady, have we not?"

Lizzie looked down and met the creature's eyes and was shaken by the shining confidence the dumb animal seemed to have in her. It was almost as though, she thought, he had *chosen* her. Lizzie squared her shoulders and gave a short nod. She had never been one to shirk her responsibilities, and besides, a dog was supposed to be the most faithful of companions, was it not? She who was friendless could hardly go wrong in acquiring one now.

"Be that as it may, madam," the official conceded. "You should have had the dog under control. You have no leash? No means of restraining it?"

Looking down, Lizzie saw the animal was wearing a battered leather collar. She seized hold of it in a firm grip. The beast did not even flinch, just continued to gaze steadily up at her. She

191

exhaled her breath. "I have him securely now," she assured them, and remembering she still had the golden guinea she had made fortune-telling, she plunged her other hand into her pocket and lifted her chin. "I will, of course, make reparation to Mr. Wilkins. However, I have not yet had the opportunity to obtain any small change. Perhaps one of you gentlemen could help me?" She stepped forward, showing the gold coin in her palm discreetly to the black-suited official.

He started. "You are ill advised as a female to go wandering around a place like this unaccompanied with such an amount on you, madam," he said disapprovingly.

Lizzie frowned at him meaningfully. Surely, he would realize that he was the one being indiscreet! She could practically feel Mr. Wilkins's gaze on the back of her head as he craned to see what money she had in her hand. The official seemed to take her meaning, for at once he cleared his throat and reached into the inner pocket of his coat.

"As to that, sir," Lizzie said, recovering her composure, "I am *not* unaccompanied. I do not think many would approach me with threat of violence when I am in possession of so very large a dog."

"There may be something in what you say," he acknowledged, inspecting the contents of his coin purse. "Here, madam," he said after picking out several coins. "Will you check it is correct?"

Lizzie did so, and then handed her golden coin over to him with thanks.

"For the official record," his companion piped up, pausing in the scribbling of his pen. "What is the name of your animal?"

Lizzie paused for only a second. "Sebastian," she said, suddenly inspired.

The man made haste to note this down in his book as Lizzie turned to Mr. Wilkins. She checked his sign proclaiming the price of his spiced nuts per portion. "How many portions of nuts do you suppose has ended up scattered on the floor, my man?" she enquired briskly of the stallholder. With the eyes of the officials on him, Mr. Wilkins clearly felt hampered in his reply. He scratched the back of his neck and mumbled a sum that the official immediately took issue with.

"She will give you a florin and not a penny more, my good man! We both know as soon as we are out of sight you will be on your hands and knees scrabbling to reclaim every kernel!"

Lizzie handed over the agreed compensation, and Mr. Wilkins thanked her rather huffily before retreating behind his barrow.

"There, now that's the end of the matter," said the man in the black suit, glancing meaningfully at Mr. Overton, who still stood hovering. His companion snapped his book shut, and they bowed to Lizzie. "Good day to you, ma'am."

Lizzie inclined her head and watched them walk some distance away before turning to the tall man stood irresolute.

"You are still here, Mr. Overton?" she asked.

"I am, madam!" he snapped. "We both know why."

"Do we? Perhaps you did not hear the official's pronouncement. He said you were not due any damages for your part in this mishap."

His face turned a mottled purple. "We both know, madam, that is not true!"

"Indeed?" Lizzie asked politely. "Perhaps I should summon him back, then, for all three are still within earshot if I was to raise my voice." Mr. Overton's lips trembled with suppressed fury. Lizzie stood silent a moment, letting the difficulty of his situation sink in. "How much do you want for the beast?" she asked softly.

Mr. Overton's back stiffened. "He is no common dog, but a rare wolf-dog—" he began.

"To my mind," she interrupted him, "he is naught but a common mongrel that somewhat resembles a German shepherd dog."

"A mongrel?" squawked Mr. Overton, clearly outraged.

"Recollect that according to official record, he is already mine," she pointed out and began to saunter away. Sebastian obediently trotted by her side, and she retained her grip on his collar with ease.

"I want two guineas and no less will I accept!" Mr. Overton snapped angrily as he capered beside her with his long, skinny legs.

"I do not have anything like as much," Lizzie retorted smartly. "I had a sovereign only and from that Mr. Wilkins's damages have been subtracted, which by rights *you* should have paid."

Overton's mouth snapped shut as he considered this. "Very well, I want what remains of your sovereign," he said grandly. "And will accept that as my payment for the animal."

Lizzie considered this. *Easy come, easy go.* "Agreed," she concurred and saw that even that did not please him. The corners of his thin lips drooped downward, as he clearly now thought he could have extorted more. "But I shall require written proof of our transaction and also witnesses. You do write, I take it?"

He glared at her. "I do, madam," he sneered.

She inclined her head. "If you will follow me this way, then I shall pay you in front of—er—one of my *family*." She almost stammered over the word, so strange was it to consider the Toomeses in such a light.

Mr. Overton muttered under his breath but moderated his long stride to match her own. They made their way in silence toward the Toomes boxing booth, and she heard his swiftly indrawn breath. "I thought you said your name was Coombe," he complained as they approached the boxing tent.

"Did you?" Lizzie uttered, glancing his way. She noticed he did not look thrilled at the prospect of tangling with the Toomes clan and could not say she blamed him.

Daphne was stood outside the entrance to the tent with a sour expression on her face. "You're back, are you?" she asked without any marked enthusiasm. Her gaze flickered over Overton and the large dog impassively. Even as Lizzie opened her mouth in reply, Jack ducked under the canvas and appeared in front of them. He did a double take at Lizzie with her hand on the hulking dog beside her.

"Ah, Jack," Lizzie hailed him with more familiarity than she had displayed heretofore. "I need you to bear witness to a business transaction between myself and this gentleman." Jack looked immediately wary, although Daphne straightened up with interest. "I am purchasing this animal from Mr. Overton," she asserted. "Do you have paper and pen?" she asked, turning back to the gentleman.

195

Overton fumbled in his breast pocket and withdrew a small notebook of cheap-looking yellowed pages and the stub of a pencil.

"Excellent," Lizzie said bracingly. "Now write: I, Stanley Overton, do willingly sell this large brown dog known as Sebastian to Mrs. Elizabeth Toomes for the sum of eighteen shillings—"

"Eighteen shillings?" Jack burst out incredulously.

"—on this day, Wednesday the twenty-sixth of March in the year of our Lord 1845," Lizzie finished smoothly.

Stanley Overton's pencil moved over the paper as he muttered the words under his breath.

"What sort of dog is that?" Daphne asked critically. "It looks half wild to me."

"Now you sign, Mr. Overton," Lizzie prompted, ignoring the interruption. "And Jack here shall sign as witness."

Overton ripped out the page and added his scrawl on the back. Before he would pass the pad to Jack, he held out his bony fingers for the money. Lizzie dropped the coins into his palm, and he passed it over to Jack, who shook his head but added his initials all the same.

"If you would print your name underneath," Lizzie told him, looking at the *J.T.* he had contributed.

Jack gave her an ironic look. "You'll have to do any writing," he said with a shrug. "If it's more than my initials you want."

"I'll do it," Daphne offered. She took the page and painstakingly printed *Jack Toomes* under his initials, then added her own details before passing the paper to Lizzie, who, glancing down, saw she had signed herself Daphne Smith in a neat hand. Lizzie returned the notebook to its owner, and abruptly, Stanley Overton turned on his heel and made off without a single further word.

Jack eyed her doubtfully as Lizzie folded the paper of ownership. "There's plenty of husbands who'd beat you black and blue for wasting eighteen shillings on a dog like that."

Lizzie opened her mouth on a sharp retort, but a great cheer went up from inside the tent, forestalling her. Jack turned and looked back over his shoulder.

"He could have spun it out for a couple more rounds," he grumbled. "That bastard never plays the game like he's supposed to."

"Will Benedict be finished soon, or should I head back to our wagon, do you think?"

"He shouldn't be too long, should he, Jack?" Daphne said quickly. She turned back to Lizzie. "I don't suppose you'd do me a favor, would you, and take a turn here collecting the entrance fees?" It was by far the friendliest that Daphne had addressed her, but even so, Lizzie was wary.

"I'm afraid I have just finished my day's employ," she pointed out firmly, moving to step around the woman.

"Hold up," said Jack, putting his hand out to stay her. "Are you saying you won't help us out here when the need arises?" His voice rose with indignation.

Sebastian set up a threatening growl that made them all step back in alarm. "Perhaps if you remove your hand from my arm, Jack?" Lizzie recommended. Jack pulled it back sharply, and the horrible noise emitting from Sebastian's throat subsided. They all breathed a collective sigh of relief.

Lizzie looked squarely at Daphne. "How long do you need me to cover your duties?" she asked. "If Benedict will soon be finished, then he will not be pleased to find I have pledged myself to sit here all evening."

Daphne opened her mouth, but before she could speak, Jack forestalled her. "That's true enough," he grumbled. "You don't want to get on the wrong side of him, Daph."

Daphne huffed out a sigh. "Long enough for me to get a bite to eat?" she offered.

Lizzie nodded. "Very well."

"Obliged, I'm sure," Daphne sniffed and hurried off.

Lizzie sought out the little three-legged stool just inside the entrance and picked up the jar of ha'pennies Daphne had stowed there. As Lizzie lowered herself onto the wooden stool, Sebastian seated himself beside her.

Jack looked them over with raised brows. "Well, no one will be arguing the entrance fee with him sat beside you, at any rate," he commented wryly before disappearing back into the tent.

It was twenty minutes later that Benedict appeared beside her, still buttoning his shirt.

"What are you doing sat there?" he asked with surprise.

Sebastian set up a low rumble, but Lizzie's hand shot out and shook his collar. "No," she said firmly. "I won't be here long," she said, addressing her husband. "I've just taken over for Daphne while she fetches herself some refreshment."

He grunted. "Who's this?"

"Our new guard dog," Lizzie said boldly. "I bought him off a most objectionable man." Wordlessly she passed him the bill of sale. Benedict glanced it over before passing it back.

"Overton?" he asked with a frown. "Doesn't he run some sort of performing animal act? Teeth like a row of neglected tombstones?"

"He does," she agreed, wincing at the description of Stanley Overton's teeth. "And vastly sorry I feel for any animal under his yoke. He was abusing this one most cruelly." They both regarded Sebastian's long nose and shaggy fur coat in silence. "He claimed he was a wolf-dog," Lizzie admitted after a moment. "Is such a thing even possible?"

Benedict shrugged. "Damned if I know. He looks like some kind of sled dog to me. Is he friendly?"

"Not especially, but he does seem to listen to me. He takes grave objection to anyone accosting me, I know that much."

"Does he, by God?" Benedict's expression lightened. "Well, it wouldn't hurt for you to have a protector to escort you about."

"Do you suppose Connie would allow me to have him accompany me tomorrow?" she asked a little doubtfully.

"I don't see why not," Benedict answered.

She gave him a sidelong look. "And the mere sight of him doesn't inspire you to violence?"

His eyebrows rose. "Why do you ask that?"

"I was informed that some husbands would feel justified in beating their wives for squandering eighteen shillings on a dog."

"I've never beaten a woman in my life, and I'm not about to start now," he answered swiftly. "You can put any concerns of that nature out of your head."

Lizzie nodded, but any reply she might have made was swiftly forgotten when Daphne reappeared and interrupted them.

Daphne eyed Benedict warily as she brushed her hands on her skirts. "Thanks for that," she muttered to Lizzie.

"You're welcome." She stood and turned back to the looming animal. "Come, Sebastian."

13

They did not tarry overlong in the fairground. Benedict bought three meat puddings for their supper, which included one for the dog. Sebastian gulped his down in two swallows and then eyed Lizzie's with a covetous gaze. Benedict was not surprised to see her give the animal at least half of her own. The beast trotted after her even more assiduously after that.

He was wholly reconciled to the animal's presence when he saw his dark shadow accompany Lizzie into the opposite field when she went to relieve herself before bed. She would come to no harm when accompanied by such a beast.

When Benedict returned from fetching water, he found Lizzie trying to coax the animal into the wagon to no avail.

"What am I going to do?" she asked in exasperation. "He simply won't come inside."

Benedict considered Sebastian impassively. "He may settle under the wagon for the night. He's likely wary of small spaces." She did not look appeased by this, until he added, "You can give him one of our blankets to sleep on." This sent her back into the wagon to fetch one, and she set about arranging it into a sort of nest for the dog as Benedict set the water on to boil.

"Here, boy!" she said, patting the blanket. "Nice and warm. Come and see." Sebastian ignored her, setting his great head onto his front paws next to the fire Benedict had lit.

"He'll settle in once the fire's banked," he consoled her.

Sure enough, that was the case. By the time Benedict had kicked over the fire and visited the opposite field before turning in, Sebastian was ensconced underneath the wagon.

"Do you think he'll be warm enough?" Lizzie asked anxiously as he joined her inside.

"I think so." He glanced up at her from his ablutions. "Overton likely kept him in a cage, which would not have been insulated against the cold."

"Hateful man!" Lizzie seethed as she fastened a particularly unbecoming cap on top of her head. "I cannot fathom why anyone would give him their patronage. I don't believe he would treat the rest of his menagerie any better."

Privately, Benedict agreed with her, however he did not wish to discuss anything so unpleasant at this point in time. While he did not intend on bothering her with amorous attentions the very night after her deflowering, neither did he wish to get into some habit of discussing all and sundry when they took to his bed. He rubbed his wet hair vigorously with a towel.

"Why are there two lines drawn in the square?" Lizzie asked suddenly as she settled herself back against the pillow. "I noticed it yesterday and forgot to ask you."

"What? In the ring, you mean?" Benedict asked, sitting on the edge of the bed and peeling off his braces.

"Ring? No, I mean the area in which you fight," Lizzie clarified.

"The ring," he corrected her as he shrugged out of his shirt.

"How can it be a ring?" Lizzie puzzled. "The ropes mark out a clear square."

He was silent as he unbuttoned his breeches and stripped down to his long underwear. "I guess because in the early days, they used to gather round the fighters in a ring," he speculated, casting his clothes aside. "But folks were always getting in the way, so they started using ropes to keep them at a distance." He pulled back the covers and climbed in beside her.

"And the lines?" Lizzie persisted. "In the center of the square, I mean, the ring."

"You have to put your toe to the line at the start of each round," Ben said. "That's what qualifies you to continue the fight. If you can't come up to the scratch, then you forfeit the fight."

"Is that where the saying comes from?" Lizzie asked in startled tones. "Come up to scratch?"

"Aye," he rumbled, finding her curiosity amusing, despite himself.

"It's from boxing terminology? Well, I never knew that."

"Why would you?" he asked with a shrug, and Lizzie did not answer, just folded her hands across her stomach. He had not meant to snub her, he thought belatedly as she fell silent. "Lizzie?"

She turned her head. "Yes?"

He had the absurd notion to ask her what she had thought of his boxing. As if it even mattered! Instead, he eyed the two unbecoming braids on either side of her head. "Why do you plait it like that?" he asked shortly.

"What?" She looked startled. "My hair? I've always worn it like this to bed," she said simply. "It's the way my aunt taught me."

"You've a man in your bed now, Lizzie," he pointed out.

She reddened. "Well," she said lamely. "My aunt never gave me that talk. If I'm supposed to be doing things differently, you'll have to teach me."

He eyed her steadily a moment and was impressed when she didn't look away. "I don't like the cap or the braids," he said finally.

Lizzie stared. "Oh." Reluctantly she sat back up and dragged the fussy nightcap off her head. Then she unfastened the end of her braids and ran her fingers through them until her hair hung about her shoulders and down to her waist in a straight fall of pale gold.

"You've a fine head of hair," he said, and even he could hear the note of warmth in his voice.

"People always tell me I could sell it," she agreed. "Once a lady approached my aunt in a book shop. She said there was enough for two wigs, but Aunt Hester said no, for it was my only beauty."

He frowned at that. "You're not to cut it," he said abruptly. She looked at him consideringly, and when her cheeks filled with color, he asked, "What?"

"You kept your long underwear on tonight," she commented. "Last night you slept naked."

"Yes," he agreed shortly. "You've had a busy day of it. I don't mean to make any demands of you tonight, Lizzie."

Her lips formed a soundless *oh*. "I thought it might be because we'd given a blanket to Sebastian and you were scared you might be cold."

That startled a laugh out of him. "No. Come here." She shuffled toward him on the mattress, and he curled his body about hers.

"What do you think of the theater?" he asked, looping an arm around her waist. "Do you enjoy it?"

"My uncle took me to see *The Road to Ruin* for a birthday treat one year," Lizzie answered.

"Never heard of it," Benedict admitted promptly. Which wasn't really saying much as he was no theatergoer, but Lizzie wasn't to know that.

"It is a play written by Thomas Holcroft."

"Sounds rather high-minded," he commented doubtfully.

"Not really, for it was a comedy although it illustrated good Christian virtues." To Benedict's mind she was further illustrating his own point. "The only other thing I've been to see is the Christmas pantomime at Drury Lane last year, but it was a very rowdy affair, and my aunt Hester was much shocked and said it had a low moral tone."

Benedict suspected The Philmore Players probably had more in common with Drury Lane than Thomas Holcroft and promptly dismissed that idea. "What about dancing?" he asked instead.

"Country dancing, do you mean?" Lizzie asked. "I have not really had the opportunity in recent years."

He thought she sounded a little wistful. "We could go," he suggested. "Tomorrow night maybe?"

"Dancing?" Lizzie turned her head to look back at him with startled eyes. "Where?"

"Fiddlers Green. It's a ballroom tent with an orchestra and a cold supper provided."

"A ballroom in a tent?" Lizzie echoed.

"Should you like that?"

Lizzie bit her lip. "I can't waltz," she warned him. "Or do any fashionable dances like the polka."

"It's just for fun." He shrugged. "No one's there to judge you from the potted palms. Everyone's just there for a good time."

"I've nothing to wear besides my green taffeta."

"So, wear your green taffeta," he responded.

"And will you wear your black suit?"

"If you want me to," Ben answered lightly. He didn't really imagine paying guests got turned away due to any dress code at Fiddlers Green.

"Then yes, I would like to go."

He gave her a slow smile. "Good, now go to sleep." He reached across and turned out the lamp and then settled against her back. They usually slept the opposite way around, he thought wryly, but Lizzie would not hug his back until she was out cold, so they would need to switch positions later.

When next he woke, sure enough, she was nestled against his back, her arm wrapped about his waist. He smiled and reached for his pocket watch balanced atop the nearest trunk. He could just about make out the figures in the gray morning light. He'd have to get up, he thought with a grimace. It was too damn tempting to lie like this for another half hour, but he didn't want her to have to wash in cold water.

The dog—if that was what they were to call it—looked up when Benedict emerged and started gathering sticks for the campfire. Sebastian remained in his spot under the wagon but watched him assiduously. Once he had the fire crackling, Ben went to relieve himself and then to fetch water.

By the time he returned with fresh water for both them and the horse, the dog was sat beside the fire eyeing him warily. Benedict crouched beside him and set the water on to boil. When the door to the wagon cracked open, Sebastian wheeled about and darted to the step where Lizzie held her hand out to him.

"Morning," she yawned, though whether to the dog or himself he wasn't sure.

"Morning," he responded. "Water will soon be heated. I didn't fetch enough for tea though. We'll have to buy some in the arena."

Lizzie nodded and stroked the dog's head. "Have you been getting acquainted?" she asked.

"Oh, he's been sizing me up alright," Benedict replied. "Hopefully, I've shown him I'm a decent provider or he'll be trying to run me off."

Lizzie laughed. "If you buy him another meat pie for breakfast, I'm sure he'll transfer his affections readily enough."

Benedict eyed the animal thoughtfully. "I doubt it," he said without rancor. "He knows his master, and it's not me."

Lizzie looked gratified, though she tried to hide it, pulling her shawl tight about her. "I've never had a pet before," she said, eyeing Sebastian fondly as he lapped up water from the bowl Benedict had set down.

He wasn't really sure *pet* was the right word, more like guardian. Still, his mind felt easier that she now had a watchdog for those moments when he wasn't around.

Half an hour later the three of them were on their way to the main field. Benedict bought them tea and currant cake from a vendor and, after perusing what was on offer, two large sausages for the dog. Sebastian made short work of them, and Lizzie had finished her cake by the time they reached Wondrous Females.

"Don't forget," he reminded her. "We're going dancing tonight."

Lizzie nodded, lingering at the entrance to the tent. "Will we still meet for lunch?" she asked hesitantly.

"Of course. We won't go to the tea tent today though. There's something else I want to show you."

She looked up quickly. "What is it?"

"You'll have to wait and see." She returned his smile a little shyly and then slipped into the tent, promptly followed by Sebastian. From the exclamations he could hear within, the large dog had clearly caused quite a stir. Benedict made his way to the boxing tent with a grin on his face.

When he returned at one o'clock, Lizzie was not awaiting him outside. Pushing past the Gone to Luncheon sign inside, he found her setting her bonnet on her head while two young women clad in filmy red garments fussed over Sebastian.

"Come, large dog!" one of them cried. "Come to Zaya!" She held out a gold bangle for his inspection. Sebastian sniffed it with the air of one humoring another. The glance he threw Benedict was distinctly sheepish, as if he knew full well he looked a fool.

"Oh, I did not mean to keep you waiting!" Lizzie exclaimed, turning and hurrying to his side. "Come, Sebastian!"

The twins called their farewells to the dog as he followed close on Lizzie's heels. Benedict offered his arm, and she took it.

"He behaved himself, I take it?" he asked, glancing at the dog.

"Oh yes! He was a great hit with Zaya and Ema, and even Connie admitted he lends me some credence as a rule enforcer. Mr. Wurtzel was a little nervous around him, it is true, but I think Sebastian is more trusting of women than of men."

"Wurtzel?" Benedict frowned.

"You remember, I told you about him? He is Salome's brother."

By great effort, Benedict managed to dredge their conversation to his mind. "I thought you said he was not really her brother."

"I never said that!" Lizzie protested, looking around nervously. "That was just something Niamh remarked," she hissed. "And I do not think she had anything to substantiate her theory."

"What does he do, this Wurtzel?"

"Do?" Lizzie looked surprised. "Squires his sister about, I suppose. I do not know what manner of business he is in. The Wurtzels are quite standoffish from the rest of us and only really speak to Connie."

He grunted. That didn't sound too bad. He did not like the idea of some man hanging about Lizzie all day when he was not there.

They stopped at a convenient stand to pick up ham sandwiches, which Sebastian ate more than his fair share of, and then headed for a far field where there were fewer acts and more wares than the ones they generally frequented.

"I do not think I've visited this area before," Lizzie remarked, looking about as they came to a stop before a stall covered in ribbons and lace.

"Pick whatever you want to spruce up your gown," Benedict offered.

"You mean—" Lizzie's eyes grew wide as she gazed down at the trimmings in seeming confusion. She made no move to choose anything.

"If you don't like anything on display here, there's plenty of others about." He gestured.

The stallholder's ears pricked up at this. "I'm sure there must be something to take the lady's fancy!" she started up, hurrying to their side. "What about this lovely bit of lace here? Would set you off a treat, that would!"

"Well—I—er…" Lizzie shot a helpless look at him. "I don't know. I don't think frills and furbelows really suit me. I am not in the first flush of youth and—"

"Nonsense!" the other woman interjected. "Got to make the most of what you've got, ain't you? Why, you're naught but a girl!"

Lizzie gazed at her despairingly. "I'm five and twenty," she corrected her. "And have never been one for ornamentation."

"Don't knock it till you try it, love!" the other responded, looking at Lizzie's severe gown. "A touch of something ain't gonna do you up like a dog's dinner, is it? You let the gentleman treat you to something pretty! Would do you some good, put a bit of color in those cheeks!"

Lizzie allowed herself to agree that some of the silk ribbon work was very pretty. "Well, perhaps something like this for the bodice or neckline," she agreed, pointing tentatively toward some pink rosette arrangements. "My best gown is of a seafoam green taffeta."

"The very thing!" the woman cried approvingly. "And if I might suggest a matching one for your hair arrangement?" Lizzie seemed much struck by this suggestion, and the stallholder drew out a box drawer of silk flowers in the manner of a magician revealing a rabbit.

"Oh, they are very pretty! But surely these ones must be more expensive?" Lizzie hesitated.

"I'm sure my pockets can stretch to a few silk flowers," Benedict interrupted. "You can have whatever you like."

"There now! He couldn't say handsomer than that, could he?" the stallholder enthused. By the time Lizzie had managed to extricate herself from the lady's clutches, she had bought a quantity of lace and embroidered tulle as well as a needle, thread, and pins, for she had no needlework box, as hers had been left behind.

"I don't know if I will even have time to sew all of this onto the dress for this evening," Lizzie confessed as they walked away. "I only hope I have not wasted your money, Benedict." Her fingers squeezed his arm, and she clutched fitfully at the paper bags in her other hand as though for reassurance.

"If you don't manage it for this evening, you can always use it another time." He shrugged. "Really you need a couple of new gowns, but we don't have much room in the wagon."

"Oh no!" Lizzie protested. "I've scarcely worn that taffeta above a dozen times. There's plenty more wear to be had from it, and besides, I have my enamel brooch and my tortoiseshell hair comb that you redeemed for me from the pawn brokers."

"One day, my Lizzie," he found himself saying, "I will buy you a diamond brooch to rival the one that light-fingered reverend pilfered."

211

She stared at him speechlessly, but before she could speak, they were interrupted. A redhead was hailing them enthusiastically from nearby. "Lizzie!" She beckoned them to where she was stood lolling next to a jellied eel stall. "Over here!"

"It's Niamh," Lizzie explained in an undertone. At Benedict's blank look, she added, "The—er—tattooed contortionist from Wondrous Females."

"Oh? Why is she calling you over?"

"I think she wants to introduce me to her man," Lizzie said. "That must be his stall; she told me about it."

Benedict looked at her pointedly. "You tell her about me?"

"Of course!"

He dropped his voice. "You tell her I'm your man, Lizzie?"

"I told her you were my husband," she responded, primming up her mouth. "I am not entirely sure that Niamh and Colin are—well—married. At least, she does not wear a ring." She glanced down at her own, and Benedict noticed again what a cheap bit of brass it was. He needed to get her a better one. "Shall we go and say hello?" She was already tugging at his arm. Casting his eyes upward, Benedict allowed himself to be towed in her wake.

14

Lizzie was jittery all afternoon. Niamh kept teasing her that she and Colin were going to turn up at the Fiddlers Green to see her in all her finery.

"We won't really!" Niamh laughed at Lizzie's red face. "My old man wouldn't spend two shillings on an evening's entertainment, more's the pity," she sighed. "We been together too long for that. You make the most of it while you can, darlin'."

They were tidying away while Ada disappeared behind the screens to dress, Connie bustling behind carrying her stays and looking wearied. Small wonder, Lizzie thought, as Connie had been parading up and down the tent all day, entreating people to come in and view the wonders within.

"There she goes to cinch La Wurtzel into her corset," commented Niamh sotto voce.

"If only we could grow so nice and round," Zaya sighed disconsolately. "Then we, too, would have coins falling upon us like rain."

"Of a certainty, that is what men desire," Ema said, nodding her head. "Very fat concubines. Only see the way their eyes stand out on stalks when they behold Salome."

"She is not *fat* precisely," Lizzie objected. "Her waist is really quite trim. It is just her hips and thighs and…" She trailed off, wanting to avoid mentioning anything indelicate.

"Her mountainous bosom," Ema supplied helpfully. "When she is in her corset, it juts out like the prow of ship." She made gestures with her hands in front of her chest that made Lizzie hurriedly avert her eyes.

"Yes," her sister concurred. "They bring many food offerings to maintain her abundance. They do not want her to lose one ounce of plentiful flesh."

Lizzie's eyes wandered over the vast quantities of chocolate boxes and cream cakes in beribboned boxes left as daily tribute to Miss Wurtzel. Every day her brother was forced to gather them up and carry them back to their quarters.

"She really does look like a classical Venus," Lizzie murmured more to herself than anyone else. Whereas Zaya and Ema were very much like delicate nymphs.

"Where is brother Wurtzel?" Niamh asked humorously. "You noticed how neither one of them stick around to help us tidy away?" She pulled a face. "Must be nice," she added sourly, "to be the star turn."

"Or the star turn's brother," Ema pointed out.

"Or not!" Zaya put in spiritedly. "One time, I see him pinch her buttocks, like this," she said, making a pincer gesture and nipping Lizzie's backside.

"Zaya!" Lizzie protested, scooting out of the way. The twins laughed heartily.

"But he could just be checking she is not losing flesh," Ema pointed out once she had wiped the tears of laughter from her eyes. "If she were to lose her mighty thighs and buttocks, then they will lose many coins."

Her sister nodded in solemn agreement. Lizzie coughed, thinking she should steer the conversation away from the subject of mighty buttocks.

"Apparently, in her last act, she emerged from a chrysalis like a great big butterfly in the Turkish tent at Vauxhall Gardens," said Niamh. "Nude, of course. At that time, her protector was a royal duke, they say."

"Protector?" Lizzie repeated.

"She was warming his bed," Niamh explained.

Lizzie tried not to look as scandalized as she felt. "But surely her brother, Mr. Wurtzel, would have objected to such an arrangement?"

"Lord, he ain't preserving her morals, Lizzie. Even if he *is* her brother, which I don't believe for one minute, he lives off her immoral earnings! Course he does!"

They all fell silent as the tent flap drew back and Mr. Wurtzel stalked in and started gathering up his sister's bags and boxes of treats. He looked to be in something of a bad mood.

"Probably he been gambling," Ema whispered as Lizzie slammed the trunk shut and pulled her own bonnet over her head. "I know that look!"

Lizzie donned the black cloak and looked around for Sebastian. The dog was sat aloof in one corner. Lizzie called him and he came toward her, carefully skirting the twins' clinging embraces. Sebastian was no lapdog and seemed to endure acts of affection rather than enjoying them. For the most part, he was happy merely to be in Lizzie's vicinity and keep a watchful eye on her.

She touched a hand fleetingly to his head. "Come, Sebastian."

"Enjoy yourself tonight, Lizzie!" Niamh called after her.

"Make sure you stand up for all the dances!" cried Ema.

"Goodbye, Sebastian darling!" chimed in Zaya.

Lizzie gave them a wave and hurried out, thinking of how long it would take her to sew her new finery onto her green gown. Now she had Sebastian to accompany her, Benedict had agreed she could make her way back to the entertainers' camp field by herself, and he would meet her there when he was ready.

Lizzie did not bother with a fire, but instead shook out her best dress and sat on the step to the wagon pinning the lace and embellishments to the neckline and bodice. Sebastian settled beneath her dangling feet and did not stir until nearly an hour later when Benedict appeared with a bagful of meat bones for him.

He leaned down and kissed Lizzie briefly on the lips, startling her greatly.

"How's it going?" he asked, glancing at her dress.

"Fine," Lizzie answered, ducking her head to hide her reaction to his spontaneous affection. "Where did you get the bones?"

"The fella that runs the meat pie stall." He handed the largest of the bones to Sebastian, who promptly disappeared with it beneath the wagon. "I'd better sort the water for washing."

Lizzie nodded, and he set about building a small fire and fetching the pail for water. Lizzie's fingers flew. The fact she had so little time meant she did not have the opportunity to debate if the trimmings were too elaborate for her tastes. Instead, she simply kept her head down and sewed like a fiend until all the little paper bags were empty. Even Mrs. Napp and Lucinda would be impressed, she thought, seeing how her needle flew.

At some point, Benedict wordlessly placed a cup of black tea at her side. When she sipped it, she was surprised. "Lemon!" she said aloud.

"That's how you preferred it, you said."

"I do," she agreed, cradling her cup. "This is lovely."

"This must be taking you back to your days with the Napps," he commented, nodding toward her dress.

Lizzie grimaced. "It's a bit different, prettifying a dress for your own pleasure and trying to sew thirty waistcoats from scratch by the end of a week."

Benedict grunted, peering under the lid of the water pot. "This is getting hot. You nearly finished?"

Lizzie shook out her dress. "What do you think?" she asked, holding it aloft. Looking at the fancy ribbon work and lace at the bodice and neck, she felt a sudden misgiving. "Is it too much?"

"Not a bit," Benedict replied promptly. "Here, let's carry this pail of water inside for you to wash and dress."

She jumped down off the step, and he lifted the water off the fire and poured it into the bucket to carry it inside.

"I'll try not to be long. I can dress my hair out here while you wash," she said, thinking of the cramped confines.

"Don't worry," he replied, placing the bucket inside the door. "We've plenty of time. I'll pour you another cup of tea to drink while you get ready."

He was as good as his word, and Lizzie felt rather spoiled as she stepped into her best stiffened petticoat and then her taffeta gown. She had no looking glass to take in the full effect; still,

217

she thought it must be the fanciest it had ever looked. She glanced down at the adorned bodice and scarcely recognized it as her rather plain Sunday best.

Pinning her enamel brooch to the frothy lace at her neckline, she suddenly wished she had a pair of white gloves to complete the look. Her black ankle boots would be hidden underneath her skirts, so they would not signify. Perhaps if she dressed her hair prettily with the silk flowers the stallholder had insisted she purchased, she could get away with her lack of accessories?

How should she dress her hair? she wondered. Lizzie had always rolled her hair very sensibly at her nape. She had never worried about trying to achieve any kind of elaborate hairstyle. Betsy used a hot poker to achieve her own sausage curls, but Lizzie had always thought them rather frivolous and certainly too girlish a look for a plain-faced woman such as herself.

She had always felt the two years separating herself and Betsy very keenly. When she had joined her aunt and uncle's household, she had been a shy child of four, recently orphaned. Their own daughter had been a chubby toddler of two who was still addressed at that point as "Baby." Lizzie had felt like an assistant to the nursemaid for several years, and then after that, her aunt's companion. There had been precious little time for parties or amusements in her life.

Picking up her hairbrush, she ran it through the length of her blond locks and swept her hair back into a softer chignon effect. Driving in her hairpins, she skewered the silk flowers around the edges of the arrangement and hoped for the best. For the first time in her life, she wished she owned a small pair of drop earrings, such as the ones her aunt wore on Sundays. Aunt Hester's were garnets, but Lizzie would rather have pearl drop earrings, then she caught her breath at the direction her thoughts were rattling in. What was she thinking of?

218

Setting down her hairbrush, Lizzie told herself sternly she was growing sadly vain and covetous. She stood up with sudden decision, and, retrieving her empty teacup, made her way out of the little door and onto the step. "What do you think?" she asked self-consciously and then turned her head so he could see the effect of her hair. "Does my hair look tidy at the back? I had no way of telling."

"It does," he told her, clearing his throat. He approached and reached up for her, lifting her down. He cupped her cheek and gazed at her steadily. "I prefer it down about your shoulders," he confessed huskily. "But it looks good this way too."

"Down?" Lizzie echoed. "I'm long past my girlhood when I could wear it so."

"There is one place you can still wear it loose," he pointed out, running his thumb along her jaw.

Lizzie fidgeted. He must mean in bed when he did not like her to wear it braided. "Isn't it about time you washed and dressed?"

Benedict released her with a laugh and clambered inside the wagon. "I won't be long," he flung over his shoulder. "Don't get distracting any passersby with your finery."

Lizzie sat on the upturned packing case and squeezed a last rather stewed half cup from the pot. She was just sipping it when Sebastian came out from under the wagon to rest his head on her knee.

"Hello, boy," she murmured in surprise and carefully stroked his ears. His pale gaze flickered to her face and away again, but he remained still, allowing her caress. Knowing he was not much of a one for physical affection, Lizzie felt profoundly touched by his gesture. He remained standing on all fours as

219

though ready to take off again, but he kept his head resting where it was.

When Benedict emerged from the wagon a few moments later in his black suit, he found them in the same pose and lifted an eyebrow. As though breaking the spell, Sebastian lifted his head and settled in front of the fire instead.

"I do hope Sebastian will not feel abandoned when we go out and leave him here tonight," Lizzie said, eyeing the large dog anxiously.

Benedict cocked his head to one side. "We've plenty of bones to keep him busy. You'll just have to be firm."

Lizzie bit her lip. "What if someone was to try and steal him from us?"

Benedict gave a short laugh. "We won't tie him up. I defy anyone to try and steal this dog."

He reached for the bag and picked out several large meaty bones which he threw under the wagon. Sebastian watched him, though he kept his head resting on his paws.

"Sebastian, you're to remain here, do you understand?" Lizzie said sternly. The animal looked at her fleetingly, then away again. "*Stay*. Do you understand?" Benedict drew on his jacket, and Sebastian climbed to his feet. "He doesn't understand," she said.

"Here, take this." Benedict drew a handkerchief from his pocket. She took it and he fetched the sack of bones. "Take another bone and show it to him."

Lizzie took his meaning and wrapped her hand in the handkerchief before gingerly retrieving a bone and calling the dog. "Sebastian, here!" She held the bone before him and then led him over to the wagon. "Now sit, Sebastian! Sit!" Reluctantly, he parked himself in front of the step and took the bone from her with careful jaws.

"Good dog, Sebastian," she praised him. He gazed at her a moment before settling down to mouth the bone. "I think he understands," she said, turning back to Benedict. He nodded and held out a hand to her. Lizzie hurried to his side and took it.

"Don't look back at him. Just keep walking," he instructed. Lizzie followed his lead, and soon they were at the stile at the end of the field. Lizzie took a surreptitious glance back and saw Sebastian's looming form still guarding the wagon. She breathed a sigh of relief.

"He really is a very good sort of dog," she asserted. Benedict accepted this without comment. "You look very smart this evening," Lizzie told him as she raised her skirts to negotiate the stile. His suit was of uniform and unrelenting black matched with a black satin tie and white shirt.

The silhouette was a good deal sleeker than the black woolen breeches and waistcoat he wore by day, but there was not even a suggestion of color even at the waistcoat. Even his tie pin was of blackest jet. On his head, instead of the top hat you might have expected, he wore a black felt derby.

"Well, we need to match," he answered lightly, handing her up onto the step. Lizzie hopped down the other side.

"Did you tell your brothers we were going dancing?"

"I may have mentioned it to Jack," he answered, swinging himself over to land beside her. "He's stepping out with some actress, by all accounts."

"Do you think we might see them there?"

He paused before shaking his head. "You don't tend to find the entertainers at the amusement tents."

"Oh. So, it will all be visitors to the fair?"

He nodded. "More than likely."

Even if there had been someone in the tent she knew, Lizzie acknowledged as they entered the Fiddlers Green a few moments later, it was unlikely she would be able to spot them. The place was in full swing, and Lizzie felt slightly dazed as Benedict towed her through the crush, a protective arm about her waist.

"Do you want to dance now, or shall I fetch us some refreshment?" he asked, raising his voice against the babble and merriment of the crowd. Lizzie gazed about in bewilderment. She had thought she would be embarrassed to take to the dance floor in a public place, but now she was here, she did not think anyone would notice her in such a tight squeeze.

Going up on her tiptoes, she suggested, "Let us have some punch first and then a dance before taking our supper."

He gave a nod. "Stay here and do not stir an inch."

She nodded, grateful for a chance to take stock and get her bearings. Benedict made off in the direction she presumed of a punch bowl, and Lizzie stared at the heaving dance floor where couples bobbed and capered madly to the tunes the musicians played. Some dancers looked to be performing prescribed steps, she noticed, and even forming country dancing formations where they swapped partners and whirled about. A good many of the couples, however, seemed to be simply doing their own thing. Some drifted about clasped scandalously close in each other's arms, though their footwork did not remotely resemble a waltz. Others simply faced one another and jigged about with more enthusiasm than skill.

There appeared to be no segregation of either party groupings or social classes. Some were dressed in silks and satins, feathers and plumes, and even face masks for anonymity. Lizzie could only suppose they must be people of fashion with reputations to uphold.

Others looked to be togged out in their shabby-genteel Sunday best, gazing about them with eyes round and cheeks red with excitement. There were some fringe characters who appeared a little less reputable, with painted and rouged faces and loud, raucous laughs, but as Benedict had said, all present seemed determined to have a good time.

Lizzie was just watching a spindle-shanked gentleman leaping and whooping with merry abandon when Benedict reappeared at her side bearing cups of fruit punch. He handed one to her, and they silently toasted one another before sipping the concoction.

"Oh, it's actually quite nice," Lizzie said, brightening as Benedict winced.

"It's very sweet," he commented before tossing his back like medicine. He discarded his cup and eyed her expectantly.

Lizzie took another cautious sip. "There is surely something alcoholic in this," she said nervously.

"Apparently, it's a champagne cocktail," he answered dryly. "But I very much doubt it contains so much as a thimbleful of champagne."

"Oh really?" Lizzie took a larger gulp. "It's delicious." She finished her cup and turned about to set it down.

Benedict laughed. "I was about to say it is more than likely laced with gin."

"Gin?" She did not have time to be alarmed, for he was already leading her out onto the dance floor. "I do not think I know this one," Lizzie said, craning to hear the tune above the noise of spirited conversation all about them.

Benedict looked unconcerned. "It doesn't really matter." He drew her firmly into his arms. "We can just dance our own steps."

Involuntarily, Lizzie stiffened, feeling his hand at her waist. Shaking off the unfamiliarity of it all, she set one hand on his shoulder as the other was enfolded in his own much larger hand.

"You ready?" he asked with a lurking twinkle in his eye.

She nodded and they started to move. Lizzie concentrated on following his lead as they glided about the bustling floor. Benedict moved easily and so assuredly he seemed almost graceful. Lizzie felt rather wooden in comparison, but after a while she found herself loosening up to the flow of the music. She was just beginning to enjoy herself when the next tune started up at a breakneck speed.

Around them, the couples starting galloping about the floor.

"Shall we sit this one out?" Benedict suggested.

"Yes, please," Lizzie replied hastily, and they forced their way out of the throng toward the trestle tables.

"It might be as well to get some supper now," he said, angling his head toward her ear so she could hear him.

Lizzie nodded, and they went toward the cold collation laid out on the head table. Waiting staff periodically refilled the dishes with cold meats, tongue, cheese, pickles, and buttered bread.

Lizzie selected a savory tart and some slices of cold turkey and waited for Benedict to finish loading his plate. Then they made their way to one of the more empty-looking tables and selected seats at the opposite end to another couple who were quietly conversing but looked up to nod politely when they saw them.

"I'll fetch us another drink," Benedict said after seeing her seated. He was soon back, and they both tucked into their cold supper with gusto.

Lizzie could not help but gaze about at the assorted clientele of the Fiddlers Green. She had never moved in such company in her life. It was somehow rather thrilling. When she had socialized, it had been with fellow members of St. Joseph's church who were sober folk much like her aunt and uncle.

She had not been to a dance party since she had grown too old for the church Christmas parties at thirteen and she had advanced to more sedate and civilized social pursuits such as attending formal evening dinners instead. Prior to this evening, it had never once occurred to her that she might have been missing out when Betsy went off on pleasure bent with the Stocktons. Now, she reappraised her previous disdain. She *had* been missing out after all.

"Another dance? Or did you want some dessert?" Benedict asked, glancing over at the dessert table where big bowls of melting ice preserved cream trifles and cakes.

Lizzie shook her head, setting down her empty glass. "Let's dance."

Once more they took to the dance floor, and this time Lizzie did not worry about possible collisions with other couples. Benedict guided them through the throng, and Lizzie closed her eyes as she swayed against him. For a moment, she wondered if the punch might be going to her head.

"Tell me," she said suddenly as the thought occurred to her. "Why would grown men wish to see a nude woman emerging from a chrysalis?"

Benedict leaned closer. "Say that again?"

"That was what Miss Wurtzel used to do apparently, to high acclaim. Try as I might, I just cannot understand why such a thing should hold any appeal."

Benedict shrugged. "I suspect the entertainment was designed for more jaded palates than my own." Lizzie cocked him an inquisitive look. "Aristocrats, likely as not," he expounded. "They're usually bored and on the lookout for something new."

"Oh." She regarded him thoughtfully. "Yes, I suppose that makes sense." She nodded. "Apparently, she was the light of love of some duke of the realm at that time."

"Light of love?" Benedict's lips quirked. "Is that the polite term for it?"

Lizzie frowned. "I think I heard the term somewhere. Perhaps it's not the correct one." She hiccupped. "I believe I might have had enough punch," she confessed, and Benedict laughed. "So." She leaned forward confidentially. "You would not be interested in seeing Miss Wurtzel appear as a human butterfly at Vauxhall Gardens?"

He shook his head. "My tastes are not so refined."

"It's funny," Lizzie rambled on. "For though she *is* very beautiful, I do not think she is as appealing as the twins, and Niamh's hair is a far prettier color. Really, I think her appeal must boil down to her magnificent figure, although I'm sure she uses some artifices to supplement nature, as it were."

At his quirked brow, she explained. "I suspect she wears some pieces of false hair to pad out her own. For when she dresses, she pins it up, and I cannot see how hair which extends down past her bottom could possibly be contained in so neat a topknot."

A smile lurked on Benedict's lips. "It sounds as though you have reasoned out the puzzle."

Lizzie narrowed her eyes. "Are you laughing at me, Benedict Toomes?"

"Who me? I wouldn't dare," he rumbled, then placed his head closer to hers. "It's funny to think that the last time I saw you in that dress was our wedding day," he murmured against her brow.

The abrupt change of subject made Lizzie's head spin in an instant. "I did not feel pretty that day," she admitted with a sigh. When he did not answer immediately, she rushed on. "I feel quite passable tonight though." For the first time in her life.

His hand clasped her waist, drawing her up tightly against him. "You look more than passable. You're the prettiest here."

Lizzie almost gasped aloud to hear such an outrageous claim. She drew back her head to look at him quizzically. "You're surely teasing me now."

"Not a bit."

She felt the caressing way his hand shifted across her back, his thumb stroking the indent at her waist. She felt light-headed and curiously free to say or do anything. "Are we flirting?" she asked as the thought popped into her head. "Only I don't think anyone ever did that with me before, so I'm not certain."

A curious expression swept over Benedict's face. "I'm not sure if it counts as flirting when you're married."

"Oh." She felt ridiculously disappointed, and even she could hear the wistfulness in her voice.

"Do you want me to flirt with you, Lizzie?" he asked in a low, intimate tone. His breath against her ear made her shiver.

"Yes," she admitted breathlessly. "I'd like to try it. Just this once." He smiled, his eyes half-closed and glinting. It seemed to Lizzie that there was suddenly no one else in the whole tent. She stared up at Benedict, and the noise of the crowd faded into the background. "What are you thinking of at this moment?" she asked on impulse.

"I'm trying to imagine you in a chrysalis," he divulged with a lazy grin.

Lizzie drew in a shocked breath. "Naked?" she asked in failing tones, glancing about them to make sure no one had overheard.

"Of course. It would be for an audience of one, mind you. I would not tolerate anyone else seeing such a sight."

"That is why I do not think Mr. Wurtzel can be Ada Wurtzel's husband," Lizzie admitted. "For surely he would not relish seeing her on display for paying spectators."

"Not all husbands are jealous," Benedict answered with a shrug.

Lizzie cocked her head, considering this, and was jostled from behind by an unsteady couple ploughing into her. Benedict

228

whisked her to the side, and a few heated words were exchanged. Lizzie noticed the other gentleman hastily owned he was at fault when he got a good look at Benedict.

"Do you want to carry on dancing?" her husband asked as the other couple retreated. Lizzie shook her head. "Another drink? Or an ice?" he offered.

"No, thank you."

He gave her a quick, considering look. "Have you had enough? Shall we head back to the wagon?"

Lizzie nodded. "I think so, yes."

Five minutes later, they were out in the cold night air. Lizzie had not brought her cloak, so Benedict removed his own jacket and draped it around her shoulders, his arm about her waist as he escorted her through the field.

"I had a lovely time," she told him with a sigh. "I think I like dancing after all."

"I've also had a change of heart," Benedict admitted after a moment. "I usually sit the dances out to smoke instead."

"Oh." Lizzie was surprised. "But you do it so well!"

"You think so?" Lizzie nodded. "So do you," he added lightly.

She shook her head. "I just followed your lead."

"There's still a knack to that," he answered. "Some ladies trample your toes and stare at their feet the whole time, making a punishment of it rather than a pleasure."

"Oh," Lizzie answered, feeling encouraged. Perhaps she was not so contemptible a partner after all. Then something occurred to her. "Are you still flirting?" she asked with misgiving.

229

Benedict laughed. "If you can't tell, I must be either very good or very bad at it. One or the other."

"I shan't tell you which I think it is," Lizzie retorted. "In case you grow quite puffed up with your own consequence!"

He squeezed her waist. "Let me carry you over the stile," he said. "It's muddy here. You'll get your skirts dirty."

Lizzie found herself swung up with little apparent effort into his arms. "It is grown a little muddy," she observed as they negotiated the obstacle. "It must have rained while we were dancing."

"We've only one more day here," Benedict observed. "So, it little matters."

"One more day?" Lizzie was startled. Benedict nodded. "Then what happens?"

"We move on to the next fair."

"Oh." She relapsed into silence. Once they were on the other side, he did not relinquish his hold of her, and Lizzie found herself gazing up at the starry night sky as he carried her back to their wagon.

15

Benedict hastily dumped the used washing water out of the basin and returned to the wagon. He wasn't leaving Lizzie time to undress tonight. They'd both visited the field, checked on the dog, and washed in cold water. As he pulled the door shut behind him, Lizzie was bunching up her stiffened petticoat and struggling to stuff it into the chest. In three strides, he was beside her, closing the lid on the cumbersome undergarment.

"Thanks," Lizzie puffed and sat on the edge of the mattress to draw off her stockings.

Benedict watched her as he stripped down to his long underwear. He drew off his vest and joined her on the bed, bare chested. When he knelt behind her, reaching for the fastenings at the front of her corset, Lizzie looked back over her shoulder.

"Thank you," she said simply as he unhooked the row of fastenings.

"My pleasure. Let down your hair."

Lizzie reached up and began drawing out the pins and silk flowers, arranging them in a neat pile atop the trunk.

He draped her stays over the top of the trunk and ran his hands down her sides which were clad now only in a thin chemise. "She emerges from her chrysalis," he murmured, and Lizzie gave a gurgle of laughter.

"I don't have any wings," she pointed out. "I emerge just as much a caterpillar as ever."

"A very captivating caterpillar," he muttered, kissing the side of her neck. "You don't need wings to captivate me, Lizzie."

He heard the hitch in her breathing. "Captivate you? You don't have to say those things, you know," she said in a constrained voice. "I know I'm not beautiful."

He frowned, drawing back his head. "I say it because I want to, no other reason." He turned her about and pressed her back down onto the mattress, running his hands over the slight swell of her breasts. "Let's take this off," he whispered, tugging at her chemise.

Lizzie extended her arms, and he pulled it up over her head. Gazing down at her, he found himself short of breath. "Beauty is in the eye of the beholder," he reminded her huskily. It was true, he did remember a time when he had thought her features sharp and plain and her coloring pale and drab in her severe gowns. Now, though, he found her high cheekbones, pointy chin, and little mouth delicate and pleasing. The fact she blushed so easily enchanted him. "You should see yourself right now."

She met his gaze, her own questioning. "Do I display to advantage half-clothed, then?" she asked doubtfully, glancing down her slender body, now clad only in plain white cotton drawers.

"God, yes," he said thickly and placed his hand on her belly. He contemplated a moment the picture his large tanned hand made against her flat stomach. When she shivered, he moved over her, covering her with his much larger body. "Cold?"

"A little."

Strange, he felt like he was on fire. Drawing the bedclothes up about them, he wrapped his body around her. "Better?"

"I'm returning to my cocoon," she joked.

He smiled against her temple. "Can I touch you, Lizzie?"

232

"Yes, of course."

Again, he placed his palm against her soft belly and then drew his hand down, sliding into the bloomers he had not yet removed. Lizzie's breathing grew ragged as he slid his hand over the thatch of hair covering her mound. "If it wasn't so cold," he said huskily, "I'd draw the covers down and take a good look at you."

"You looked last time," she reminded him in stifled accents.

"It was definitely worth a second look," he murmured. "Besides, I could barely see, the light was so low." He sifted his fingers through the intriguing hair, then dipped his middle finger into her cleft. Lizzie gasped and jolted beneath him as he found her little pearl and slicked it with her moisture. He concentrated then on her every breath and whimper as he stroked and worked her with his fingers. His fingers were deep inside Lizzie's delightfully slippery cunt, and *he* was the one shaking at the sensation. God, he wanted to put something else of his inside her. Something that was so hard it hurt.

"Tell me," he said gruffly, "that you wanted me all along." He knew it wasn't true, but he wanted to hear it all the same. "Say it now."

She gave a soft sob. "Benedict," she whimpered, and he felt a rushing in his head. That was almost as good.

"Say my name again."

"Ben—oh!" He heard the catch in her breath and felt the jolt that ran through her. She was coming on his fingers, and he felt light-headed at the sensation of the tight spasmodic clasp of her, even though she'd rushed ahead when he'd meant to keep teasing her awhile yet, mindless with need.

233

Pushing his fingers deep, he clenched his jaw and concentrated on the distant merry-making of the fair in the background. He could hear it even from the distance of four or five fields away. He felt blisteringly aware of everything, even the steady rasp of his own breath.

"Fuck, I need to be inside you," he swore. "I meant to take it slower, but I'll spill in the sheets if you don't take me now."

She started to struggle, and he felt his heart plummet a moment, thinking she was trying to get away from him. Then he realized she was trying to free herself from her bloomers.

"I don't deserve you, sweetheart," he said shakily, stripping the cotton garment down her legs. When he resettled between her bare thighs, he was breathing hard. "Are you sure you're ready?" He knew for a fact she'd come, but it had happened so quickly he still felt he was rushing her.

She nodded. "Yes," she whispered, and he reached down, taking himself in hand, poising his shaft at her entrance.

Once he'd worked the tip inside her, he braced himself to go slow, for he knew she had found this part uncomfortable the last time. "Wrap your legs around my back, Lizzie. I need you to open up to me."

He felt a fierce surge of joy when she did so, and he started to push his way inside her, concentrating on the pressure of her fingers clutched on his hips. "Tell me if I go too fast or if anything hurts." She nodded, and by the time he was fully sheathed, the sweat was beaded at his brow.

"Oh, Lizzie," he groaned. "You feel so good. It's a lucky thing we skipped dessert, for I'm about to slake my lust on you like a regular glutton at a banquet."

"A glutton?" she echoed, sounding mystified.

"Aye, a glutton," he agreed, reaching up and plucking at her little pink nipples. "Feasting on these little raspberry tarts, though by rights, I ought to have eaten that dripping honey cake between your legs."

Lizzie's mouth fell open. "Benedict!" she spluttered.

"Hmmm?" When she could not answer, he lowered his head to her breasts. "Offer them up to me, Lizzie." The sight of her slender fingers cupping her breasts for him almost had him spilling inside her. He groaned. "Fuck!" He'd done it again and pushed himself too far. His cock jerked inside her as he sucked her perfect breast right into his greedy mouth.

"Oh!" Lizzie moaned.

His nostrils flared. He'd make her come again now. That would redeem his pride. He closed his teeth gently around her nipple and teased it with his tongue. Lizzie's thighs tightened fitfully about his hips, and he lavished his attention on the other breast.

"Nnnnnnh!" she gasped and threw back her head. He felt the nice, deep squeeze of her cunt and knew himself to be lost and that was before he felt the press of her heels into the small of his back. *Christ.* She was doing it, he thought, light-headed with elation. She was coming on his cock. His nostrils flared as he slammed his hips into her, and Lizzie cried out, her fingers biting into his sides, her hair tossed against his pillow.

"Benedict!"

His eyes were riveted to her face. Suddenly, he needed to kiss her, even though both of them had tipped past the crisis point already. Threading his fingers through her silky hair, he angled her face and took her lips beneath his own. It felt strangely intimate to kiss at this point. Kissing usually came earlier than

235

this, he thought dimly, much earlier. But for some reason, he wanted it now as they crossed the finish line together.

Lizzie's arms slid around his back, clasping him to her in an embrace that undid him completely. Reluctant to relinquish her lips, he gave her one last lingering kiss before collapsing on top of her, breathing hard.

*

Benedict woke early, wrenched from his sleep by the unpleasant conviction he had missed a step in the flight he was descending. His spine jerked and he woke blinking in the gray morning light. He reckoned it was about five thirty. Lizzie was tucked into his side sound asleep, her one arm wound about his waist as was her habit.

Likely he had woken so early because it was the last day of the fair, he told himself uneasily. It would be a long day, and this time tomorrow they would be packing up their things to get back on the road. He had not even discussed with Frank which of the smaller fairs they would travel to next. His thoughts bounced around, searching out the reason for his unease.

He was not hungover. He had only had a few glasses of the punch and certainly not enough to turn his head. He felt fine, he told himself, so why did he feel this deep disquiet? Reluctantly, Benedict forced himself to go over anything he might have said or done the previous evening.

There it was. He flushed in the dark remembering the things he had tried to make Lizzie say to him. *Tell me you wanted me all along.* He squirmed with embarrassment as he recalled his own words. Why the hell had he wanted her to say that? He'd never needed assurances from anyone before.

Besides, it was ridiculous to demand anything of the sort and moreover was tantamount to making the poor girl admit she'd coveted her own cousin's fiancé, something he knew damned well she had not. He dwelled deliberately a moment on Lizzie's previously pinched and disapproving expression whenever she had deigned to look his way.

Instead of feeling the resentment he had previously, though, his reaction was highly colored by how he felt about her now. Inconveniently, he felt himself growing hard, and he turned his head toward her, despite the fact it was not light enough yet for him to make out her features clearly.

As though aware of his scrutiny, Lizzie stirred in her sleep, turning more firmly into him, burrowing her face into his chest and throwing her leg over his. Benedict sucked in his breath before blowing it back out again. She'd be the death of him, he thought wryly, and steeled himself to lie beside her perfectly still for another half hour before rising.

He just about managed it. By the time she opened the door an hour later, he had boiled the water and was scooping the tea leaves into the pot.

"Good morning."

He glanced up warily and found her wrapped in a blanket off the bed, her hair still loose about her shoulders. "I've water for you here," he said, clearing his throat and standing.

She took the water with thanks and shuffled back inside to wash and dress. Benedict scratched the back of his neck, still gazing at the door she'd shut after her. Sebastian yawned, and Benedict glanced at the dog, only to find the beast regarding him steadily.

"I suppose you want another bone," he muttered, retrieving the sack which was decidedly lighter than when he'd carried it back

237

the previous day. He held one out for Sebastian, who clamped his jaws around it and dropped down on his haunches beside the fire.

Lizzie joined them there ten minutes later in a dress of dark gray wool, her hair once more demurely coiled at her nape. She sat on an upturned wooden crate and reached for the teacup he slid toward her wordlessly.

"Thank you," she murmured and settled back to enjoy the hot drink. "It seems funny," she commented a moment later, "to think our view will be a completely different one after today." Benedict grunted, and she fixed her eyes on him. "I've been thinking about what you said last night—" she started, and Benedict shot to his feet.

"You don't need to set any great store by anything a man might say to you in bed," he heard himself say abruptly. "That kind of talk… It doesn't really mean anything."

Lizzie blinked and stared at him a heartbeat then she said blankly, "Oh." Then, "I see." Something about the way she said it bothered him, and even more so, the way she averted her face a moment from him. He opened his mouth again but found himself at a loss for words. When she turned to face him again, she was perfectly calm and even had a small smile for him. "Thank you for explaining," she said simply and picked up both their empty cups, carried them over to the basin of water, and employed herself there washing them clean.

Benedict stared after her, feeling if anything, worse than he had on first waking. *Shit*, that didn't come out right.

"I must go and visit with your grandmother at some point today," Lizzie's raised voice carried over to him. He had the feeling she was talking simply to fill the awkward silence, but

238

after his unpardonable clumsiness, thought he had better humor her in any case.

"Why?" he asked, frowning.

"To return her headscarf for one thing and ask if I can keep her black cloak."

"I see."

"When do you think would be the best time for me to go in search of her?" Lizzie asked, looking back over her shoulder.

Benedict shrugged irritably. "She both rises and goes to bed early, if memory serves."

Lizzie nodded, reaching for a drying cloth and employing unnecessary care over the cups. "Shall we head for the main field now?" she asked brightly, and he answered her with a wordless nod. He told himself it did not bother him when Lizzie chose to cling to the dog's collar instead of his arm.

They had crossed into the main field, and he was helping Lizzie down from the stile when a stifled cry had them both turning their heads. Benedict saw a plump, middle-aged woman in a purple dress staring at them with her mouth open.

"Annie!" Lizzie exclaimed, straightening up and pushing Benedict's hands away from her waist.

Annie? Benedict looked from Lizzie's expression of dismay to the other woman's obvious stupefaction with raised brows. Was no one to speak?

"Lor' bless you, Miss Lizzie," the other stammered, recovering her wits. "I scarcely recognized you for an instant." She stole another incredulous glance at Benedict, and it occurred to him he did dimly recognize the woman, though from where he could not quite recollect. Annie swallowed convulsively. "And you'll remember Dick," she said, pulling at her escort's arm.

The man beside her, sporting a pair of fluffy sideburns, pulled on his braces and cleared his throat.

"Of course," Lizzie replied unevenly. "You are Mr. Blake, the butcher's assistant, are you not? I believe you made the deliveries to Sitwell Place."

"That's right," the other agreed cheerfully, looking Benedict up and down. "I been walking out wiv Annie some six months now in all. How do?"

"I did not realize," Lizzie murmured. Then she seemed to pull herself together. "I'm sure, Annie," she said, half turning toward Benedict, her expression self-conscious in the extreme, "that you remember Mr. Toomes."

"O' course I do!" Annie responded, bobbing up and down. It was at that moment that he remembered her, crouching at the keyhole when he opened the parlor door after breaking his engagement with Betsy. She was the Andersons' maid.

He gave a curt nod, observing the way Annie stared at Lizzie. Then she seemed to notice something that made her gasp aloud, and she staggered against her swain.

"'Ere careful, old girl!" Dick protested, extending a steadying arm about her reeling figure. "You turnin' faint?"

Benedict followed Annie's gaze and deduced she had seen the brass ring on Lizzie's third finger. It struck him once again with uncomfortable force that the thing looked cheap and was beneath her.

"You haven't been frequenting the waxwork tent, have you?" Lizzie asked with a feeble attempt at humor. "Only I saw a woman carried out of there half-insensible the other day."

"She works there," Benedict cut in, feeling he ought to have some share of the conversation. "Her name's Nancy, and she faints at least five times a day to attract passing custom."

"Does she really?" Lizzie asked, turning to him. He was pleased to see the color was returning to her white face. "Well, what an ingenious stratagem." Her voice had a faint wobble in it, but otherwise she was trying to rally from the shock of seeing a familiar face from her not-so-distant past.

He turned back to the couple. "You'll have to excuse us now," he said smoothly. "Only my wife and I have places we need to be." He heard the hitch in Lizzie's breathing, but she managed to stammer out her goodbyes as he dragged her back toward Wondrous Females. "Are you alright?" he asked in low tones once they had left the couple behind them.

"What? Oh yes, of course," she answered. "Thank you," she added distractedly, and he saw the hand that was not tucked in his arm reach out for Sebastian's collar, squeezing it tight. She took a shuddering breath. "I do not think you realize, but she will certainly talk about the fact she has seen us," she said in an uneven voice.

"Will she?" he asked, feeling irritated the dog was a source of comfort to her rather than her own husband.

"Of a certainty! You probably don't understand how these things work, but she will tell Cook and the boot boy and the gardener..." She bit her lip.

"I expect she will. She was certainly listening at the door when Betsy and I broke off our engagement."

Lizzie's eyes grew rounder. "I see," she choked out. "The thing is, it will undoubtedly get back to my aunt Hester. And in turn she—she—"

"Will tell your cousin," he continued when she seemingly could not.

Lizzie's gaze flew to meet his, and her own was wretched in the extreme. "Yes," she said feebly.

"This distresses you?" he asked coolly. "I had not realized you were hopeful for a reconciliation with the Andersons."

Her gaze grew startled. "A reconciliation?" she echoed. "No, I had not dared to ever hope for that."

Her response jarred him. That was something she wanted, then? "You have another family now," he pointed out, although he did not mean the Toomes clan precisely, just himself.

Lizzie's shoulders slumped. "I had better go in," she said, glancing toward the Wondrous Females tent. "Connie will be scolding me if I am late."

"Connie be damned," he said sharply. "I haven't bought you any breakfast yet."

"I'm not hungry," Lizzie responded and hurried away from him without even fixing up a meeting point for lunchtime. He opened his mouth to call after her, but something about her tense bearing and the way she clung to the dog for dear life dissuaded him. By the time he reached the boxing tent, he had worked himself into a fine temper, and Jack did a double take on seeing him.

"I take it the dancing was not a success?" his brother commented with a wry twist of his lips.

"What?" Benedict swung around to glare at his younger brother. "The dancing was fine."

"What's with the ugly look on your face, then?"

Benedict shrugged out of his jacket and threw it over the rope. "We just bumped into someone from Lizzie's past," he answered with a scowl, glancing away.

"Oh ho! An old beau, I'll warrant, from the frown on your face. I pity the poor bastard that gets in the ring with you this morning, eh, Frank?" Jack said, hailing their older brother.

Even in his current bad mood, Benedict recognized Frank was not looking his best this morning. He hadn't shaved, and his hand shook as he raised a silver hip flask to his lips. As he lowered it, he sent a hangdog expression their way.

"Hair of the dog," he mumbled, running a hand through his untidy hair.

"Since when do you drink hard liquor before nine in the morning?" Benedict asked.

"You were out drinking last night, weren't you?" Frank demanded belligerently. "We haven't all got pretty wives to distract ourselves with. Not anymore, at any rate."

"You leave off looking at what's mine. You've got Daphne, haven't you?" Benedict retorted nastily. "Everyone seems to think she's taken Maggie's place where you're concerned."

"Daphne?" Frank pulled up short. "Is that what you think?"

"Everyone thinks it."

Frank looked a little green around the gills as he lowered himself onto a low wooden stool with a groan. He dropped his head into his hands. "I haven't touched her," he groaned. "I swear it. Not even once." He breathed in and out raggedly. "I haven't been with another woman since Maggie."

Jack looked up sharply at his words. "What about Ivy, that time at Nye's?" he asked.

"Oh, I tried it alright with pretty Ivy, but when it came to the actual deed, I couldn't stomach it. I paid her double and she promised not to tell anyone." Frank looked shame-faced. "At the time, I thought that was my lowest point, but every day since has felt just as bad."

"That state of you," Benedict growled. "You're not fit to be seen in the tent."

"Ben." Jack's voice was low with entreaty. "Leave off him."

"Someone needs to give him a talking-to and seems to me you're all tiptoeing round him!"

"Well you're not the one to deliver it," Jack fired up. "It's clear you're spoiling for a fight this morning, and Frank's not the one to give it you!"

"No? What about you, then?" Ben snarled. "I'm sick of wasting my time with slow tops. Why don't you get in the ring with me this morning? If you've got the stomach for it."

"I'll not deny you," Jack retorted promptly. "Come on, then! Let's have you!"

"Oh God," Frank moaned and grabbed a bucket. He heaved, and both brothers turned to watch him impassively.

"That's the idea, Frank," Jack said heartily as he shrugged out of his braces. "You'll feel better directly."

"I'm dying," Frank wheezed.

"Well you won't have to worry about working the crowd this morning," Benedict told him coldly. "Me and Jack will put on an exhibition match, so you can just take it easy."

"Not if you half kill him, I can't!" Frank retorted before another wave of nausea had him bent over double.

"Lord, he ain't gonna kill me, Frank," Jack said blithely. "He just wants to let off some steam." He cast a sly look Benedict's way. "That little wife of his is holding him at arm's length, so he needs some kind of outlet."

"Fuck off, Jack."

Jack laughed merrily. "Oh, she's brought you low, brother. Maybe you should let me take her dancing. Bet I could put a smile on her face."

"You—"

Frank shot up from his seat and got between them. "Save it for the ring," he bit out before raising a scarf to his mouth. His brothers eyed him warily, but he managed to lower it without gagging. "Jack, go out and explain to Daphne that we don't need her to find any contenders this morning."

Jack nodded briskly and made for the entrance.

"Don't you hurt him, Ben," Frank said direly. "I'm trusting you to have some fucking self-restraint."

Ben curled his lip, but in fact, his anger was no longer at boiling point or even a low simmer. "Oh, sit down, you fool, before you pass out."

16

Lizzie found Wondrous Females in disarray. Zaya and Ema were sat side by side on Salome's couch watching as Connie roamed from one end of the tent to the other like an uncaged tiger. "That bitch! She can't do this to me!" she seethed. "I'll have her up in court for breach of contract!"

Niamh ushered Lizzie in with a finger to her lips. "Don't breathe a word!" she warned in a hushed whisper as Lizzie abruptly dropped down beside Niamh to perch on her pedestal. "Connie's breathing fire this morning." Niamh looked gleeful.

Sebastian slunk under the couch and poked his head out from between Ema's legs. The twins surreptitiously bestowed caresses on him as Connie muttered dire threats and viciously kicked out at a striped hat box that Lizzie thought belonged to Ada Wurtzel.

"What's happened?" Lizzie murmured out of the corner of her mouth.

"Darling Ada's done a moonlight flit for some tour of Europe," Niamh replied in barely audible tones. "She had a letter delivered here by some errand boy first thing."

Connie was now viciously tearing something that looked suspiciously like a letter into tiny pieces and finished by jumping up and down on top of it, her face a mottled purple with rage. Suddenly she wheeled around, as though only just noticing her avid audience.

"Get out of my sight, you jackals!" she screeched, flinging her arms in the air. Sebastian's lip rose on a growl, but Lizzie called him sharply and all five of them fled from the tent.

"Phew!" said Niamh, slowing down as soon as they were at least three tents away. "Did you ever see such a temper?"

The twins giggled. "Her face was like a big ball of fire," said Ema, blowing out her own cheeks. "Steam was about to start pouring from her ears!"

"But if she had really flown at us," Zaya put in, "then dear Sebastian would have nobly defended us!" Sebastian promptly wheeled about and darted through the twins' legs, making them squeal with delight. The running had excited him, and he bounded about them like a puppy with his tongue lolling out.

"If she means to sue," Lizzie said with dignity, for she did not think it became her to run away like a frightened child. "Then it was very foolish of her to destroy that letter which would have formed the bulk of evidence for her case."

"Lord, she ain't really going to sue, Lizzie," Niamh told her, hooking her arm through hers. "Connie's all talk. Anyway, we got the day off, girls. What we going to do wiv it?"

"Alas," said Zaya, turning tragically toward them. "Today is the last day of the fair and the day that Connie was meant to pay us all! What will we do now with empty pockets?"

"Do?" echoed Niamh. "Why, you can thank your lucky stars that you've got a prime article like old Niamh for your friend and work colleague, that's what." She reached into her bodice and extracted a bunch of envelopes. "I picked up our wages soon as I walked into the tent this morning and seen what way the wind was blowing, didn't I?"

247

Ema and Zaya screeched and threw themselves about Niamh's neck. "You have saved us!" they crowed, bringing their envelopes to their lips and kissing them. Niamh passed Lizzie's to her with a wink. "Yes, I know," she gloated. "And this way we don't have to help Connie pack up the tent tonight neither! By the time she's simmered down, we'll be long gone, and she can bloody well hire some muscle to do it for her!"

Lizzie interrupted the twins' high glee to ask if Connie would not be rather angry the next time they saw her. "She will have dismounted her high horse by then," Zaya said with a dismissive wave of her arm.

"And besides," her sister chimed in. "She can have no one to blame for that save herself. She chased us off like a ferocious old dragon, did she not? And now we will have a half day holiday!"

Rather more than a half day, Lizzie thought, but did not voice it. "Where will we go?" she asked doubtfully. Mercifully, Niamh and the twins had not had chance to change into their costumes that morning, so they were not wearing outlandish or revealing garb.

Still, Lizzie thought, looking at the laughing slender twins with their long, dark braids, they drew the eye. Even now, heads were turning to stare at them as they gamboled about with Sebastian. Luckily, the fact they had such a large and fierce escort would put off any would-be admirers, Lizzie hoped. As for Niamh, she carried herself with a sort of brash assurance that meant only the boldest of men would approach her.

"Where won't we go?" Ema answered gaily.

"First we must have both sausage and egg," Zaya asserted. "And then bread and butter."

"And a nice pot of tea," Niamh added. "There's a tea tent in the next field."

"None of you are wearing bonnets," Lizzie remarked with misgiving.

Niamh reached up and patted her flame-red hair. "Oops," she remarked. "Must of left it behind in the rush. Well thank gawd you ain't got that awful fright of an 'at on this morning!" Niamh laughed. "Or we'd have had to cut our ties wiv you."

Zaya slipped her slim hand into Lizzie's. "She is only joking, Lizzie," she murmured, squeezing her fingers. "We would not leave you behind even if your bonnet was ever so ugly."

"Course not!" Niamh agreed. "She's one of us, ain't she, girls?"

"Oh yes," Ema agreed breathlessly from in front. She had her hand on Sebastian's collar and was being run hither and thither by him in some sort of frantic game.

"Careful," Lizzie called in warning. "He'll have you over!"

They managed to make it into the tea tent in one piece and settled around a table, though Lizzie felt they were the object of a few stares. As she took her first sip of tea, it suddenly occurred to her that Annie and her swain might be lurking somewhere inside the tent. She took a quick furtive glance about but could see no sign of them.

They ate a large breakfast, though a good deal of it seemed to disappear under the tablecloth to Sebastian. After that, the twins insisted they go to the waxwork tent so Lizzie could be terrified by the ghoulish Bluebeard tableau. The man on the door recognized Niamh and waved them through without paying admission. "Only make sure one of the pretty ones faints on the way out," he whispered to Lizzie.

The twins cackled over the grisly display, but Lizzie felt herself taken quite queasy at the profusion of dismembered limbs. She blamed it on the late, heavy breakfast and possibly the aftereffects of last night's punch. When she had woken that morning, she had felt quite seedy, and that was before Annie's upsetting appearance. She took several deep breaths and managed to navigate the tent without embarrassing herself.

Zaya and Ema quarreled about who should be overcome, so Niamh ended up bundling Ema out and Lizzie half dragging Zaya.

"Oh!" Niamh cried. "Whatever shall we do? These poor young ladies have been scared insensible!"

This had the unfortunate effect of causing several young gentlemen to bound over to lend their manly aid. Zaya and Ema fluttered their eyelashes and sighed so prettily that the male admiration was increased tenfold and they then seemed unable to shake them off.

By the time they reached the theatrical tent, they still had the most persistent three in attendance. Lizzie and Sebastian eyed these newcomers with disfavor, but Niamh just laughed and said the twins were having a high time. "Besides," Niamh whispered, nudging Lizzie in the ribs, "we'll just let them pay for everything from here on out."

Lizzie stiffened and opened her mouth to object strenuously to this but found her herself whisked through the entrance and a bag of peanuts thrust into her hands. Zaya dragged her down onto a bench.

"It is already started!" Ema whispered excitedly. "Come, Sebastian!"

Inside the tent was pandemonium. Clowns with painted faces moped over beauties in elaborate wigs. There was a plotting villain who the audience booed and pelted with orange peel and nutshells and a ghost in a winding sheet who kept popping up from behind fake trees. Lizzie watched in gathering bewilderment as she felt the beginnings of a headache form behind her temples.

It didn't help that around her the young people kept getting up and down and tripping over each other's feet. It seemed to Lizzie just as chaotic on their bench as it was on the stage. The young men seemed determined to make the most of their opportunity to sit in a darkened tent with their arms about the twins' slender waists, and as there were three of them, this meant frequent swapping of seats and much indignant whispering about "it being my turn now, old man."

Lizzie placed a hand on Sebastian's neck as he growled with irritation, but really, she felt just as impatient with it all as he. A brief intermission while the scenery was changed gave Lizzie a chance to give her excuses. At first the twins were inclined to argue, but when she used Sebastian as her excuse, they allowed that poor dear Sebastian might not like the noisy surroundings. One of the young men politely offered to escort her, but Lizzie declined with haste.

"We'll see you at Putney Heath, then, for the next fair," Niamh said, kissing her cheek. "Be sure to give Connie's tent a wide berth now or she'll have you in there doing all the packing."

Lizzie nodded and made her way back out into the fresh air with a sigh of relief. It took a moment for her eyes to adjust from the dim interior, and it was while she was stood blinking in the light that someone sidled up to her.

"Given your swains the slip, then?" asked a voice to her right. Sebastian turned sharply, but apparently recognized the newcomer, and so did Lizzie after a split second, for it was Daphne.

"Hello, Daphne," she responded coolly, not caring for the woman's overfamiliar tone or what she was implying.

"I seen you gadding about with your gentleman friends. Guessed you didn't have quite so much starch in your drawers as you made out, or he wouldn't hardly have married you, would he? I still can't see how you hooked him, mind you," the other carried on snidely.

Lizzie felt herself bristle but didn't want to give Daphne the satisfaction of launching into explanations. "And why are you so far from the boxing tent?" she asked instead. "I thought you took the entrance fees."

Daphne sniffed. "They didn't put on much of a show today as it 'appens. Packed up early, didn't they. After they'd knocked merry hell out of each other, that is."

Lizzie felt a lurch of alarm. "After they'd what? What time is it anyway?" she asked, gazing about in consternation.

Daphne smirked knowingly. "Lost track of your day, did you? Well, that's what happens when you're enjoying yourself."

Lizzie turned a look of exasperation on her. "Are they packing up the boxing saloon?" she asked outright.

Daphne looked her up and down and folded her arms. "Wouldn't you like to know?" she asked with a decided sneer.

Lizzie turned on her heel and headed in the direction of the boxing tent. She thought Daphne called jeeringly after her, but she paid her no heed and did not catch her mocking words. With Sebastian trotting along beside her, they soon reached the tent, or rather the spot where the tent had once stood.

Lizzie stared about her in consternation, turning in a full circle as she looked for any sign of the Toomes family, but there was none. She felt a momentary panic well up inside her when suddenly she heard someone shout her name. Whirling about with tears in her eyes, she saw Benedict standing a few yards away and took off toward him with a choked cry.

She saw a flash of surprise in his eyes the instant before she was caught up in his arms and held tight. "Lizzie?" he asked in muffled tones as she hung about his neck. She shook her head, feeling words were beyond her at this point. "What is it? What's happened?"

"Nothing," she managed to choke out, struggling to regain control of herself. "I just—I thought you'd left without me," she admitted, dropping her arms and attempting to disentangle herself. To her consternation, she found herself hoisted rather more firmly into his arms.

"Well, that was foolish," he answered coolly and swung around with her still in his arms toward the beer tent.

"Where are we going?"

"We're joining Jack and Frank in the Adam and Eve for a farewell drink." He looked back over his shoulder and whistled to Sebastian. "Where have you been anyway? I went to Connie's tent earlier and there was no one to be seen."

"There was a bit of an upset," Lizzie admitted, plucking at his shoulder. "The Wurtzels have run away to the Continent, and Connie flew into a fury about it."

His stride checked. "Not with you?"

"With all of us," Lizzie clarified. "She screamed at us all to clear out, so we did."

By this point they were inside the beer tent, and Benedict slid her down his front until she was stood on her own two feet. "What happened to your face?" Lizzie asked with surprise, noticing the red marks about his cheekbones.

"Jack happened," he said, seizing her hand in his. "He's turned out a lot better boxer than I thought he would, only don't tell him I said so."

Lizzie opened her mouth but did not get the chance to voice her words as she was tugged in his wake until they reached a table near the bar area.

"Lizzie!" cried Jack, who looked to be in high spirits, though he sported both a split lip and a swollen eye. He patted the seat next to his own. "Come and sit! We're celebrating."

Frank seemed to be in a lot more subdued spirits, but he gave her a tired smile and added his entreaties for her to sit, removing his cap and pulling out her chair. Sebastian shot under the table and sat there looking alert with his ears sticking straight up in the air.

"What are we celebrating?" Lizzie asked, seating herself as some beer was sloshed into her mug from the pitcher.

"The best takings in two years, that's what," Frank said as Benedict pulled up another seat and set it next to hers.

"A successful reunion of the Toomes brothers," Jack said, wiping the foam from his moustache with the back of his hand.

"You should shave that off," Benedict said critically, dropping into his chair. "It looks ridiculous."

"I've been told it lends me a rakish air," Jack said, twiddling the ends. "What say you, Lizzie? We'll have a female opinion, if you please."

Lizzie regarded him thoughtfully. Jack was far better looking than any of the three young men who had been dogging Ema's and Zaya's steps all day, but certainly too youthful for a handlebar moustache. He could not be more than three and twenty. "I think it detracts from your boyish appeal," she said truthfully.

"There, you see," Benedict said, though he looked a little askance at her mention of "boyish appeal."

"She's bound to back you," Jack complained, but his hand dropped from fondling his moustache and he grinned all the same.

Frank sat up, seeming determined to make an effort. He picked up his mostly full tankard. "To Greenwich," he said rousingly.

They all lifted their mugs and repeated the toast, taking gulps of their beer. Lizzie was surprised to find hers rather refreshing.

"This is much nicer than the stuff Mrs. Napp had," she commented as Frank and Jack fell into discussing the merits of leaving that very evening as opposed to the next morning. Benedict dragged his seat closer to hers and draped an arm over the back of her own. "How was your day?" he asked.

"Strange," Lizzie responded truthfully. "Yours?"

His gaze swiveled from her own to contemplate Jack a moment. "Unexpected."

"That too," Lizzie agreed.

He turned back to her, lifting his drink to his mouth. "How did you spend your time?"

Lizzie colored guiltily but hoped the shadowy surroundings obscured her reaction. "Uneasily," she admitted. "I kept thinking Annie would jump out from behind every waxwork.

255

Or Connie," she added. "The others seemed to think it was imperative we stayed out of her sight. Funnily enough though, it was Daphne who sprang out at me in the end."

"Daphne?" He frowned, lowering his beer.

"She saw us going into the theater tent," Lizzie said frankly. "The girls had gained some admirers by this point, and Daphne seemed to think I was doing something I ought not. She was...gloating about it. Like she had one up on me."

Benedict set his tankard down with a thump. "What did she say?" he asked shortly.

"Nothing much, it was more what she implied," Lizzie said evasively. "That I was being underhand or keeping company I shouldn't." Benedict eyed her in silence a moment and Lizzie rushed on. "Truthfully, I felt miserable all day. I'm not really sure why."

Benedict's hand slid from the back of her seat to shift comfortingly over her back. "It wasn't your fault one of Connie's acts did a bunk," he said gruffly. "She had no right to lose her temper with you like that."

Lizzie nodded. "I know."

"It wasn't your fault Annie happened upon us this morning either," he added and shifted closer, and she felt his breath on her cheek before he kissed her fleetingly there.

"Humph!" an explosive exclamation interrupted them. "So here you all are! Swilling beer and canoodling! I might have known!" Ma Toomes stood before their table with her hands on her scrawny hips. Daphne swung out from behind the malevolent old woman with a defiant look on her face.

"Ma, Daphne," said Frank warily. "Take a seat."

Benedict pulled on Lizzie's hand, tugging her onto his lap. "Have this one," he said, kicking it toward his grandmother.

Ma seized on it at once and plumped herself down. "What about a chair for Daphne?" she demanded.

Frank came wearily to his feet. "Take this one, Daphne," he offered and went in search of another. Daphne sat herself down with a great show of rearranging her skirts.

"Jack, go and fetch your old grandmother another pitcher of beer," the old woman said with her eyes fixed speculatively on Lizzie's face.

All of a sudden, Lizzie knew that Daphne had told Ma Toomes what she had seen earlier. She felt a sudden fervent gratitude that she had seen fit to confess all to Benedict, for she could see the old woman had a mind to cause mischief between them. Boldly, she passed an arm about Benedict's shoulders and felt him relax against her.

Jack sighed but stood up anyway and made his way toward the bar.

"You might not look quite so cozy when you hear what that little wife of yours has been up to this day," Ma said, narrowing her eyes.

"Whatever she gets up to, it's no business of yours," Benedict replied in a bored voice.

"No business of mine?" Ma Toomes spat out. "We raised you to respect your elders!"

"You didn't *raise* me at all," he responded coldly. "And we both know it, so don't come that with me, old woman. You keep your distance from me and mine."

257

Ma Toomes had gone rigid in her seat. She glared at Benedict. "So resentful always!" she burst out. "It was barely more'n a year you was gone from us and that no fault but your own!"

Lizzie felt Benedict stiffen. "It was more than two years I was gone," he replied in a dangerously quiet voice, and Lizzie felt confused, for surely, he'd told her his prison term had been nine months.

The old woman tossed her head angrily. "Such nonsense! Your pa fetched you back in the end, and if you'd anything to say, you should have said it at the time and cleared the air." She glared at him. "Not you though. No, you never breathed a word to any of us. Just let that hatred fester in your heart till there was no room for nothing else!"

"No room for you, you mean," he corrected her in a low voice as his hand shifted from Lizzie's waist to her hip, clasping her firmly.

Ma Toomes's eyes flashed. "Oh, yet you've room for your stuck-up little bride, haven't you?" she sneered. "Shunned your own family once you got out so's you could court her. *Far* too good to mix with your own flesh and blood, ain't she? Well, what if I told you she's no better than she ought to be, Benedict Toomes? What then?" She folded her arms and regarded him with an exuberance that was unpleasant to see.

Benedict reached for the pitcher and poured himself some more beer with a steady hand. "You could tell me she was the devil himself and I'd still take her part over yours," he answered with a shrug. The old lady's eyes flashed, but even as she opened her mouth to respond, Benedict interrupted her. "There's nothing you could say that could turn me against her, so don't even try."

Something in his tone of voice had both Lizzie and Ma Toomes catching their breath. "I may as well tell you now that I'd

258

believe her word over the evidence of my own eyes," he finished simply. "So, you may as well save your breath."

Lizzie turned to stare at him quite flabbergasted by this claim.

"I seen her!" Daphne burst out, no longer able to keep her silence.

"What's this?" Frank asked, returning with a chair. "What's to do?"

Daphne pointed an accusing finger at Lizzie, but before she could get her words out, Ma Toomes stopped her. "Hold your tongue, you fool!" she hissed. "Didn't you hear what he said?"

Daphne's face turned puce. "B-but," she stammered. "I—"

"I said *quiet*!" Ma bit out, whipping around in her seat.

Daphne sprang up from her chair, her fists clenched, nearly overturning the table. Sebastian let out a rumbling growl, leaping to his feet.

"Careful!" Jack cautioned, returning with a second jug of beer. Daphne made a sound of suppressed fury and rushed from the tent.

"Stupid girl!" Ma muttered under her breath.

"What's got into her?" Frank asked in bewilderment as he sat himself down.

"Pour me a drink, Jack!" Ma demanded, rapping her bony knuckles on the table.

Jack refilled the cups, throwing a puzzled look toward Benedict and Lizzie as he did so. Ma tossed her beer back, wiped her mouth with a grubby mittened hand, and then surged to her feet.

She gave a short nod to all present and then marched out of the tent.

"What the hell was that about?" Jack burst out.

When no one spoke, Lizzie drew a deep breath. "Your grandmother was just trying to drive a wedge between Benedict and myself," she answered calmly, reaching down to pat Sebastian's neck. "But she did not achieve her aim."

"Why would she do that?" Frank asked uneasily.

"Same reason she did it to you and Maggie," Benedict answered, reaching for his beer. "Because she likes to have the upper hand."

"She never tried to get between me and Maggie!" Frank objected, looking thunderstruck.

"Didn't she?" Benedict remarked, taking a swig of beer.

"No, she didn't!" Frank insisted. "It was—" He gazed down into his own drink. "Something else."

Jack frowned but said nothing, and they only stayed to finish the pitcher before bidding a rather subdued farewell and going their separate ways.

17

"What do you fancy for your supper?" Benedict asked her as they walked across the field in the direction of the campsite.

Lizzie considered a moment. "A baked potato," she answered. "You'll have to let me buy it this time," she said. "For I've had my wages. Or do I just give them straight to you?" she asked uncertainly. She had never received a pay packet before and was not precisely sure of the etiquette.

Benedict shook his head. "You hold on to it. I'm sure you've plenty of things you need to spend that on for yourself."

Lizzie looked up at him in surprise. "Such as?"

"I'm sure there's a hundred things," he replied with a shrug, towing her in the direction of a baked potato stall. It was a curious stand on four legs with a little spout at the top emitting steam. A fire bucket kept the large tin container which housed all the potatoes warm, and there were various compartments with little lids containing the butter, pepper, and salt.

Once they had bought two potatoes and had them wrapped in newspaper, Benedict bought a meat pie from another vendor and another bag of bones for Sebastian and they made their way back over the fields toward their wagon.

"Have your family always traveled the fairs?" Lizzie asked as he helped her down from the stile.

He was silent a moment before answering. "No. My great-great-grandfather was a tenant farmer. He had five sons. My great-grandfather was the youngest and ran away at thirteen to join a traveling fair. Eventually he owned his own jellied eel stall. His son, my grandfather, was the first boxer in the family."

"And your father carried on the tradition?"

"That's right, he and his brother, Ted."

"Where is your uncle now?"

"Dead," he answered briefly. "But he was the true talent of the two. My father was never more than passable and that was before he took to the drink."

"Oh." Lizzie, noticing his expression, thought she had better lighten the mood. "And what of your generation?" she asked. "I suspect it's you that possesses the true boxing talent out of you three brothers."

A reluctant smile twisted his lips. "Why do you suspect that?" he asked.

"Mostly because you seem to be the one carrying the performance on your shoulders. Frank does the announcing and Jack the betting book."

"They both take their turn in the ring when the need arises," he answered. "While I was in prison, they got by without me ably enough."

"I don't know about that," Lizzie mused, thinking of Jack's previous angry words. "I received the distinct impression things have not been easy for them without you." Benedict snorted. "Besides," she added in a lighter tone, "I benefitted from some expert commentary on your performance in the ring, so I know you are something quite special."

"What expert commentary?"

"There was a gentleman in a fancy waistcoat stood beside me when first I saw you fight. He was talking to his friend and I overheard him." She thought he checked his step, but then he seemed to recover himself. "It is a bit muddy, isn't it?"

262

"A bit." He paused before adding, "Tell me about this gentleman."

"He bet on you every time," Lizzie replied promptly. "Moreover, he told his companion that you would defeat every man in the tent."

"He had a fancy waistcoat?" Benedict asked in an odd tone.

"He did. It was a pattern of silver thread in the shape of little seashells in delicate blues and silvers."

It occurred to her that his expression was oddly intense. "What have I said?"

"Maybe nothing," he said slowly. "But maybe something."

"I don't understand."

"Boxing at fairgrounds was not always the full extent of my ambition, Lizzie." She waited for him to speak, and after a moment he continued. "I used to fight for real money before I went to prison. Prizefighting, I mean. Against other boxers. Real boxers."

"You do not anymore?" Lizzie asked when nothing else seemed forthcoming. "Does possessing a criminal record prohibit you from competing, then?"

He laughed at that. "No. If it did, there would be precious few contenders." He eyed her warily. "They're a checkered bunch, Lizzie, myself included."

"Why do you not prizefight anymore?" she persisted, refusing to be sidetracked.

He cleared his throat. "I fell out with the man who arranges most of the fights. Fell out with him badly. Said some things…

I was in an ugly mood that night. It was the same night I got arrested. He washed his hands of me. I'm finished now."

Lizzie caught her breath. Something in his voice made her feel oddly defensive of him. "He did not contact you once while you were in Exeter jail?"

Benedict gave a short laugh. "No," he said, shaking his head. "After the row we had, I never expect to hear from him ever again."

Lizzie hesitated. She wanted to ask why they had fought but had a shrewd notion any such enquiry would be firmly repulsed.

"I wanted a shot at the title," he said suddenly, surprising her. "Nat booked me for a lot of fights, good fights with high money stakes. But he never saw me as champion material, Lizzie. I never got to fight for the title. Not once. That rankled with me. It took root inside me, and over time, I couldn't see anything else he'd done for me. Only what he hadn't."

"You grew embittered," she murmured.

He gave a short nod. "Finally, it burst out of me, like poison from a wound. I burned my bridges that night in the worst possible way. I struck out at whoever crossed me and all but destroyed a fancy hotel barroom. That's how I wound up in prison for nine long months." He grew silent, and Lizzie felt herself abruptly sobered by their conversation. "That's the manner of man you married, Lizzie," he said in a low voice. "A man that bit the hand that fed him."

Lizzie looked at him. "Yet you regret it now," she replied thoughtfully. "And fully own you were the party at fault."

"Nine months is a long time to cool your heels. Only a complete fool would not see he was to blame for his own downfall in such a matter."

"Have you considered contacting this man at all since your release?" she asked tentatively.

"No." His abrupt answer held a note of closed finality. "That part of my life is over and done with now."

Lizzie frowned. Instead of climbing down and apologizing, he would simply write off a huge part of his life. His dream, even? She found such a thing hard to fathom. Especially when he knew himself to be the one who was in the wrong.

They had reached the wagon by now. "Sit down," he told her, drawing the packing cases up. "I'll soon have the fire going."

"You forget I have not done a stroke of work today," she pointed out. "Besides, it'll be quicker if we work together."

They had soon gathered up a pile of sticks, and Benedict started the fire before fetching water for Florence the horse and Sebastian. Then he made a second trip for their own water. Lizzie managed to set up the tripod and chain above the fire before his return, and he set the water on to boil as she fetched the blankets from the wagon, for the evening had turned chilly.

They were soon sat beside the blaze, bundled in blankets and eating their supper while the water boiled for a pot of tea. "I can see why the fairs do not run over the winter period," Lizzie observed. "For this kind of living must be a good deal harder then. Where do you live during the off season?"

Benedict threw another log on the fire. "Lodgings usually."

She badly wanted to ask what he had meant to do with Betsy while he was touring with the booth, but something held her back. "Do you usually lodge in London?" He nodded. "Your family too?"

"It depends. Ma has some family in Shropshire. Sometimes she'll head that way for a couple of months."

She wanted to ask what Benedict had meant when he claimed his family had not raised him, but again, some instinct bade her hold her tongue. Another thought occurred, so instead, she asked, "What *was* the possible significance you attached to the man in the fancy waistcoat?"

He swallowed his last mouthful and scrunched up the newspaper. "It occurred to me it could have been Nat Jones," he admitted.

"Nat Jones?"

"The fight promoter I told you of. The one I fell out with. He's known for his flamboyant dress, particularly his waistcoats."

"Oh, I see." Lizzie pondered this a moment. "If it was him—" she began.

"It probably wasn't." His tone was dampening, but still Lizzie persisted.

"But only suppose for a minute that it was. Would that not mean that he was considering giving you another chance?"

He was silent a moment. "I don't see why he would. In my experience, it's best not to get your hopes up about such things. That way lies disappointment." She could see what he meant, of course. Biting her lip, Lizzie resolved not to press him, so when he did speak, it took her by surprise. "Besides," he added, "he might have come to see Jack box." He touched the graze that had formed on his cheekbone. "I never gave him enough credit before now."

"Jack's as good as you?" Lizzie asked.

"He could be, if he trained hard enough, with the right person."

"Your uncle trained you?" Lizzie guessed shrewdly. "Your uncle Ted?" He nodded. "Could *you* train Jack?"

Benedict shrugged. "Maybe."

Picking up on his reluctance to further discuss his family, Lizzie let the matter drop. The trouble was, if they did not discuss his family, she was a little apprehensive about what topics that *did* leave on the table.

Recalling some of the things she had come out with the previous evening left her feeling rather foolish. Her ears felt hot when she thought about her tipsy ramblings about what men liked. She was fairly certain she had mentioned Ada Wurtzel's bottom at one point. As she drank her tea, Sebastian leaned heavily against her side, and Lizzie wound an absent arm around his furry neck.

"I hope Sebastian will come into the wagon on the journey tomorrow for he certainly cannot run alongside us the whole way," she commented aloud.

"He seems intelligent enough and won't want to be left behind," Benedict said, casting the dregs from his cup aside.

Lizzie nodded. "Perhaps if he won't go inside, he will sit up on the step beside us."

Benedict nodded. "We've an early start in the morning so…" His words trailed off.

Lizzie nodded and helped clear away before adding another blanket to Sebastian's nest beneath the wagon. The dog accompanied her to the field opposite and then settled in his blankets with another bone.

Lizzie washed, donned her nightgown, and brushed her hair before Benedict joined her. Her thoughts kept returning again

267

and again to his astonishing words in the beer tent. *There's nothing you could say that could turn me against her, so don't even try.* Could he truly have meant that? She bit her lip as she climbed between the cold covers and curled herself into a ball. After all, he had not been in bed when he said it. He said you could not set store by any words a man said when he was in your bed, but out of it, presumably you could.

Behind her she could hear Benedict washing in the basin. His words had left her almost breathless especially after the way her own family had turned on her so swiftly, but perhaps again, she was seeing too much in what he'd said.

After all, it was plain to see his relationship with his grandmother was a poor one. Maybe he had simply meant there was nothing Ma Toomes could say that would set him against her because he disliked the old woman so much and did not trust her?

She hugged her knees and thought that this was distinctly probable. Benedict blew out the lamp and climbed into the bed beside her, and Lizzie breathed out as he crowded around her shivering body.

"You've given too many blankets to the dog," he murmured, pulling her firmly into his arms.

"No, I haven't," Lizzie disagreed at once. "For he does not have anyone to curl up with as we do."

He grunted, resting his chin against the top of her head. "Did you really think I'd left you behind earlier?" he asked after a moment of silence.

Lizzie paused, then realized what he was alluding to. "Just for a minute," she admitted.

"I wouldn't do that." When she did not reply, he jolted her in his arms. "Lizzie?"

"What?"

"Tell me you believe me."

"You told me not to though," she reminded him.

"What?"

"You told me I could not believe a word a man said to me when he was in bed with me."

A stunned silence greeted these words, then to her surprise, he released her and sat up in the bed.

"Benedict?" Moments later, she heard a match strike and the lamp was relit. Lizzie rolled onto her back and blinked up at him. "What are you doing?" she asked in bewilderment.

He turned back to her, his expression frustrated. "Lizzie, we need to talk."

Lizzie drew the blankets up to her chin and regarded him doubtfully. "Are you going to get out of bed, then?" she asked. There wasn't much room for him to sit anywhere else except on one of the two fixed trunks.

He scrubbed his face with his hand. "When I said that, I did not mean that precisely," he started. "I meant simply that when a man is trying to get you into his bed, his words can't be trusted."

Lizzie regarded him blankly. "No one ever tried that with me," she pointed out flatly. "And besides," she added, giving him a frank look, "I don't think that *was* what you meant."

He narrowed his eyes at her. "Why?" he asked in steely tones.

"Because, you weren't trying to get me into bed at that point. It was very first thing in the morning." When he continued to glare at her confrontationally, Lizzie added, "I said I had been thinking over what you said to me and *you*—"

He flung his hand up for silence and looked away. If she did not know any better, Lizzie would think he was blushing. He breathed out noisily. "Very well," he bit out. "You have me there. I was embarrassed, so I said the first thing that sprang to mind to discredit what I'd previously said."

He'd been embarrassed? Lizzie clutched the blankets and gazed at him in bewilderment. "I don't think I quite follow you," she admitted. Benedict was practically grinding his teeth by now, she noticed with misgiving.

"I was embarrassed," he repeated doggedly. "Because I'd said, nay, I'd asked some things of you that I ought not have." His gaze swerved away from hers, and Lizzie realized he was still abashed by the memory. She cast her mind back to the previous night. *Tell me that you wanted me all along.* That was what he'd said. Her frown cleared. That was what he was so ashamed of?

"Oh," she said. "Well, we need never mention it again if you feel so badly about it."

He looked conflicted to say the least. "Tell me what you were going to say this morning," he said, folding his arms and bracing himself as though for the worst.

She was quiet a moment, bringing the speech she would have made to mind. "I—well, I was going to explain that it never even occurred to me in those days. To view you as a man, I mean." She shook her head, dissatisfied with her choice of words. "What I mean is," she tried again, "I did not consider men as anything to do with me. I was twenty-five years old and devoted to a life of charity and good works at my aunt's side. I thought that Reverend Milson—"

"Lizzie," he interrupted in a warning voice. "Watch your step." Lizzie gazed at him in confusion. What had she said? "Never mind. Continue," he said through gritted teeth.

"I didn't know, I just didn't know how things could be between a man and a woman," she admitted. "But if I had known—" She bit her lip and hesitated.

"Go on," he said gruffly.

The tips of Lizzie's ears burned at the confession she was about to make. "Then I would have wanted what I knew I couldn't have." She paused. "I would have wanted you."

"Lizzie," he groaned and covered his eyes with his hand. Lizzie gazed at him with misgiving. Had her words not pleased him, then? "Do you mean to say, I could have had those words this morning? If I had not—" He broke off. "If I had not been such a damned coward."

Lizzie continued to feel bemused. "How were you cowardly?" she wondered aloud.

"Say it again," he demanded, reaching for her and dragging her against him, his hands roaming up and down her back and sides. "You're covered in gooseflesh," he murmured distractedly. "I need to get you warm."

"I would have wanted you," she mumbled against his shoulder. "If I had known who you truly were. If I had known you were like this."

He shivered, seemingly more from her words than the decided nip in the air. "Let me take care of you," he said, wrapping his arms around her. "God," he groaned. "My day would have been so very different if I had only let you speak this morning."

Lizzie blinked against his neck. "How would it?" she asked.

"Well, for one thing, I would not have snapped and snarled like a cur at everyone who crossed my path." She still didn't quite understand but looped her arms about his waist in any case. "And I probably wouldn't have dragged Jack in the ring for another."

"But it sounds as though that turned out to be a good thing," she reminded him. "For you realized your brother's improvement, did you not?"

He brushed this off with a rumbling sound. "Let's not have any more misunderstandings of that sort between us again," he said firmly. "We'll make sure we clear the air at the outset in future." Lizzie nodded and he tipped her face up, looking down at her intently. "Tell me truly," he said gruffly. "Are you upset that your aunt will discover we're married?"

Lizzie blinked. "You mean from Annie?" Seeing his expression, she realized it must have been preying on his mind a good deal more than it had her own. "I own that I was a little discomforted at first," she admitted slowly. "But in truth, I thought you would be more upset by it than I."

"Me?" He sounded stunned at the very idea. "Why should I?"

"Betsy," she pointed out quietly, attempting to disentangle herself. He would have none of it, however, and clasped her all the tighter to him.

"Maybe we should talk about Betsy," he suggested in a low voice.

Now it was Lizzie who felt a momentary panic, but it would be pointless to try to stop her ears. Instead, she swallowed and renewed the pressure of her hands against his chest. With some reluctance, he released her, and she shuffled back on the mattress, putting some distance between them.

He watched her retreat without comment. "What do you want to know?" he asked. His expression was open and unguarded, and Lizzie felt suddenly emboldened.

Still, the words that tumbled out of her mouth astonished even her. "Did you kiss Betsy as you kiss me?" Her face immediately grew hot as she waited for his reply.

"Never," he replied. "I treated her with the utmost respect at all times."

"What does that mean?"

"I never stuck my tongue in her mouth."

Lizzie's face was bright red now. "Oh," she said. "I see." Was the way he kissed her not respectable, then? Partly to cover her confusion, and partly out of genuine curiosity, she blurted, "Why did you tell me to watch my step earlier?" she asked. "When I mentioned Reverend Milson."

"Because I'm jealous," he ground out. "I don't like that you admired Milson, even if it was like a frustrated spinster."

Her brows flew together at that. "I was not a frustrated spinster!"

Her denial seemed to amuse him, for a smile tugged at his lips. "Oh yes, you were," he disagreed lightly. "Otherwise, you would not have come so prettily and so often on that night I took your virginity."

"I don't know what you mean!"

"Most virgins don't enjoy it, Lizzie. But you did."

"Benedict!"

He laughed at her indignant tone, reaching out and catching her up to him. At the first contact between them, he let out a sigh of relief. "I'm a fool," he groaned as he took her lips beneath his own. "We've an early start tomorrow," he said regretfully. Then, as though he could not help himself. "Tell me again."

Lizzie hesitated. "Will you turn out the lamp?"

"I will once you say it," he responded, his gaze snaring hers. She caught her breath at his words.

"I would have wanted you, if I had known it would be like this, Benedict Toomes."

The smile he flashed her was reward enough. He kissed her again lingeringly and turned out the lamp.

18

The next morning, Benedict woke feeling surprisingly light in spirit. Considering he had fallen asleep half-hard and lying next to the object of his desire, this was nothing short of a miracle. He disentangled himself from Lizzie's sleeping form and set about the morning preparations. The field was a lot sparser with many carts and wagons having moved on already to their next venue.

Some, though not all, would be headed to the much smaller fair at Putney Heath that was their own destination. Sebastian lifted his head and watched Benedict go about his familiar routine. It was only when the water was bubbling over the fire that the animal deigned to rise from his blankets and join him next to it. Even then, Benedict did not fancy it was to seek his company, but rather because Lizzie's dog thought it was time he had his first bone.

He had just obliged by fetching him one when he found himself hailed by his older brother. Frank was disheveled and unshaven as he hurried across the field toward him. Sebastian looked from one of them to the other with his great jaws clamped around the bone. For a moment, he hovered undecided but then skulked under the wagon with his prize.

"Ben, you'll have to come," Frank said. "You'll never guess who's here and wanting to speak to you."

Benedict's heart plummeted to his boots. "Not the old man?" he asked with an abrupt reversal of mood.

"What? Lord no!" His brother clapped him on the shoulder. "It's Nat."

"Nat?" Benedict was startled. Whatever he had expected his brother to come out with, it was not that. "Nat Jones?"

"Who else?"

"What does he want with me?"

Frank tugged at the open neck of his shirt. "Ben, it's an olive branch he's offering. Nothing more, nothing less. We told him, Jack and I, that things have changed with you. You're married and settled down now; things are steadier."

Benedict eyed his brother shrewdly. Frank was nervous and clearly apprehensive. "Tell me what he wants," he said, crossing his arms.

"I won't lie, Ben. It's a minor fight he's offering you, way down the bill and not the purse you're used to either." Frank swallowed and drew another breath. "We all know you deserve better, but—"

"I'll do it."

"You will?" The relief in Frank's bloodshot eyes was palpable. "Good for you, brother," he said warmly, clapping him on the back. "Good for you."

"Where is it?"

"Not far from here, at some farmer's barn in Surrey."

"When?"

"Tonight."

That brought Benedict up short. He cast a wry look at his brother. Clearly, Nat was looking for a last-minute fill-in. Someone billed must have fallen through. Frank assiduously avoided his eye. "You and Jack fighting?" Benedict asked after a moment, letting him off the hook. After all, what was the point in making Frank squirm?

"Jack is." Frank rubbed his nose. "I'm not fit to get in the ring, and we both know it."

Well, here was plain-speaking and no mistake. Benedict eyed his brother warily. "You going to do anything about that?" he asked after a moment's pause.

Frank cleared his throat. "I reckon I'd better." Ben nodded. "You coming, then? We shouldn't keep him waiting any longer."

"I'll just go and have a word with Lizzie. She's still asleep."

As though on cue, the door opened and Lizzie peered out, her hair loose and a shawl wrapped about her shoulders. She gave a start on seeing Frank and drew back hastily inside as though she was naked or something.

Benedict shook his head and approached the door, knocking on it lightly. "I've hot water here for you to dress," he said. "I'll hand it up, but I've just got to go back with Frank to their wagon for ten minutes." She nodded. "Come here." Lizzie approached the door. "Give me a kiss."

"Benedict," she murmured in reproach, her eyes flying over his head to see his brother was no doubt within eyesight. Yet still she leaned down to oblige. He reached up and caught the back of her neck, holding her face to his for a fraction longer than was really necessary.

"I won't be long." She looked flustered but accepted the bucket of hot water with thanks, gave him and Frank a wave, and retreated inside to dress. "Watch over her," he bade the dog as he and Frank took off over the field, though in truth the animal did not need telling. It occurred to him that it was a good thing

277

Lizzie had acquired Sebastian, or he would not be so easy in his mind leaving her unattended as he often had to.

They soon reached the Toomes family wagons. This field, too, had emptied. Benedict could see Nat Jones's yellow tailcoat from the other side of the field. He was stood conversing with Jack, and though he looked up with an easy smile as they approached, Benedict could see the guardedness in his expression as he extended his hand to him.

"Ben."

"Nat."

"Frank filled you in?" Nat asked, sending a quick look in Frank's direction.

"He has," Benedict agreed. "I'm willing."

He saw the flash of surprise in Nat's face before he concealed it. "It's an early bout; I won't deceive you," he warned. "To warm up the crowd."

"Frank said." Benedict cleared his throat. "I'm grateful you thought of me," he said, and though his voice sounded a little gruff, it was steady at least. "In light of how we parted ways."

Again, he thought Nat looked startled. Clearly, he had not expected him to allude to the previous bad blood between them. "Not at all," he said politely. "You always delivered in the ring," he said. The inference was clear that it was outside of it that Benedict's behavior was a problem.

"Capital! That's decided, then," Jack said a little too heartily. His two brothers did their best to get him through the next five minutes which was mostly an exchange of conversation about boxers Benedict had not kept in contact with.

"Ben saw Dabney recently, ain't that right, Ben?" Jack jockeyed him along.

"That's right."

"When was that?" Nat asked with interest.

"Late February. He was looking at investment opportunities."

"Theaters, Ben said," Jack chimed in. "Can you imagine old Clem owning a theater?"

Nat laughed. "I wouldn't put anything past him, in truth."

It wasn't until their farewells that Nat brought up the match again that night. "Johnston's green," he said briefly. "I'd appreciate it if you'd let him put in an honorable showing. I've known his father all my life."

Ben nodded, though he had no intention of carrying anyone through a fight. He guessed Nat's original intent had been for Frank to fight this Johnston, but his brother had let him down by not being match fit. Nat must have really been in a corner, Benedict reflected as he watched the fight promoter walk away, to give him a second chance.

The only hiccup in proceedings had been afterward when Frank had assumed Ben would let Lizzie travel with him instead to Putney Heath. "You and Jack can take your wagon into Surrey, and I'll have Lizzie up beside me and set up the booth at Putney." This had earned a flat no from Benedict.

Frank had frowned. "You can surely trust me with your wife, Ben," he had said in an injured tone. "I can sleep outside or find another bunk for the night."

"It's not you, but the old woman," Benedict had answered curtly. "I don't trust you to hold her off. Not when—" He broke off.

"When I couldn't guard my own wife against her?" Frank asked tightly.

Benedict looked away. He could not deny that *was* what was on his mind. "I'll not have Lizzie browbeat or used as a skivvy," he said instead. "And I won't have that Daphne round her either."

"Hold hard," Jack interceded, stepping forward. "There's another way around this without us all falling out. How about if I took *our* cart to Surrey and Ben comes in with me? Frank, you could drive Lizzie and her wagon and set up her camp at Putney separate from Ma and Daphne, same as we did here. Then Frank can bunk in with one of the Farini brothers overnight till we get back. They're off to Putney, and I bet Tony and Pietro would oblige alright."

Frank glanced at Benedict while he considered this. "I'm willing, though it seems strange to leave her camped on her own without protection."

"She's got that dog," Jack pointed out. "It'd rip anyone's throat out that crossed her."

"I'd have to speak to her first," Benedict said after a moment, and he saw his brothers exchange speaking glances. He didn't really give a damn if they thought him overprotective. He wouldn't put Lizzie in another man's wagon overnight if he could help it, or at the mercy of a vicious pair of harpies. "I'm heading back."

Frank nodded. "We're finishing packing up anyway, so let us know what you decide."

When he got back, Lizzie was up and dressed and sat drinking tea with Sebastian's head resting on her knee. "There's tea in the pot," she said cheerfully. "I'll pour you a cup."

He sat on the crate next to hers. "Something's come up," he announced abruptly and then clammed up. Only when she had passed his drink to him did he continue. "It's strange when you consider we were only talking about this yesterday," he said with a frown.

Lizzie drew her cloak closer about her. "Oh?" she said encouragingly. She hadn't put her bonnet on yet, so she sat bare-headed, her fair hair neatly coiled and pinned. He preferred it loose, but it still looked well.

"It's a fight," he added.

Her eyes leaped to his. "Really?" He nodded. "So then, that's a good thing?" she asked, scanning his face uncertainly. Benedict nodded. "Yet, you look as though you have reservations," she said slowly.

"It's tonight, in Surrey."

Lizzie tipped her head to one side. "That is not so far. Will it interfere with our plans for the fair at Putney Heath?"

He had a strange reaction to the way she said "our plans," like a warmth spreading through his chest. "It would mean you having to go on ahead with Frank," he explained. "Jack and I would join you there tomorrow."

She nodded. "That does not sound so very disruptive," she ventured, earning his swift frown. "Does it?"

"I don't like the thought of you spending the night without me."

"Oh." She glanced down at the dog sat beside her. "I have Sebastian, and you said your brother Frank would accompany me."

Benedict nodded. "He'd drive the wagon and set up camp for you."

"Then what is your objection?" she asked calmly.

What was his objection? "You're not used to this life," he pointed out. "You're still adjusting."

"Yes," she agreed. "But it's only one night, and this is important, isn't it?"

"The fight? Not really. I'm just a last-minute stand-in. Nat wanted Frank, but he's not up to it."

Lizzie gave him a very direct look. "But that's not the issue, is it? It's this waistcoated person giving you another chance."

Benedict's gaze dropped from hers. She had seen right to the heart of the matter. "Even if I do make a good showing, there's no guarantee he'd book me again," he said gruffly.

"There are very few guarantees in this life," she answered promptly. "Besides, this is more an opportunity for you to vindicate yourself than anything else. After what happened last time, I mean." Benedict said nothing. "Did you tell him you would do it?"

"I did."

"It's settled, then."

"I could change my mind."

"But I don't think you should," she urged. "I'm sure you're doing the right thing. Even if it leads to nothing, this is a way for you to be easy in your own mind over what happened and—"

Benedict caught her arm and tugged her off her own crate and into his lap. "I know," he agreed, closing his arms tight about her. "But I still don't like leaving you all the same."

282

"I'll be fine," she reassured him. "And waiting for you at Putney." He nodded and Lizzie bit her lip.

"What is it?" he asked.

"Nothing," she said hurriedly, but he saw the color that rushed to her cheeks.

"Tell me."

She reached up and lightly rested her hands on his shoulders. "If I was not so…prim and proper, would you ever take me to watch you fight?"

Striving to ignore the powerful effect her unprompted touch had on him, he drew in a sharp breath. "You dislike the boxing tent," he reminded her.

"Yes, but you said this was different."

He winced. "It's a good deal rougher, if anything. This fight's in some barn and likely unlicensed."

"You mean it is an illegal gathering?" Lizzie asked, drawing back.

"It's in the middle of nowhere," he explained. "I doubt there will be any trouble with officials." When she continued to look alarmed, he added, "They only trouble with things like permits for the official fights. It's a bigger purse involved for the fighters when they've paid less overheads."

"I see," she replied, though she still looked unconvinced.

To lighten the mood, he murmured, "Besides, you're not prim and proper where it counts, Lizzie mine." At her uncomprehending look, he added, "In my bed."

"Benedict!"

283

He laughed and pulled her forward to kiss her soundly. "If I win, I'll buy you a new ring," he muttered as he drew back.

"A new ring?"

He caught her wrist and held her left hand up. "Aye, a gold one this time," he said, eyeing the brass ring with disfavor.

"I would rather we had curtains," Lizzie replied, glancing at the wagon.

"Curtains?"

She nodded. "For the little windows."

"If you want curtains, then we'll get curtains."

"I could sew them, if—"

At this point, a piercing whistle interrupted them. They both turned and saw his brothers approaching. Lizzie made as though to stand, but Benedict's clasp of her waist prevented it. He turned on the crate to face them, his grip firm about her.

"What have you decided?" Frank asked as they drew close.

"I'll take you up on your offer," Benedict answered. "You accompany Lizzie and see her settled at Putney, and I'll go with Jack."

Jack visibly brightened, rubbing his hands, and Frank looked relieved.

"That's settled, then," said Lizzie. "Shall I make another pot of tea?"

19

Lizzie's biggest worry about the journey was how to get
Sebastian up into the wagon. However, when he realized that it
was Frank and not Benedict who would be sat up beside her, the
dog was quick to force his way between them.

"I think you should point out I'm your brother-in-law," Frank
joked as Sebastian gave him a dark look. "I think his sense of
propriety is offended."

Lizzie was so relieved to get the animal up on the footboard that
she laughed at this witticism, and Frank looked gratified.
Hearing the sound of an approaching cart, he turned in his seat
and glanced behind them.

"It's Ma and Daphne. They'll follow along behind us."

Lizzie braced her feet against the struts as Benedict had taught
her and wrapped an arm about Sebastian's neck.

"You ready for the off?" Frank asked, and at her nod, he flicked
his rein and gave Florence encouragement. The large horse
obligingly began to move forward.

"How far is it from here to Putney Heath?" Lizzie asked as they
meandered their way across the field toward the cart track.

"Some twelve miles or thereabouts."

"And how long do you suppose that will take us?"

Frank gave her a rueful glance. "A good part of the day, I'm
afraid. It's slow going with the wagons."

"At least it's not raining," Lizzie said, glancing up at the sky
which was gray and full of clouds.

"Not yet anyway," Frank agreed.

Just then, they went over a bump in the ground which jolted Lizzie. She gripped the edge of the seat tighter and caught her breath.

"Sorry about that." Frank winced. "It'll be easier when we're on even road."

Lizzie assured him that she would not be dislodged from her perch, and once they were on the open road, they were able to converse more easily.

"How did you like Greenwich Fair?" Frank asked her, his eyes still on the road.

Lizzie considered the question a moment before answering. "I think it's an interesting life you lead," she said slowly. "With never a dull moment."

"It's your life too now," Frank pointed out.

"Yes," she agreed.

He flashed her a curious look. "Did you never think to dissuade Ben from this life? From what he's said, his savings are still intact, and it's clear you hold great sway over him." Lizzie hesitated, unable to explain that in fact she was never in a position to influence Benedict's way of life.

"I don't say that you counselled him against seeing us on his release," he said quickly. "I'm not so foolish as to set that blame at your door." From the way he said this, Lizzie could tell that someone *did* in fact blame her for the fact Benedict had stayed away from his family. She guessed Frank was thinking of Ma Toomes.

"I know full well that he's always been…conflicted about his family, shall we say," Frank continued, unaware of her ruminations.

Questions burned on Lizzie's tongue. *Why should Benedict be conflicted?* Indeed, why was it that he did not feel so bound by family obligations as his brothers clearly did?

"It's not my place to challenge how my husband makes a living," Lizzie said after a moment's pause. "Or to try and break any existing familial bonds."

"Or lack of them," Frank said grimly.

Lizzie shot him a look. "I think he is close to you and Jack though," she said carefully.

"Aye, it's our father and grandmother he cannot tolerate," Frank answered tightly before directing a troubled look her way. "Forgive me, I should not have said anything," he sighed. "It wasn't fair of me, and if Ben knew I'd said anything, he'd have my guts for garters. God knows, I have my own things I prefer not to discuss."

"You mean your wife's disappearance," Lizzie guessed, then wondered if she ought not to have.

Frank grimaced. "There's no mystery about it. She ran off and left me." Lizzie sat in silence, respecting that the topic was off-limits, when to her surprise, he carried on. "I never would have dreamed that old Ben would make a more considerate husband than I." His voice shook slightly, but any anger he felt seemed to be directed toward himself. "He's been careful with you. In a way that I…was not."

"Careful?"

"Considerate," Frank explained. "It didn't even occur to me to shield Maggie from Ma and our father. Looking back, I threw her in at the deep end and left her there to flounder." He swallowed. "I suppose I thought that was her role. To put up with them, I mean. As I do."

Lizzie was silent a moment before asking, "Did you never try to discover her? It's clear you miss her badly."

Frank breathed out loudly. "It's too late," he said with a wealth of bitterness. "Far too late to turn back the clock."

"Why do you say so?" When he would not answer, only shake his head, Lizzie said boldly, "I do not think Benedict would sit back so resigned, if I were to attempt such a thing."

Frank gave a short laugh. "You would not get further than five miles before he dragged you back again."

"Yet you cared for Maggie," she persisted. "Why is it so different with you?"

"Benedict would not come after you if you had done what Maggie did, I assure you."

Lizzie felt stung and almost argued back that Benedict would come for her whatever she had done. Then she considered his words, for something about them sounded strangely inconsistent. "Everything I have heard about Maggie said she was hardworking and downtrodden. What is it you imagine she has done which is so unforgiveable?"

Frank had stiffened. "Who's been talking to you about my Maggie?" he demanded hotly, before coloring and looking away. "Nay, that's not right," he muttered. "For she's not mine. Not anymore." When he looked at her again, his expression was shuttered and closed. "She cheated on me with another man and then ran off with him, that's what. I may not have been the perfect husband, but few men would tolerate such a betrayal, including Ben. Such a thing cuts deep with a man."

She could not say why, but something did not ring altogether true to Lizzie. She might have had a narrow upbringing, but there was plenty of gossip and speculation among her aunt's acquaintance and the flock of St. Joseph's. Such was the nature of gossip, that if Maggie *had* played her husband false and run off with another man, it seemed to Lizzie that Niamh or Connie, both forthright women, would have said as much to her. Instead, they had merely talked of Maggie being worn out and lacking the gumption to stand up to her husband's family. These facts were not half as juicy a tidbit to impart as infidelity.

Of course, she reflected, it might just be that neither woman knew the full truth of the matter. She did not really know enough to comment, and so Lizzie lapsed again into silence and drew up her hood when it started to drizzle with rain. With some wriggling, she managed to free up enough of her cloak to wrap it around Sebastian's shoulders and envelop him beneath the voluminous black cloak with her.

Once again, she remembered that she had not yet returned the garment to Ma Toomes and suffered a pang of remorse. She really must speak to the old woman presently, however disagreeable the task may be. Sebastian suffered her close embrace, and after a while, she began to feel grateful for the warmth of his body seeping into hers beneath the cold April sky. The only moment of alarm the journey gave her was when a cart passed carrying several sheep. Sebastian trembled with excitement and seemed to gird himself up to spring from his seat after them.

"No, Sebastian!" Lizzie told him and seized him even tighter. As soon as the cart was out of sight, he subsided against her once more, yawning ostentatiously as though such a thought had never occurred to him. "I'm not fooled," she told him darkly. "I know you considered abandoning your post, you wicked creature."

Frank gave a chuckle, his former mood seemingly passed. "You let him alone," he said comfortably. "We can none of us go against our natures, more's the pity."

Lizzie was not so sure about that. Was not every Christian tenet to revolt against the base nature of man, with its impulses toward greed, revenge, and selfishness? She brooded on this a moment before Sebastian rested his head against her shoulder. Reaching up, Lizzie stroked his muzzle to show all was forgiven.

They reached Putney Heath before nightfall, and once they had found a spot Frank approved of, he sprang down and shared some words with the wagon behind them containing Daphne and Ma Toomes. Though she could hear Ma's cracked voice upraised with indignation, Lizzie could not make out the words and did not trouble herself overmuch. She felt tired and wanted to stretch her limbs but could not do so until Frank unhitched the wagon. To her surprise, on his return, he leaped back up into the driving seat and set Florence in motion once again.

"Are we not stopping here?"

He cast her an apologetic look. "Ben was quite specific. Your pitch is to be separate from ours."

Enlightenment dawned. "Oh," she said. No doubt that was what the old woman was being so scathing about. "I hope Ma did not give you too much grief," she said shrewdly. "No doubt she thinks I believe myself too good to set up camp next to her."

Frank flushed and she knew she had hit the mark. "Don't worry," he replied awkwardly. "I told her it was Ben's

290

instruction, not yours. She wouldn't dream of trying to bend his ear like she does mine."

It was not long before he had tethered Florence and stabilized their wagon in a spot about a five-minute walk from the Toomeses. As Lizzie checked on any items that might have been dislodged inside, Frank grabbed the pails and went off in search of water for her. There was not much to set to rights for their possessions were so meager that most had fitted inside the two trunks that were fixed to the floor.

As Sebastian sniffed all around their new spot, Lizzie scoured about for branches for the fire and had made quite a pile by the time Frank had returned carrying the water. He soon had the fire lit and the water on to heat.

"What will you do for supper?" Frank asked. "I could fetch you some of our stew."

Lizzie paused in the act of throwing the last of her twigs into the flames. "Oh no, thank you," she said hastily, thinking of Daphne's likely reaction to her partaking of their food after snubbing their company. "There's half a loaf inside I can toast with some butter and jam."

"Well, so long as you're sure." He hesitated. "It doesn't seem right leaving you alone like this."

"I have Sebastian," she said as the large dog ambled over at the suggestion of his name. "Where will you sleep tonight? Have you made arrangements?" She thought he would find it a tight squeeze in with two women.

"I have, don't worry about me. Tony Farini said I could bunk in with him."

"The Farini Family Acrobats?" Lizzie said, remembering their tent from Greenwich.

"That's right."

"Well, thank you for all your help today, Frank," she said, and, after a moment, offered him her hand.

Frank took it with a rueful smile and shook it. "I'm sorry if I came across a bit brusque," he started as Lizzie simultaneously came out with, "I'm sorry if I said anything I ought not."

They both laughed.

"No, of course not," he said.

"Not at all," Lizzie responded.

"You know where we are if you *should* need anything."

Lizzie nodded. "What time do you suppose we can expect Benedict and Jack back tomorrow?"

"I can't imagine they would get here much later than midday," Frank answered. "I'll be sure and fetch you some water in the morning."

Lizzie nodded. "That would be very good of you."

She ate her solitary tea by the campfire with Sebastian gnawing on his bone at her feet. When it came time to turn in, she was disappointed to find she still could not coax the dog to accompany her inside. It seemed the step was as far as he would go. Instead, she arranged Sebastian's blankets for him and bade him good night before climbing into the wagon.

Wrapping the sheets around herself, Lizzie opened her bible and read awhile, seeking comfort from the good book as had always been her habit. She had been too busy eking out her new life to really miss St. Joseph's, but she was determined that her faith would remain constant, even if regular church attendance was no longer guaranteed.

After extinguishing the lamp, she lay awake a good deal longer than she thought she would after such a tiring day being jolted around on the road. She would have to do some laundry soon, she thought, for she had run out of clean underwear and the skirts of her navy dress were muddied. The thought of attempting laundry without the aid of a heated copper was a daunting one, but it would have to be faced, nonetheless.

At least she would not be expected to launder for the entire family as it seemed likely poor Maggie had been. Frank seemed nice enough, but she did not envy his wife's drudgery. Really, who could blame Maggie for running away under such circumstances?

Resolving to ask Niamh about it on the morrow, she rolled onto her side and dragged the blankets up and over her shoulder. It was a little after ten o'clock. She had no idea if Benedict would yet have fought in his match. She was sure he would win; she just hoped he managed to be gracious about it and rebuild some bridges with his former acquaintance. Deep down, she knew this was important to him, however much he claimed it was all over and done with.

She could not help a twinge of misgiving when she remembered the event was unsanctioned by the law. If there were to be some trouble, would her husband not suffer harsher consequences due to his being so recently released from prison? It was a disquieting reflection. What would happen to her if Benedict was clapped in irons again? She had no family of her own to support her, and Benedict had deliberately kept her apart from his.

She rolled onto her back and lay there a moment, filled with uneasy thoughts and fears. Strange, she thought suddenly, she could not remember doing this since she had left Mrs. Napp's. This past week at Greenwich, she had not lain awake once weighed down with worries. Even at Sitwell Place, Lizzie had been a worrier, often lying sleepless well into the early hours. Somehow, lying tucked into Benedict Toomes's side was not conducive to nameless dread.

Closing her eyes, Lizzie allowed herself, just for a minute, to remember how he had sat her in his lap and told her he would buy her a new wedding ring, a gold one this time. Without opening her eyelids, she felt for the brass ring on her third finger and turned it about like a talisman or good luck charm. *Let him come safely home to me*, she wished in silence.

Then she gasped, her eyes springing open. *Home.* Did she think of this small space on wheels as her home now? She gazed about her at the shadowy interior. There was next to nothing to it. Two trunks and a bed, that was all. The contents of the trunk were clothing and a few basic household essentials only. And yet…what there was felt homely in a way that Sitwell Place, for all its attendant comforts, never had, not to her.

At the end of the day, it had been the house of her aunt and uncle. She had been there under sufferance. No, she thought, rolling onto her other side. That wasn't fair. They had been gracious about doing their duty by their niece. When all was said and done, perhaps she had been as much a charity case as the Napps. The thought surprisingly did not make her feel any worse. Had she already known this all along, she wondered, on some unspoken level?

She had at one point, lying on the floor in Mrs. Napp's overcrowded bedroom, wondered if her aunt and uncle would have thrown out their own child if it had been Betsy who had seen Reverend Milson help himself to that brooch instead of her. She considered it again now impassively and fancied she knew the answer only too well.

Squeezing her eyes shut, she told herself it was pointless raking over this old ground. She had been disowned and was nothing to them now. She had a new family, and by that she did not mean the Toomes family as such.

She had Benedict, that much was true, but she also had Sebastian and new friends like Niamh and the twins. Her brothers-in-law, too, she felt instinctively would become closer to her over time, for even if Benedict was not aware of their import to him, it was clear the Toomes brothers were close in their own fashion.

Lizzie knew she was not the type of person to draw others to her with natural warmth or an engaging manner, but against all the odds, she did think she had found a new place to belong. Strangely enough, it was at Benedict Toomes's side. When she finally fell asleep, she did so hugging her pillow tight and thinking of her husband.

She woke early the next morning, but even so, she had scarcely dressed and relieved herself in the adjacent field when Frank turned up to collect their buckets for water. Lizzie handed them over and set about gathering firewood. When she had a decent pile, she selected the last of the meat bones from Sebastian's store and then set up the cast iron rigging to go over the fire with the chain and hook for the kettle.

She was fetching the box of matches from inside the wagon when Frank returned.

"Let me do that for you," he offered and soon had the fire lit and water on to boil.

"It does not look terribly busy," Lizzie commented, gazing three fields away where a very few tents stood fluttering in the breeze.

"There will be more going up. We haven't set up our booth yet." At Lizzie's surprised look, he explained, "It doesn't get started till midday here, except for on Wednesday."

"Really? Oh." For a moment, she wondered what she was going to do with herself for the next few hours. Then she remembered her resolve the night before. "I'll dedicate the morning to a wash day then, I think."

Frank offered to fetch her more water, and she accepted his offer gratefully. After checking on Florence and feeding her from a bag of oats and corn that Benedict kept in the wagon, Lizzie set about collecting up the laundry that needed doing. When she had a substantial pile, she delved back into the trunk for the bar of lye soap she had seen in there before going back outside to tackle the laundry.

It was hard going, and it was when she was elbow deep in suds, her skirts tied about her calves, that she had her first visitor. Ma Toomes came strolling about the corner of the wagon with a pipe sticking out the corner of her mouth.

"So you ain't so fancy you can't turn your hand to a bit of scrubbing when the occasion calls for it, I see," she said with a disparaging glance at the nearby thornbush over which Lizzie had draped her first lot of clean washing.

"Good morning to you," Lizzie responded after a moment, straightening up. Sebastian bounced up from his seated position to give a loud bark.

Ma Toomes eyed him warily. "That dog of yours needs tellin', unfriendly varmint." Her pipe waggled as she spoke.

"He's just doing his job," Lizzie replied, shushing Sebastian. He made a loud rumbling in his throat as he sat back down on his haunches, letting them know he was close at hand.

"I'll take a drop of tea if you've not got anything stronger," the old woman said, dropping down onto a convenient tree branch. Lizzie eyed Ma Toomes's disreputable appearance with resignation as she stretched her legs out next to the fire, showing her hobnail boots and gray woolen stockings.

Rinsing the soap from her wrists and arms, for it was harsh stuff, Lizzie dried her hands and set about refilling the kettle and hanging it above the fire. "You'll have to excuse me while I collect some more firewood," she commented. Ma Toomes shrugged, and removing her pipe from her wrinkled mouth, she set about repacking it with fresh tobacco as Lizzie foraged for branches.

"I've still got your cloak and headscarf," Lizzie commented as she returned with an armful of sticks. "I keep meaning to return them to you but have been getting distracted."

Ma grunted and puffed furiously on her pipe until the bowl smoked. "A nice granddaughter you've turned out to be!" she muttered, sounding aggrieved. "If it wasn't for that doxy of Frank's, I'd starve in a hedge before you did your duty by me!"

Lizzie set out the teapot and cups. "Is Daphne Frank's doxy?" she asked calmly, letting her skepticism show. "He doesn't talk about her that way. When he first mentioned her to us, he called her a sort of stepsister."

"She don't see it that way!" Ma Toomes retorted.

"Yet she sleeps in your wagon."

Ma's eyes glinted. "Stop trying to change the subject, girl."

"Maybe I have not been terribly dutiful," Lizzie acknowledged.

"You haven't lifted a finger! Not so much as a stocking of mine have you darned!"

297

"As I understand it, Frank's wife was exceedingly dutiful, yet you did not appreciate her in the slightest." The words flew from Lizzie's lips before she had the chance to check them.

Ma clamped her pipe between her teeth and tilted her chin up aggressively. "I'll own Maggie were a good girl," she muttered, narrowing her eyes. "Not like you, my fine lady."

"Yet you did not appreciate her efforts until she had flown."

"There's a pecking order to be followed. I did my fair share when I was a girl, now's my time to be waited on a bit," she bridled.

"That may well be," Lizzie answered lightly. "But my husband has made it plain that I am not the one to do the waiting."

"Pah!" Ma Toomes burst out. "Let's see if he's still singing that tune in a twelvemonth when the shine's worn off you!"

"Maybe he thinks if I'm not worn to a frazzle, I'll keep my shine longer?" Lizzie suggested mildly.

The old woman contemplated her a moment in moody silence. "Properly got him on leading strings, haven't you? You must be feeling mighty proud of that fact, for Lord knows, you're no beauty."

Lizzie poured some of the hot water into the pot and swirled it about before emptying it out. "Perhaps his attraction to me runs deeper than my superficial appearance?" she suggested.

The old woman snorted. "Don't be naïve, girl!" Lizzie shrugged and measured out three teaspoons of tea leaves from the tin and into the pot. "I know exactly how you snared him, as it happens," the old woman said smugly. When Lizzie poured the hot water into the pot without comment, she continued malevolently. "It's that hankering for respectability that the workhouse gave him," she pronounced with disgust. "Those places install it in you if they catch hold of you young enough. It's not really the lad's fault."

Lizzie looked up at that. "The workhouse?"

"Didn't know about that, did you?" answered Ma with satisfaction. "Well, you don't know everything about Benedict Francis Toomes, do you? For all, you're his sweetheart." She spat this last word with the utmost contempt.

"I don't understand," Lizzie admitted. "Benedict told me his great-grandfather ran away to join the fair, and his family had followed in that trade ever since."

Ma Toomes blinked. "Well, that's right enough," she allowed grudgingly.

"Then how is it that Benedict wound up in a workhouse when he was young? Did you fall on hard times?"

The old woman looked cagey. "Don't you get mentioning it to him!" she cautioned. "For it's not spoken of in general, and he won't thank you for it." She hesitated, her thin lips working as she seemed to undergo some inward struggle. "I blame that time for the rift between Ben and the rest of us," she said at last bitterly. "The time he spent there drove a wedge between us all. He resented us and never forgave his father for it."

"Do you mean…?" Lizzie broke off uncomprehendingly. "Can you be saying that it was *only* Benedict that was admitted to the workhouse? No, that cannot be."

The old woman looked away. "As it happens, it was."

"How?" Lizzie demanded. Benedict was the middle son, so she could imagine no easy circumstance in which he could have been separated from his family.

"It's not for me to tell you," the old woman clammed up suddenly.

"When he was a child you said," Lizzie said slowly, and suddenly she remembered the heated exchange in the beer tent. "He said you never raised him," she remembered. "He said—"

"That's not true!" Ma burst out hotly. "He was all of eight years when he went in and no more'n ten and a half when he came back out again."

Lizzie stared at her. *Two and a half years.* "And he was the only one of the three brothers?" she asked, feeling stunned. "How could that happen?"

"It ain't my story to tell!" the old woman grouched. "Where's that tea, girl?"

Lizzie clutched her skirts between her fingers as she strove to remain calm. "I *shall* ask him, you can be sure of that," she warned as she poured tea unsteadily into a cup. "And your tea will be weak as you have not given it time to brew." She passed the cup across at the glaring old woman.

"Huh!" Ma Toomes muttered darkly. She considered Lizzie over the rim of her cup as she sipped it and grimaced. "I've a sister and a niece in Shropshire," she said in an abrupt change of subject that made Lizzie's head spin.

"Oh?"

"Benedict ain't the only one who craved a respectable life," she sniffed. "So did Mabel. Married a farmer, she did. Dull fellow, dull but steady."

"I see. You think Benedict takes after your sister? By marrying into staid respectability?"

Ma Toomes gave a shout of laughter. "You've plenty of faults, but dullness ain't one of 'em. No, I seen the way he looks at you," she said, screwing up her mouth. "I've eyes in me head, don't I?" She shook head. "But I do say as that's how you got your clutches into him in the first place. Hankering for respectability." She nodded. "That's what the workhouse does for you."

Involuntarily, Lizzie thought of Betsy. Was that why Benedict had become engaged to her cousin? The solid respectability of Sitwell Place was beyond question. "You're quite wrong," she heard herself say aloud. "When Benedict married me, I was engaged in slopwork and living hand to mouth with eight other females in two rooms in the east end of London." She saw Ma Toomes's eyes widen and felt a momentary satisfaction in scoring the old woman off.

Ma soon recovered, however. "Well, madam, you may have been brought low," she answered dismissively. "But it's plain enough what stock you come from." She fell into a brooding silence for a moment before adding bitterly, "The Toomes men never have much luck with marriage." Lizzie remembered her railing on this subject before. Something about Benedict's mother and Maggie both running off and leaving their husbands.

"His father's always been a fool where women are concerned," Ma started up again abruptly. "Always thought more of whatever bit of petticoat had his attention than he ever did of his own kin. It was a dark day that he allowed Ben to go through the gates of that place. Wrought all manner of damage on our family, it did. Short-sighted, that's what Jedidiah Toomes was and always shall be. He thought it would learn Ben a lesson, but all it taught him was to nurse a grudge and see himself as separate from us all."

"Shall I ever meet him, do you think?" Lizzie asked, gathering Jedidiah was her father-in-law.

"Not if Ben can help it. He loathes his pa like poison. Always did, even when he was a boy." Ma Toomes paused. "I don't say his father was a saint. He never had much work in him, my Jed. Too fond of the bottle too. He's not the one to keep his old mother in comfort in her old age."

"Where is he now?" Lizzie asked curiously. "Does he still work the fairs?" If so, surely their paths would cross at some point.

Ma Toomes gazed out across the field opposite her. "He'd taken up with some slut last time I saw him," she said disparagingly. "Daphne's mother, as it happens. They were running a pickled whelk stall and talking about moving to the coast." Dimly, Lizzie remembered Frank telling them this before about Daphne's mother being Pa Toomes's latest woman.

"He was the one as introduced Daphne into the family," Ma said dryly. "Jed had some notion she would suit Frank better than Maggie. He's the one who told lies to Frank about her taking up with another man." Lizzie stared at Ma as the old woman steadily returned her gaze. Did she know what she was admitting? Lizzie wondered. That they had sabotaged Frank's marriage and conspired to get rid of his wife behind his back? "Mebbe I should have stood firm against the scheme," Ma said mutinously. "But, truth to tell, Maggie's martyred act was getting on my nerves!" She hitched her shoulder irritably. "She didn't have your spirit, girl. Never argued back, did Maggie, just fell into her mopes. And she had no cause to be so timid, for Frank never raised a hand to her, that I'll swear."

Lizzie gazed at the old woman aghast. "Frank is torn up about her leaving," she managed to gasp out. "Benedict says he's started to take to drink."

Ma Toomes took a deep breath in and out. "I know that, you little fool! Why else do you think I'm tellin' you all this? First Jed messed up Ben, and now he's done the same to Frank!" She gnashed her teeth together angrily. "I thought I'd run you off and rely on Daphne to hold things together, but all things considered, you're the better bet." She gave Lizzie a level look. "Daphne hasn't managed to snare Frank, and hell would freeze over before Ben let you go, so I'm retiring from the ring." She cast her eyes up and down Lizzie impartially. "You'll carry it off, I have no doubt."

"What do you mean?" Lizzie asked, feeling alarmed.

Ma Toomes threw her scrawny arms in the air. "I'm too old to sort out this mess! So, I'm leaving it to you to sort this family out."

Lizzie stared as Ma rose to her feet and cast the remains of her teacup away. "I'm leavin'," she said abruptly, "before the boys get back. You can keep that cloak, if you've a use for it. My gift to you."

"Where will you go?" Lizzie stammered. What would she even tell the brothers? "Into Shropshire?"

Ma gave a mirthless chuckle. "Aye, and it'll give Mabel the shock of her life. Always said she has a place for me at her farmhouse table, has Mabel. She never really thought I'd take her up on it though," she said with satisfaction. "That's the thing about respectable folks," she remarked caustically. "Always a slave to their duty. Oftentimes, it comes back to bite 'em in the backside!"

"Well, at least you won't wind up in the workhouse," Lizzie pointed out and received a vicious glare in response.

303

"Well!" Ma Toomes expostulated. "Good luck to you! You'll need it. And if that no good son of mine ever does turn up like a bad penny, you'll send him away with a flea in his ear, if you've got any sense." She looked Lizzie up and down again and nodded, stomping off in the direction from which she'd come.

"Wait!" Lizzie half rose off her wooden stool, but what could she do except call a feeble goodbye after her? Sebastian barked, but did not move from his spot next to the fire, so it was clearly a half-hearted gesture even from him.

Had Ma even told Frank and Daphne she was leaving? Lizzie sank back down onto her seat and gulped the last of her tea down in hopes of fortification. Her head felt in a whirl that Benedict's grandmother could think she was the one to sort things out. She bit her thumbnail, lost in thought. Only the lingering taste of the soap reminded her she was but halfway through her washing. With a frustrated sigh, Lizzie returned to the washtub and plunged herself back into her work.

20

They did not reach Putney until long past four o'clock, and Benedict was restless by the time they turned their wagon down the lane that led to the heath.

"For the love of God, would you settle down, Ben?" his brother sighed in exasperation. "It's your fault we're so late after all! You're the one who insisted we went shopping."

Jack spoke nothing but the truth, and the number of parcels bundled up in the back of the wagon bore testament to his words. Still, Benedict was itching with impatience by the time his brother set him down next to his own wagon.

"Will you come over to ours later to catch Frank up with how things went?" Jack asked as Benedict unloaded his parcels from the back.

"Will I be damned," he muttered, jumping down. "I've better things to do. You can brag to him of your triumph all by yourself."

"What of *your* win?" Jack asked with a grin.

"Jesus, Jack, he was nothing but an untried boy. That win was hardly something for me to brag about."

"I don't know about that," Jack said slowly. "Nat seemed well pleased with how you handled it."

Benedict shrugged. "I kept it clean and I didn't humiliate the boy. Nothing more, nothing less."

"I still say you acted handsomely," his brother insisted. "And I wasn't the only one."

"Well, be that as it may." Benedict glanced over his shoulder, but no one was stirring from the direction of the wagon. Not even the dog. "I'll bid you farewell now."

Jack nodded. "I bet you *do* go and brag to Lizzie, all the same." He grinned and gee-upped the horses before Benedict could respond.

Shaking his head at Jack's nonsense, Benedict carried his packages over to the wagon and deposited them inside. A pile of crisp laundered washing was neatly folded on top of the nearest trunk, and if he wasn't mistaken, the items strewn over the nearby bushes were also theirs.

Ben made his way toward them and found them mostly dry. To his surprise, most of the items there were his own. Gathering them up, he carried them inside and then started setting up the campfire. He would get things sorted here and then walk over to meet Lizzie at the end of her shift.

He soon had a pile of firewood ready. After collecting the water, he unwrapped the new set of steps he had bought, and he set them down next to the wagon. Having run through the list of tasks, he made his way toward the fairground where things appeared to be in full swing.

Glancing at his pocket watch, he thought it must be about time Lizzie was done for the day and made his way toward Connie's tent. To his surprise, he found Lizzie already stood outside and in deep conversation with the redhead she had introduced him to previously.

Only Sebastian seemed to notice his approach, his tail thumping against the ground in a lazy wag. Quickening his pace, Benedict called out her name and saw his wife start guiltily at his approach.

"Oh, Benedict," she said, turning toward him with an outstretched hand. He grabbed it firmly and pulled her into his embrace.

"Has something happened?"

"Hmmm?" She gazed up at him.

He cast a glance over his shoulder toward the tent and found the redhead watching them with amusement. "You in Connie's bad books again?"

"What?" She looked aghast. "No! How about you?" Her expression grew suddenly anxious. "It went off alright, didn't it? The fight, I mean."

He nodded. Had she been worried about him? And why did that make him feel warm all through? A smile tugged at his lips. "Couldn't have gone better, actually."

She sighed and gave him an answering smile. "That's alright, then."

He lowered his face to hers, couldn't help himself. The kiss was tender and lingering. It didn't belong in an open field, surrounded by crowds, but there was little he could do about that. When he drew back, Lizzie's eyes were closed, and she swayed slightly in his arms. "You finished here?"

Lizzie blinked, nodded, and turned to wave at Niamh, who laughed and called something about a *pair of lovebirds* before pulling her shawl about her shoulders and setting off in the opposite direction.

"What were you two talking about that you looked so serious?" Benedict asked, pulling her arm through his. Sebastian trotted at their heels.

307

Lizzie's color heightened. "I was asking her about Maggie," she admitted in hushed tones.

"Maggie?" Whatever he had expected her answer to be, it wasn't that.

"Yes, and Benedict, you will never guess." Her voice shook with excitement and she went up on her tiptoes, angling her mouth toward his ear. "I've found out where she is!" Her eyes gleamed. "Shall we go for some refreshment so I can tell you all about it?"

It was a struggle, but somehow, he managed to murmur the affirmative. *Fuck Maggie and Frank*, he thought sourly as he towed Lizzie off to feed her. He didn't want to talk about either of them. *Fuck the tea tent too*, he thought. He needed a real drink.

The good thing about receiving Lizzie's confidences was as soon as they were seated in the beer tent, she brought her chair flush against his and leaned right into him. The bad thing he thought, slipping his arm around her back, was that her excited chatter was about his bloody family.

"—and Niamh says that Maggie definitely had the impression that Frank was untrue to her," Lizzie said breathlessly. "For Aggie told Niamh. So, *that* you see, is why Maggie went with her to Southend!" She leaned back to gauge his reaction to this piece of news.

Who the fuck was Aggie? Luckily at this point, the server approached with their pitcher of beer which stemmed the excited flow. Benedict poured their drinks, and Lizzie accepted hers with thanks, taking a sip and looking at him expectantly.

He wondered if it was safe to admit ignorance over Aggie. Had she mentioned an Aggie before? "Who's Aggie?" he said, throwing caution to the wind.

"Oh, didn't I say?" Lizzie lowered her glass. "Aggie was a performer in the Wondrous Females tent. The Living Skeleton, only in reality she was just rather gaunt with sunken eyes and they used greasepaint to accentuate the fact. Apparently, she was Maggie's particular friend and confidante."

That did ring a bell, though he hadn't known the name of his sister-in-law's friend. Then again, why the hell should he? Benedict took another swig of beer. "And what's at Southend?" he asked, frowning in concentration.

"Aggie's sister's boarding house," Lizzie replied patiently. "Oh, and Maggie. That's the whole point. You see, Aggie took Maggie with her when she quit this life and went to help her sister run it."

Benedict's head spun. *Aggie and Maggie?* You couldn't make this up. "What's the sister called?" he muttered with some acidity. "Peggy?"

Lizzie looked a little taken aback. "I don't think Niamh mentioned her name, now that you ask. Is that important?"

Benedict shook his head. "No," he answered quickly. "Forget it."

Lizzie nodded and took another sip of her beer. "So, I've been thinking about it," she said seriously. "And I think I know what our next step should be."

Benedict regarded her moodily. "Our next step?"

"Yes," she agreed, sitting up straighter. "Let me know if you agree. I think we need to determine once and for all if Frank is innocent. My own inclination is that he is, but I think we need to make absolutely sure before I write to Maggie—"

"You want to write to Maggie?" he echoed.

"Yes, because if she was lied to, Benedict, then she needs to know." She placed her hand on his arm and looked so sincere that any acerbic words on his tongue shriveled away. "She was the wronged party, and I don't like to tell you this, but there was something of a conspiracy against her, against them both, if Frank was innocent." Someone from a noisy party behind them jostled against the back of Lizzie's chair, pitching her forward against him.

"Sorry, love," sang out a woman's voice as Benedict glared in that direction.

"That's quite alright," Lizzie assured her. "Perhaps this isn't the best place for me tell you all this, it is rather noisy," she said ruefully as she disentangled herself.

"Maybe you should sit on my lap?" he suggested. "Then I could hear you better." He met her enquiring gaze with perfect blandness.

"Oh, you think that would help?"

"It would definitely help me."

Lizzie rose jerkily out of her seat and sat herself on his lap. The self-conscious look on her face should not have this effect on him, he realized dimly, but it made absolutely no difference to the fact he was getting hot under the collar.

Lizzie cleared her throat and leaned into him. "So, what do *you* think?" she asked, bringing her face closer to his.

"Hmmm?"

"About Frank."

His eyebrows snapped together. "What about him?"

"If he *is* innocent of what they told his wife? That he betrayed her, I mean."

Only by a huge effort did Benedict manage to get his mind on the issue at hand. "He didn't," he answered, rather gruffly. "He hasn't had anyone since Maggie. Apparently, he tried to bed some whore, but he couldn't get it up." Seeing the way Lizzie bridled made him realize he'd put things rather crudely. "That was after she'd left him," he clarified, clearing his throat. "Not before."

Lizzie bit her lip. It was plain she did not consider this as the action of an altogether innocent man. "I must say I'm rather disappointed in Frank, but I suppose he *did* think she had left him for another man," she said with a sigh.

"Did he?" It was the first he'd heard of it. "Who told you that?"

"Frank."

"Frank did?" The idea of them having a heart-to-heart about the state of Frank's marriage was so jarring to him that for a moment he couldn't think how to respond.

"Yes," she sighed, then her faraway gaze seemed to focus on him anew. "Benedict," she said impulsively.

"Hmmm?"

"You agree, then? That I should write to Maggie and apprise her of the true facts?"

"Why not just give Frank the address in Southend and let him sort out his business?" he asked abruptly. Lizzie shook her head, avoiding his eye. He reached up and caught her chin until their gazes met. "Why?" he demanded.

"I think the least we can do is allow Maggie to make her own mind up about returning or not," Lizzie replied slowly. "I do not think Frank was as good a husband as you are," she said, completely flabbergasting him. "I'm not entirely sure he deserves her."

And just like that, the gathering thundercloud at his brow evaporated into nothing. "You think I'm a good husband, Lizzie?" he asked in gravelly tones, all thought of defending his brother going abruptly out of the window.

She nodded, her gaze so clear after uttering so startling a statement that he wasn't sure his ears hadn't been deceiving him. "Of course," she said, seemingly oblivious to the fact he was profoundly shaken. Sebastian chose that moment to poke his head out from underneath the table. "I think you had better feed us," she said wryly. "All I've had since breakfast is an apple and some cheese."

Twenty minutes later, they were walking through the fair, sipping hot soup and eating buttered rolls. There was a lot less choice tonight with the reduced number of stalls, but Sebastian seemed happy enough with his meat pudding, which he swallowed in three great mouthfuls, and then glued himself to Lizzie until she followed that up with half of her sponge cake. She cast a guilty look at Benedict. "I'm afraid Ema and Zaya have taught him some very bad habits about begging for tidbits."

"If it upsets his stomach, you'll know about it," he answered dryly and left it at that.

At one point, she tugged him toward a stall that sold writing implements and sundries, and he watched without comment as

312

she bought a sheaf of paper and a pen. They were soon meandering their way back to the wagon, and Lizzie uttered an exclamation on spotting the new steps. "When did you get these?" she asked, running to inspect them. "Oh, they're perfect! Just the right height. You must have measured before you left."

"I just guessed." It was ridiculous to preen over such a thing, but Benedict found he was markedly inclined to bask in her approval.

"Did you fetch in the clean washing or did someone steal it?" she asked suddenly, turning toward the bushes.

"I fetched it in."

The look she bestowed on him was glowing. "I'll get the tea things," she said, mounting the steps with her light tread. "What are all these parcels?" she called from inside.

"Just things for the wagon, you can open them," he answered as he set about lighting the fire.

"Really?" He wished now he had bought her something more exciting, but they had only stopped at a general and hardware store. You wouldn't guess it from her reaction though. "This fabric, I love it!" she called out to him. The woman in the store had recommended it, but Benedict did not feel inclined to point this out. "It will be just perfect for the curtains!"

He heard the ripping of paper and guessed she had found the chamber pot next. He heard her clear her throat. "Very functional," she commented, and he heard her slide it under the bed. He wasn't so worried about her going over the fields now she had the dog to accompany her, but even so. He did not like to think of it late at night if he was not around.

"A new blanket! This is a nice one. *Not* for Sebastian this time."
More ripping of paper. "You bought more tea and lemons!" Her
head poked out of the door. "You will have to tell me what I
can buy for the wagon now I've money to spend."

"I don't think there is anything else at present. Come out and
keep me company."

"Are you going to tell me about your fight?" she asked, coming
back down the steps with the tea tray.

"There's not much to tell."

"Because your win was inevitable?" she asked with a slightly
teasing tone to her voice he wasn't sure he'd heard before.

He smirked but answered seriously. "My opponent was
inexperienced. He's had good trainers, though, and in a couple
of years he'll be a force to be reckoned with."

Lizzie added the tea leaves to the pot. "His introduction to the
business has been very different to yours, then."

"I grew up around boxing, for the most part." She looked up
quickly, then fiddled with the cups and saucers. "What?"

She shook her head. "It's nothing. I just remembered something
you said the other day to your grandmother." The mention of
his grandmother seemed to sink her deep in thought, and a
frown appeared on her brow as she finished preparing the tea.

Benedict was already half resigned to further elaboration on the
subject by the time he heard her take a deep breath for resolve.

"Benedict, before you tell me any more, there is something I
must tell you about your grandmother. She must have done it by
now, for she said she would before you and Jack returned."

Benedict quirked an eyebrow at her. In truth, he had nothing more to tell her about his wholly predictable fight. "Let's get it out of the way, then," he said, thinking he should have brought some beer back with him to the wagon. Instead, he raised his cup to his mouth.

"She's gone," she said simply.

He swallowed his tea down the wrong way. "Gone?" he repeated once he had coughed to clear his throat. "What do you mean?"

Lizzie looked grave. "She left." He set his cup down again on the packing case with a heavy thud. "This morning she came around to our wagon while I was doing the washing and told me she was leaving to take up her sister's offer for her to live with her in Shropshire."

Benedict stared. "It's the first I've heard of it."

"That Ma Toomes had a sister, you mean?"

He shook his head. "No, that Great-Aunt Mabel would have her. I know Ma winters there most years, but I thought they were always pleased to see the back of each other." He frowned. "God help them," he commented finally. "Neither of them ever has a good word to say about the other."

"It seemed as though she had simply had enough of this life." Benedict looked at her sharply, but Lizzie's expression was open and untroubled. "She said she could not depend on her son to support her in her old age but that her sister had always offered her a place by her hearth. Or words to that effect."

Benedict gave a short laugh. "She has not relied on my father for many a year. It's Frank she leeches off, and Jack to a lesser extent."

"Well, it appears she has now relinquished her hold over them."
Lizzie hesitated. "I think she regrets how things went with
Maggie and means to clear the field."

"It would be the first thing she ever regretted in her life,"
Benedict said scathingly. Lizzie folded her lips and said
nothing, though her gaze remained intent on him. "Well, she's
gone," he said challengingly. "Anything else I should know?"
Again, she hesitated, and Benedict braced himself. "What is it?"
he asked with foreboding.

"She did let slip that—well, your father was behind the attempt
to oust Maggie." Lizzie kept her eyes on the teaspoon she held.
"It seems he had lately taken up with Daphne's mother and
thought that Daphne would suit Frank far better."

Benedict brought his hand down sharply on the packing case,
making the tea things jump. Sebastian sat up from his spot by
the fire and watched them narrowly. Once he saw that
Benedict's anger was not directed toward his mistress, he
relaxed slightly, but did not lie back down. Lizzie remained
calm. She lifted her gaze to meet his. "The old man was behind
it?" he asked tightly.

She nodded. "Apparently so."

Benedict swore for a full minute, and that did make Lizzie
wince. Once he had his temper under control, he said in low
tones, "No doubt he thought he could manipulate Frank easier if
he had someone speaking directly into his ear."

"I'm sure you are right. I suspect the tale that Maggie ran off
with another man originated with him also, for neither Niamh
nor Connie had ever heard of such a rumor."

"I don't believe such a tale exists!" Benedict burst out hotly.
"She wasn't the sort."

316

"Frank believed it," Lizzie said simply. "And what's more, it's what he believes motivated her to leave, though he may have been too ashamed to admit it to you or Jack."

Again, Benedict swore. "That bloody fool!" He sat simmering for a moment. When he looked up, he was resigned. "Go and get your paper and pen." After all, Frank was going to the devil at an alarming rate. Maybe Maggie's return *would* sort him out.

Lizzie flew up the steps and returned within seconds with her stationery and a candle which she passed to Benedict. He lit it for her and set it in a saucer to give her light enough to write her letter. He felt irritated that their evening had been given over to family matters, but perhaps it was just as well to get it over with in one go, then they could concentrate on the two of them.

He watched as her nib scratched across the page. She wrote determinedly and neatly, as she did everything else in life. Before long, she had covered three pages with her even handwriting, and Benedict wondered why she could not have put the matter into three simple lines. He would have done.

She looked up at one point. "Maggie can read?"

He shrugged. "If she can't, she can always find someone who can."

Lizzie frowned, no doubt thinking the subject matter sensitive. "I hope she will not think I'm taking a liberty by writing to her."

"You're doing her a favor," he retorted shortly.

"Do you mind if I write that you endorse my writing to her?" He gave a brief shake of his head, and she added a postscript and blotted the letter. "I'll get Charlie to take it along for posting tomorrow," she said, sitting back with a sigh.

"Charlie?" he asked, rather more sharply than he'd intended.

"He runs errands for Connie and comes to the tent most days for any commissions from the girls." At the look on Benedict's face she added, "He's twelve."

His expression rapidly cleared. "Oh."

She stretched and sat back on her low seat. "And now you *really* must tell me how things went with the waistcoated gentleman."

Benedict glanced at her. "I'll tell you inside. It's getting cold. I put the water on to heat while you were at your letter."

Lizzie glanced at the bubbling pan in surprise. "Is it not a little early for bed?"

"No," he replied. "No, it is not."

"Oh, very well," she said, gathering up what was left of her paper and ink. "I suppose your fight would take it out of you."

21

"Benedict," Lizzie began tentatively as she brushed her hair before bed.

He slung his boot over his shoulder. "What?"

"If I was to run away, you would come after me, wouldn't you?"

He gave a short laugh. "I'll put it this way, you wouldn't get far."

Lizzie pursed her lips thoughtfully. "What if…?" She cast a quick glance at him.

He stilled in the act of unbuttoning his shirt. "What?"

"Well, what if rumor said another man was involved." At his narrowed eyes, she added quickly, "Of course, you would know there was nothing whatsoever in such idle gossip."

He was quiet a moment, but it looked as though it caused him some effort. "Why would you be leaving me, then?" he asked gruffly, tugging his shirt out of his breeches.

"Say…I felt underappreciated or overworked?" Lizzie ventured, thinking of everything she had heard about Frank's wife.

Benedict moved so suddenly he was a mere blur. The next thing he knew, she was blinking up at him, still clutching her hairbrush as he held her about the waist. "Are you feeling that way, Lizzie?" he asked tightly.

"No! Of course not!"

His eyes raked over her. "You'd tell me?"

Lizzie spluttered. "You may be assured of that!" she retorted. "When do I ever spare you my opinion?"

A smile tugged briefly at his lips but vanished just as quickly. "What are you trying to tell me at this moment, then?"

"I'm not *telling* you anything," she stressed. "I'm merely trying to gauge how you would feel if—" She broke off. "Forget it, I was being foolish. And besides, you more than do your fair share about the place."

He gazed down at her as though assessing the truth of her words. Whatever he saw in her face seemed to assure him. He gave a short nod and released her, shrugging off his shirt.

"I can tell you what I wouldn't do," he answered grimly. "I wouldn't fall apart at the seams and hit the bottle like Frank seems to have."

Yes, but Frank and Maggie were a love match, Lizzie thought with a pang. She and Benedict were decidedly not. She had no answer to the interrogative look he threw at her.

"Very well, then," he continued after a moment. "In answer to your question, I would first fetch you back and then seek out the source of the gossip and cut it off at the root. Satisfied?"

Lizzie considered this as he unfastened his breeches. "What if the source were someone deeply connected to you?" she asked slowly, even as he started to shake his head. "By familial bonds of the strongest kind."

"They couldn't be more closely connected than a man to his wife," he said simply.

Lizzie reeled as she considered the fact that Benedict might think her the closest person to him in the world. He could not mean that, surely. Something of her thoughts must have shown in her expression, for he looked at her quizzically as he climbed in the bed. "This is news to you?" he asked. "Come here."

Lizzie cleared her throat and set down her hairbrush. "Well, no, I just would have thought that people you were raised with might have a prior claim on your loyalties..." she said, stepping to the bed and lifting the blanket. "After all, we do not know each other terribly well and—"

His fingers closed about on a fistful of her nightgown, tugging her down on top of him. "We know each other inside out," he growled as their bodies came into contact with each other. "I'm the *only* man who's ever known you, Lizzie, or ever will."

"You mean biblically, of course."

"You think that meek-faced vicar knew you better than me?" he demanded against her ear.

"Well—" She broke off with sudden diplomacy.

"What does he know about you that I don't?" he asked tersely. "Tell me."

"No, no," Lizzie replied weakly. "I did not mean that!"

"Tell me!" he reiterated, closing his arms about her fast.

"Well." She blew out her cheeks. "Just inconsequential things really. Like my favorite verse, sermon, season... That sort of thing. But I did not mean Reverend Milson, in any case. I was thinking of my uncle who raised me."

Benedict snorted. "If he knew a damn thing about you, then he would know you did not lie about that bloody brooch."

Lizzie had no reply for that. "I suppose that is true enough," she conceded quietly and rested her head against his shoulder. His fingers squeezed convulsively at her waist, and they lay silent a moment.

"Why did you tell him those things?" he asked in a surly voice.

"What things? Who?" she asked absently.

He pinched her hip. "Milson. Why did you tell him personal things about yourself?"

Lizzie considered this. "Well, he came to dine with us once a week," she answered truthfully. "Polite table conversation usually revolves around such things."

"You usually embroider slippers for dinner guests?" he asked with an edge to his voice.

Lizzie raised her head in surprise. "Who told you about that? Those were a Christmas present!" she retorted, feeling unaccountably embarrassed. The curl of his lip showed he was not appeased. "It is a perfectly respectable practice for a parishioner to give a handmade gift—"

"What if your vicar was old and infirm?" he interrupted. "Instead of young and smug with an oily grin?"

"Reverend Milson's predecessor, Canon Wilner, was seventy when he retired, and I also embroidered him slippers for Christmas!" she informed him icily. Benedict grunted, his hand sliding from her hip to cup her backside. Lizzie caught her breath. "I could make you some next Christmas, if you so desire," she joked feebly.

"You'd better."

Lizzie drew her head back to regard him with surprise. "You want slippers?"

"Of course." He shrugged. "I can wear them for the four steps it takes from the wagon door to the bed."

Lizzie burst out laughing, and he yanked her forward to stop her mirth with his lips. When he released her, she was breathless. "You'll be telling me you want polite conversation from me next."

His shoulder rose and fell. "You'd better tell me those things while you're at it."

"What things?"

"Your favorite flower," he growled. "And whatever the hell else you told that slimy bastard."

"Benedict!" She struggled in his arms, but as he held her hard against him her efforts were not having the effect she had anticipated. "There's no need to use such language!" she objected primly. "My aunt and uncle were present the entire time and so was Betsy! I don't remember you objecting to his presence at Sitwell Place when my cousin was your affianced!"

The next thing she knew, she had been rolled underneath him. "I don't give a damn if Betsy sat on his lap clad only in her drawers," he said roughly as he dragged her nightgown up her legs.

"Benedict!"

"She was never mine. Not like you are." His hand was between her legs now, petting and stroking her there.

Lizzie caught her breath. "You w-wanted to marry her," she pointed out.

"Not really," he breathed out. "The fact I ended up engaged to her at all was just a matter of bad timing."

Lizzie found herself listening hard. The confessional tone in his voice caught her off guard. "What do you mean, bad timing?" she asked with a hitch in her voice.

His fingers stilled, and instead, he cupped her mound possessively with his palm. "Just what I said."

"I don't understand," Lizzie persisted.

He exhaled noisily. "Are we having this conversation now?"

"Apparently," Lizzie responded tartly.

He rolled off her so he lay on his side facing her. After a moment, he placed his hand on her hip as though he could not bear for them to have no contact. "I met Betsy at a dance last spring in Chelsea. She was there with some cousins, I think? One had a loud braying laugh like a donkey."

Lizzie nodded. "Our cousins the Stocktons. Harriet's laugh is quite unfortunate."

"You weren't there," he said accusingly.

Lizzie sniffed. "I do not care for the Stocktons," she said primly.

A smile curved Benedict's lips. "So disapproving, Lizzie. Why?"

Lizzie hesitated. "I just don't." She plucked at the blanket. "Besides," she said, avoiding his eyes, "they did not invite me. I was not considered merry company." Before Benedict could say anything, she added quickly, "Betsy did not say she met you at a dance."

"Likely her parents would not have approved of a public masquerade ball."

Lizzie sucked in a shocked breath. "No indeed! And if that is not *just* like Cousin Harriet to organize such an entertainment! She knows full well Uncle Josiah would not have agreed to such a thing."

"Where were you that night?" he asked, surprising her.

Lizzie shrugged. "In general, I stayed home when Betsy went to stay with them. She went for a whole month last March. I collect that must have been when your paths crossed."

He grunted. "We met up the next day as a group, and the acquaintance went on from there."

Lizzie frowned and rolled onto her back. Benedict immediately crowded into her side.

"What?" he asked, pulling her back into his arms.

"It feels strange. Hearing how you courted Betsy," she said abruptly.

He breathed out shakily. "It wasn't anything really," he said, drawing her close. "If I had not been caught up in that brawl a couple of weeks later, we would never have got engaged."

"How do you make that out?" Lizzie asked.

"Your cousin started writing to me in jail. I was miserable and feeling lonely." He shrugged. "She wrote pretty enough letters. It was just…an entanglement."

"Yet you would have married her, if not for the events of that unfortunate dinner party," she pointed out, feeling a coldness steeling over her.

"No," he said, shaking his head. "No, I was already looking for a way out by that point."

Lizzie shivered and he dragged her hard against him. "You say that now," she persisted. "But at the time you—you made her promises." When she peeped up at him, he was regarding her gravely.

"Ask me what Betsy's favorite flower was, Lizzie."

"What is Betsy's favorite flower?" she whispered.

He shrugged. "I have no idea. Now tell me yours."

"It's violets."

"Favorite season?"

"Autumn."

"What was the rest?" he asked.

"I don't remember now," she murmured. "I daresay it does not signify. You tell me yours now."

"My favorite flower?" he asked humorously.

"Yes, why not?"

"The daffodil?" he answered after a pause. He sounded more like he was asking than telling.

"Favorite season?"

"Spring."

"When is your birthday?"

"September 4. Yours?"

"July 12."

"Hmm." He regarded her a moment in silence. "The Stocktons are idiots, Lizzie. Your company is the best of all."

Her jaw dropped and she stared at him before a sudden suspicion struck. "We're in bed," she reminded him. "Does that mean I can believe you or not?"

"Well, as I've already got you where I want you, you can believe me."

"Is that how it works?"

"In general." He regarded her through frowning brows. "How about you just believe me anyhow, Lizzie? I've no intention of deceiving you now or in the future."

Lizzie thought about this. "If I *had* been at that masquerade party," she said slowly. "Do you think you would have noticed me, Benedict Toomes?"

He gave her a searching look, as though realizing she was testing him. "It depends," he replied seriously. "On whether you'd have sat there all prim and disapproving, threatening to tell your uncle on your return."

He answered so frankly she winced. "*Or,*" he carried on steadily. "If wearing a mask and having a glass of punch would have freed you up to enjoy yourself, like you did at the Fiddlers Green." Lizzie met his gaze. "I'd have noticed you then, alright."

His words set her heart racing, even though she was not so sure if that was true. The fact he had thought her the prettiest present at the Fiddlers Green was because his opinion was already biased in her favor. Still, she could not bring herself to utter any of this when he was looking at her with such an expression.

"You think so?" she asked instead and found herself placing a hand against his chest.

"I know so," he breathed out. "I couldn't take my eyes off you that night." Lizzie felt the strangest sensation of warmth spreading throughout her limbs from the inside out.

"I don't feel cold anymore. You remember I told you that once when we were sat by the fire? That I felt cold inside, not outside?"

"Were we talking about family?"

"Yes. You told me you weren't close to yours, and I said I thought I was, but not anymore."

"I remember."

"I think it's because you're my family now."

His arms about her tightened. "Yes," he agreed in a raspy voice. "And you're mine."

"Benedict…" She did not get the chance to speak anymore, for he pressed his mouth to hers, and actions became more important than words between them.

22

The next morning passed quietly enough. Lizzie kept expecting Frank or Jack to appear and announce that Ma Toomes had disappeared, however nothing occurred to disturb the harmony between herself and Benedict.

He nipped out early to get more meat bones for Sebastian. On his return, he fried some bacon over the fire and made them sandwiches from a fresh loaf he had purchased nearby. They drank tea, and over this simple meal he told her that he felt he had closed the chapter that was his prizefighting career with some dignity at least.

It was plain that Benedict did not anticipate being contacted again any time soon and considered this last appearance to have been a fluke occurrence and nothing more. Lizzie took a more optimistic view, but this she kept to herself, for she could tell it was something he could not allow himself to contemplate.

His feelings ran deep about his old ambitions, and she guessed he could not bear the disappointment if he allowed himself to grow hopeful. "Did you see any of your old boxing friends and acquaintances?" she asked.

Benedict swallowed his mouthful. "A couple. Dabney and Pfeiffer," he elaborated, then no more.

"I'm glad you managed to display yourself to advantage," she said, setting down her plate. "Your boxing could not fail to have impressed all who saw you."

He smiled at this and reached across to grab her hand before kissing it and releasing it again. She fetched the fabric for the curtains and got to work, for the fair did not start until midday which gave her enough time to cut and sew at least one pair, considering how small the windows were.

By the time they walked hand in hand across the field toward the fairground at midday, she had cut out both pairs of curtains and started lining them. The fair at Putney was a weeklong affair, so she fancied she would finish her sewing before they moved onto their next engagement.

"How long will it take us to reach Oxford?" she asked.

"Oxford?"

"Yes, for Connie said the next fair was Banbury."

"Is that where they're headed?" Benedict asked without much interest.

Lizzie halted abruptly, forcing him to do the same. "Is that not where we are headed?"

Benedict shook his head. "We always go from here into Hampshire. There's a fair at Andover we attend every year."

"Hampshire?" Lizzie was dismayed. "But Connie definitely told me they were headed for Banbury the day after tomorrow."

Benedict looked amused. "Do you think all the acts follow the same route, Lizzie? It's obvious we would part ways at some point. We're staying put here at Putney for the whole week. We'll see them at the fair after that, or at some further point down the road."

"But what about my job?"

"We'll find you something else to do." He shrugged. "Or nothing at all. I made a good sum of money yesterday, so we're far from hard up. Our living costs are very low." Lizzie could not hide her disappointment, and he slipped his arm about her waist. "This life on the road is all about change. Each fair is different. Besides," he added thoughtfully, "if you're expecting a response from Maggie, it's Andover she'll expect us to be from mid-April." He dropped a kiss on her cheek. "Don't look so glum. You'll worry Sebastian."

Lizzie managed a smile, for the dog was regarding her intently. She dropped her hand to stroke his head, and they passed into the busy fair.

Connie and Niamh were inclined to be philosophical about their parting of ways, but the twins were inconsolable, casting their arms about both her and Sebastian's necks and wailing.

"But what will we *do*?" they demanded. "Without our protectors?"

"First Alfred, then Ada, and now Lizzie," Connie said sourly. "I'm used to being left in the lurch!" She slammed the lid of a trunk, muttering to herself.

"Can't you persuade the Toomeses to change their route?" Niamh suggested, half in jest. "You got Benedict wrapped around your finger, sure enough."

"I think they've been going to Andover for years and years from what he said," Lizzie said mournfully. "I'm really going to miss you all."

"It's the nature of this life," Niamh sighed. "With never the same view from your window one week to the next."

"I don't mind that part," Lizzie said. "It's people I miss, not places."

The twins gathered around Connie. "Why can we not go to this Andover?" they clamored. "Then we need not be parted at all!"

331

"You want me to change my plans all on Lizzie's account?" Connie demanded, looking incensed. "She's hardly my Salome now, is she?"

The twins pouted. "Salome, Salome!" Ema sniped. "It's always about Salome!"

"After all, there is no Salome right now!" Zaya muttered.

"No, but I'm interviewing one in Oxford, aren't I?" Connie said smartly. "So put that in your pipe and smoke it!"

Ema rolled her eyes. "Lizzie, why can you not consume a mountain in chocolates and then you could be our Salome? Your hair is far more beautiful than Miss Wurtzel's ever was."

Connie burst out laughing, and Lizzie braced herself, expecting some detrimental comment about her looks. "You think that husband of hers would permit her to sit around in the altogether, to be ogled by all and sundry? Do me a favor. He'd see us shut down first."

"She's right," Niamh agreed. "He looks sick as a dog having to part with her most mornings. Casts longing looks over his shoulder as he walks away and everything."

"Oh, stop it," Lizzie said uncomfortably. "He does not."

"You wouldn't know, for you never look," Niamh teased.

"Besides," Zaya huffed sadly. "I do not think Lizzie would ever grow big enough hips and thighs, even if she ate a whole mountain of candy. For she does not have the right frame for it."

They all turned to survey Lizzie critically. "I don't know why you're looking at me like that!" Lizzie said spiritedly. "For I have no intention of even trying!"

The rest of the afternoon passed without much event. Charlie came for any commissions and for a fee took her letter for Maggie. He promised faithfully he would post it that very day. The only other occurrence was Lizzie having to escort a hysterical young woman out of the Wondrous Females tent all of a flutter.

The troublesome female in question had insisted on proclaiming in a loud, know-it-all voice that the goddess Anvi's extra arms "were clearly not real but fake appendages suspended on strings." Upon which, Ema had reached around from behind her twin and seized the girl's wrist in a hard grasp, as Zaya began to laugh in a quite terrifying manner.

The visitor had screamed so loudly that quite a crowd had gathered at the tent entrance, trying to push their way in to find the source of the commotion. Sebastian rushed toward them barking loudly, which seemed to restore some order.

"Let her go!" Lizzie had insisted as the poor girl started to gibber.

Zaya crossed her arms. "She should not have insulted the goddess!" she said, sticking her little chin in the air.

"She apologizes most sincerely, oh wondrous goddess!" a young man in spectacles stammered.

"You I like," the goddess announced, making the young man blush. "For you speak handsomely." She extended one of her other hands toward him, and after a moment's confusion, he kissed it reverently. "I will release this foolish mortal for your sake."

The young man bowed gratefully, and Ema released her victim. Lizzie half dragged the fainting young woman out into the fresh air outside the tent as the young man propping up her other side scolded her soundly.

"If that doesn't just serve you right, Jennifer!" he complained, wiping his brow with his handkerchief. "Wherever I take you it is always the same! Causing scenes and showing off! I'm sure I don't know why I bother!"

"Ohhhhh," Jennifer moaned. "Her fingers burned into my skin, Cedric. I'm sure she cursed me!"

"She did not curse you," Lizzie said firmly.

The girl's frightened eyes rolled toward her. "How can you be sure?" she wailed and began to weep noisily.

"If she had cursed you, there would have been a good quantity of colored smoke filling the tent," Lizzie improvised. "I have seen the goddess curse many people, and you she did not curse, for she liked the look of your companion."

Cedric's rather thin chest puffed out at this. "There, there you see," he said comfortingly and patted her gloved hand. "Let me buy you a cup of hot, spiced wine. You will feel better presently, I daresay."

"The very thing!" Lizzie approved. "Or a nice cup of hot sweet tea for the shock she has had."

Cedric thanked her profusely, and when she drew her hand away from a vigorous handshake, she found he had tipped her handsomely.

"Only let this be a lesson to you, my dear," she heard him taxing the unfortunate Jennifer as he led her away.

When Lizzie returned to the tent, she found the queue outside the tent was heaving and three times as long as it had been before. Connie nodded to her as she and Sebastian passed by her in the entrance. "Nicely done, my dear," she said. "We'll miss you at Banbury."

Lizzie felt quite sentimental by the time she'd finished for the evening. As the fair did not start until twelve, it was long past nine by the time things were wound up in the Wondrous Females tent.

Suppressing a yawn, Lizzie made her way toward the Toomes Brothers Boxing Saloon when, to her surprise, she noticed a familiar figure lurking outside. It was the solid respectable figure of Josiah Anderson. "Uncle!" she uttered in astonishment.

He gave a violent start on hearing her voice and wheeled about. "Lizzie!" he gasped faintly, his eyes raking over her.

"Were you looking for me?" she asked, quite flabbergasted to see him in such surroundings.

He swallowed, his whiskered chin quivering. "I am," he admitted hoarsely.

Lizzie turned to look at the boxing tent, which was clearly in full swing. Cries and shouts rang out from the rowdy patrons within. Daphne stood at the entrance, momentarily distracted by the stream of people waiting admittance. She tossed her hair and laughed uproariously at something some wag said to her.

"It looks like it will be a good while until Benedict will be finished for the evening," Lizzie said, eyeing the queue. "Should we go for some refreshment, Uncle?"

Her uncle looked frankly relieved. "I will own, I think that a good notion," he said, unbending slightly in his rigid stance.

"I believe I saw a tea tent in this direction," Lizzie said, leading him resolutely away from the boxing saloon. She could not imagine such a place would earn her uncle's good opinion. Indeed, she imagined he was loathing every minute of the noisy fair. What on earth had brought him here? she wondered distractedly. Had he come to check on her welfare?

Five minutes later, they were sat looking at each other over a small table in a quieter, though still busy, tea tent. Sebastian sat at Lizzie's knee, alert and on guard, as though he had picked up on her own tension. "Shall I pour?" Lizzie asked when her uncle sat grave and silent. He acquiesced with a quick movement of his hands before placing them both on the tablecloth before him.

"How did you know to find us here?" Lizzie marveled. "I know Annie saw us at Greenwich, but for you to trace us here is quite another thing."

Her uncle swallowed and seemed incapable of speech for a full minute. "I made…enquiries," he said with effort. "And found the most likely sites for you to have moved onto were either here or Chelmsford. I traveled into Essex yesterday, fruitlessly. Today, well." He gestured toward her. "My quest is over," he said heavily and without joy. "For I have found you."

Lizzie placed the teapot down and surveyed him quizzically. "You sound rather as though you had found a corpse than your living niece," she commented wryly.

Her uncle's cheeks turned purple. "All wrongdoing is sin, but there is sin that does not lead to death," he intoned hollowly.

"Indeed?" Lizzie said coolly. "Is that what you sought me out to inform me?" She held out his teacup, and he could not quite meet her eyes as he took it from her.

"You are right to upbraid me," he said after a moment's heavy silence. "I am all too well aware of my own part in bringing you low. You were in quite desperate straits, and Mr. Toomes took despicable advantage of that fact. I can only suppose he meant to be revenged on us by ruining you. I am well aware that such a course of action would never have occurred to you, if you had not been cast out friendless and alone—"

"Uncle—"

He held up a forbidding hand. "No, Lizzie. I am fully sensible of my role in your downfall, and there can be no denying it is a considerable one."

"But you see—"

"Allow me to say my piece, my child," he insisted.

"Only if you will allow me to respond in kind at its close!"

He blinked at this, but nodded he was willing. "I suppose that is only fair and part of my penance," he said heavily.

Lizzie sighed and folded her arms. "Continue, then. I will hear you out however erroneous your conclusions."

He ignored this, carrying on doggedly. "I cannot, of course, ever admit you again into my home. Not while Betsy remains there, an innocent who could be contaminated by such company. There are, however, certain worthy institutions where you could seek refuge—"

"I'm going to have to interrupt you there, Uncle Josiah!" Lizzie put in smartly. She pulled off her left glove and brandished her hand. "I am not even remotely ruined, and Betsy need have nothing to fear from my society." She saw his watery gaze alight and fasten on the ring there. "Until my marriage, I resided in female-only lodgings with people who stood true friends to me in my hour of need. I neither require your help or that of any worthy charity, I assure you."

His chest heaved. "Am I to understand that Mr. Toomes has made you his wife?"

"You are."

His rheumy gaze rested on her heavily. "Annie did mention he made such a claim, but I assumed this was mere subterfuge—" He broke off. "Well, that is something, indeed, that he has given you the protection of his name. Yet, despite this mark of respect, I find he has still seen fit to bring you into this low company."

Lizzie checked the hot words that sprang to her tongue. "His family is also part of this company," she pointed out quietly. "I am sure you would not encourage me to look down on my husband's own kin."

Uncle Josiah shook his head. "When I negotiated the terms of Betsy's marriage, Benedict Toomes told me he had fully renounced all such associations. I saw deeds to a respectable house, details of investments and savings that would assure her future. Yet you he sees fit to drag from one immoral cesspit to another." He shook his head again. "I fear you have made a bad bargain, Lizzie."

"Well, I had no one to negotiate on my behalf, did I?" she responded tartly and saw him color. "I had no fond father to fight my corner, for your brother is dead." That shaft, too, sank home, and her uncle's mottled purple cheeks took on a waxy glow. Lizzie took a quick breath. "But Benedict Toomes did marry me in God's house and our union was duly witnessed, so you need have no fear for my immortal soul, even if I am surrounded with what you deem to be low company."

She stood and her uncle hastily leaped to his feet. "I assure you, Uncle, that my role in what happened does not trouble my conscience and neither does it keep me awake at night plagued

338

by fears of judgment. I was always a good niece to you and my aunt and did my best by my cousin despite a lack of any true sympathy or understanding between us. As for the actions that saw me thrown from your house, I abided by the tenets and principles of the faith you raised me in. I spoke nothing but the God-given truth and refused moreover to bear false witness, something you saw fit to punish and ostracize me for."

Her uncle's breathing was ragged by this point, and his eyes darted anywhere they could to avoid her own. "What's worse is that I think you must have known deep down. No one was more shocked than I by Reverend Milson's perfidy."

"You shall not say so," her uncle said feebly. "The reverend *must* be beyond reproach. Our community has invested heavily in his cause and—"

Lizzie broke him off with a sharp laugh. "He's a thief, Uncle. If you have invested heavily in him, then I feel sorry for you. Such a course of action will surely end in disaster. The one on the road to ruin is you, not I." She gave him one last truly pitying look and then turned on her heel.

"Wait!" he called after her hoarsely, but Lizzie did not attend. She hurried straight out of the tea tent with Sebastian on her heels and collided into a figure lingering in the entrance.

Lizzie was already apologizing when she realized it was Daphne loitering there. "Are you spying on me again?" she demanded with sudden suspicion. Daphne bridled, looked as though she would deny it for a moment, but then seemed to suffer a change of heart.

"What if I am?" she challenged. "Someone needs to keep an eye on what you're up to! I saw you sneaking off with yet another man! The Toomeses may think you're something special, but I knows better!" she sneered, plunking her hands on her hips.

Lizzie regarded her with exasperation. "I haven't got time for this right now, Daphne," she said, glancing over her shoulder to make sure her uncle wasn't about to appear. She started to move away, but Daphne kept apace with her.

"So, who was he, then? Your latest fancy man?"

Lizzie ignored her, her brain teeming with the information her uncle had just imparted. Apparently, she had been wrong in thinking Benedict had lied about having money and a house to secure Betsy's hand in marriage. Uncle Josiah said he had seen deeds and accounts. Had they been falsified? Or was it possible Benedict had a secret life he had not told her of, one where he did not live in a wagon touring from fair to fair?

Lizzie's mind reeled. Daphne buzzed on the edge of her thoughts like an annoying fly, flinging accusations and suspicions at her. Sebastian's ears were stood up, and he looked alert and watchful as he gazed between the two women. They had crossed the field and were entering the campsite now. Lizzie swung around and faced Daphne squarely.

"I should probably tell you that I've written to Maggie and told her the truth."

Daphne's haranguing abruptly stopped. "*What did you say?*" she demanded shrilly.

"I told her that Frank's father and grandmother lied and that he had not betrayed her."

Daphne forced a leer onto her face, though it was clear she was shaken. "That's what you say, but I knows different."

340

"I don't think so. I don't suppose he's looked twice at you," Lizzie retorted.

A furious look passed over the other woman's face, and she surged forward with a vengeful screech, bowling Lizzie clean off her feet. "You rotten, interfering little bitch!"

Lizzie lay a moment, stunned and winded. No sooner had Daphne dropped her full weight on top of her than she landed a wild punch to Lizzie's face.

There was an explosion of white and Lizzie realized she had been punched in her left eye. Abruptly, Daphne gave a horrible gurgling scream as something barreled into her in a blur of dark fur, knocking her off Lizzie.

Lizzie struggled to her knees. "Sebastian!" she croaked, crawling over to where Daphne lay still and limp as a rag doll. Sebastian's eyes rolled, showing his whites, his great jaws clamped about Daphne's neck.

"Oh my God!" Lizzie cried in a shaken voice. Then her blurry vision cleared, and she saw Daphne's terrified expression and realized she was still alive. "Release her, Sebastian. *At once!*" She had to get a hand to Sebastian's collar before he would draw back and even then it was with a show of resistance. "Back, Sebastian!" She shoved the animal behind her, and he made a disgruntled noise in his throat.

Lizzie wrenched the flimsy scarf from Daphne's neck to check what she was sure would be a horribly mangled throat, but to her relief the skin was unpunctured.

Daphne's terrified eyes gazed up at her. "Am I done for?" she choked out. "I can feel my life's blood trickling down me neck!"

"That's drool," Lizzie explained, extracting her handkerchief from her sleeve. "He drooled all over you but has not drawn any blood." She mopped at Daphne's neck and showed her. "See?"

Reassured, Daphne burst promptly into tears. "'E's dangerous, that brute!"

"Keep your voice down. He might take it into his head to tear your throat out next time."

Daphne's eyes widened and she put a hand to her neck with a gasp.

"You should not have attacked me," Lizzie said severely, and for the first time she felt the throb of her own eye. "You punched me in the face," she said incredulously.

Daphne sniffed. "Well, you've gone and properly queered me pitch, so I'd say we was even."

Lizzie flopped down beside her and felt around her eye. It already felt slightly puffy. She gave a groan. "What am I going to tell Benedict?"

"Never mind that," Daphne sniffed. "Who's going to take over my duties?" she demanded. "You? The only man you've ever enticed is Benedict Toomes! Going to pick up all my cooking and cleaning after the Toomes menfolk and caring of the old gal, are you?" She snorted.

"Certainly not, I have my own man to take care of," Lizzie answered coolly. "As for Ma, she's cleared out."

Daphne's mouth dropped open. "What?" she squawked.

"She didn't sleep in the wagon with you last night, did she?"

"Well, no, but—"

"There you are, then. She'll be halfway to Shropshire by now. Probably hitched a ride on a hay wagon. She won't be coming back."

Daphne was clearly flummoxed by this news. "She would have told me!" she rallied.

"No, she wouldn't," Lizzie replied with a quiet firmness which seemed to take the air out of the other woman's sails.

Daphne's shoulders slumped. "What about me?" she demanded aggressively. "What am I supposed to do now? You tell me that, my fine lady!"

Lizzie regarded her a moment in heavy silence. "Is there any way that you and Maggie could make up your differences?" she asked wearily. After all, Daphne *was* very good at drawing in the spectators to the boxing tent, and Lizzie had a sneaking suspicion Maggie would be just as useless at that as she was.

"Hardly!" Daphne scoffed. "You know what my old mum told her. What I let her believe about her husband and me carrying on," she muttered angrily. "Soon as Frank finds out, I'll be out on me ear!"

"Could you join your mother and Pa Toomes wherever they've gone?" Lizzie suggested. "At the seaside."

"What? Just roll up there, another mouth to feed after they told me they'd handed Frank to me like a ripe plum? Oh, yes, vastly pleased to see me, they'd be!" she said bitterly.

"Well, realistically, what *are* your choices?" Lizzie asked.

Daphne rested her chin on her hands a moment, sunk in thought. "I reckon I'm due some reparation for the past year I've spent skivvying for this family," she muttered sulkily. "Threw a good number of punters their way too, I did. And let

343

me tell you, before Benedict returned to the fold, they weren't putting half as good a showing as they are now! Scraping the barrel they was, some days."

"I can well believe it," Lizzie admitted. "But I don't have any money to give to you."

Daphne tapped a finger against her chin. "What if you was to help me now?" she suggested boldly. "What if we was to hitch up that wagon that me and Ma been sharing to one of the cobs, and I showed a clean pair of heels before the menfolk returned?"

Lizzie considered. Perhaps, all told, it would be for the best. An ugly scene was sure to ensue once Frank's wife returned armed with the truth. And Pa Toomes was the one who had devised the scheme to get rid of his daughter-in-law. In some lights, Daphne could be seen as something of a pawn, simply trying to get by in life.

"Very well," she responded after a moment's consideration.

Daphne blinked. "You're a cool one, ain't you?" she marveled. "I half feel sorry for the poor bugger what falls afoul of you." She dropped her hand from her neck, and Lizzie saw it was showing some redness. There would be nasty bruising on the morrow.

"We had better not delay," Lizzie said briskly. "If we pack up your things and get you on the road, Jack and Frank will think you and Ma departed together. That way they won't kick up a fuss about the missing horse and wagon."

Daphne nodded and clambered to her feet. Once there, she stuck down a hand to Lizzie, who took it, for she felt a little dizzy, and clambered to her feet. "Sebastian," she called, looking around. He bounded forward with his tongue lolling out, and Lizzie heard Daphne's sharply indrawn breath. "Here, boy."

Twenty minutes later, Lizzie and Sebastian watched the wagon pull out onto the track and head out toward the road. Daphne turned in the seat and waved. "No offence," she cried. "But I hope to God our paths never cross again, Lizzie Toomes."

Lizzie nodded. "Good luck to you, Daphne!" she called, and then turned and headed for their own wagon.

Lizzie felt worn out and fed up. "I don't know why you're looking at me like that," she said to Sebastian as she gathered sticks for the fire. Deep down she knew alright. Benedict would be looking for her in the main arena. For the life of her, Lizzie could not muster the energy to return there now. It had been a long day, and she just wanted to curl up in front of the fire and nurse her wounds.

"I don't feel guilty at all," she insisted as Sebastian continued to gaze at her expectantly. Grabbing him a bone out of the sack, she threw it under the wagon and set about lighting the fire. Once it was done, she fetched herself a blanket and wrapped it about her head and shoulders, hoping the growing shadows and the folds of the cloth would hide her swollen eye.

I saw deeds to a respectable house… Yet you, he sees fit to drag from one immoral cesspit to another. Lizzie closed her eyes as she remembered her uncle's words. When first she'd married Benedict and seen the wagon, she had assumed *this* had been his home. It seemed now that was not the case at all.

Or was it? She pulled her blanket about her, feeling more and more confused. Maybe he had lied to the Andersons and then tired of all the subterfuge and that was why he had broken things off with Betsy? Certainly, her cousin would not have lasted more than twenty-four hours in this life. Then again,

345

maybe if Benedict had married Betsy, he would not have expected her to live this life at all. Her mouth twisted. *There was no "maybe" about it.*

To her astonishment, she felt the tear running down her cheek and angrily swiped it away. She certainly wasn't going to sit here crying about the fact her husband might had deceived her.

A heavy footfall had Sebastian starting up from under the wagon and Lizzie half turning in her seat.

"There you are!" Benedict exclaimed. "I've been twice around the field looking for you! What made you come back here without me?" He surveyed her bundled form with concern and crouched down before her. "Feeling ill?" His hand was at her brow before she could answer.

"I'm not ill."

He drew back and looked at her searchingly. "You're sure? You don't look yourself."

She shook her head and he frowned. "Have you eaten?"

"I'm not hungry."

"Tell me what's wrong," he said, narrowing his eyes. "You look like you've been crying."

But all Lizzie would do was shake her head. After a moment, she heard him move away. When he returned, he did so with a pan of water which he set over the fire before fetching more wood.

Lizzie supposed she should go and fetch the tea things, but for some reason she remained huddled where she was, her eyes trained on the fire.

"Is it your woman's time?" he asked in a low voice as he threw logs onto the growing flames.

This startled Lizzie out of her torpor. "No!"

"Is this about Banbury, then?" he persisted.

Banbury? Lizzie gazed at him blankly a moment before remembering this particular bone of contention. "Nothing is wrong!" she lied and made as though to stand. "I'll fetch the teapot."

"I'll get it."

It was while Benedict was brewing up that Sebastian bounded up and started barking. He stopped as soon as he saw Jack appear around the side of the wagon.

"They've gone, upped sticks and left!" Jack announced. "Ma and Daphne both. Took both the wagon and the brown mare."

For a moment, Benedict met her gaze wordlessly over the fire, and she remembered that he already knew about Ma leaving the previous day for Shropshire. Silently, Lizzie cursed the fact she had blabbed to him about that. However, when he spoke, it was only to offer Jack a cup of tea in the blandest of voices.

"Didn't you hear what I said?" his youngest brother remonstrated, dropping down onto a convenient seat.

"I did," Benedict admitted as he spooned sugar into a cup. "Daphne was at the boxing tent earlier," he pointed out slowly.

"She was," Jack agreed. "But I never saw her after five and that much I'll swear."

When Benedict squeezed the last of a lemon into her cup and held it out to her, Lizzie roused herself to speech. "When was the last time you saw your grandmother?" she asked, accepting the cup and avoiding Benedict's eyes.

Jack rubbed the stubble on his chin thoughtfully. "I wouldn't like to say for sure," he admitted. "I saw her yesterday alright, but I couldn't swear I even clapped eyes on her today."

Benedict grunted. "You got any notion why they'd take themselves off?"

"None," Jack said. "I wanted to ask the same of you."

"It's nothing to do with us," Benedict said coolly. "Ask Frank." Then something seemed to catch his eye, for he tensed up and stepped around the fire, whipping away Lizzie's blanket and dragging her to feet. "What's this?" he asked sharply, tilting her head and looking fully into her face. "Someone's struck you!"

Sebastian gave a warning growl, and Lizzie spoke to him quickly. "Sebastian!" He lowered his head to his paws and lay back down.

Jack gave a low whistle. "That's going to be quite the shiner tomorrow, Lizzie my girl."

"Don't call her that, she's not your girl!" Benedict snapped, making his brother chuckle. "And it's no joking matter." He turned back to Lizzie. "When did this happen? In Connie's tent? Some customer got rough with you?" His face grew grim. "You should have fetched me if there was any trouble. I want the name of the bastard that hit you."

"It wasn't there. You've got it all wrong," Lizzie said, struggling to free herself from his grip.

"Tell me how, then?"

"Benedict…" Jack started but halted when his brother swung around to look at him.

348

"Do something useful, can't you?" Benedict bit out. "Go and buy me a raw steak."

"What about Ma and Daphne—" Jack began, but again did not get to finish for his brother had skewered him with a furious glance. "Alright, alright," he said, raising his hands and backing away. "I'll leave you to tend the wounded."

Benedict turned back to her with kindling eye. "Tell me now," he rapped out in clipped tones. "But I may as well say it straight, you're never to set foot in that tent again—"

"It wasn't anything to do with Wondrous Females!" Lizzie protested. He opened his mouth, but she cut him off. "It was Daphne," she admitted. "But—" His violent swearing cut off her words. "Benedict!" she gasped and clapped her hands to her ears. When he moved as though to fling away, she reached out and caught hold of him. "Where are you going?"

"To have a little word with Daphne," he gritted out.

"She's gone, remember?"

That caught his attention. "Gone?" He scowled. "Thought to save her own skin, I suppose."

Lizzie surveyed the murderous look on his face with alarm. "Benedict… Calm down. People pummel you every day and I do not fly off the handle like this."

"That's my job, Lizzie. She had no right to lay a finger on you."

Lizzie plucked at the sleeve she still grasped tightly. "I told her what I had done. Written to Maggie, I mean," she admitted. "That was what incensed her."

"Sit down," he urged, lowering her onto the three-legged stool. "I'm going to fetch water and a clean cloth."

349

Lizzie murmured some agreement and exchanged a wary look with Sebastian as her husband took off muttering darkly under his breath. She could not imagine that one swollen eye could merit all this fuss and felt frankly embarrassed by the whole business. Sebastian ducked his head and did a fake-looking yawn, clearly unwilling to admit his own role in proceedings.

Benedict returned with a bowl of cold water and dabbed at her eye with a cloth to clean it. When next he spoke, it was in a low, terse voice. "You should not be exposed to such company. I was mad to bring you here."

It was uncanny how closely his words echoed her own uncle's. Lizzie tipped her head to one side. "I disagree—"

"No, I've learned my lesson," he cut her off. "I'll write to Edwards on the morrow and get the tenants out of Winchester Street."

Lizzie caught her breath. "Winchester Street?"

He turned abstractedly. "It's the house I own."

Lizzie almost reeled. "House?" Now, he saw fit to mention this alleged house? "I thought the wagon was your home."

He ignored this. "As soon as I can, I'll have you installed as mistress there."

Inexplicably, Lizzie felt a surge of panic. "Don't I get any say in this?"

"I'll have to finish up the season here, but I can join you later. I'll speak to Frank and Jack about buying me out of the booth."

"Now just a minute, Benedict!" Lizzie interrupted him hotly. "Don't you think we should discuss this with cooler heads?"

His eyes refocused on her and took on an exasperated expression. "Haven't you heard a word I've said?" he demanded. "This is what I should have done at the very outset. I was mad to drag you into this life." He snatched up the cloth and started wringing it out with a savagery that surprised her.

"No, it isn't, Benedict!" she protested. "Is this the house you told Betsy you had bought for your married lives together?" she asked stiffly.

He froze. "What?"

"She mentioned something about it, but I thought you must have deceived her."

"I never—" He broke off. "She never even saw the place!"

Lizzie shook her head angrily. "Well, I don't want to live there!" she burst out mutinously.

Benedict ground his teeth. "Fine, I'll sell that house and buy another, then. Tell me what sort of house you *do* want."

"I don't know that I care to live in any house when my husband continues to tour."

It was at this point that Jack appeared carrying a brown paper parcel done up with string.

"Got your steak," he said, presenting it with a flourish. "How's the patient?"

"Your brother is making an inordinate amount of fuss about naught but a tiny scuffle," Lizzie said with a kindling eye.

"Hold still!" Benedict scolded her, taking the raw steak from his brother.

"You solved the mystery yet? Of how it happened?" Jack asked him humorously.

"I have. Daphne belted her and then took off into the night."

"What?" Jack was thunderstruck. "Daphne did? Why in God's name?"

"What are you doing with that piece of meat?" Lizzie asked with misgiving as Benedict cast the paper and string into the fire.

"Hold still."

Lizzie recoiled from the wet, cold press of the steak against her eye, but Benedict's firm grip would not allow her to retreat from his ministrations.

"So the two of you came to blows?" Jack said, scratching his head. "Maybe we should put her in the ring, eh, Ben? The Fighting Toomeses and no mistake."

"The only one she fights with is me," Benedict said through gritted teeth. "And that's with words, never fists."

"Benedict wants to send me away!" Lizzie burst out angrily.

"What?" Jack's face fell. "Then what was the point in Daphne clearing out?"

Benedict turned sharply to his brother. "That vicious bitch would have stayed over my dead body!" he said with such seething anger that even Jack fell back a step.

"Yes, well," his younger brother said hastily. "That may be so, Ben, but you can't deny she was damn useful to us about the place, cooking and cleaning. Not to mention drumming up business for the tent. But well, if she's gone now, then that's all there is to it."

"You haven't even asked me who it was instigated the fight," Lizzie pointed out in an odd voice.

Benedict's eyes flickered a moment. "That's because I don't care," he admitted.

Jack spluttered. "Ben!"

"So, was it you who started it?" Benedict responded, a challenging gleam in his eye.

Lizzie's gaze fell before his own. "I—well, I provoked a verbal fight with her," she admitted.

"That's not the same thing and you know it," he responded and unscrewed a bottle of ointment which smelled very pungent.

"Why did you quarrel?" Jack asked her curiously.

"Because of Maggie," Lizzie responded. "Ow! That stings!" Benedict was applying it to a spot on her temple that she hadn't even realized was grazed.

"I know it does, sweetheart," Benedict replied gravely. "But I want your face to heal."

His tone was so tender that Lizzie caught her breath and Jack backed away with alarm. "Right," he called back in a cheerful voice. "I'll head back and er—leave you to it. I'll fill Frank in with what's happened with the womenfolk."

"Good night," Lizzie called after him, though she kept her eyes on Benedict's face. "I'm not being sent away to some house I've never seen while you finish the year touring with your brothers." It was hard to sound firm and reasonable when she had a piece of raw steak stuck to half her face, but she attempted it anyway.

"We'll talk about it later." He refilled the kettle over the fire and fetched her cloak from the wagon, tucking it about her. "I'm going to fetch us some food," he said abruptly. "You're going to eat it, and then we'll turn in early. Don't take that off your eye."

Lizzie fumed silently as he tilted her head back to the angle he thought necessary to keep the meat applied to her eye and then walked away. "Outrageous!" she muttered, kicking her foot against a pail of water. "As though I have no say of my own!"

Sebastian's ears went back, and he flashed her a sheepish look as he lowered his muzzle onto his front paws. "You weren't much help either!" she grouched, leaning across to test the weight of the teapot. When she'd determined there was another drop to be squeezed out of it, she helped herself to another cup and navigated sipping it with some difficulty with her head tipped back.

Hearing footsteps, she squinted into the darkness and saw Frank approaching, a troubled expression on his face. Sebastian bounded up and circled around the newcomer making huffing noises which Lizzie recognized indicated excitement more than hostility. Clearly Frank thought so too, for he did not look concerned by the dog's attentions.

"He's gone to fetch us some supper," Lizzie explained, seeing Frank look about for his brother. She thought he looked a little relieved to hear this as he patted distractedly at Sebastian's head. The dog tolerated this for a moment only before returning to sit beside the fire.

"Can I see?" Frank nodded to her face as he crouched down beside her.

"It's really nothing," Lizzie said as she lifted the steak momentarily to reveal her eye.

He flinched, his expression growing even more grave. "I can't believe Daphne did that," he said, swallowing. He looked away briefly as though steeling himself for bad news. "Can you explain to me—the remark you made to Jack."

"Which remark?" Lizzie stalled, though she could guess well enough.

"About why this happened," Frank continued doggedly. "Jack said, well, he seemed to think that…" He trailed off as though unable to continue. "That it was something to do with Maggie."

"I confronted Daphne about what Ma told me yesterday."

Frank's eyes flew to hers in painstaking enquiry. "What did Ma tell you?"

"That your father decided to replace Maggie with Daphne, so they fed your wife a bunch of lies."

Frank collapsed down onto the seat Benedict had vacated. He passed a shaking hand over his brow. "Pa did that?" he croaked and then lapsed into heavy silence. "He told Maggie that me and Daphne—" Lizzie nodded. "And he told me the people were talking about how she was carrying on behind my back." His voice rasped until it sounded like his throat closed over.

"Yes, so I gathered from what you told me the other day. He worked on your pride, I suppose. Your grandmother said Jedidiah Toomes had first messed up Benedict by letting him go into the workhouse and then you by getting rid of your wife."

Frank started violently at her mention of the workhouse. "For God's sake," he said hoarsely, looking about. "Do not mention that place to Benedict. She never should have told you of that."

"Of course she should!" Lizzie said briskly. "Benedict's secrets are safe with me. And besides, he will tell me of it himself, with time. After all, he says that no one is closer to a man than his wife."

Frank stared at her before covering his face with his hands. "I can't believe—" he started in a choked voice. "That Maggie thought I played her false. And with *Daphne*."

"Well, Daphne is a very handsome woman," Lizzie said, taking a final sip of cold tea.

"You never met my Maggie. Daphne couldn't hold a candle to her." He brooded a moment in silence. "All this time, I thought it was that plain-faced friend of hers turning her against me, never my own father."

"Aggie?" asked Lizzie with interest. "The Living Skeleton?"

"Aye, her. Maggie was always running off to her and telling her all her woes. That was about the time she stopped talking to me altogether."

"Well, it sounds like there were already some cracks in your marriage before your father started prizing them even further apart," Lizzie remarked dryly.

Frank grimaced. "It was all my fault. We married very young and I...I never stuck up for her like I should have."

Sebastian leaped upright, and they both turned to see Benedict approaching with a parcel wrapped up in paper.

"Battered fish," he said, holding it aloft.

Lizzie would have preferred to hear a little more of Frank's thoughts before her husband's return, but seeing the meaningful look Benedict angled his brother's way, Frank soon departed, leaving them to their food.

"What did he want?" Benedict asked, throwing a look after Frank. "He wasn't bothering you to know where Ma went?"

"He never mentioned her once," Lizzie replied truthfully. "He wanted to check on my eye."

Benedict grunted. "That's alright, then." He washed his hands and then turned the steak over. The coldness made Lizzie flinch, but he murmured soothingly to her. "It's bringing out the bruise."

They ate their supper largely in silence. When they had finished, Benedict carried a bucket of hot water inside the wagon for her and carried her over to the door.

"I'm not infirm," Lizzie objected, but was ignored.

"Do you need me to help you into your nightgown?"

"Of course not!" she spluttered. "I meant to do some sewing this evening on the new curtains."

"No," he interrupted her. "You're resting that eye tonight and that's my final word."

Lizzie leaned back and regarded him narrowly, though she suspected the effect might be ruined by the fact it was only through the one eye.

"I'll join you in ten minutes," he murmured unperturbed and swung her inside the wagon. In truth it was more like five. Lizzie had scarcely tied the bow at her neck before he was opening the door and slamming it shut behind him.

"Sebastian's settled."

"And Florence?" she asked. She had felt a bit guilty seeing Daphne depart with the brown cob. She had no idea if Frank or Jack had a favorite among their horses.

357

"Both are fine."

She had wondered if he might press her for more information about Ma or Daphne, but Benedict seemed wholly unconcerned about either of them. She climbed into the bed. "I can't possibly keep this on my face all night. What shall I do? Remove it before I fall asleep?"

Benedict murmured some agreement to this as he undressed, and Lizzie stared up at the ceiling with one eye, fiercely trying to think of counterarguments in case he tried forbidding her from work tomorrow. Goodness only knew when she would next see her friends! She was determined, in any event, that she would not be prevented from sharing their company while she still had the opportunity.

Mercifully, however, her husband did not even attempt to raise the subject; he merely settled beside her and wrapped an arm about her waist. "Go to sleep," he growled, almost as though he could hear her busy thoughts.

23

Benedict left Lizzie outside the Wondrous Females tent the next morning without bothering to voice any objections he knew she would disregard. Her eye was not swollen this morning, though the area underneath and in the inner corner was a bright mottled red. She let him inspect it and apply a little ointment before they left their fireside, and then she expected him to act as though nothing ailed her.

Hearing a stifled expletive, Benedict turned back to see Connie had come bursting out of the tent after him, but Lizzie had a hold of her arm and was gabbling into her ear at top speed. Connie relaxed and disappeared back into the tent. It occurred to Benedict that his wife's employer must have thought he was the one who had given Lizzie the eye. He was both impressed and surprised that Connie had sought to tackle him about it. Connie Brown had always been a man's woman, but evidently, Lizzie had won her over.

And she wasn't the only one, he thought when both his brothers asked after Lizzie as soon as he entered the boxing tent. Jack followed this up with a flurry of complaints about having no one to make their breakfast or light the fire for them that morning.

"Do it yourself, you lazy bastard," Benedict growled.

Jack pulled a face. "That would mean getting up earlier," he grumbled.

Frank said nothing, but Benedict noticed he was quiet and distracted all morning. The midweek point at Putney Heath was an all-day event, from ten in the morning until ten at night. He wasn't surprised when his older brother drew him to one side before lunch and told him he would need to take some time away from the booth at some point soon, and that he and Jack would have to hold the fort.

"For how long?" Benedict asked with a frown. If Frank was talking of going off, how was he supposed to make his own plans for settling Lizzie at Winchester Street?

"I don't know yet," Frank admitted. "I haven't firmed up how I'm to go about it."

Benedict raised his brows, and Frank drew himself up. "I'll need some time off, to go in search of her, Ben. You must see that."

"Which one?"

Frank bristled. "Maggie, of course!"

"Oh? And where will you start?"

"I suppose I'll have to make some enquiries. There was that friend of hers that worked for Connie." Frank frowned. "I haven't seen her in months, come to think of it. Then there was that one Farini sister. Sophia, I think?" He scratched his neck. "It's a starting point anyway."

Benedict debated a moment telling him all that he knew, but for some reason held his tongue. After all, he didn't need another reason for Lizzie to be pissed at him. He had given her plenty already, what with the house he owned and hadn't told her about. "Well," he prevaricated. "You'll need to lay your plans first. No point rushing off half-cocked."

Frank nodded. "Aye, I know."

"If you mean to speak to anyone at Wondrous Females, then you'll have to do it today." At Frank's curious look, he explained Connie's company were packing up to leave for Banbury tomorrow.

"Right," Frank said. "Thanks for the tip."

Benedict's mood did not improve at lunchtime when he headed over to Connie's tent only to find it empty and a sign pinned to the entrance saying they were closed and would return next year. He stared at it a moment before peering inside to check if Lizzie had waited for him. She had not. Not only that, but everything was tidied away neatly into packing cases and trunks. They must have spent the morning packing up. He bought a ham sandwich and returned to the boxing tent in a somewhat worse mood.

"That was quick," Jack said, looking up at his reentrance.

"Lizzie's gone off to lunch without me," he admitted, unwrapping his sandwich.

Frank looked up from where he was sat drinking oxtail soup but made no comment.

"What have you done to rile her up?" asked Jack, who was not so tactful.

"Bought a house," Benedict admitted, dropping down onto an upturned box that doubled up as a chair.

Frank spluttered on his soup. "You did?"

"It was before we got married," Benedict added defensively in the face of his brothers' incredulous stares.

"Is that what she meant yesterday when she said you were planning on sending her away?" Jack asked. "I thought that blow to the head had scattered her wits."

"You're what?" demanded Frank. "Why in God's name would you do that?"

"It's cutting off your nose to spite your own face, if you ask me!" Jack agreed.

"Because," Benedict said, swallowing his mouthful of sandwich, "this isn't a fit life for her. She deserves better."

"So, you're leaving again too, are you? Again?" asked Jack testily.

"The first time I didn't have much choice about it," Benedict reminded him. "I was in prison."

"Well, when you put it that way, you're not exactly a fit husband for her either, are you?" his younger brother responded. Benedict leaped off his box and Frank got between them. "I only meant," Jack clarified, "that she married you in spite of your prison sentence, you bad-tempered bastard."

Benedict simmered down, just a tad. "She was in a tight spot," he admitted, returning to his seat, and picking it up off the floor. "I took advantage of that fact." He hesitated. "When I married her, she had no clue I'd be dragging her around the fairs."

Jack whistled, but Frank shook his head. "That's not really something you ought to spring on a person, Ben."

"I know that. When I married her…" His brothers both looked at him expectantly, and he found he couldn't say the words *I didn't like her that much.* He'd respected her, but he hadn't liked her. Not then.

"You were scared she'd turn you down flat if she knew the truth?" Jack guessed.

Benedict decided to let that stand. "Something like that, maybe," he muttered.

"Well, she seems to have taken to it well enough," Frank commented, scratching the side of his face.

Jack snorted. "He coddles her something awful!"

"I do not!"

"That's nothing to be ashamed of," Frank put in reasonably. "I wish I'd taken a leaf out of your book." Benedict lapsed into silence.

"She ever said she's not happy with this life?" Jack asked. "Cos if you ask me, she was hopping mad yesterday when you said you'd send her away."

Benedict rubbed his eyes. "She can't take over for Daphne outside the tent," he said shortly. "If that's what you're thinking. And she's certainly not picking up your cooking and cleaning."

"She doesn't even do yours!" Jack retorted. "Has she cooked you a single meal since you were wed?"

"I don't expect her to," Benedict retorted and saw his brothers both were taken aback. "That's not why I married her." They seemed at a loss of how to respond to that. "She was raised in a house with a cook and a maid," he added grudgingly. "I doubt she'd even know where to start."

"Oh," Frank said lamely. "Well, she's picking things up as she goes along, I daresay."

Benedict shrugged. Such things didn't concern him overmuch.

"How will you afford to keep her in such a style, with cookmaids and the like?" Jack asked. "You heard from Nat about any future fights he might be able to put your way?"

"No," Benedict cut him off. "And nor is he like to. But I've a good sum of money put by. I need to make some decisions how to invest it and what line of business to go into." Even as he said it out loud, he knew his words lacked conviction. What business did he know of except for boxing? Or want to know for that matter? He sat stock-still a moment, letting this sink in.

Was that the reason why he'd never managed to settle on anything these last couple of months? He'd had enough opportunities dangled before him by Edwards, his man of business, and others keen for his input. Clem's mad scheme about a theater had been another, but nothing had appealed.

Sitting here in the tent, opposite his brothers, he experienced a moment of clarity. He didn't want to be anywhere else. That was one of the reasons why he'd felt so bloody relieved when he'd joined them at Greenwich. He'd thought at the time it was the last-minute escape from marrying Betsy, but part of it had been returning to the family fold all along. He felt dazed at the realization.

"I want to stay with the booth," he admitted abruptly. "Turning my hand to anything else just wouldn't feel right."

"Good," replied Frank, looking relieved. "But, Ben," he hesitated. "I don't think you'll do so well with her stashed elsewhere."

"Of course not!" he snapped, rubbing his face. "I didn't think things through."

Jack chortled. "Well, at least you'll own you put a foot wrong in this regard. It'll be some consolation to poor old Frank that you don't know *everything* there is to know about being the world's perfect husband."

Benedict darted a quick glance at Frank, who looked a little pained. "I'm far from perfect," he said gruffly. "As you both know."

"We're glad you're sticking around, Ben," Frank said sincerely. "Things will be easier now we're all of one accord when it comes to the old man." His expression grew grim. "I certainly won't be making excuses for him now I know the trick he served me over Maggie. I'll be the first to run him off if he turns up again."

The brothers lapsed into silence as they contemplated the prospect of their father.

"Though for my part," said Jack, sticking out his chin. "I don't think our mother was much better, if you look at how she left you, Ben."

Benedict bristled and saw the warning look Frank sent to their younger brother. Breathing in, then out again, he let his idealized picture of his mother slowly fade away. "No," he said thoughtfully. "No, I suppose she wasn't."

*

It had been a strange sort of day, all told. Benedict was making his way toward the Wondrous Females tent when he spied Sebastian in the distance. Quickening his pace, he soon saw the dog was, as usual, on his mistress's heels.

Lizzie was sandwiched between her redheaded friend and Connie Brown. They seemed to be headed back in the general direction of their own tent, though taking a rather circuitous route. Connie said something and the redhead threw back her head to laugh uproariously.

Benedict caught up with them just as they were approaching their tent.

"Oh, Benedict!" Lizzie said, pitching forward and almost barreling into him. He closed his arms around her automatically and thought he got a whiff of gin. "I said he'd be waiting for me, didn't I?" she asked of the other two, attempting to turn about and nearly tripping over Benedict's feet. He tightened his grip on her waist to steady her.

Connie guffawed. "We've been celebratin'," she said with a defiant air. "And wishing our dear Lizzie all the best, until we reunite again."

Benedict glanced back down at Lizzie's vacant smile. Her eye looked none the worst, for all it had turned a deeper purple. "Been enjoying yourself, have you?" he asked, quirking a brow at her.

Lizzie tipped her head back. "I have," she sighed. "Connie bought us such a lovely pitcher of fruit punch."

"Two pitchers," the redhead corrected her.

Lizzie's eyes widened. "Did we drink two whole pitchers?" she marveled.

"Goes down awful easy, don't it?" Connie cocked a knowing look at Benedict. "You'd best take your leave of us now, Lizzie girl. That man of yours will be wanting to drag you off for your supper."

"What about packing up the tent?" Lizzie asked, but Connie seized hold of her and kissed her cheek. "I've already hired a couple of burly hands to see to it. Until next time. Be off with you."

Niamh kissed her other cheek. "Take care of yourself, Lizzie darlin'. We'll soon be all back together."

Benedict led a tottering Lizzie away. "We'd better get something substantial inside your stomach," he remarked wryly. "Or you'll be feeling the worst for it in the morning, and we've an early start."

Lizzie was hanging off his arm and humming a tune. Suddenly she came to a standstill. "Where's Sebastian?" she remarked, looking around. "Oh, there he is."

Benedict steered her toward the food stands. She had a potato with minced meat and gravy, and they made their way back to the wagon with a meandering step. She ate most of her food and then set down the last of it for Sebastian to finish off. Benedict handed her up into the wagon as she was yawning her head off.

"I'll bring the water in for you to wash as soon as it's ready." She nodded, removing her bonnet and sitting on the edge of the bed.

"There's just one thing I can't figure out," she said, frowning with concentration.

"What's that?"

"What kind of a marriage did your grandmother and grandfather have?"

Benedict gazed back at her. "A rotten one," he answered after a pause.

"Oh." Her frown cleared. "That makes *perfect* sense to me."

Instead of saying anything further, she flopped back onto the bed and rolled onto her side.

Benedict watched her a moment in silence. Then, realizing nothing else was forthcoming, he pulled the door shut and set about fetching the water. It seemed they would not be clearing the air tonight about the house on Winchester Street.

It didn't take him long to feed and water the horse, and he smoked awhile as he waited for the water to heat. He debated helping himself to Lizzie's writing supplies to send some new instruction to Edwards, but what was the point in throwing out his tenants if they weren't going to live there for at least another nine months?

He cast the butt of his cigarillo away, removed the water, and put out the fire. Letting himself into the wagon, he found, as he knew he would, Lizzie fast asleep. He lit the lamp and moved to the bed, swiftly unlacing her boots. She stirred but did not wake. He moved on to her stockings and then her dress and underclothing, until he had her swathed in her nightgown and tucked under the covers.

When he dabbed at her eye area with some water to clean it and then followed this up with the ointment, she flinched and murmured. "Shhh, let me do it," he soothed her.

His words seemed to do the trick, and she relaxed back onto the pillows with a sigh. Benedict glanced toward her wash bag but knew she would not appreciate him trying to tackle her with either hair or toothbrush. Pulling out any obvious hairpins he could see, he realized this would simply have to do for her evening's toilette.

Moving back over to the washbasin, he saw to his own wash and then stripped down to his underwear for bed. When he pulled back the blankets to climb in, she rolled onto her side toward him and cuddled into him. Benedict lifted his arm to accommodate her and then settled it about her, resting his hand at her waist.

He'd sell the damned house if that was what she wanted. After all, what was the point of keeping it if she didn't like it? While it was true, he had bought the house with marriage in mind, he had not precisely thought of Betsy, but rather some vague idea of what he thought a gentleman's residence should be.

At the end of the day, he was under no illusions about his own claim to the title of gentleman. He had none. The best thing he could do at this point was simply be led by Lizzie in what was acceptable to her and what was not. Gazing into the darkness at their current cramped conditions, he found it hard to believe her standards could be all that exacting. After all, she seemed content enough in this tiny box. With him.

24

Lizzie woke abruptly, her eyes heavy and a bad taste in her mouth. She lay a moment in confusion before realizing she was safely in her bed. Though, now she came to think of it, she could not remember climbing into it. Glancing to her side, she found she was alone in the bed. Where was Benedict?

Sitting up, she could see light streaming through the small window at the foot of the bed and guessed it was midmorning. He must be up and about already!

Swinging her legs off the mattress, Lizzie grimaced, feeling her sore head. Raising her hands to massage her temples, she realized she had imbibed rather too *much* fruit punch. She had not brushed her teeth the previous night either, she thought with a groan and moved across to the wash basin which stood on the trunk. The water was cold, but she plunged her hands into it and scooped the water into her face.

That woke her up. She spluttered and swung around for her face towel which she found after a moment's groping about. Then she set about cleaning her teeth with the small horsehair brush she used for that purpose. Her store of tooth powder was running low, she noted. Usually, she made this once a month with her aunt, from powdered castile soap, camphor, and charcoal, but she would need to make her own supplies in future. Perhaps she ought to make a list of ingredients she would need for that and her mouth rinse?

Consulting the small square mirror Benedict used for shaving, she saw the purple of her eye looked a little more yellowish in hue today. Catching sight of her hair, which resembled a rat's nest, Lizzie gave a muffled squeak and grabbed her hairbrush. Each time she passed it through her locks, she snagged it on another concealed hairpin. She would never drink fruit punch again, however delicious. The mere thought of it this morning turned her stomach.

By the time she had thoroughly washed with soap, dressed her hair, and donned her underwear, she heard a fumbling at the door and snatched up her dress to hold it before her. Benedict's face appeared framed in the doorway.

"You're up," he said, climbing inside. "I bought you a currant bun," he said, setting it on the side. "How are you feeling?"

"Better now I've washed and cleaned my teeth."

He nodded. "You'll feel even better when you've eaten something. Come here and let me look at your eye."

Lizzie dropped her dress onto the bed and stepped around it to stand before him. Benedict tipped her head back and gazed down at her eye. "It looks a little better, I think," she said self-consciously.

He grunted and turned away to the door. "Come out when you're ready, the kettle's on."

Lizzie made haste to dress, though her every movement felt sluggish and clumsy. When she joined Benedict moments later by the fire, he was already pouring the tea into their cups. She took a seat, and Sebastian touched his nose to her knee. Lizzie fondled the dog's ears, and he settled beside her to gnaw his bone.

"Thank you," Lizzie said, taking her teacup and warming her hands against it. "I'm sorry about last night."

"Don't be," he answered with a shrug. "Everyone needs to cut loose once in a while."

Lizzie colored and avoided his eyes. She had a feeling he was waiting for the opportunity to say something. She had thought it must be a scolding about her disgraceful intoxication, but clearly that had *not* been it.

She racked her brains for what else it could be. The only other thing she had done that he didn't know about was meeting with her uncle in the tea tent. She felt a sudden panic that someone else might have seen her there and told him of it.

She eyed Benedict uneasily as he kicked his boot against a pile of logs next to the fire. These weren't fallen branches but had been chopped. "Here's a pile for you to keep adding to the fire today." Lizzie looked up at him in surprise. Was she to stay put, then? His face grew stern. "I want you to stay here and rest today, Lizzie."

"But I feel fine now!"

"Connie and the others have moved on, so there's no reason for you to come into the fair. You can sit here quietly and…finish your sewing," he suggested.

Lizzie opened and closed her mouth. Was he angry with her? "Is this about my uncle's visit?" she blurted in a panic. "Because if so, I doubt very much I will ever see him again."

Benedict's frown deepened. "Your uncle?" he repeated, looking thunderstruck. "What do you mean?"

It dawned on Lizzie that she was barking up the wrong tree. Her wits were most definitely blunted today. "Oh," she said lamely. "You didn't mean that."

"When did he visit?" Benedict demanded.

"It was before Daphne punched me, so it sort of slipped my mind, you see."

"It slipped your mind?" he repeated incredulously. Then his expression grew grim. "What did he want?"

Lizzie waved a hand. "Oh, it was just a misunderstanding—" she started, but Benedict crouched down before her, forcing her to meet his eyes.

"What—did—he—want?" he repeated direly.

"To escort me to some sort of charitable institution for fallen women," Lizzie admitted with a sigh. "At least I think that was the gist of it."

"*What?*" Benedict exploded.

"He appeared to be under the impression we were only masquerading as a married couple."

Benedict seemed to be having some difficulty catching his breath. Lizzie watched him with some concern. "I set him right, of course," she hastened to explain.

"He wanted to take you off—"

"No, no—"

"And you did not come and fetch me?" he demanded wrathfully.

"Benedict, it wasn't really like that! He just wanted to do his Christian duty by me. Once I had explained—"

He dragged her up out of her seat, his hands gripping her upper arms. "If he or anyone else from your past should ever appear again, I want you to fetch me, Lizzie. Do you understand?"

Lizzie nodded. "Yes."

"I want your word on that," he said grimly.

"Yes, I promise."

He glared at her wordlessly for a minute, and Lizzie thought it was touch and go. Then he hauled her against his chest.

"Son of a bitch," he swore viciously, and then his mouth was on hers, hot and demanding, his fingers wrapped around her jaw, urging her participation.

Lizzie reeled under the onslaught and clung to his shirtfront for dear life. He was not gentle, but for some reason, she found she did not mind so much. When he tore his mouth from hers, she almost sobbed aloud with disappointment.

"We'll speak more about this later," he said with a scowl. Lizzie nodded dumbly, pulling her shawl back around her shoulders for she had almost lost the garment in their tussle. "Don't let the fire die out," he said direly. "And put some more ointment on that eye!"

He flung off in high dudgeon, and Lizzie watched him stride away with some consternation. Glancing back down, she saw Sebastian had not even troubled to raise his head from his paws. His eyes flickered to meet hers for an instant before he glanced away, looking embarrassed by the scene he had been forced to witness. Clearly, Sebastian was only too well aware she was in no danger from her husband however much he might carry on.

Putting a hand to her spinning head, Lizzie lowered herself back onto her seat. She raised her cup to her lips with a shaking hand. She would finish her tea and then fetch those half-finished curtains outside to complete. The fair was at Putney Heath for another three days, she thought. How was she supposed to occupy herself during that time now the Wondrous Females tent had moved on?

Lizzie sat sewing beside the fire for the next couple of hours. She finished her curtains and even had a go at fixing them to the windows. Admittedly, the results were mixed. There were none of the traditional fixings in place, and only a piece of twine slung across to hang them from. Lizzie surveyed the result with dissatisfaction. She would have to ask Benedict to take a look at it. Maybe with some better string they would hang better.

Returning outside, she considered what she could turn her hand to next. Glancing at the sky, she guessed the time to be about four o'clock. If she did not put another log on the fire, then it was about to go out. Lizzie debated a moment. What she really needed to do was prepare some more tooth powder and mouth rinse. For that she would need peppermint oil and cloves as well as the ingredients she had already noted down.

After all, why should she not do a little shopping for some household items? They needed soap, more lemons, and sugar too. Connie had paid her yesterday, and she still had not spent most of her previous wages. There were sure to be some shops nearby, and she could easily ask for directions.

Her mind made up, Lizzie returned to the wagon for her cloak and bonnet before setting off in the opposite direction to the fairground, Sebastian close on her heels.

25

Benedict's heart thudded painfully in his chest. He peered around the cabin again for the third time. She was definitely gone. Then he noticed the new curtains. Both sets. That calmed him a little. She couldn't have been gone long, and if her intention had been to leave him, then she would hardly have waited to finish them first.

Jumping down onto the ground, he forced himself to rationalize this. The dog was gone too. If she had been snatched by relatives, they would not have taken an animal that would plainly have been hostile to his mistress's abductors.

Benedict looked at the pile of logs which he'd left her. It was only half-diminished. It was that point that he heard his name called. Looking up, he scanned around until he saw her in the distance just coming through the trees at the opposite end of the field. It was undoubtedly Lizzie, for the huge, shaggy gray dog was at her side. She waved.

He took off at a quick jog. "Where were you?" he shouted as soon as he was sure she could make out the words. She held up her arms wordlessly, and he noted the parcels done up in string. *Shopping*. She'd been shopping. He closed the distance between them and took the largest parcels from her. "What have you been buying?"

"Oh, just a few things I needed. Nothing terribly interesting. I got us some more sugar. Have you been back long? I rather underestimated how far I would have to walk to reach the nearest store."

Benedict cleared his throat. "Not long, but long enough," he admitted. He avoided her look of enquiry.

"I've bought supplies to make tooth powder and rinse. I can make up a batch tomorrow," she said brightly. "Did you see I finished the curtains?" He nodded. "I'm not sure I secured them terribly well. We might need some new string put up."

"I'll take a look at it," he said grudgingly.

Lizzie seemed to notice something was amiss at this point and treated him to a long look. "Was everything alright at the boxing tent?" she asked dubiously.

"Fine," he answered shortly. They had reached the wagon by now.

"I got a new bag of meat bones for Sebastian mmfff—" Her words broke off as Benedict chose this moment to drop the parcels and drag Lizzie into his arms for a punishing kiss. Well, that was how it started anyway. He walked her back into the wagon and pinned her against the side of it, pressing into her and letting her feel just how riled up he was.

"Benedict!" she gasped as soon as she was able, only to find herself scooped up and slung into the wagon. She scrambled to her feet at once, her eyes flying to his.

"Take your clothes off," he said, picking up the largest of the two packages. "Which one of these is his bones?" he asked, nodding toward Sebastian.

Lizzie pointed to his left hand. "That one." Then she turned and washed her hands and face in the basin on the side.

He ripped into the parcel and threw a bone down for Sebastian, who pounced on it at once with savage enjoyment. Then he climbed into the wagon after her, shedding his waistcoat and neckcloth as soon as he was inside. The washing water on the side was cold, but he plunged his hands into it anyway and performed a perfunctory wash.

377

"Strip, Lizzie," he said without turning. He knew she was still fully dressed for she was standing entirely still.

She took a steadying breath. "It only just occurred to me that I should have left you a note," she began calmly. "But I didn't think—"

"No, you didn't!" he agreed, stripping off his shirt and braces. "Though seeing a letter would likely have given me a heart attack too!"

Lizzie surveyed him a moment, looking puzzled. "Why?"

"Because I would have assumed the worst," he growled.

"The worst?"

"That you had taken off and left me!" He was entirely frank with her. It seemed the best way, going forward.

Lizzie's mouth dropped open. "Why on earth would you assume that?" she faltered.

He unbuttoned his breeches. "Get on the bed."

"What? Why?"

"So, you can console me for the nasty shock you gave me."

"Console you?"

"Aye, console me. With that sweet little body of yours."

He let his eyes travel over her deliberately. Lizzie's mouth shut, and she reached behind her to make a start on the bead buttons at the back of her neck. She had made precious little progress by the time he was down to his long underwear and flung her on the bed. Lizzie gave a squawk as she bounced, for if he had not followed her down, his knee planted between hers, she would likely have ended up on the floor.

"I'm not undressed!" she panted.

"No, you're not, are you? Let me help you with that."

"Don't you rip my dress, Benedict Toomes! I only have this one and the navy one for weekdays!"

"I'll buy you a new one."

Lizzie made a muffled sound of annoyance as he yanked her dress open at the back, drawing it over her head and flinging it over the side of the bed. "One of every color," he added. "I'd like to see you in brighter colors, Lizzie, to match your hair."

Lizzie seemed so startled by this pronouncement that she made not one murmur as he ran through the hooks and eyes of her corset, and then her stays, chemise, petticoat, and bloomers followed her dress over the edge of the bed.

Only when she lay back on the bed entirely naked did she murmur his name half-reproachfully, her cheeks very pink.

He let his eyes devour her slim body with its bright gold hair, from her high, perky bosom to her slender ankles. "Take down your hair."

Lizzie reached up and unpinned the neat arrangement. He watched with satisfaction as she leaned over to set a handful of pins on the top of a trunk.

"Finally," he said. "I get to see you in all your glory by daylight."

"In all my glory?" she repeated weakly as he shed his vest. "Are you sure you're seeing me clearly?"

"You're the one in my bed, aren't you?"

"Yes," she admitted. "But…"

"But what?" he asked, grabbing her ankle and pulling her down the bed. "This is how you should greet me at the end of a working day."

Lizzie spluttered. "Naked?"

"Why not?"

"We haven't lit the fire even, or—"

"Later," he growled. "There's time enough for that." He grabbed her knees and pulled them apart.

"Benedict!"

"Your hair isn't your only beauty, Lizzie," he said, running his fingers through the hair between her legs. "But it is one of them."

Her breathing hitched and she closed her eyes, "I—I'm not—"

"Put your hands on your breasts, Lizzie. Squeeze those pretty nipples for me."

She hesitated a moment, then did as he asked, her breathing shaky as he tweaked and sifted through the soft hair on her mound.

"When I married you, I endowed you with all my worldly goods, Lizzie. Everything of mine is yours. Do you understand? *Everything*." She bit her lip and nodded, but kept her eyes closed. "Look at me." When her eyes sprang open, he shifted down the bed until he was kneeling at the edge.

Lizzie gazed at him as he lowered his head slowly and deliberately and replaced his fingers between her legs with his tongue. "Benedict!" She half groaned, half whimpered his name as he took his time, tracing her cleft, his breath hot against her cool skin.

When her thighs kept trying to close about his ears and her hips were moving restlessly to encourage him, he knew he had pushed past her inhibitions. He ran his tongue lingeringly through her wet petals and groaned. Panting, he turned his face to rest against her soft inner thigh for a moment. Drawing an uneven breath, he said lasciviously, "Whatever will I do, Lizzie mine? The more I lick, the wetter you get."

Lizzie gazed down at him, her indignant face flushed, her bosom heaving. He was fucked if he knew why, but the spark in her eye made him burn hotter than ever. "Tell me," he said thickly. There he went again. Wanting to know what was on her mind. It really made no sense, yet here he was, wanting to hear her thoughts.

"You know exactly what you're doing to me, you wretch!" she told him with spirit.

"Getting you worked up, you mean?" he answered with a laugh. "Yeah, I do. I'm starting to know exactly what treatment this naughty pussy likes."

Lizzie drew in a shocked breath. "Benedict!"

He laughed again. "You'll be the death of me," he commented, moving swiftly up the bed and positioning his pulsing cock at her entrance. "Now tell me you're going to come all over my cock like a good girl, and I'll give you what you want."

She gave a needy whimper, and he couldn't hold back like he should to tease her anymore. "Close enough," he grunted and thrust inside her. Lizzie arched her back and wailed. He had to cover her mouth with his hand or everyone in the campsite would know what a lucky bastard he was. "Coming already?" he grunted and willed himself to withstand the pleasure as she clenched around him so hard he had to steel himself against the rich satisfaction it afforded him or he would embarrass himself.

Benedict clenched his buttocks and bit his lip as he strove to keep a lid on it. "That's alright, Lizzie," he told her huskily when he was sure he had himself under control. "You can come. But I'm not going to join you just yet." When the violence of her orgasm began to relent, he gave a few stiff bucks of his hips, just enough to send her climax spiraling again. Lizzie sobbed against the back of her hand as she arched against him in the throes of bliss.

"That's it," he rasped as he ground his hips against hers. "I want *everything*. Give it to me. It's mine by right." Her eyelids drifted shut as she fluttered against his cock, sobbing softly. Only then did he lower himself down over her and take her mouth in the hot, wet kiss he wanted.

"Fuck, you're perfect," he grunted. "I want to come inside you so bad." If he had any sense, he ought to pull out to be on the safe side. He wanted to make her come at least twice more before he joined her, and he didn't like to think how close he was to failing in that goal. The fact was her tight little body was too perfect, and the instant he was inside her it was all too easy to lose control.

"Why don't you, then?" she asked in that relaxed and sated voice that always made him edgy with need. "I'm not stopping you." He gazed at her flushed cheeks, the pale hair tumbling about her face.

"Oh, I will, don't you worry. But not till I'm ready." He pulled out of her, earning a disappointed sigh. "How do your arms and legs feel? Any strength left in them?"

"Hmm?" Her arms slid around his back, trying to pull him closer.

"Siren," he growled. "Stop tempting me."

"Siren?" she repeated.

"That's what you remind me of," he said, kissing her neck and then sucking her pink nipples into his mouth one after the other, listening to her ragged breath, "with your pale body and bright hair. I saw a painting once. You were covered in seafoam in the midst of a raging storm and very, very beautiful."

"Aren't they treacherous?" Lizzie asked, shifting restlessly against him. "Mermaids, I mean?"

Benedict shrugged. "You tell me, I'm not much for book-learning." He squeezed her backside.

"I think they drown sailors," Lizzie answered thoughtfully. She wrapped her arms about Benedict's neck. "They wind their naked limbs about the brawny sailors and drag them down to a watery doom."

He answered her smile with his own and took her lips in another kiss. "I could drown in you, but I'll own that doesn't sound much fun. I never figured out what you were supposed to do with a fish tail, mind you. Get up on your knees, Lizzie."

"My knees?"

He helped her up and then turned her about.

"Benedict," she said suddenly, looking back at him over her shoulder. He stilled at once. "The curtains do cover the windows, don't they?"

His snorted. "You think I'd let anyone else see you like this?"

She relaxed and he positioned himself behind her. "Get on your elbows, I don't want you to fall on your face."

"What are you—? Oh!" His fingers were between her legs again, petting and toying with her.

He rested one foot against the floor and reached down to position himself at her cleft. No way was he going to last through another of Lizzie's climaxes, he thought, but maybe this position would help him last a little longer. "You okay?" he asked tersely.

"Yes."

"You trust me?"

"Yes."

"If you don't like it, just tell me. We'll switch back." She nodded and he started to push into her, grabbing a firm hold of her hips and starting a slow grind. When Lizzie began to pant, he gritted out, "Too much?"

She shook her head, making her silky hair fly about her shoulders. "No."

Thank God for that. He felt the sweat begin to bead at his brow as he watched her undulating back. "You like this, Lizzie?"

"I'm not—yes!" she blurted. "Yes. I like it."

"You just never disappoint me, do you?" he rasped. "You about to come, Lizzie?" he asked, feeling the telltale quivers. She answered him with a low wail, and he planted himself deep, bracing his foot against the floor as he braced himself to withstand her shuddering climax. She was still sobbing when he flipped her over and pushed back inside her.

"I want to see your face," he grunted when she blinked up at him in surprise at the rapid change of position.

"Oh," she whispered, and he pressed his mouth to hers and finally allowed himself his release.

Afterward, they lay in a tangle of limbs, and he pulled the blankets up and over them, kissing her shoulder and settling against her. He would get up in a minute and see to what needed doing. Lizzie fell into a deep sleep as soon as he wrapped his arms around her. An hour or so later, Benedict dragged himself out of bed, lit the fire, and heated the water.

One of Lizzie's parcels looked distinctly loaf shaped, and he was tempted to see if he could make some supper out of that. He washed and roused Lizzie to do likewise, though she grumbled and tried to push him away at first. "You need to come wash and eat," he insisted, and finally, she rolled onto her back and regarded him.

"What time is it?"

"A little after eight."

"In the morning?"

"At night."

"Oh." She dragged herself out of the blankets, and he helped her don her nightgown.

"Is this bread?" he asked, lifting the parcel.

"Yes. There's a small cheese and some apples in another."

Benedict felt the other parcels until he found the right ones, then he carried them outside to slice. By the time he had prepared a plate of sliced apple and cheese, he figured she would likely be washed. He knocked on the door and passed the plate inside.

"Are you coming in to eat this with me?" she asked. "Or do you want me to come out there?"

"I'll come back inside once I've seen to the horse and made the tea."

Lizzie nodded and he joined her half an hour later to find her sat up in bed and swathed in a shawl. She had brushed her hair but left it loose.

"Animals are seen to," he said, pulling the door shut and slipping off his braces. He had not troubled to don a shirt. He had his wash, listening to Lizzie crunching on her apple.

Lizzie yawned. "Good," she murmured.

He soon joined her under the covers where she was dozing back off again. "Lizzie?"

"Hmmm?"

He hesitated. They hadn't really cleared the air about Winchester Street, but he was strangely reluctant to rock the boat now they were back in tranquil waters. Taking another bite of bread and cheese, he decided he'd better let her sleep. It was only fair after he'd exhausted her like that. Setting the plate down on top of the trunk, he rolled into her and dragged her pliant body against him. She sighed and Benedict smiled into her hair.

It would be alright. He just had to find the right words.

26

Lizzie spent the next morning mixing her tooth powder and mouth rinse solution. She made enough for Benedict also and put the little supply of bottles in the bottom of the second trunk, surrounded by linen. Hopefully, they would be safe that way from breakage during their ride to Andover. They had only two more days left here at Putney, and the next journey would be a substantially longer one and take a day and a half.

She found she wasn't too worried, for Benedict would be at the reins this time instead of Frank, and she felt the trust between herself and Sebastian had grown stronger with each day. She would not be in a constant state of panic this time that he would attempt to jump down from the moving cart.

Hearing a stifled "woof" from him, Lizzie glanced across to see him bounce up from where he had been lying next to the fire. Someone was approaching in a dark gray coat with a shabby-looking fur collar, clutching a battered valise.

"Here, boy!" Lizzie snapped her fingers, and Sebastian came to her side. It was a woman, a very beautiful-looking woman with sherry-colored eyes and curling chestnut hair. She had an anxious look in her eyes and came to an abrupt halt a few feet away.

"Are you Mrs. Benedict Toomes?" she asked in an attractive low voice.

"I am," Lizzie answered as a sudden suspicion entered her head. "Are you Maggie?" she asked with suppressed excitement.

The woman bit her lip and nodded. "I am," she said in a wobbly voice. "I got your letter."

"You must have set off at once," Lizzie marveled. "I never expected you to come so soon. I mean I *hoped*…"

"Aggie didn't want me to come," Maggie admitted. "She said I had a home with her and her sister, Winifred, but, well, things have changed."

"Please, come and sit by the fire, and I'll toast you some bread and cheese and make a pot of tea."

"I couldn't eat anything," Maggie said, but she approached with a nervous glance at the dog and took Lizzie's hand.

"Pleased to meet you."

"Likewise." Maggie gave a strained smile.

"Please be seated." The kettle was already over the fire, so Lizzie set about preparing the pot and setting out the cups. "My letter must have surprised you a good deal," she said, hoping she was striking the right note and not embarrassing her sister-in-law.

"I—yes," Maggie answered stiltedly. "I can't tell you how many times I've read it. Enough to learn it by heart." Her gaze lowered, and she sat in perfect silence as Lizzie poured the kettle.

"You were happy at the boarding house?" Lizzie prompted when Maggie clammed up again.

"Not happy exactly." Maggie frowned. "Most of the time I was miserable as sin, but Aggie's a kind soul, and her sister was grateful for all the help she could get, getting the place up and running. I was kept busy which didn't really give me time to brood."

"You said things had changed. Can I ask what things?" Lizzie asked curiously.

388

"Well, your letter changed things a good deal," Maggie answered frankly, her brow wrinkling. "And something else I never expected," she confessed ruefully. "Aggie met a man, and they started walking out together of an evening." She lapsed into silence a moment before starting up again in a rush. "We shared an attic room, you see, and being left alone got me to thinking again."

Maggie fiddled with her glove. "Aggie was going to marry and move on with her life, but I was stuck. Married yet not married." She shot a glance at Lizzie. "And of course," she choked out, "I kept thinking Frank *had* moved on. With that *woman*, and that hardened my heart against anything else…" She paused as Lizzie passed her a cup and saucer of tea. "Then I got your letter." She stared at Lizzie with mounting curiosity. "I must say you're not at all what I would have expected for Benedict," she said slowly.

"Because I'm not pretty?" Lizzie asked without resentment.

Maggie promptly blushed up to the roots of her hair. "No! That wasn't—" She broke off in confusion. "It's just—forgive me. I don't know what I meant."

"That's alright," Lizzie assured her. "You're not what I was expecting either." Maggie reminded her of a Renaissance painting with her vivid coloring.

Maggie opened her mouth and then closed it again. "It's not fair for me to ask you for an explanation when I could give you none," she admitted wryly.

Lizzie smiled. "It's just everyone described you as such a wrung-out drudge," she admitted. "But you're so young and vibrant and beautiful."

Maggie's color ebbed and flowed. "That's kind of you to say. I think I have got back a bit of my color. Winifred was so grateful for everything I could do about the place. She couldn't praise me highly enough. I got the chance to catch my breath and start taking a bit of care of myself. You know, just small things like putting cream on my hands and face of an evening. Time to wash and brush my hair out nice."

"Frank took you for granted," Lizzie said. "That's what Benedict said."

"Yes, he did," Maggie agreed. "But I let them walk all over me. His father and that latest woman of his wore me down, expecting me to fetch and carry for them while Frank turned a blind eye. 'They'll be leaving us soon,' he'd say. 'Just a few more days, Mags. Then they'll be gone.'" She sighed. "But days became weeks, and weeks became months. Frank likes things easy, and he was never any good at standing up to his old man. Jack's not more than just a lad, but in the past, Benedict had always been there. He gave his father short shrift, I can tell you. Always ran him off in the end, but there…" She sighed. "Ben was in prison, and so they hung on and on and just wouldn't leave." Maggie pulled a face. "I got so's I couldn't take it anymore. It probably wouldn't have been so bad if Gracie hadn't had that daughter of hers with her."

"Gracie is Daphne's mother?"

"That's right," Maggie confirmed. "And a nasty pair of vipers they were too, with their sly comments and constant jibes. I reckon Daphne must have told her mum from the outset that she wanted my Frank. Pa would love to sink his hooks into Frank good and proper," she said bitterly. "He's a lazy old villain and no mistake. No work in him. If he could leech off Frank for the rest of his days, he would."

Maggie's expression became tighter, and she lifted her chin. "I thought she'd succeed too, with me out of the picture. But then I got your letter." She swallowed and darted a look at Lizzie. "You still stand by everything you said?"

"I do," Lizzie assured her. "In fact, I confronted Daphne about it."

"You never did!"

"How do you imagine I got this?" Lizzie asked, gesturing to the yellowing bruise about her eye.

Maggie set her cup down with a clatter. "You fought?"

"Well," Lizzie said dryly. "She punched me in the eye, and I survived to tell the tale. Daphne fled into the night."

Maggie gasped and beheld her with open awe. "Why, she could make two of you!" Then Lizzie's words seemed to register. "You mean she's gone?" she asked excitedly. Clearly, she had not relished the prospect of seeing Daphne again.

"Oh yes," Lizzie said. "Long gone. But if you'll allow me to advise you, Maggie, I do not think you should be in any hurry to step back into your previous role." She regarded her sister-in-law frankly.

Maggie's face fell. "What would you advise, then?" she asked slowly.

"That you keep Frank on tenterhooks for a while," Lizzie responded promptly. "Let him court you a bit and tell him you do not mean to be worn to a frayed edge serving his family."

Maggie flushed. "I couldn't leave you to shoulder the burden, Lizzie," she said awkwardly.

"Me?" Lizzie gave a short laugh. "I've done no more than brew a cup of tea for my in-laws. Benedict told me from the outset that we were our own separate concern."

Maggie regarded her with round eyes. "You mean, you do not live all together?" Lizzie shook her head. It seemed to take Maggie a few minutes to absorb this startling news. "Then forgive me, but how can you know that Frank and Daphne—"

"Frank and Jack shared one wagon and Ma Toomes and Daphne the other. Besides, Benedict told me himself that Frank had never so much as looked at Daphne that way. He could not be deceived."

Maggie's shoulders relaxed. She stared down at her cup and saucer and then back at her valise. "But if I have not come back to Frank, then I do not know where I will go," she said hopelessly.

"Well, as to that, I'm sure some other female performer must have a spare bunk to lend you. You must have had other friends apart from Aggie. If my friend Niamh were here, I could ask her, but they've gone on to Banbury."

"There's no one stood my particular friend like Aggie," Maggie said mournfully. Her gaze faltered before Lizzie's steady one, and she seemed to reconsider. "I was friendly with Sophia and Lily Farini at one time. Of the Farini Family Acrobats. I don't suppose they are here?"

"Yes, I'm certain they are," Lizzie answered gladly. "I've seen their tent myself. If you like, we could go and find them after we've finished our tea. I have money if they ask for board from you."

Maggie made a quick gesture with her hands. "Oh no, I have money," she said, looking embarrassed. "Winifred insisted on paying me despite the fact I hadn't finished out the month. You must not think me a charity case."

Lizzie assured her she did not, and they duly set off for the main field with Sebastian in search of the Farini tent.

It was an hour or so later when Lizzie was stood at a lemonade stall with Maggie and Sophia Farini that she felt someone grab her arm, and she turned around to find her husband glowering at her.

"What are you doing here?" he demanded. "I just walked back to the wagon in search of you."

Lizzie nodded her head meaningfully toward Maggie, and Benedict glanced blankly at her companions. "Hullo, Mags," he said briefly and turned back to Lizzie. "Well? Are you done here, or can we get something to eat?"

"Excuse me," Lizzie murmured in embarrassment to the two women, tugging his arm and dragging him aside. "Benedict," she said in an urgent undertone, "Maggie has traveled all this way to try and resolve matters with Frank—" she began only to find herself cut off midstream.

"So I supposed," he answered levelly. "And we should leave them to it." He looked over Lizzie's shoulder toward Maggie. "Frank was tidying things away in the boxing tent when I left him. He's likely not strayed far." Lizzie opened her mouth, but Benedict wrapped an arm about her shoulders. "Lizzie's coming with me now," he said firmly. Sebastian trotted over to his side. Lizzie just about managed to wish a flustered-looking Maggie good luck before she found herself towed away.

"You weren't very friendly," she pointed out.

"She needs to fight her own battles, Lizzie. You can't do it for her."

393

"I know that, but I think she was hoping for some support."

"We need to stay well out of it. It's their affair." He paused before the beer tent. "Do you want tea?" he asked abruptly.

"No, for I've drunk two cups in the last hour already."

"Thank God for that," he muttered and plunged inside the tent, pulling her after him.

Lizzie frowned. "I'm only trying to help. Maggie said that in the past *you* always exercised a beneficial influence and that things only broke down because you were in prison—"

"That's bullshit," Benedict cut her off. "I've never done anything to interfere with Frank's marriage."

"I think she meant more in regards of you seeing your father off before he outstayed his welcome."

Benedict snorted. "Well, that had nothing to do with Maggie and Frank. I can't abide my father and never have."

Lizzie shot him an exasperated look. "I know you and Jack are worried about your brother, so I don't know why you're pretending otherwise." When he said nothing, Lizzie persisted. "When we first arrived here, you seemed very put out that Maggie was not around anymore."

He swung her around to face him. "What do you mean, *I* was put out?"

Lizzie looked at him with surprise. "Well, just that. Jack said she was worn ragged, and you said that Frank ought to have looked after her better. And you always seemed to resent Daphne being around."

"What Frank gets up to is his affair, not mine," Benedict pointed out, pulling out a chair at a side table. "I felt sorry for

Maggie, true enough, but she needs to grow her own backbone; you can't take that role on for her."

Lizzie was a little taken aback. She dropped into her seat. "Well, no, but—"

"And I'll not have her running to you constantly expecting you to dry her eyes and take up the cudgels for her."

"What makes you think she'll do that?"

"Because that's what she was always doing before with her little friend. The plain-faced one who used to work for Connie."

"Because I'm the plain-faced one who works for Connie now, you mean?" Lizzie answered before she'd had chance to bite the words back.

"What did you say?" Benedict looked incensed.

"Oh, nothing." Lizzie tried to fob him off. She had been rattled and spoken the words in haste.

Mercifully at that moment, someone came over to take their order. As soon as they'd gone, Benedict leaned in closer.

"Repeat to me what you just said," he seethed.

"I suppose you mean Aggie, the Living Skeleton," Lizzie replied, avoiding the eyes boring into her own.

He shook her arm. "Tell me!" he repeated.

"I don't want to!" Lizzie burst out hotly. "It's just that no one saw fit to mention how beautiful Maggie is, that's all!"

"So what if she's beautiful!" Benedict thundered back. "I've never looked twice at her in that light, and if she's going to cause trouble between us, then I'd just as soon she hadn't shown back up at all!"

"Cause trouble between us?" Lizzie echoed, mystified. "How would she do that?"

"She already seems to have!"

Lizzie looked away as the server appeared and fiddled with her wedding ring as the pitcher of beer was set down and the glasses.

Benedict poured the beer out and scowled at her. He lifted his glass before setting it back down again untouched. "I don't think of you as plain," he said abruptly. "You should know that by now."

Lizzie colored hotly. "I don't know why I said that," she mumbled. "Can you please just forget I said it?" He took a sip of beer and Lizzie tried again. "Maggie has not caused any trouble between us, Benedict," she said, reaching for his hand. "And you've never said anything to make me feel insecure. Please don't be cross."

He was still a moment and then turned his hand to tighten his fingers about her own. "I want you to let this business between Maggie and Frank play out now without interference, Lizzie. You've done your part in writing that letter. We need to iron out our own grievances."

Lizzie stared, and he lifted an eyebrow. "We do?" she asked uncomfortably.

"If we didn't, you would not have just made that comment," he said grimly.

Lizzie raised her glass with a hand that was not entirely steady. "Very well," she said, though when he looked at her a little impatiently, she lowered it again. "Now?" she asked, casting a glance around the busy beer tent.

"It might be easier than in that box on top of one another." He shrugged, looking away.

Lizzie drew her hand out of his and straightened her shoulders. "My uncle said when you offered for Betsy you promised to set her up in her own home. All this time I thought you must have exaggerated your prospects. Now I find—" She glanced down at her hands. "That is not the case."

She paused a moment, mustering her courage to voice the next part. "I suppose at my lowest ebb it occurs to me that maybe you meant to use me on the road for a twelvemonth and then trade me in for a better prospect when you settle down to your prosperity. My uncle mentioned the word *revenge* in connection with our union."

She heard his swiftly indrawn breath. "Is that it?" Benedict asked harshly. "I want you to get it all off your chest once and for all."

Lizzie looked up, meeting his cool hazel eyes. She felt her own color must have drained away leaving her very pale and plain. She bunched her hands together, hard. "I know you did not admire my looks or personality at Sitwell Place, Benedict. And let us be frank, I thought you were a dreadful man, but we married anyway," she concluded painfully. "Due to circumstance."

"Circumstance?" he echoed. "Is that what you think?" He gave a bitter laugh. "I brought about my own change of circumstances, Lizzie. And let me tell you plainly, your own prospects changed the minute I saw you face down that table full of smug hypocrites. That changed *everything* for me."

"What do you mean?" Lizzie croaked.

At that moment, there was a commotion in the crowd next to their table, and Jack came bursting through it.

"Benedict, thank God!"

Benedict's mouth tightened. "Whatever it is, I don't want to know right now!"

"Trust me," Jack panted. "You'll want to know about this!" Benedict opened his mouth to deny it, but did not get that far. "It's Nat!" Jack blurted. "Nat Jones! He's here with a bunch of his fancy backers. They've come to watch you fight, Ben." His brother's voice shook. "This could be it. If you impress them now, this could be a real shot for you at the big time."

Benedict went very still, and Lizzie reached across to touch his sleeve. His eyes shot to meet hers.

"Go," she said simply. "We can finish this later."

He started to shake his head. "No, Lizzie, we haven't cleared the air."

"Benedict," she urged. "It's fine. We can pick this up later. This sounds important."

"So is this!"

Seeing his frustration, she squeezed his arm. "We've got the rest of our lives for matrimonial strife," she joked weakly. "I'm not going anywhere, and we can take a walk later and finish this…conversation."

He swore, low and profane. "I shouldn't have raised all this between us right now," he said, grabbing her hand and pressing it to his lips. He closed his eyes fleetingly. "The timing couldn't be worse."

"No, this is a good thing," Lizzie insisted. "I will spend the time arranging my thoughts so I'm coherent later. I was ill prepared for this conversation." She hesitated. "You made some very good points," she said softly. "And you're right, we need to have this out properly."

"Ben!" Jack burst out in an agony of anticipation. "They're waiting at the tent!"

"Lizzie—"

"Just go, Benedict." She managed a smile. "I have Sebastian to escort me back, and we'll sort this out later. I promise."

She watched him being swallowed up into the crowd as he sent one last backward glance her way. She glanced down at Sebastian. "Come on, boy."

Sorely tempted as she was to find out what was happening between Maggie and Frank, Lizzie turned her steps toward the exit, intending to head for the wagon, when she heard her name. The voice that called it almost made her miss her footing. She halted and turned slowly about.

No, she had not been mistaken about those sweet, high tones.

It was her cousin, Betsy.

27

It took a moment for Lizzie to register that Betsy was not alone but accompanied by two others. As Lizzie stood frozen immobile, Betsy gave a smile and stepped forward, looking extremely neat in a fur-trimmed cloak and a bonnet of sage green. "Cousin," she said and extended a dainty gloved hand. Lizzie stared at the yellow kid glove and then met Betsy's gaze.

"What do you want, Betsy?" she asked aloud.

A soft gasp behind them drew both their attention, and Lizzie noticed with surprise that Aunt Hester was stood nearby looking agitated with a handkerchief held to her mouth.

"Aunt," Lizzie blurted. "What are you doing here?" It seemed incongruous in the extreme to see her respectable aunt stood surrounded by gaily colored striped tents. Aunt Hester's tastes in life had always been so puritan.

Lizzie's gaze traveled on to the third person who stood supporting her aunt. It was not her uncle, but a much younger man dressed in a gray tweed suit. She vaguely recognized him as Mrs. Lessing's nephew, though she could not recall his name just now.

Seeing the direction of her gaze, the young man said with a polite bow, "Perhaps you do not remember me, Miss Anderson, but we were introduced at a garden party last summer. I am Mrs. Lessing's nephew, Frederick Mountford. Perhaps you remember me?"

"Of course," Lizzie answered automatically, though in truth, her memory of him was dim. All she really remembered was Betsy saying what a shame it was that so handsome a young man should have to dance attendance on his disagreeable old aunt in the hopes of inheriting.

Now it seemed Betsy did not mind so much, if the warm eye she was casting over him was any indication. "You must not address my cousin as such, Mr. Mountford," she said gently. "For she is a married lady now, is that not so, Lizzie? And as such, her name is Mrs. Toomes."

"Your pardon, Mrs. Toomes," Frederick Mountford said with a charming smile, and Lizzie nodded. When the awkward silence stretched, he cleared his throat. "I hope you would not think it impertinent for me to suggest we all repair somewhere we can have some quiet conversation?"

"Oh yes!" Betsy cried at once, sounding relieved. "That sounds the very thing, does it not, Mother?"

Hester Anderson did not reply, for her eyes were still fixed on Lizzie in mute appeal, though she seemed wholly incapable of speech.

Lizzie sighed. "I do not mean to appear rude," she began. "But—"

"Please, Lizzie!" Betsy burst forth, clasping her hands before her. "We—we must speak with you of this matter! I beg of you!"

Sebastian barked, not appreciating the suddenly tense atmosphere. Lizzie looked from Betsy, to her distraught aunt, to Frederick Mountford, who had a concerned pucker between his brows. "Oh, very well," she conceded, reaching down to grasp Sebastian's collar. "I can give you half an hour of my time, I suppose."

Lizzie turned about and led them in the direction of a tea tent, noticing for the first time the dried mud splatter at the hem of her cloak. That must have been from her jaunt to the shops yesterday. She would need to take a brush to that, she thought wryly, considering the contrast between her smart cousin and herself.

Reaching up, she straightened her bonnet and considered the fact she was likely not looking her best. The bruising around her eye was now a jaundiced shade of yellow, and her gray gown had been on the shabby side before it had left Sitwell Place.

By the time the four of them were seated about a table, Lizzie was feeling decidedly at a disadvantage. She listened to Betsy give an order for tea and muffins all round and stroked Sebastian's neck when he sat alert and watchful. They sat mostly in silence until their order was brought to the table, and then Betsy broke the silence by pouring and handing around the tea with determined cheerfulness. "This one is for you, Mother, this for Mr. Mountford, and here is yours, Lizzie."

Lizzie took hers with a murmur of thanks but refused the muffin. The plate stood untouched as Betsy let out a deep sigh. "The truth of the matter is, Lizzie, that we stand to lose *everything*. Father won't come to ask for your aid, for he says he is too ashamed." Betsy bit her lip. "He hasn't really been the same since he came to visit with you earlier in the week," she said in the manner of one making a confession.

"On that occasion, on his return, he shut himself up in his study and would not come out for three hours. I will admit, I quite feared you'd been dragged out of a river or something of that nature," Betsy admitted. "For when he came home, he was pale as milk and trembling all over. 'Father,' said I, 'what ails you?'

'Not now, my child, not now' was all the response he would make me.

"Then, when finally he did emerge, what do you think? Not a bite of supper would he take but insisted that Mother and I come into the parlor and pray for forgiveness for the wrong we'd done you." Betsy bit her lip. "At the time, I don't mind telling you, Lizzie, we thought you'd met with some terrible end. I won't lie to you, Lizzie, Mother and I tried to resist and say we were not to blame and then—" Betsy paused, licking her dry lips. "Then Father told us that if we would not pray for forgiveness for our role in casting you out among wolves, then we should pray for our own salvation, for our pride was surely putting it in grave peril. Then he said he was going out at once to speak to his fellow elders about how things stood with the church financially.

"He said, and I will never forget his face, Lizzie, 'If Reverend Milson is a crook, then we are ruined, my dears, quite ruined. For I have made all our investments over to him as have a good many of our community.' Then he turned and went out of the door, and Mother and I ran to watch him walk down the street. And I tell you, Lizzie, he looked a broken man."

Aunt Hester gave a moan and covered her face with her hands. Lizzie glanced at her in alarm. "Surely things were not as dire as he supposed?" she faltered.

"No," Betsy said gravely. "For they were a good deal worse. Reverend Milson has embezzled all of the church funds, Lizzie, and dipped into a good many charitable pots. Worse than that, Father found that almost all of the church elders had been persuaded to invest in the reverend's private accumulation schemes as Father had. Mr. Hedgcomb, Mr. Scott, Mr. Fitzallen, all of them.

"They, too, had seen no return in a twelvemonth but had not raised the alarm due to the fact they had such implicit trust in him. Other prominent members of the congregation have also been taken in." She hesitated. "The richer of the widows—" She broke off at an involuntary gesture Mr. Mountford made.

The breath caught in Lizzie's throat. That Reverend Milson could have been stealing on such a large scale was truly horrifying. "I can scarcely believe such a thing is possible," she muttered.

Aunt Hester dropped her hands from her face. "Who could believe that such wickedness exists in the world," she said hollowly, "when it wears the guise of honesty?"

"His mask did slip before though, Lizzie. To you," Betsy pointed out. "You saw beneath the façade, and none of us would believe you."

"There are none so blind as those who will not see," intoned Aunt Hester.

"Yes," Lizzie agreed sadly. "But if I had not seen it with my own eyes, I daresay that I, too, would have been hard to convince."

"You are generous, Lizzie," Betsy said. "More generous than we. Now I, too, know how Papa felt when he saw you previously." She smiled sadly and reached across to briefly clasp her mother's hand. "May we earnestly beg your forgiveness, cousin?"

Lizzie swallowed and nodded. "You have it," she said. "Is that the extent of your errand today?" She frowned. "To ask my forgiveness?" Their urgency had seemed a good deal more pointed than that.

For the first time, Betsy's gaze faltered. "Alas," she answered with a small laugh. "I wish that were true, but…" She glanced at Frederick Mountford, and he gave her an encouraging look. "In truth, that was only the first of the boons we wished to beg from you. You see, Mrs. Lessing's legal man is currently compiling the church's evidence against Reverend Milson. We have eyes watching him, and it is believed that at any moment he may try to flee the country on a passage steamer bound for the Americas. Time is of the absolute essence in our case."

"Yes?" Lizzie still could not see where her cousin's narrative was taking them.

"It occurred to us that the only case we could currently bring against him successfully is the charge of attempted theft regarding Mrs. Lessing's diamond brooch. If he were clapped in jail awaiting trial for those charges, that would give our legal people time to prove the additional frauds and embezzlement." Betsy twisted her clasped hands in her lap.

Enlightenment dawned. "Oh," said Lizzie, her brow clearing. "I see, and I am your only material witness."

"Several members of the dinner party that night will attest to its being discovered in Reverend Milson's pocket, but you were the only one who actually saw him steal it."

"That is true," Lizzie agreed slowly. "But will the police not think it odd that we waited a whole month before bringing it to the attention of the authorities?"

"Doubtless they will," Betsy agreed. "But we mean to be fully frank and open." She hesitated. "Once it is explained that my parents threw you out—" Aunt Hester moaned aloud again and shut her eyes. "Then I do not think they will wonder that you were not in a position to report the theft and give Queen's evidence until now."

Lizzie nodded, though her expression was troubled. "Can I not simply give you a statement?" she asked. "It is not entirely convenient for me to make my way to a police station at present."

Betsy darted another quick look at Mr. Mountford. He shook his head.

"I beg your pardon, Miss Anderson," he said, looking at Lizzie. "But I am afraid we would need you to proceed with us at once if the miscreant is to be apprehended."

Lizzie opened her mouth, but Betsy forestalled her.

"My cousin is not Miss Anderson anymore, Frederick," she reminded him briskly. Lizzie glanced quickly at Betsy's face, but her bright gaze was fixated on Frederick Mountford.

"I apologize, Mrs. Toomes."

Lizzie nodded absently, wondering if his aunt was due to lose considerably more than a brooch this time if Reverend Milson was not prevented from fleeing the country. Mr. Mountford certainly seemed very invested in the outcome.

"It is at Millbank station that we have lodged our complaint," he continued smoothly. "We have told them that we hope to have you attend an interview this very afternoon. They have indicated that is the only circumstance in which they will be able to clap him in irons." Mr. Mountford's tone was faintly apologetic. "Our every hope depends on you, Miss—that is, Mrs. Toomes," he corrected himself.

"I see." Lizzie's mind raced. She had promised Benedict not half an hour ago that she would "stay put" for the rest of the day. "You must understand that I cannot leave with you without first consulting my husband."

"You will bear witness, Lizzie?" her aunt asked, half disbelieving.

"Of course I will," Lizzie replied. "After all, you showed me twenty-one years of kindness in your home, Aunt Hester."

"Before one act of very grave unkindness," her aunt gasped and then burst into tears. Lizzie patted her shoulder, but otherwise left Betsy to comfort her as she spoke hurriedly with Mr. Mountford.

"I need to make for the boxing saloon where my husband works," she explained. "Will you await me here?"

"I will accompany you," he responded quickly, and she saw that Frederick Mountford had no intention of letting her out of his sight. As it had not been her intention to give him the slip, Lizzie did not allow this to trouble her.

"I won't be long," she said, getting to her feet. "Shall we meet you at the exit in fifteen minutes? I may have to wait for my husband to reach the end of his current bout." Betsy gave her a grateful nod, and she, Sebastian, and Mr. Mountford headed for the Toomes Brothers Boxing Saloon.

She kept a brisk pace ahead of Frederick Mountford, otherwise she had a suspicion she would feel he was escorting her as an armed guard. She would not say his manner was officious, but he clearly thought himself the master of the situation. Probably, she thought, due to her aunt's current collapse and Betsy's cloying manner toward him. Lizzie's expression grew even more determined. He would certainly not be taking charge of her!

To Lizzie's surprise, she found Maggie sat at the entrance with the collection tin. She gave a guilty start when she saw Lizzie.

"Oh, I—I just said I would help Frank out this afternoon—" she began, but Lizzie did not have time to tarry.

"It is not my place to judge your actions, Maggie," she said as patiently as she could under the circumstances. She no longer had the smallest hope that Maggie would spend a couple of nights under Sophia Farini's roof. "I need to have a word with my husband, so this gentleman and I are just popping inside for a moment."

Maggie's eyes widened with panic. "Oh, I wouldn't do that, Lizzie! Frank said this is a crucial moment for Ben's future. You wouldn't want to do anything to jeopardize that, surely!"

Lizzie paused just the barest moment at Maggie's words, but she knew what she had promised. Benedict would absolutely hit the roof if she went off now without telling him.

"I'm afraid I must be the best judge of that," she said firmly and pressed on, though once inside the tent flap, she could see it was packed out, the baying crowds noisier than ever. Sebastian barked in agitation, and Lizzie patted his neck and grabbed his collar.

She turned back to Frederick Mountford, who had reached out to grasp her arm. "You will have to stay close," she shouted. "Lest we get parted in the crowd."

He nodded and set his jaw resolutely as they began to push forward into the jostling crowd.

"Let's hear it for Charlie, gentlemen," boomed Frank. "This man gave his all, though it wasn't enough to stop the Harbinger of Doom! He gave it a good try."

A chorus of boos and jeers rang out, and Lizzie craned her neck to see a bloody-nosed bruiser being helped from the ring. Her gaze sought out her husband, who was stripped to the waist, pacing about the roped-off area with a barely contained energy which put Lizzie in mind of a visit she had once paid to the London Zoological Gardens. Some of the bigger cats had seemed to embody the same restlessness as they stalked their pens.

"Is there any man here can challenge him?" Frank asked. "He's fresh as a daisy, gentlemen, and ready for the next contender, if anyone dares!"

"Over 'ere!" yelled a raucous voice to Lizzie's left. "My friend here will take him on!"

A few cheers rang out, and Lizzie saw Frank walk to the edge of the roped-off area. "Your name, good sir?" he shouted.

"It's Jim!" roared another who stood head and shoulders above his companions. "Jim North, and I can take any man here, Toomes included!"

Lizzie saw Frank's eyes narrow, and he shot a look toward the row of suited gentlemen thronging the ropes to the one side of the ring. She could just about make out the lavender and silver waistcoat of Nat Jones in the midst of them. She fancied he had an amused gleam in his eye, but that might have just been down to her own imagination.

"Jim!" Frank shouted, recovering quickly. "Long time no see. One of our boxing brethren is among us today, I see."

"Thought you said he takes all comers!" shouted one of North's companions. "Or is it only amateurs Toomes will face?"

The crowd grew even more animated at this back and forth. Lizzie saw Benedict's lips move, and Frank crossed the ring to speak quickly in his ear. Whatever he said, Benedict seemed to be disregarding. His hazel eyes were dwelling on North with a cold sort of disinterestedness that almost bordered on contempt for his fellow man.

Before seeing him in the ring, Lizzie had assumed fighters must be hot-headed and quick to anger, but Benedict seemed just the opposite. She knew the exact moment his gaze fell on her. The quick blink of his eyes, and then he was surging forward, shouting to Frank.

"He's seen us," she said weakly to Mountford, though she was not sure he heard her, the crowd was so rowdy. North was shouting and bawling all manner of insults behind them which was sending the crowd into a frenzy. Lizzie struggled but could not seem to make any headway now they had reached the thickest part of the audience. Sebastian growled low in his throat, but she doubted anyone could hear him among the noisy throng.

Suddenly, to her relief, she realized the men in front of her were parting ways, and she saw Benedict coming through. At his approach, they hastily fell back a step. It was not just she who relaxed at his approach, for Sebastian ceased plunging and straining under her grasp. As soon as Benedict reached her, he seized hold of her and dropped any semblance of cool indifference. "Who the fuck is that?" he barked, nodding at Mr. Mountford though his eyes did not leave Lizzie's face.

"It's complicated," she yelled back. "He brought my aunt and cousin with him. They want me to go with them now to the police station—"

"No," he answered tightly. "Not without me."

"Mr. Toomes, I must protest—" Frederick Mountford began, and Benedict swung round on him with an expression that blazed. If he'd had room, Mountford would undoubtedly have retreated. As it was, he could only fall back against the press of bodies behind him.

"Would that not be rather awkward for you?" Lizzie asked him, dropping her voice as much as she could with so much background noise. "It's not just my aunt, but also Betsy that came—"

"I don't give a fuck about Betsy," he answered swiftly.

Lizzie caught hold of Benedict's arm. "They need me to testify against Reverend Milson," she explained. "They fear he is about to flee the country." She hesitated, horribly conscious of the chaos around them and Frank hanging over the ropes with an expression of anguish on his face.

She was messing things up for Benedict's career, she thought with a pang. She found herself stroking his arm in a vain attempt to calm him. "It won't take long, dearest," she heard herself placating him. "I just need to make a statement."

"Not without me," he repeated in a calmer, though no less deadly, voice.

"Very well," Lizzie agreed desperately. "How many more bouts must you win today?" Frederick Mountford opened his mouth but lacked the courage to voice his objection.

"Just this last one," her husband answered grimly, his gaze flickering over Lizzie's shoulder to where North's faction were creating quite a commotion.

"Surely the *Harbinger's* not scared of a little real competition?" Jim North sneered to accompanying backslaps and encouragement.

411

"Then we shall wait," Lizzie said brightly. "Until you have knocked down this rude man and can accompany me to the station."

Benedict's gaze focused on her again, and Lizzie saw he was looking icy cold once more. She gave him a determinedly cheerful smile. "I daresay it won't take you long."

His eyes seemed to warm for a fraction of a second, his hand tightening about her wrist and dragging her forward. Lizzie did not even have a chance to check if Frederick Mountford had kept up with them or no, for the next thing she knew, she and Sebastian were up against the front of the ropes and Benedict had stepped back inside the square.

He gave the nod to Frank, who turned back to the audience. "Challenge accepted!" The crowd erupted, and Lizzie groped for Sebastian's collar at her side. Benedict turned a full circle in the ring, his gaze pinning Lizzie when she would have looked over her shoulder to check if Mr. Mountford were there.

Eyes on me, he mouthed to her.

Lizzie nodded, her throat suddenly dry. Why this was reminding her of the first time they were intimate, she could not say. Except that he had wanted her eyes on him on that occasion too, she remembered suddenly. Lizzie swallowed and did not let her gaze drop away, no matter how boldly he stared at her.

Sensing Sebastian's agitation, she reached down to pat his head, though her gaze never wavered from her husband. "Easy, boy," she murmured as the North party came forging forward, all bluster and bombast.

"Toomes won't find this prospect such an easy conquest," a whiskered gentleman nearby opined.

412

"Don't be so sure," his companion replied. "Care to make a little side wager, Algie?"

Lizzie was dimly aware that North had entered the ring and stripped off his shirt, showing a barrel chest bristling with hair to match his bushy beard. She had no eyes to spare for him, however, for she somehow knew Benedict was conscious of her gaze on him.

She had no sooner steeled herself for the spectacle than it had begun. Benedict seemed to launch himself at his opponent in a sudden onslaught of blows which the other man, for all his bragging, seemed ill prepared.

"Good lord!" the whiskered gentleman puffed. "Seems to have taken that chap's remarks to heart, don't he?"

Actually, Lizzie thought, *he's just in something of a hurry*.

North, finding himself with his back to the ropes, roared like a bear and lurched forward, swinging wildly, only to find his great fists dodged and his ribs struck in quick succession with three brutal body blows.

"Did ye see that?" the whiskered gentleman demanded as his friend simultaneously exclaimed, "Cracked his ribs, I'll warrant!"

Surely not, Lizzie thought with dawning horror, but North was certainly wheezing with discomfort as he tried to fend off the procession of jabs Benedict was directing at his head.

"Winded, by gad," her neighbor pronounced dolefully. "He's blowing like a bellows!"

As soon as North managed to get his fists up to protect his face, Benedict returned to slamming his fist into North's ribs. Lizzie winced. It seemed almost cruel to watch. The fickle crowd had

413

turned again and was now enjoying the bigger man's humiliation.

North rallied again, managing to throw out a few punches, but Benedict dodged and sidestepped, countering them with his own which seemed to be a good deal more effective.

No one was surprised when, moments later, a right landed on North's jaw that sent him sprawling to the ground.

"Clapped out," her neighbor said sadly. "Fellow's done for."

Lizzie swallowed and lifted her chin when Benedict swung about and looked straight at her. Their gazes clashed a moment, and then he turned back to watch his fallen opponent. Frank crouched down over North, speaking to him in measured tones.

To Lizzie's alarm, the large man struggled into a seated position before clutching his ribs and groaning. Frank straightened up, still talking, and when the crowd saw North vehemently shake his head, they set up a disappointed groan. Frank crossed his arms and then pulled them apart. "It's all over, gentlemen," he pronounced loudly.

Lizzie's shoulders slumped with relief. Benedict leaned over the back ropes. When he straightened back up, Lizzie realized he had been retrieving his shirt and jacket.

"I must say," the whiskered gentleman complained, watching Frank help the fallen man to his friends on the other side of the square. "That blasted ruffian did not last half as long against Toomes as that brickmaker chap he faced off against before this!"

His friend laughed. "Toomes would not feel he had to hold back against a fellow professional."

414

"My God!" breathed a voice behind them. Lizzie glanced back to see Mr. Mountford was stood behind her. He had removed his gray bowler hat to wipe his brow with a silk handkerchief.

Lizzie did not give him her attention for long as Benedict was walking toward her. Wordlessly, he passed his clothes to her and started wiping a cloth about his neck and face and then over his chest and arms. Lizzie extracted his vest from the pile, which he pulled on over his head, followed by his shirt, which she helped him button, followed by his waistcoat.

Frank came hurrying over. "Ben, will you come and have a word with Nat's backers?"

"No," he answered shortly, tying his neckerchief. "They saw what they came to see. Let them console their man North." When Lizzie opened her mouth, he shot her a warning look and she left her words unspoken. Taking his jacket from her, he slung it over his arm and reached for her hand. "Let's get out of here."

Out of the corner of one eye, Lizzie saw Frederick Mountford following in their wake. She kept one hand on Sebastian and let Benedict propel the three of them forward. The crowd seemed to part automatically for him, though a few brave souls attempted a backslap or a shoulder squeeze as he passed by.

Lizzie felt half deafened by the time they left the tent. She nodded to Maggie as they passed her, but she had her mouth half-open and did not attempt to speak.

"We're meeting my aunt and cousin at the exit," she explained. "Did I introduce you to Mr. Mountford, Benedict?" she asked, hoping she was not still shouting.

Benedict half turned his head and nodded.

"A pleasure, sir," yelled Mountford, hastening to fall in step beside them. "This is very good of you, indeed."

"It's my wife you need to thank," Benedict responded grudgingly.

"Will it matter that you did not take the time to converse with Mr. Jones's friends?" Lizzie asked anxiously. "Frank seemed to think—"

"Very little," Benedict retorted. "They didn't come to talk to me." He spat and Lizzie hoped it was not blood. Very few of Mr. North's punches had seemed to land, but she was sure even a graze from those huge fists would wreak some damage.

"Did they bring Mr. North to test you, then?" she asked, and he cocked an eye at her.

"Picked up on that, did you?"

"I did not see Jack at all."

Benedict gave a short laugh. "He was buried under a mountain of bets."

"A bookmaker would have made a pretty penny on such a match," Mr. Mountford interjected and was ignored.

"Will you not put your coat on?" Lizzie fretted. "There is quite a chill in the air."

Benedict glanced down at his jacket over his arm as though he had forgotten all about it. He stopped to pull it on, and Mr. Mountford, catching sight of Betsy and Mrs. Anderson in the distance, ran on ahead to assure them they were on their way. Sebastian barked after him disapprovingly.

"Who the hell is that anyway?" Benedict grouched.

"He is the nephew of that lady whose brooch the reverend pilfered. He was not there that night. He lives in Lincolnshire, I believe, and is his aunt's heir."

"Thought she got her brooch back," Benedict commented, seizing hold of her hand once more.

"She did," Lizzie sighed. "But it seems a good many of the congregation, Mrs. Lessing and my uncle included, have invested their money in Reverend Milson's various schemes." Benedict pulled a face. "I'm sorry for dragging you into this," Lizzie blurted. "You ought to be celebrating with your brothers, not on your way to a police station."

Benedict snorted but made no other reply. When they reached the gate at the end of the field, they found Mrs. Anderson looking fit to drop. Betsy hurried forward on seeing Benedict. "We did not mean to trouble you, Mr. Toomes," she exclaimed in a high, unnatural voice. "I hope this is not an inconvenience." She looked from Benedict to Frederick Mountford, and Lizzie found herself wondering if the formal address was for his benefit.

Compared to Benedict, Frederick Mountford seemed bland and unsubstantial to Lizzie. She marveled that Betsy's eyes should be so drawn to him. Then again, there was no accounting for taste. She dimly remembered a time when she had thought Betsy mad for looking at Benedict Toomes. She cast a quick look at her husband's face. With a pang, she realized this situation must be awkward for him as well.

"Hello, Betsy," he said shortly. "Mrs. Anderson," he said, nodding toward the older lady. Lizzie's aunt made an incoherent noise behind her handkerchief.

"If we walk to the end of the road, I'll hail us a cab," Mr. Mountford said, clearing his throat. Betsy and her mother clung

417

on to either side of him as Benedict and Lizzie led the way, Sebastian trotting beside them.

28

It was some two hours later that they returned by the same route. Benedict tipped the cabbie and helped Lizzie down from the carriage. Sebastian jumped down behind her, and they made their way back toward the camping field.

"Did you not wish to see if your brothers were still in the beer tent?" Lizzie suggested tentatively. Benedict shook his head. "Mr. Jones may have left some message for you with Frank," she pointed out.

He shot her a look. "Well, if he did, it can wait. You've been sat in a draughty station for two hours. I want to get you back in the warm."

Lizzie felt touched by his words, though it seemed a strangely anticlimactic end to their eventful day. "I wonder how Frank and Maggie are getting on," she wondered aloud. When he made no reply, she squeezed his arm. "My aunt seemed a good deal grateful to us for attending today. Do you think the police will apprehend Reverend Milson on my statement?"

"I neither know nor care," he answered promptly. "If there's a court appearance, we'll have to cross that bridge when we reach it." Lizzie bit her lip. "Did she say anything to you?" he asked abruptly.

"My aunt? She expressed her gratitude, but her emotions made her somewhat unclear in the main part."

"I mean about being reconciled," he interrupted her.

"I—that is, not really." Lizzie frowned. "Betsy said my uncle was too ashamed to come and see me today."

"Well, at least one of them feels as they should!"

Lizzie glanced at him uneasily. "Should you wish us to cut the acquaintance?"

Benedict threw her an exasperated look. "*They're* the ones who threw *you* out, Lizzie! They had a bloody cheek turning up and expecting you to save their necks now. What do you think they made of the fact you're sporting a black eye and I'm dragging you round the fairs with me?"

Lizzie blinked. "I'm not sure I understand you."

He gave a harsh laugh. "I doubt they have any illusions about the life you're living. If they had a scrap of decency about them, they'd have been begging to take you back under their roof. Yet they didn't, did they?"

Lizzie hesitated. "I don't want to go back under their roof. I'm content where I am." She looked at his expression, dark and angry. "Was it difficult?" she asked abruptly.

"Yes, very. You're too good for the likes of them."

"I meant…seeing Betsy," she elaborated, glancing down at Sebastian.

Benedict made no reply, and Lizzie's heart sank, though his footsteps picked up now the wagon was in sight. She thought someone called his name and tried to turn to see who it was, but Benedict did not let her. He practically hurled her up the steps to the wagon. "Benedict!" she protested, but he was already turning around and addressing Jack, who had come running up.

From what she could make out, he was giving his brother short shrift. Lizzie disappeared into the wagon and fumbled for the matchbox. She had no sooner lit the lamp than Benedict ran up the steps.

"Was Jack—" she began but did not get to finish her sentence.

420

"Never you mind about Jack," he said, setting down a bottle and two glasses on the trunk. "I'm going to sort out some hot water, and then it seems to me we need to straighten a few things out."

"Now?" Lizzie asked, attempting to turn about and look at his face, but his hands were closing over her shoulders, dragging off her cloak. Lizzie divested herself of her bonnet and placed it on the trunk nearest the door.

"Get on the bed," he said tersely.

Lizzie opened her mouth and then closed it again. He hadn't told her to undress, and indeed, he kept his own jacket on. Lizzie sank onto the mattress, watching him curiously as he knelt at her feet and unlaced her boots.

Straightening up, he reached for the bottle and popped the cork in a business-like fashion. "Are we celebrating?" she asked curiously and received no answer.

He poured her a glass into the shallow champagne glass and set it down beside her. "Drink this. Frank's fetching us some supper. I won't be long." He reached across for her shawl and bundled it about her before making for the door.

Lizzie gazed after him in some consternation. "Don't forget to feed Sebastian!" she called after him, though she did not know why precisely, for he never did forget. Reaching for the glass of champagne, she took a sip and debated changing into her nightgown, but indeed it was very early, and what if Benedict invited his brothers to share their supper?

Before she knew it, she had drunk half the glass of delicious bubbles. Setting it down, she reclined against the pillows, reflecting she had not eaten since a savory cheese scone at lunchtime. Five minutes later, Benedict reappeared with a paper bag.

"Your supper," he said, handing it over. "I've fed the dog."

Lizzie opened her mouth to question him further, but he had already disappeared again. Tutting loudly, Lizzie ate a Cornish pasty and, guessing that she was not going to be socializing again this evening, changed into her long cotton nightgown. Drinking the other half of her glass, she unpinned her hair and brushed it out, pulling on a pair of woolly bed socks to keep her feet warm.

Before long, Benedict reappeared with a basin of hot water which he set on the side for her. "Come and wash." She did so, and he refilled her glass, shrugging off his own jacket.

"Are you not having any?" Lizzie asked as she lathered her hands with the new cake of fragrant soap she had bought.

"I will after."

"After?" Again, she received no answer, and Lizzie turned back to finish washing her face and neck. "I've finished," she told him in subdued tones as she dabbed at her chin with a towel.

"Get comfortable," he said in clipped tones, and tore off his own neckcloth and waistcoat before taking her place at the basin. Lizzie slid up the bed until she was sat up by the pillows.

"Don't forget your champagne," he told her as he splashed the water about. Lizzie ignored the fizzing glass, for she wanted no more of it until she had heard what he had to say.

Finally, he was drying himself off and walking around the bed in his breeches and long-sleeved vest. He dropped down onto the mattress directly in front of her and stared at her a moment. "Our conversation was interrupted earlier," he started. "We still need to set things straight between us."

He paused. "First of all, though, I want to thank you for not going off without fetching me this afternoon." Lizzie nodded warily. She had a feeling he was getting the good out of the way before the bad. She felt almost unspeakably jittery about what might come next. "Get under the covers if you're cold," he said with a frown, mistaking her nerves for shivering.

Lizzie reached for her shawl instead and draped it around her shoulders. "Continue," she said with a calm she did not feel.

"It wasn't hard for me to see Betsy this afternoon," he said bluntly. "There's nothing between us now and there was precious little there to start with. Under normal circumstances, I would never have entered into an engagement with her. Almost from the beginning, I knew it felt wrong, but I thought settling with anyone would, until I met you. It would never have worked out between Betsy and me. You do know that, Lizzie?"

Lizzie flushed. "I hadn't really considered it."

He regarded her with some skepticism. "You expect me to believe you didn't counsel her against marrying me at every turn?"

Lizzie's color grew even deeper. "Well, of course I did, but that was my own prejudice against you at work."

A faint smile curved his lips. "And you knew full well Betsy and me would never have lasted. We had nothing in common and barely knew each other."

Lizzie pulled a face. "The same could be said about the two of us when we made our vows," she pointed out.

Benedict shook his head. "No, I knew you alright. I knew your substance."

Lizzie felt suddenly breathless. "What do you mean?" she quavered.

"I knew what you were made of—here," he said and placed a hand carefully over her breastbone. Lizzie stared at him, feeling the warmth from his palm spread out. He was quiet a moment, keeping his hand where it lay. "Ask me about the house, Lizzie."

"The one on Winchester Street?" He nodded and she took a deep breath. "Why didn't you tell me that it existed?"

He frowned but did not look angry. "I bought it in preparation of going respectable," he said slowly. "Marriage came under that heading, as did retiring from boxing, but I promise you, I never once thought of Betsy either at the point of purchase or in the month I spent living in that house. In truth, I felt indifferent about it. It didn't feel real. It certainly didn't feel like my home. But if you were there maybe…" He broke off and took a deep breath. "I think I need to tell you something now, something I haven't told anyone before."

Lizzie's head swam, and for the craziest moment, she thought he was going to tell her he loved her. When he spoke, she realized her mistake of course; his tone was all wrong for that sort of thing.

"There's a reason why I don't feel so close to my family as my brothers do," he said, his gaze not quite meeting hers.

Lizzie drew her knees up, dislodging his hand and wrapping her arms about her legs. "And why is that?" she asked, fortifying herself and feeling strangely grateful to Ma Toomes for preparing her for this moment.

He paused, seeming to measure his words. "I loved my mother a good deal," he said on an outward breath. "When she left my father, I was eight years old and I went with her. Just me, you understand? She left both Frank and Jack with Pa."

Lizzie sucked in a breath. "Why did she take only you?"

"Because I begged her to. I returned to the wagon unexpectedly one morning and found her packing to leave. She tried to lie and tell me that she was just going to visit with friends, but I knew she didn't have any. I told her if she didn't take me, I'd run and tell Pa she was leaving him."

He fell quiet a moment before continuing. "At first, it was fine. We were on the road together. We slept in barns, and I looked out for her. She danced for money in the villages at the taverns. Then we stopped awhile in one village. She took up with a musician who lived above the blacksmiths. She was merry and laughed a good deal. He wasn't so bad, all told. Then one morning, I woke up and she was gone. They'd moved on without me."

Lizzie drew in a noisy breath. "Why?"

He shrugged. "Didn't want me slowing them down, an extra mouth to feed over winter months, who knows? Whatever the reason, I had no one and was considered a burden on the parish. Can't say as I blamed them; I wasn't from round those parts."

"What happened to you?" Lizzie asked, sitting up straight, though she already had an idea thanks to Ma.

Benedict's face was expressionless. "I told them I had a family, knew their name and their direction, for even at that age I knew the fairs by the month of the year. It was September and they would be at Stourbridge. Even though my Pa couldn't read, I knew a letter addressed to him there would reach him, and he could find someone there to read it to him."

"And they wrote to him?"

425

"They did." Lizzie waited. After a moment, he continued. "We had the reply by the end of the following week. He said he could not spare the fare for my journey and would not travel to our neck of the woods fully for a twelvemonth. In the meantime, he recommended they should place me in the workhouse until it was convenient for him to fetch or send for me."

Lizzie caught her breath. "No!" Benedict nodded, his expression wooden. "Is that what happened? They put you in the workhouse?"

"They did."

Lizzie launched herself across the divide between them, throwing her arms about his neck. "How dare they? How *dare* they?" she repeated on an angry sob. "No wonder you hate him. *I* hate him!" Benedict gave a choked laugh, wrapping his arms about her. Neither spoke for a long moment. "He did not fetch you for a long time, did he?"

"It was over two years," he said quietly.

"They had better hope that I *never* meet that wicked man!" she seethed.

He chuckled again, but then grew quickly sober. "I think it was in the workhouse that I decided I wanted different things to my family," he admitted. "To kick my father out, then eventually leave the booth and the fairgrounds behind me altogether. Get a house, a wife." He paused. "Children of my own who would go to school."

Lizzie's breath caught. "I'm glad you achieved your revenge and kicked him out," she said warmly. "Though how your brothers dare speak to you of family loyalty…" She trailed off.

"Next time Jack accuses you of that, I shall have plenty to say to him, that's all!"

Benedict smirked, rubbing his hand up and down her back. "Hmm, well. I think we're working our way toward some kind of understanding, me and my brothers, I mean," he murmured.

"I do not think the rift between you is as wide as you imagine," Lizzie said from his shoulder. "It seems to me the three of you are really quite close."

"We'll be fine," he agreed with a note of finality. "Let's not get sidetracked."

"And *we'll* be fine also," Lizzie said stoutly as she drew back, patting his chest. "Whether you wish to remain on the road or to settle in your house on Winchester Street."

He looked at her very intently. "You mean that?"

"Yes," she said firmly. "I do."

"I can easily sell the house if it's not to your taste."

She shook her head. "I'm sure it's a very fine house."

He looked relieved. "Nat Jones did leave a message with Frank. He means to back me, to the top this time."

Lizzie gasped. "You mean, you will get your championship fight?"

He nodded. "It'll take twelve months or so before I get my shot, but I'll get it. He gave me his word."

"That's wonderful! Hence, the champagne." He nodded, still watching her, his expression serious. Lizzie hesitated. "Benedict, why then do you look like that?" she asked, deciding to take the bull by the horns.

"Like what?"

"I don't know exactly, but not like a man who has just achieved his life's ambition, that's for sure."

He smiled a little grimly. "Maybe because now it's within my grasp, I've realized it's not my heart's ambition at all," he said slowly.

She caught his subtle change of *life* to *heart* and caught her breath. "It isn't?" He shook his head. "Then, what is?"

He reached out and caught her hands in his. "Lizzie," he began. "When I determined to make you mine," he carried on calmly, "I reasoned it out quite coolly. I may have thought my motive was a little involved." He winced. "But it turns out things were a lot more straightforward than I knew." He paused, as though mustering his thoughts. "Your honesty, your sheer obstinate, *bloody-minded* determination to do what you felt to be right, never mind what anyone else thought about it, flying fully in the face of adversity, and not backing down an inch. All of it resonated deeply with me. Here."

He picked up her own hand to press it to his chest. Lizzie's mouth fell open as she felt the emotion vibrate in his voice as he spoke. "I felt it here, and I knew you were the one for me. And every day, every hour, and every minute I have spent with you since has confirmed that instinct one hundredfold. You're the one for me." She nodded dumbly. He took a deep breath.

"I can tell you now, Lizzie, your hair is *not* your only beauty. Not to me." He dropped her hand and reached across to cup her chin. "This firm little chin, these dainty lips," he said, tracing them with his thumb. "These intelligent eyes, this determined nose... I find beauty in all of it. I could look at your face all day long and find no fault with it. And you *know* I like your body. When I'm champion, I'll have your portrait painted by someone who can do you justice." Lizzie stared at him. His expression, so fiercely sincere, robbed her of words completely.

He thought she was beautiful? An idea occurred to her so astonishing that it made her tremble. "Benedict," she quavered. "Are you sure it's not just that you're, well…" She licked her lips. *Just say it.* "In love with me?"

He held her gaze, the ghost of a smile playing about his mouth. "Of course I am, Lizzie," he said, astounding her. "I think I fell in love with you the very moment you called that reverend out, causing merry havoc at that damn dinner party."

Lizzie's mouth dropped open. "What?" she squeaked.

"If it wasn't fully at that moment, then it might have been when you barged past me the next morning with your chin high in the air. Or maybe," he mused, "it was when you swung your bag at that thug's head in Poultney Street." When she continued to sit there open-mouthed, he sighed. "It might have been a combination of all three moments. I don't know. I just know I spent the nights that week lying awake until the early hours, plotting and scheming how I could break my engagement to the wrong girl and get *you* where I wanted you."

Lizzie swallowed convulsively. "You mean, you wanted it to be *me* in the church that morning?" she enquired incredulously.

He nodded. "I knew I wouldn't rest night or day until I'd made you mine."

So, she was not a last-minute substitute at all! "I thought—that is—I had no idea you felt that way!"

"I know," he said simply. "I scarcely realized the truth myself. And I didn't want to scare you. It was quite a turnaround."

"You didn't worry it might just have been a passing fancy?" she marveled.

He shook his head. "No."

"How could you be so certain?"

"I just was, and that conviction has held firm ever since." Her gaze fell beneath his own. He waited until she met his eye again before speaking. "As soon as I started getting those feelings, I began noticing more and more things about you that I liked. Not just the way you look, but your gutsiness, determination, everything about you. *Everything.* I love you, Lizzie. I won't know true happiness until you feel the same way I do."

Lizzie's head reeled. She put out her hand blindly. "Wait," she said, and he caught her hand in a comforting grip.

"Forever if I have to," he assured her, kissing her fingers. "Though I hope it won't take that long."

"When you say you thought your motive was a little involved in marrying me, what did you mean?"

Benedict winced. "Trust you to home in on that."

"You meant to get some measure of revenge on me, didn't you? Confess."

He smirked. "I did. You irritated me to no end with your glares and disapproval at Sitwell Place. I meant to make you pay for that, but you made all my plans go awry. From the very first."

Lizzie huffed out a breath. "I didn't really know you then," she began awkwardly. "I thought you a terrible villain."

He laughed. "I know. And now?"

"Now…" Lizzie avoided his gaze. "Now it's different," she admitted. "Very different. I feel I should be very cross to hear anyone say *anything* against you."

"You're well disposed toward me, then?" he asked teasingly, reaching across to thread his fingers through hers.

"Yes," she agreed quietly. "Though, mind you, I'm not at all sure when that happened either. Maybe it was because you didn't kick up a big fuss when I spent all my money on a dog. Or maybe," she considered aloud, "because you didn't set me prancing in my drawers or telling fortunes as your grandmother told me you would."

When he reached for her, she stayed his hand. "Wait!" He dropped it at once. "I'm lying," she said, feeling the hot, red flush spreading across her face. She looked him in the eye. "I know exactly why I fell in love with you, Benedict Toomes."

His gaze snapped to hers, all playfulness gone. "You do? Why?"

"It's because you set me above everyone else," she sobbed, feeling suddenly overcome with emotion. "No one ever did that for me before."

He jerked her forward into his lap. "Lizzie," he groaned and took her lips in an achingly tender kiss. "I set you above everyone else because you *are* above everyone else to me. Now say it properly. And look me in the eye when you do it."

"I love you," she said breathlessly. "It's strange to even remember a time when I did not."

His eyes softened, and he lowered his head to kiss her again lingeringly before drawing back, his eyes agleam. "You called me dearest earlier in the tent," he said. "Did you realize?"

Lizzie's startled gaze flew to meet his. It wasn't like her to use endearments. "Did I?"

He nodded. "I liked it. Do it again."

"Yes, dearest." He smiled at her, his hazel eyes warm for once and aglow with feeling. Lizzie felt her chest flutter. The Harbinger of Doom, Benedict Toomes, was in love with her, and he wasn't troubling to hide the fact.

"Now I feel like I've achieved my heart's content," he said with satisfaction. "Tomorrow we head out of Putney," he said. "And before we leave London, I'm going to buy you a new gold ring and the biggest bunch of violets you ever saw in your life."

"Dearest…"

He crushed his mouth to hers, bearing her down onto the mattress. Lizzie slipped her arms around his neck, holding him close. "Are you sure we should not be celebrating with your brothers?" she asked as he began placing kisses down her neck.

"I don't want to be with anyone else right now. Only you. Always you."

Lizzie sighed as he untied the ribbon at her neck. "Neither do I," she admitted. "Oh, Benedict."

Much later, as they lay naked and wrapped in each other's arms, Benedict remembered the champagne and they toasted one another in the lamplight.

"My beautiful mermaid," Benedict murmured, running his fingers through her unbound hair. "I want to drown in you for the rest of my life."

Lizzie laughed. "I still can't decide if that's a romantic notion or not."

"I think I shall have you painted as one," he mused. "Naked. Sat on a rock, combing out your long golden hair."

"Naked?" Lizzie yelped.

"Wearing a string of pearls that goes all the way down to here," he said, trailing his fingers down her stomach and between her legs.

"Benedict!"

He laughed. "Or should it be emerging from a chrysalis?" he teased, setting down his champagne glass and shifting over her.

"It would have to be a miniature," Lizzie said anxiously. "So you could keep it in your pocket where no one else could see it."

"I'd have a hard time letting an artist see it," he growled. "Let alone anyone else."

Later again, Lizzie lay plastered against his chest, her face buried in his neck. Feeling bold, she kissed him there, and his hand reflexively squeezed her waist. "I feel so happy," she murmured against his jaw. "I want everyone else in the world to be as happy as we are."

He laughed. "They won't be. What we have is rare." His hand drifted over her bottom to rest there. "Very rare."

"I hope Jack did not have to sleep under a canvas spread over some sticks," she said as the thought occurred. "I do not think Maggie will have made Frank wait even one night before reconciling. I suspect my pep talk was a waste of breath." Benedict grunted and she pinched his earlobe. His eyes flew open to look at her.

"What?"

"Nothing, just…familiarizing myself with what's mine."

His face relaxed again, his eyes drifting shut. "You can be as familiar as you please, Mrs. Toomes," he rumbled. "I'll deny you nothing."

"I suppose really it is a good thing she's back," Lizzie sighed. "It's not as though I have time to be cooking and cleaning after Frank and Jack."

Benedict frowned. "There was no question of that."

"Besides, they still love each other," Lizzie said breezily. "I do hope Ma is doing alright at her sister's." He made no response to this. "And even Daphne. At the coast." His breathing was deep and even by this point, and she wondered if he was drifting off to sleep.

"I think Betsy has her eye on Frederick Mountford," she confided. "Though it may come to nothing if his aunt has lost all her money." She rested her chin against his chest, and Benedict murmured something noncommittal. "Are you falling asleep?" she asked.

"Say something interesting if you want a response," he retorted.

She tweaked his chest hair and he smirked, though he did not open his eyes. "Maybe I'll commission a plaster statue of you, if you are to have a portrait of me," she mused. "Naked, of course, in the Greek style."

Benedict's eyes snapped open. They held a distinctive gleam. "Would that be with or without a fig leaf?"

Epilogue

Eight Months Later, Winchester Street, London

It was Christmas Eve at Winchester Street. Evergreens and ribbons hung from every picture frame and banister. Lizzie was sat her writing desk, scribbling furiously at the list of parlor games she was devising for the Napps, who were coming to Christmas dinner the next day as their guests of honor. Sebastian lay on his side along the handsome hearthrug in his new red leather collar.

Yes, she had thought of something for everyone, she thought, casting a quick glance down the list, from the youngest of the Napps, to the oldest of the apprentices. She had forgotten no one in the quantity of crackers, whistles, and paper hats she had accumulated over the past week. She and Molly had added so many silver charms to the Christmas pudding that she was now starting to worry they might constitute a choking hazard.

She drew back her chair and rang the little bell for Molly, their maid of all work, who appeared in the doorway. "Oh, Molly," she said, getting to her feet. "Will you help me to hang these paper streamers in the dining room? I thought if we did them now, then it would be less things for us to remember in the morning."

Sebastian cast a look over his shoulder at them, yawned, and then closed his eyes again, choosing the comfort of the hearth over duty. He did not feel the need to follow his mistress's every move these days.

Molly nodded brightly. "Yes, Mrs. Toomes," she agreed. "And then you and the master can enjoy them tonight when you takes your Christmas Eve supper in there together."

"Oh, what a nice idea," Lizzie murmured, not mentioning the Christmas Eve Benedict had outlined he wanted in recompense for his house being overrun with Napps the following day. It had involved a cold supper, eaten picnic style in the intimacy of their bedroom. Besides, Molly would never know, as she had a half day holiday and would be spending the evening at her mother's.

Unknown by anyone else, Lizzie had another reason she did not want to be balancing precariously on chairs just now. She thought of the present she had wrapped for Benedict only that morning. An intricate, hand-knitted baby's blanket in the softest white wool which she had made in secrecy on the smallest knitting needles she could buy. She was simply bursting to tell him her news but had saved it for an extra-special surprise for their first Christmas together.

"Did you finish that milk jelly for Eliza?" Lizzie asked, thinking suddenly of the youngest Napp. "That is her particular favorite."

"Oh yes, Mrs. Toomes," Molly assured her. "And the blancmange."

"Excellent."

"I got all the ingredients for that bowl of smoking bishop you wanted for the old lady too."

"Mrs. Napp will be pleased." Lizzie smiled. "You remember everything, Molly."

Lizzie checked her reflection in the gilt framed hallway mirror as they passed through, admiring her pretty gown of soft pink. She thought it lent her skin a rosy color that flattered her complexion. She patted the arrangement of her hair dressed in matching ribbon and lace. Benedict still preferred it down, but she was starting to feel more comfortable wearing ornamentation these days. At her ears, she wore the amethyst and gold teardrops her husband had bought her for her birthday.

She was very much looking forward to their day of celebrations on the morrow, but she was also looking forward to her own private celebrations that evening with just her Benedict. She gestured to a central point on the ceiling where she wanted the streamers affixed, and Molly obligingly stood on a chair. Lizzie was just passing up the first of the streamers when she heard a tap on the window and whirled around to see Benedict beckoning to her from outside.

Her heart gave a leap at the sight of him, as always. He was wearing a new tailored suit today which showed off his athletic build to perfection. Other than a light graze above his right cheekbone, a leftover from his last fight three weeks ago, he looked the very image of respectable affluence today. Though, perhaps his shoulders were rather broad for a true gentleman of leisure.

"Sorry, Molly," she apologized, setting the streamers on the table. "We'll have to finish this later. I won't be long." She hurried back out into the hall and carried through to the kitchen and then out of the back door.

Her husband was lurking there with a suspicious gleam in his eye. "You were rather long at the barber's," she commented. "Though they made a good job." She liked it when they left it long enough to show the curl. "I'm glad you did not go back to that man in Wendover Street. He hacked it off far too short last time."

"I have something to show you, wife," he said, leaning down and pressing a kiss to her lips. As she drew back, she noticed he was holding a sprig of mistletoe over her head.

"Is it the mistletoe?" she laughed. "We've a great bunch of it suspended in the parlor. I was hoping Jack might come after supper tomorrow and dance with Mrs. Napp's apprentices. The poor girls could use some excitement in their lives."

"He can dance with Miss Lucinda Napp," Benedict answered with feeling. "Then I shan't have to."

Lizzie laughed. "Her mother told me that Cindy's now courting a baker's apprentice. A very steady young man called Herbert, so you will soon be replaced in her affections."

"Thank God for small mercies," he answered briskly. "Anyway, enough about the Napps, we've got all day with them tomorrow. The first of your Christmas presents awaits."

Lizzie looked at him with surprise. "Are we doing that now? I thought we were exchanging them this evening."

He shook his head. "You're to receive the first of yours now," he said, tucking her arm through his and leading her through the kitchen garden and into the courtyard where Florence was stabled.

"You buy me too many presents," Lizzie tutted, thinking of the painting he had bought her only last week that now hung in their bedroom above the bed. It showed a storm-tossed sea with several sea nymphs sporting in the waves. Lizzie had thought it was rather too risqué for the parlor, although she was not convinced, as Benedict was, that the mermaids resembled her so very much.

He shook his head. "Not possible." They followed the path down to the end of the garden, and Lizzie halted in astonishment, catching sight of what stood there. "What do you think?" he asked.

"That's not ours!" she exclaimed, looking at the gaily painted wagon. "Is it?" She spun around to look at his face.

"It is now."

She turned back again. "It has a chimney!"

"It has its own stove."

Lizzie ran down the garden path to peer in at the windows. "I love it!" she cried. "Can we go inside?"

"Of course," he said, laughing at her enthusiasm. "We can do whatever we want. It's ours."

"There's a key for the door?" She watched him unlock it, and he swung her up inside. When she saw the interior, she gasped. "It's so grand!" She gazed about in wonder at the canopy over the bed and the cunningly carved wooden fixtures and fittings, so cleverly wrought. "Oh, I love it!" she said, clapping her hands. "Is it really ours?"

He wrapped his arms about her waist and rested his chin on her shoulder. "We could always sneak out here and sleep in it after Molly's left for the night," he suggested. "Just you and me."

Lizzie sighed happily. "Yes, that sounds perfect," she murmured, looking back over her shoulder at him. "A midnight tryst."

He leaned in for a kiss which she happily bestowed. Lizzie had vastly enjoyed the last month spent at Winchester Street, which was a very handsome and well-proportioned house. It had been pleasant to be able to host family and friends in the fine-sized parlor and around one's own dining table. Indeed, she was looking forward with pleasurable anticipation to another three months living in comfort before the next season started.

Still, she was already anticipating when they would next be able to take to the road again. Benedict had simply shrugged and said they would rent the house out for six months of every year. "And if children come, we'll rethink things. I don't want you struggling when that time comes."

Remembering his words now, Lizzie bit her lip. She hoped he wasn't going to be difficult about her pregnancy. She adored taking fully immersive baths instead of strip washes and having their fires ready laid in handsome fireplaces. Somehow, though, she felt she enjoyed these things all the more *because* she did not always have the benefit of them.

And there was something very intimate and simplistic about living with one other person in so very confined a space. She missed that sometimes now they had their own dressing rooms. On occasion she had to go in search of Benedict even when they were under the same roof. You never had that problem when all you had was a wagon and a campfire.

"What are you thinking of?" he murmured.

"Our old wagon," Lizzie improvised. "What will we do with it now?"

"Give it to Jack?" Benedict suggested. "He needs his own space with Frank and Maggie carrying on like a pair of regular lovebirds."

Lizzie nodded her head in agreement. "Good idea. They should have arrived in Southend by now." Her sister and brother-in-law were spending Christmas at Maggie's friends' boarding house. Frank had been teetotal for nine months and was anxious to make a good impression on the friends who had taken her in during their time apart.

"Sure to have," Benedict agreed.

"Do you still think they will be back in time for our New Year's dinner party?" Lizzie asked, faintly anxious for the familiar faces she knew. Some of Benedict's prizefighting fraternity were attending their New Year's celebrations this year, and Lizzie did not yet have all their names straight in her head. She had met a brace of them over the last few months, and some of them were rather alarming.

Nat Jones would be there, and his "lady friend," Dot. Then, too, there would be Benedict's friend Clem Dabney, who Lizzie had met several times and thought a handsome rogue. Goodness only knew who he would bring with him, for every time she had met him, he had a different lady on his arm. Just lately he had invested in a theater which everyone said should keep him supplied with a different dancing girl for every night of the week. Lizzie had taken exception to that, but Benedict had winked at her and told her Nat was only joking.

The Andersons they had not seen much of, nor had they made any festive plans. They had paid a rather stiff, formal visit the previous week to Winchester Street and partaken of a light luncheon of thinly sliced sandwiches. Everyone had been rather awkward with one another, except for Benedict, who had not seemed to be at any pains to be particularly agreeable.

Her uncle was plainly still mortified by the events that had transpired, but Lizzie and her aunt had done their best to carry things off between them. Betsy had been full of her engagement to Frederick Mountford, but there had been some constraint about that, for her father had turned reserved and disapproving whenever that young man was mentioned.

When Uncle Josiah had stumped out of the room to take a turn about the garden with his pipe, Betsy had confided in them. Frederick's aunt, Mrs. Lessing, had still not given her approval to their match, so it had not been formally announced, a fact her father did not appreciate.

Aunt Hester had explained, with two spots of bright color in her cheeks, that the young couple were having to "bide their time," and as Lizzie knew, her uncle "abhorred any kind of subterfuge" and thought Frederick should announce his intentions and stand independently on his own two feet.

Betsy chimed in again at this point, extolling the futility of Frederick being cut off without a shilling from his aunt's will. Especially, she had added, when their own finances were still so up in the air. Benedict had rolled his eyes, but Lizzie had quickly asked how the legal case against Reverend Milson was proceeding and thus averted any disaster.

Her aunt had lamented for the remaining hour about their woes, and it transpired there was still a good deal of doubt if they would ever be able to fully recoup their losses. Indeed, they might well have to sell their house and downsize to somewhere far smaller. Lizzie had felt guilty for feeling relieved at the close of their visit. As she had waved them off at the front doorstep, her aunt had mentioned something about inviting them for a return visit in a couple of months' time.

"See if you cannot delay that visit until the end of February," Benedict had recommended as they closed their front door after them. "If you can't spin it out until March."

Looking about her now at the intricate interior of their new wagon, Lizzie sighed.

"It's a lovely present, Benedict," Lizzie sighed. "Thank you so much."

"It's not really your present," he murmured as he kissed her again. "It's just our traveling home away from home. There's more personal gifts upstairs I'll give you this evening."

"You shouldn't have," she scolded him. "The thing I've got you is homemade and not anything fancy."

"You've already given me everything I always wanted," he said as he lifted her down from the caravan.

Lizzie smiled to herself. *Not yet*, she thought*, but soon.* "You will win your championship next year, so there's still plenty for you to look forward to," she reminded him. The title match was scheduled for March. She would be showing by then, she thought ruefully, and there would be no chance of Benedict allowing her to watch him win. The baby would be coming along in June, so it would be a busy twelve months for their family.

"I look forward to every day with you," he said, kissing the back of her hand.

"I received a Christmas card from the twins this morning, dearest," Lizzie informed him as they walked back up the garden path. She had to practice throwing out casual endearments to him, for they did not come easily, though she was getting better at it.

Her latest stratagem was to write him small love notes which she concealed about his person, in his waistcoat pocket, or tucked in the brim of his hat for him to find at times when he was away from her. They had started out rather stilted and uninspired, but recently she was growing a good deal bolder.

The trouble was striking a balance, so he would be gratified but not so inflamed he turned on his heel and came straight home to her, leaving poor Mr. Edwards, his man of business, bewildered and a bunch of documents unsigned. Some days she did not get the balance entirely right which led to her being interrupted in some household duty and carried upstairs to the bedroom at very strange hours of the day.

"They are wintering at Brighton and sent me a whole list of the entertainments they have planned for the season." She smiled fondly thinking of Ema and Zaya and the scores of admirers they would no doubt be making at the seaside resort. Their scrawled postscript had been a written appeal for news of "darling Sebastian."

"Didn't you say Connie's at Brighton?" Benedict asked absently.

"No, Connie's at Eastbourne," she corrected him. "Niamh and Colin are in lodgings at Epsom, so I hope we will see them soon. I was thinking of inviting them for Boxing Day or maybe the day after that." He nodded, opening the kitchen door for her to precede him inside.

"Benedict," she said impulsively, turning to him. "Would you like your Christmas present now?"

"I thought you'd never ask."

"It's in the front parlor," she said, feeling unaccountably nervous.

He cocked an eyebrow at her, as though picking up on her abrupt change of mood. "Lead the way."

When they entered the parlor, she crossed the room and opened the drawer in the oak sideboard. Retrieving her package, done up in paper and ribbons, she turned back and held it out to him. "I've been making it myself," she blurted. "In the last month, whenever you were out."

He took the package from her and turned it over a moment before untying the ribbon. "It doesn't feel like slippers," he commented, and Lizzie laughed, remembering her promise to make him some.

"It isn't," she admitted. "I'm going to make those for your birthday."

"You made this?" he asked, casting the paper aside and shaking out the delicate white shawl. "It's very fine work," he began admiringly and then froze, his gaze snapping to hers. "Is this what I think it is?" he demanded. "Lizzie?"

She bit her lip and nodded. "A baby's shawl."

"When?" he demanded.

"June time."

"Lizzie," he said in a choked voice, placing the shawl down carefully over the back of a chair and drawing her into his arms. "Come here. You amazing woman." He sounded awestruck. "June. So soon?"

"Yes." They stood locked in each other's embrace before the fire for a good long moment.

"I can't believe it," he said huskily.

"You'll be a world champion *and* a father in a few months," Lizzie said with satisfaction.

He made a choked sound and then drew back, his expression turning swiftly from tender to stern. "You'd better enjoy our night in the new wagon tonight, Mrs. Toomes," he told her, drawing back. "Because that's as close as we're going to get to touring the countryside for the next year at least."

"Benedict…"

"No, Lizzie, I mean it," he said. "I shall see Edwards first thing in the morning."

Lizzie regarded him with exasperated amusement. "I doubt Mr. Edwards will be in the office on Christmas Day, Benedict."

"First thing on the twenty-seventh of December."

She debated arguing with him before laying her hands on either side of his face. "Yes, dearest," she soothed him.

"And what did you mean by saying you'd only got me a small gift?" he demanded. "It's the biggest gift you could ever give anyone. That set of pearls I got you is nothing compared to it."

"Yes, but it is more a joint gift for the both of us, really," she pointed out. Then she realized what he'd said. "Pearls? Did you really get me pearls, Benedict?"

"When will we tell people?" he demanded, ignoring her reaction to his gift of jewelry. His hand moved from the small of her back to rest against her still-flat stomach.

"I think…in another month's time," she suggested. "So, we have a few weeks of just the two of us knowing."

He nodded, his eyes full of emotion. "Yes," he said, resting his brow against hers. "That sounds perfect."

Lizzie smiled up at him. "Are you happy, my love?"

He caught her up in his arms. "I couldn't be happier, Lizzie mine."

THE END

I do hope you enjoyed this story. If so, perhaps you would be kind enough to leave me a rating on Amazon, Goodreads, or Bookbub, or to sign up for my newsletter via my website:
www.alicecoldbreath.com

Also, please do check out some of my other stories!

Many thanks, Alice.

If you want to read more about Victorian Prizefighters, then the next book in the series is Clem's story:

A Contracted Spouse for the Prizefighter

Theodora knows in her heart that she has star quality but sadly, no-one else in her theatrical family feels the same way. When her sister, leaves to get married, Theo is promptly axed from the bill and expected to take a back seat in the family business.

Clem Dabney, aspiring theatre owner and ex-prizefighter has built up his supper and song business as far as he can take it. In order to expand he now needs a theatre. When Theodora appears before him with her outrageous proposition, he sees his chance and devil take the consequences.

Their marriage is purely a business arrangement, so Theo is not worried about Clem's reputation and Clem is not concerned about Theo's distinct lack of feminine charm. Now that's all settled and out of the way, both agree things should be straightforward enough… Why then, is Clem acting the jealous husband when Theo finds herself among a throng of new admirers?

If you liked this story, you might enjoy some of my others:

THE BRIDES OF KARADOK SERIES:

The Unlovely Bride by Alice Coldbreath

Lenora Montmayne leads a charmed life as the most beautiful woman at King Wymer's court, surrounded by admirers. And then disaster strikes. The red pox sweeps the summer palace at Caer-Lyones, and Lenora's fair face falls victim to its ravages. Without her looks, what does Lenora have left to her?

If ever there was a knight the crowd loves to hate, it's Garman Orde. Even his own family despises him. Then one night a heavily veiled lady offers him an extraordinary bargain. And he finds out that Lenora Montmayne was never just a pretty face.

Her Bridegroom, Bought and Paid For by Alice Coldbreath

Aimee Ankatel, younger daughter to the richest merchant in all Karadok, has eyes only for the heavily scarred Lord Kentigern. Her heart beats louder when she watches him compete in the field.

When her father lends funds to the Crown and promises her a glittering match with a nobleman, she daydreams of making the ill-fated knight fall in love with her. After all, if Aimee's father buys back Kentigern's lands and castle for a dowry, surely that would make her an acceptable bride to him?

Any idealistic dreams of youth Kentigern once had were lost long ago in battle when he was disfigured and blinded in one eye. His destiny was a cruel one, his homelands confiscated for his part in the Northern uprising, and now he ekes out a lonely nomadic existence, traveling from one tournament to another.

Never would he have dreamed that all he had once lost could be put in his hands again by some upstart merchant wanting a stud and a title for his pretty daughter. Never in his wildest dreams would he have imagined a reversal of fortune that included a wife like Aimee.

www.ingramcontent.com/pod-product-compliance
Lightning Source LLC
Chambersburg PA
CBHW020828030726
47496CB00001B/144